GREEN MANSIONS

GREEN MANSIONS

❦❦❦❦❦❦

by W. H. HUDSON

INTERNATIONAL COLLECTORS LIBRARY

Garden City, New York

GREEN MANSIONS

PROLOGUE

IT IS a cause of very great regret to me that this task
has taken so much longer a time than I had expected
for its completion. It is now many months—over a
year, in fact—since I wrote to Georgetown announc-
ing my intention of publishing, *in a very few months*,
the whole truth about Mr. Abel. Hardly less could
have been looked for from his nearest friend, and I
had hoped that the discussion in the newspapers
would have ceased, at all events, until the appearance
of the promised book. It has not been so; and at this
distance from Guiana I was not aware of how much
conjectural matter was being printed week by week
in the local Press, some of which must have been
painful reading to Mr. Abel's friends. A darkened
chamber, the existence of which had never been suspected in that familiar house in Main Street, fur-

nished only with an ebony stand on which stood a
cinerary urn, its surface ornamented with flower and
leaf and thorn, and winding through it all the figure
of a serpent; an inscription, too, of seven short words
which no one could understand or rightly interpret;
and finally, the disposal of the mysterious ashes—that
was all there was relating to an untold chapter in a
man's life for imagination to work on. Let us hope
that now, at last, the romance-weaving will come to
an end. It was, however, but natural that the keenest
curiosity should have been excited; not only because
of that peculiar and indescribable charm of the man,
which all recognised and which won all hearts, but
also because of that hidden chapter—that sojourn in
the desert, about which he preserved silence. It was
felt in a vague way by his intimates that he had met
with unusual experiences which had profoundly affected him and changed the course of his life. To me
alone was the truth known, and I must now tell,
briefly as possible, how my great friendship and close
intimacy with him came about.

When, in 1887, I arrived in Georgetown to take up
an appointment in a public office, I found Mr. Abel
an old resident there, a man of means and a favourite
in society. Yet he was an alien, a Venezuelan, one of
that turbulent people on our border whom the colo-
nists have always looked on as their natural enemies.
The story told to me was that about twelve years
before that time he had arrived at Georgetown from

some remote district in the interior; that he had journeyed alone on foot across half the continent to the coast, and had first appeared among them, a young stranger, penniless, in rags, wasted almost to a skeleton by fever and misery of all kinds, his face blackened by long exposure to sun and wind. Friendless, with but little English, it was a hard struggle for him to live; but he managed somehow, and eventually letters from Caracas informed him that a considerable property of which he had been deprived was once more his own, and he was also invited to return to his country to take his part in the government of the republic. But Mr. Abel, though young, had already outlived political passions and aspirations, and, apparently, even the love of his country; at all events, he elected to stay where he was—his enemies, he would say smilingly, were his best friends—and one of the first uses he made of his fortune was to buy that house in Main Street which was afterwards like a home to me.

I must state here that my friend's full name was Abel Guevez de Argensola, but in his early days in Georgetown he was called by his christian name only, and later he wished to be known simply as "Mr. Abel."

I had no sooner made his acquaintance than I ceased to wonder at the esteem and even affection with which he, a Venezuelan, was regarded in this British colony. All knew and liked him, and the reason of it was the personal charm of the man, his kindly disposition, his manner with women, which pleased them and excited no man's jealousy—not even the old hot-tempered planter's, with a very young and pretty and light-headed wife—his love of little children, of all wild creatures, of nature, and of whatsoever was furthest removed from the common material interests and concerns of a purely commercial community. The things which excited other men—politics, sport, and the price of crystals—were outside of his thoughts; and when men had done with them for a season, when like the tempest they had "blown their fill" in office and club-room and house and wanted a change, it was a relief to turn to Mr. Abel and get him to discourse of *his* world—the world of nature and of the spirit.

It was, all felt, a good thing to have a Mr. Abel in Georgetown. That it was indeed good for me I quickly discovered. I had certainly not expected to meet in such a place with any person to share my tastes—that love of poetry which has been the chief passion and delight of my life; but such an one I had found in Mr. Abel. It surprised me that he, suckled on the literature of Spain, and a reader of only ten or twelve years of English literature, possessed a knowledge of our modern poetry as intimate as my own, and a love of it equally great. This feeling brought us together, and made us two—the nervous olive-skinned Hispano-American of the tropics and the phlegmatic

blue-eyed Saxon of the cold north—one in spirit and
more than brothers. Many were the daylight hours we
spent together and "tired the sun with talking";
many, past counting, the precious evenings in that
restful house of his where I was an almost daily guest.
I had not looked for such happiness; nor, he often
said, had he. A result of this intimacy was that the
vague idea concerning his hidden past, that some unusual experience had profoundly affected him and
perhaps changed the whole course of his life, did not
diminish, but, on the contrary, became accentuated,
and was often in my mind. The change in him was
almost painful to witness whenever our wandering
talk touched on the subject of the aborigines, and of
the knowledge he had acquired of their character and
languages when living or travelling among them; all
that made his conversation most engaging—the lively,
curious mind, the wit, the gaiety of spirit tinged with
a tender melancholy—appeared to fade out of it; even
the expression of his face would change, becoming
hard and set, and he would deal you out facts in a
dry mechanical way as if reading them in a book. It
grieved me to note this, but I dropped no hint of
such a feeling, and would never have spoken about it
but for a quarrel which came at last to make the one
brief solitary break in that close friendship of years.
I got into a bad state of health, and Abel was not
only much concerned about it, but annoyed, as if I
had not treated him well by being ill, and he would

even say that I could get well if I wished to. I did not take this seriously, but one morning, when calling to see me at the office, he attacked me in a way that made me downright angry with him. He told me that indolence and the use of stimulants was the cause of my bad health. He spoke in a mocking way, with a pretence of not quite meaning it, but the feeling could not be wholly disguised. Stung by his reproaches, I blurted out that he had no right to talk to me, even in fun, in such a way. Yes, he said, getting serious, he had the best right—that of our friendship. He would be no true friend if he kept his peace about such a matter. Then, in my haste, I retorted that to me the friendship between us did not seem so perfect and complete as it did to him. One condition of friendship is that the partners in it should be known to each other. He had had my whole life and mind open to him, to read it as in a book. *His* life was a closed and clasped volume to me.

His face darkened, and after a few moments' silent reflection he got up and left me with a cold good-bye, and without that hand-grasp which had been customary between us.

After his departure I had the feeling that a great loss, a great calamity, had befallen me, but I was still smarting at his too candid criticism, all the more because in my heart I acknowledged its truth. And that night, lying awake, I repented of the cruel retort I had made, and resolved to ask his forgiveness and leave it to him to determine the question of our future relations. But he was beforehand with me, and with the morning came a letter begging my forgiveness and asking me to go that evening to dine with him.

We were alone, and during dinner and afterwards, when we sat smoking and sipping black coffee in the verandah, we were unusually quiet, even to gravity, which caused the two white-clad servants that waited on us—the brown-faced subtle-eyed old Hindoo butler and an almost blue-black young Guiana negro—to direct many furtive glances at their master's face. They were accustomed to see him in a more genial mood when he had a friend to dine. To me the change in his manner was not surprising: from the moment of seeing him I had divined that he had determined to open the shut and clasped volume of which I had spoken—that the time had now come for him to speak.

❧ 1 ❦

Now THAT we are cool, he said, and regret that we hurt each other, I am not sorry that it happened. I deserved your reproach; a hundred times I have wished to tell you the whole story of my travels and adventures among the savages, and one of the reasons which prevented me was the fear that it would have an unfortunate effect on our friendship. That was precious, and I desired above everything to keep it. But I must think no more about that now. I must think only of how I am to tell you my story. I will begin at a time when I was twenty-three. It was early in life to be in the thick of politics, and in trouble to the extent of having to fly my country to save my liberty, perhaps my life.

Every nation, someone remarks, has the government it deserves, and Venezuela certainly has the one it deserves and that suits it best. We call it a republic, not only because it is not one, but also because a thing must have a name; and to have a good name, or a fine name, is very convenient—especially when you want to borrow money. If the Venezuelans, thinly distributed over an area of half a million square miles, mostly illiterate peasants, half-breeds, and indigenes, were educated, intelligent men, zealous only for the public weal, it would be possible for them to have a real republic. They have instead a government by cliques, tempered by revolution; and a very good government it is, in harmony with the physical conditions of the country and the national temperament. Now it happens that the educated men, representing your higher classes, are so few that there are not many persons unconnected by ties of blood or marriage with prominent members of the political groups to which they belong. By this you will see how easy and almost inevitable it is that we should become accustomed to look on conspiracy and revolt against the regnant party—the men of another clique—as only in the natural order of things. In the event of failure such outbreaks are punished, but they are not regarded as immoral. On the contrary, men of the highest intelligence and virtue among us are seen taking a leading part in these adventures. Whether such a condition of things is intrinsically wrong or not, or would be wrong in some circumstances and is not wrong, because inevitable, in others, I cannot pretend to decide; and all this tiresome prolusion is only to enable you to understand how I—a young man of unblemished character, not a soldier by profession, not ambitious of political distinction, wealthy for that country, popular in society, a lover of social pleasures, of books, of nature—actuated, as I believed, by the highest motives, allowed myself to be drawn very readily by friends and relations into a conspiracy to overthrow the government of the moment, with the object of replacing it by more worthy men—ourselves, to wit.

Our adventure failed because the authorities got wind of the affair and matters were precipitated. Our leaders at the moment happened to be scattered over the country—some were abroad; and a few hot-headed men of the party, who were in Caracas just then, and probably feared arrest, struck a rash blow: the President was attacked in the street and wounded. But the attackers were seized, and some of them shot on the following day. When the news reached me I was at a distance from the capital, staying with a friend on an estate he owned on the River Quebrada Honda, in the State of Guarico, some fifteen to twenty miles from the town of Zaraza. My friend, an officer in the army, was a leader in the conspiracy; and as I was the only son of a man who had been greatly hated by the Minister of War, it became necessary for us both

to fly for our lives. In the circumstances we could not
look to be pardoned, even on the score of youth.

Our first decision was to escape to the sea-coast; but
as the risk of a journey to La Guayra, or any other
port of embarkation on the north side of the country,
seemed too great, we made our way in a contrary
direction to the Orinoco, and downstream to Angostura. Now, when we had reached this comparatively
safe breathing-place—safe, at all events, for the moment—I changed my mind about leaving or attempting to leave the country. Since boyhood I had taken
a very peculiar interest in that vast and almost
unexplored territory we possess south of the Orinoco,
with its countless unmapped rivers and trackless
forests; and in its savage inhabitants, with their ancient customs and character, unadulterated by
contact with Europeans. To visit this primitive
wilderness had been a cherished dream; and I had to
some extent even prepared myself for such an adventure by mastering more than one of the Indian
dialects of the northern states of Venezuela. And
now, finding myself on the south side of our great
river, with unlimited time at my disposal, I determined to gratify this wish. My companion took his
departure towards the coast, while I set about making
preparations and hunting up information from those
who had travelled in the interior to trade with the
savages. I decided eventually to go back upstream,
and penetrate to the interior in the western part of

Guayana, and the Amazonian territory bordering on
Colombia and Brazil, and to return to Angostura in
about six months' time. I had no fear of being arrested in the semi-independent, and in most part
savage region, as the Guayana authorities concerned
themselves little enough about the political upheavals at Caracas.

The first five or six months I spent in Guayana,
after leaving the city of refuge, were eventful enough
to satisfy a moderately adventurous spirit. A com-
plaisant Government employee at Angostura had
provided me with a passport, in which it was set down
(for few to read) that my object in visiting the interior was to collect information concerning the native tribes, the vegetable products of the country, and
other knowledge which would be of advantage to the
Republic; and the authorities were requested to afford
me protection and assist me in my pursuits.

I ascended the Orinoco, making occasional expeditions to the small Christian settlements in the neighbourhood of the right bank, also to the Indian villages; and travelling in this way, seeing and learning
much, in about three months I reached the River
Meta. During this period I amused myself by keeping
a journal, a record of personal adventures, impressions of the country and people, both semi-civilised
and savage; and as my journal grew, I began to think
that on my return at some future time to Caracas, it
might prove useful and interesting to the public, and

also procure me fame; which thought proved pleasurable and a great incentive, so that I began to observe things more narrowly and to study expression. But the book was not to be.

From the mouth of the Meta I journeyed on, intending to visit the settlement of Atahapo, where the great River Guaviare, with other rivers, empty themselves into the Orinoco. But I was not destined to reach it, for at the small settlement of Manapuri I fell ill of a low fever; and here ended the first half-year of my wanderings, about which no more need be told.

A more miserable place than Manapuri for a man to be ill of a low fever in could not well be imagined. The settlement, composed of mean hovels, with a few large structures of mud, or plastered wattle, thatched with palm leaves, was surrounded by water, marsh, and forest, the breeding-place of myriads of croaking frogs and of clouds of mosquitoes; even to one in perfect health existence in such a place would have been a burden. The inhabitants mustered about eighty or ninety, mostly Indians of that degenerate class frequently to be met with in small trading outposts. The savages of Guayana are great drinkers, but not drunkards in our sense, since their fermented liquors contain so little alcohol that inordinate quantities must be swallowed to produce intoxication; in the settlements they prefer the white man's more potent poisons, with the result that in a small place like Manapuri one can see enacted, as on a stage, the last act in the great American tragedy. To be succeeded, doubtless, by other and possibly greater tragedies. My thoughts at that period of suffering were pessimistic in the extreme. Sometimes, when the almost continuous rain held up for half a day, I would manage to creep out a short distance; but I was almost past making any exertion, scarcely caring to live, and taking absolutely no interest in the news from Caracas, which reached me at long intervals. At the end of two months, feeling a slight improvement in my health, and with it a returning interest in life and its affairs, it occurred to me to get out my diary and write a brief account of my sojourn at Manapuri. I had placed it for safety in a small deal box, lent to me for the purpose by a Venezuelan trader, an old resident at the settlement, by name Pantaleon— called by all Don Panta—one who openly kept half a dozen Indian wives in his house, and was noted for his dishonesty and greed, but who had proved himself a good friend to me. The box was in a corner of the wretched palm-thatched hovel I inhabited; but on taking it out I discovered that for several weeks the rain had been dripping on it, and that the manuscript was reduced to a sodden pulp. I flung it upon the floor with a curse, and threw myself back on my bed with a groan.

In that desponding state I was found by my friend Panta, who was constant in his visits at all hours;

and, when in answer to his anxious inquiries I pointed to the pulpy mass on the mud floor, he turned it over with his foot, and then, bursting into a loud laugh, kicked it out, remarking that he had mistaken the object for some unknown reptile that had crawled in out of the rain. He affected to be astonished that I should regret its loss. It was all a true narrative, he exclaimed; if I wished to write a book for the stay-at-homes to read, I could easily invent a thousand lies far more entertaining than any real experiences. He had come to me, he said, to propose something. He had lived twenty years at that place, and had got accustomed to the climate, but it would not do for me to remain any longer if I wished to live. I must go away at once to a different country—to the mountains, where it was open and dry. "And if you want quinine when you are there," he concluded, "smell the wind when it blows from the south-west, and you will inhale it into your system, fresh from the forest." When I remarked despondingly that in my condition it would be impossible to quit Manapuri, he went on to say that a small party of Indians was now in the settlement; that they had come, not only to trade, but to visit one of their own tribe, who was his wife, purchased some years ago from her father. "And the money she cost me I have never regretted to this day," said he, "for she is a good wife—not jealous," he added, with a curse on all the others. These Indians came all the way from the Queneveta mountains, and were of the Maquiritari tribe. He, Panta, and, better still, his good wife, would interest them on my behalf, and for a suitable reward they would take me by slow, easy stages to their own country, where I would be treated well and recover my health.

This proposal, after I had considered it well, produced so good an effect on me, that I not only gave a glad consent, but, on the following day, I was able to get about and begin the preparations for my journey with some spirit.

In about eight days I bade good-bye to my generous friend Panta, whom I regarded, after having seen much of him, as a kind of savage beast that had sprung on me, not to rend, but to rescue from death; for we know that even cruel savage brutes and evil men have at times sweet, beneficent impulses, during which they act in a way contrary to their natures, like passive agents of some higher power. It was a continual pain to travel in my weak condition, and the patience of my Indians was severely taxed; but they did not forsake me; and, at last, the entire distance, which I conjectured to be about sixty-five leagues, was accomplished; and at the end I was actually stronger and better in every way than at the start. From this time my progress towards complete recovery was rapid. The air, with or without any medicinal virtue blown from the cinchona trees in the far-off Andean forest, was tonic; and when I took my walks on the hillside above the Indian village, or later, when able to climb to the summits, the world as seen from those wild Queneveta mountains had a largeness and varied glory of scenery peculiarly refreshing and delightful to the soul.

With the Maquiritari tribe I passed some weeks, and the sweet sensations of returning health made me happy for a time; but such sensations seldom outlast convalescence. I was no sooner well again than I began to feel a restless spirit stirring in me. The monotony of savage life in this place became intolerable. After my long listless period the reaction had come, and I wished only for action, adventure—no matter how dangerous; and for new scenes, new faces, new dialects. In the end I conceived the idea of going on to the Casiquiare river, where I would find a few small settlements, and perhaps obtain help from the authorities there which would enable me to reach the Rio Negro. For it was now in my mind to follow that river to the Amazons, and so down to Para and the Atlantic coast.

Leaving the Queneveta range, I started with two of the Indians as guides and travelling companions; but their journey ended only half-way to the river I wished to reach; and they left me with some friendly savages living on the Chunapay, a tributary of the Cunucumana, which flows to the Orinoco. Here I had no choice but to wait until an opportunity of attaching myself to some party of travelling Indians, going south-west, should arrive; for by this time I had expended the whole of my small capital in ornaments and calico brought from Manapuri, so that I could no longer purchase any man's service. And perhaps it will be as well to state at this point just what I possessed. For some time I had worn nothing but sandals to protect my feet; my garments consisted of a single suit, and one flannel shirt, which I washed frequently, going shirtless while it was drying. Fortunately I had an excellent blue cloth cloak, durable and handsome, given to me by a friend at Angostura, whose prophecy on presenting it, that it would outlast *me*, very nearly came true. It served as a covering by night, and to keep a man warm and comfortable when travelling in cold and wet weather no better garment was ever made. I had a revolver and metal cartridge-box in my broad leather belt, also a good hunting-knife with strong buckhorn handle and a heavy blade about nine inches long. In the pocket of my cloak I had a pretty silver tinder-box, and a match-box—to be mentioned again in this narrative—and one or two other trifling objects; these I was determined to keep until they could be kept no longer.

During the tedious interval of waiting on the Chunapay I was told a flattering tale by the village Indians, which eventually caused me to abandon the proposed journey to the Rio Negro. These Indians wore necklets, like nearly all the Guayana savages; but one, I observed, possessed a necklet unlike that of the others, which greatly aroused my curiosity. It was

made of thirteen gold plates, irregular in form, about
as broad as a man's thumb-nail, and linked together
with fibres. I was allowed to examine it, and had no
doubt that the pieces were of pure gold, beaten flat by
the savages. When questioned about it they said that
it was originally obtained from the Indians of Parahuari, and Parahuari, they further said, was a moun-
tainous country west of the Orinoco. Every man and
woman in that place, they assured me, had such a
necklet. This report inflamed my mind to such a degree that I could not rest by night or day for dreaming golden dreams, and considering how to get to that
rich district, unknown to civilised men. The Indians
gravely shook their heads when I tried to persuade
them to take me. They were far enough from the
Orinoco, and Parahuari was ten, perhaps fifteen, days'
journey farther on—a country unknown to them,
where they had no relations.

In spite of difficulties and delays, however, and not
without pain and some perilous adventures, I succeeded at last in reaching the upper Orinoco, and,
eventually, in crossing to the other side. With my
life in my hand I struggled on westward through an
unknown difficult country, from Indian village to village, where at any moment I might have been murdered with impunity for the sake of my few belongings. It is hard for me to speak a good word for the
Guayana savages; but I must now say this of them,
that they not only did me no harm when I was at

their mercy during this long journey, but they gave me shelter in their villages, and fed me when I was hungry, and helped me on my way when I could make no return. You must not, however, run away with the idea that there is any sweetness in their disposition, any humane or benevolent instincts such as are found among the civilised nations: far from it. I regard them now, and, fortunately for me, I regarded them then, when, as I have said, I was at their mercy, as beasts of prey, plus a cunning or low kind of intelligence vastly greater than that of the brute; and, for only morality, that respect for the rights of other members of the same family, or tribe, without which even the rudest communities cannot hold together. How, then, could I do this thing, and dwell and travel freely, without receiving harm, among tribes that have no peace with and no kindly feelings towards the stranger, in a district where the white man is rarely or never seen? Because I knew them so well. Without that knowledge, always available, and an extreme facility in acquiring new dialects, which had increased by practice until it was almost like intuition, I should have fared badly after leaving the Maquiritari tribe. As it was, I had two or three very narrow escapes.

To return from this digression. I looked at last on the famous Parahuari mountains, which, I was greatly surprised to find, were after all nothing but hills, and not very high ones. This, however, did not depress me. The very fact that Parahuari possessed no imposing feature in its scenery seemed rather to prove that it must be rich in gold: how else could its name and the fame of its treasures be familiar to people dwelling so far away as the Cunucumana?

But there was no gold. I searched through the whole range, which was about seven leagues long, and visited the villages, where I talked much with the Indians, interrogating them, and they had no necklets of gold, nor gold in any form; nor had they ever heard of its presence in Parahuari, nor in any other place known to them.

The very last village where I spoke on the subject of my quest, albeit now without hope, was about a league from the western extremity of the range, in the midst of a high, broken country of forest and savannah and many swift streams; near one of these, called the Curicay, the village stood, among low scattered trees—a large building, in which all the people, numbering eighteen, passed most of their time when not hunting, with two smaller buildings attached to it. The head, or chief, Runi by name, was about fifty years old, a taciturn, finely formed, and somewhat dignified savage, who was either of a sullen disposition or not well pleased at the intrusion of a white man. And for a time I made no attempt to conciliate him. What profit was there in it at all? Even that light mask, which I had worn so long and with such good effect, incommoded me now: I would cast it aside and be myself—silent and sullen as my barbarous host. If any malignant purpose was taking form in his mind, let it, and let him do his worst; for when failure first stares a man in the face it has so dark and repellent a look that not anything that can be added can make him more miserable, nor has he any apprehension. For weeks I had been searching with eager, feverish eyes in every village, in every rocky crevice, in every noisy mountain streamlet, for the glittering yellow dust I had travelled so far to find. And now all my beautiful dreams—all the pleasure and power to be—had vanished like a mere mirage on the savannah at noon.

It was a day of despair which I spent in this place, sitting all day indoors, for it was raining hard, immersed in my own gloomy thoughts, pretending to doze in my seat, and out of the narrow slits of my half-closed eyes seeing the others, also sitting or moving about, like shadows or people in a dream; and I cared nothing about them, and wished not to seem friendly, even for the sake of the food they might offer me by-and-by.

Towards evening the rain ceased; and rising up I went out a short distance to the neighbouring stream, where I sat on a stone, and casting off my sandals, laved my bruised feet in the cool running water. The western half of the sky was blue again with that tender lucid blue seen after rain, but the leaves still glittered with water, and the wet trunks looked almost black under the green foliage. The rare loveli-

ness of the scene touched and lightened my heart.
Away back in the east the hills of Parahuari, with the
level sun full on them, loomed with a strange glory
against the grey rainy clouds drawing off on that
side, and their new mystic beauty almost made me
forget how these same hills had wearied, and hurt,
and mocked me. On that side, also to the north and
south, there was open forest, but to the west a different prospect met the eye. Beyond the stream and
the strip of verdure that fringed it, and the few scattered dwarf trees growing near its banks, spread a
brown savannah sloping upwards to a long, low, rocky
ridge, beyond which rose a great solitary hill, or rather
mountain, conical in form, and clothed in forest almost to the summit. This was the mountain Ytaioa,
the chief landmark in that district. As the sun went
down over the ridge, beyond the savannah, the whole
western sky changed to a delicate rose-colour that had
the appearance of rose-coloured smoke blown there
by some far-off wind, and left suspended—a thin, brilliant veil showing through it the distant sky beyond,
blue and ethereal. Flocks of birds, a kind of troupial,
were flying past me overhead, flock succeeding flock,
on their way to their roosting-place, uttering as they
flew a clear, bell-like chirp; and there was something
ethereal too in those drops of melodious sound, which
fell into my heart like raindrops falling into a pool to
mix their fresh heavenly water with the water of
earth.

Doubtless into the turbid tarn of my heart some sacred drops had fallen—from the passing birds, from that crimson disc which had now dropped below the horizon, the darkening hills, the rose and blue of infinite heaven, from the whole visible circle; and I felt purified and had a strange sense and apprehension of a secret innocence and spirituality in nature—a prescience of some bourn, incalculably distant perhaps, to which we are all moving; of a time when the heavenly rain shall have washed us clean from all spot and blemish. This unexpected peace which I had found now seemed to me of infinitely greater value than that yellow metal I had missed finding, with all its possibilities. My wish now was to rest for a season at this spot, so remote and lovely and peaceful, where I had experienced such unusual feelings, and such a blessed disillusionment.

This was the end of my second period in Guayana; the first had been filled with that dream of a book to win me fame in my country, perhaps even in Europe: the second, from the time of leaving the Queneveta mountains, with the dream of boundless wealth—the old dream of gold in this region that has drawn so many minds since the days of Alonzo Pizarro. But to remain I must propitiate Runi, sitting silent with gloomy brows over there indoors; and he did not appear to me like one that might be won with words, however flattering. It was clear to me that the time had come to part with my one remaining valuable trinket—the tinder-box of chased silver.

I returned to the house, and going in seated myself on a log by the fire, just opposite to my grim host, who was smoking and appeared not to have moved since I left him. I made myself a cigarette, then drew out the tinder-box, with its flint and steel attached to it by means of two small silver chains. His eyes brightened a little as they curiously watched my movements, and he pointed without speaking to the glowing coals of fire at my feet. I shook my head, and striking the steel, sent out a brilliant spray of sparks, then blew on the tinder and lit my cigarette. This done, instead of returning the box to my pocket I passed the chain through the buttonhole of my cloak and let it dangle on my breast as an ornament. When the cigarette was smoked I cleared my throat in the orthodox manner, and fixed my eyes on Runi, who, on his part, made a slight movement to indicate that he was ready to listen to what I had to say.

My speech was long, lasting at least half an hour, delivered in a profound silence; it was chiefly occupied with an account of my wanderings in Guayana; and being little more than a catalogue of names of all the places I had visited, and the tribes and chief or head men with whom I had come in contact, I was able to speak continuously, and so to hide my ignorance of a dialect which was still new to me. The Guayana savage judges a man for his staying powers.

To stand as motionless as a bronze statue for one or
two hours watching for a bird; to sit or lie still for
half a day; to endure pain, not seldom self-inflicted,
without wincing; and when delivering a speech to
pour it out in a copious stream, without pausing to
take breath or hesitating over a word—to be able to
do all this is to prove yourself a man, an equal, one
to be respected and even made a friend of. What I
really wished to say to him was put in a few words at
the conclusion of my well-nigh meaningless oration.
Everywhere, I said, I had been the Indian's friend,
and I wished to be his friend, to live with him at
Parahuari, even as I had lived with other chiefs and
heads of villages and families; to be looked on by
him, as these others had looked on me, not as a
stranger or a white man, but as a friend, a brother,
an Indian.

I ceased speaking, and there was a slight murmur-
ous sound in the room, as of wind long pent up in
many lungs suddenly exhaled; while Runi, still unmoved, emitted a low grunt. Then I rose, and detach-
ing the silver ornament from my cloak presented it to
him. He accepted it; not very graciously, as a stranger
to these people might have imagined; but I was satisfied, feeling sure that I had made a favourable impression. After a little he handed the box to the person sitting next to him, who examined it and passed
it on to a third, and in this way it went round and
came back once more to Runi. Then he called for a

drink. There happened to be a store of casserie in the house; probably the women had been busy for some days past in making it, little thinking that it was destined to be prematurely consumed. A large jarful was produced; Runi politely quaffed the first cup; I followed; then the others; and the women drank also, a woman taking about one cupful to a man's three. Runi and I, however, drank the most, for we had our positions as the two principal personages there to maintain. Tongues were loosened now; for the alcohol, small as the quantity contained in this mild liquor is, had begun to tell on our brains. I had not their pottle-shaped stomach, made to hold unlimited quantities of meat and drink; but I was determined on this most important occasion not to deserve my host's contempt—to be compared, perhaps, to the small bird that delicately picks up six drops of water in its bill and is satisfied. I would measure my strength against his, and if necessary drink myself into a state of insensibility. At last I was scarcely able to stand on my legs. But even the seasoned old savage was affected by this time. *In vino veritas*, said the ancients; and the principle holds good where there is no vinum, but only mild casserie. Runi now informed me that he had once known a white man, that he was a bad man, which had caused him to say that all white men were bad; even as David, still more sweepingly, had proclaimed that all men were liars.

Now he found that it was not so, that I was a good man. His friendliness increased with intoxication. He presented me with a curious little tinder-box, made from the conical tail of an armadillo, hollowed out, and provided with a wooden stopper;—this to be used in place of the box I had deprived myself of. He also furnished me with a grass hammock, and had it hung up there and then, so that I could lie down when inclined. There was nothing he would not do for me. And at last, when many more cups had been emptied, and a third or fourth jar brought out, he began to unburden his heart of its dark and dangerous secrets. He shed tears—for the "man without a tear" dwells not in the woods of Guayana: tears for those who had been treacherously slain long years ago; for his father, who had been killed by Tripica, the father of Managa, who was still above ground. But let him and all his people beware of Runi. He had spilt their blood before, he had fed the fox and vulture with their flesh, and would never rest while Managa lived with his people at Uritay—the five hills of Uritay, which were two days' journey from Parahuari. While thus talking of his old enemy he lashed himself into a kind of frenzy, smiting his chest and gnashing his teeth; and finally seizing a spear, he buried its point deep into the clay floor, only to wrench it out and strike it into the earth again and again, to show how he would serve Managa, and any one of Managa's people he might meet with—man, woman, or child. Then he staggered out from the door to flourish his spear; and looking to the north-west, he shouted aloud to Managa to come and slay his people and burn down his house, as he had so often threatened to do.

"Let him come! Let Managa come!" I cried, staggering out after him. "I am your friend, your brother; I have no spear and no arrows, but I have this— this!" And here I drew out and flourished my revolver. "Where is Managa?" I continued. "Where are the hills of Uritay?" He pointed to a star low down in the south-west. "Then," I shouted, "let this bullet find Managa, sitting by the fire among his people, and let him fall and pour out his blood on the ground!" And with that I discharged my pistol in the direction he had pointed to. A scream of terror burst out from the women and children, while Runi at my side, in an access of fierce delight and admiration, turned and embraced me. It was the first and last embrace I ever suffered from a naked male savage, and although this did not seem a time for fastidious feelings, to be hugged to his sweltering body was an unpleasant experience.

More cups of casserie followed this outburst; and at last, unable to keep it up any longer, I staggered to my hammock; but being unable to get into it, Runi, overflowing with kindness, came to my assistance, whereupon we fell and rolled together on the floor. Finally, I was raised by the others and tumbled into my swinging bed, and fell at once into a deep, dreamless sleep, from which I did not awake until after sunrise on the following morning.

❧ 2 ❧

IT IS FORTUNATE that casserie is manufactured by an extremely slow, laborious process, since the women, who are the drink-makers, in the first place have to reduce the material (cassava bread) to a pulp by means of their own molars, after which it is watered down and put away in troughs to ferment. Great is the diligence of these willing slaves; but, work how they will, they can only satisfy their lords' love of a big drink at long intervals. Such a function as that at which I had assisted is therefore the result of much patient mastication and silent fermentation—the delicate flower of a plant that has been a long time growing.

Having now established myself as one of the family, at the cost of some disagreeable sensations and a pang or two of self-disgust, I resolved to let nothing further trouble me at Parahuari, but to live the easy, careless life of the idle man, joining in hunting and fishing expeditions when in the mood; at other times enjoying existence in my own way, apart from my fellows, conversing with wild nature in that solitary place.

Besides Runi, there were, in our little community, two oldish men, his cousins I believe, who had wives and grown-up children. Another family consisted of Piaké, Runi's nephew, his brother Kua-kó—about whom there will be much to say—and a sister Oolava. Piaké had a wife and two children; Kua-kó was unmarried and about nineteen or twenty years old; Oolava was the youngest of the three. Last of all, who should perhaps have been first, was Runi's mother, called Cla-cla, probably in imitation of the cry of some bird, for in these latitudes a person is rarely, perhaps never, called by his or her real name, which is a secret jealously preserved, even from near relations. I believe that Cla-cla herself was the only living being who knew the name her parents had bestowed on her at birth. She was a very old woman, spare in figure, brown as old sun-baked leather, her face written over with innumerable wrinkles, and her long coarse hair perfectly white; yet she was exceedingly active, and seemed to do more work than any other woman in the community; more than that,

when the day's toil was over and nothing remained
for the others to do, then Cla-cla's night work would
begin; and this was to talk all the others, or at all
events all the men, to sleep. She was like a self-
regulating machine, and punctually every evening,
when the door was closed, and the night-fire made
up, and every man in his hammock, she would set
herself going, telling the most interminable stories,
until the last listener was fast asleep: later in the
night, if any man woke with a snort or grunt, off she
would go again, taking up the thread of the tale where
she had dropped it.

Old Cla-cla amused me very much, by night and
day, and I seldom tired of watching her owlish countenance as she sat by the fire, never allowing it to
sink low for want of fuel; always studying the pot
when it was on to simmer, and at the same time attending to the movements of the others about her,
ready at a moment's notice to give assistance or to
dart out on a stray chicken or refractory child.

So much did she amuse me, although without intending it, that I thought it would be only fair, in
my turn, to do something for her entertainment. I
was engaged one day in shaping a wooden foil with
my knife, whistling and singing snatches of old
melodies at my work, when all at once I caught sight
of the ancient dame looking greatly delighted,
chuckling internally, nodding her head, and keeping
time with her hands. Evidently she was able to appre-

ciate a style of music superior to that of the aboriginals, and forthwith I abandoned my foils for the time and set about the manufacture of a guitar, which cost me much labour, and brought out more ingenuity than I had ever thought myself capable of. To reduce the wood to the right thinness, then to bend and fasten it with wooden pegs and with gums, to add the arm, frets, keys, and finally the catgut strings—those of another kind being out of the question—kept me busy for some days. When completed it was a rude instrument, scarcely tunable; nevertheless when I smote the strings, playing lively music, or accompanied myself in singing, I found that it was a great success, and so was as much pleased with my own performance as if I had had the most perfect guitar ever made in old Spain. I also skipped about the floor, strum-strumming at the same time, instructing them in the most lively dances of the whites, in which the feet must be as nimble as the player's fingers. It is true that these exhibitions were always witnessed by the adults with a profound gravity, which would have disheartened a stranger to their ways. They were a set of hollow bronze statues that looked at me, but I knew that the living animals inside of them were tickled at my singing, strumming, and pirouetting. Cla-cla was, however, an exception, and encouraged me not infrequently by emitting a sound, half cackle and half screech, by way of laughter; for she had come to her second childhood, or, at all events, had dropped the stolid mask which the young Guayana savage, in imitation of his elders, adjusts to his face at about the age of twelve, to wear it thereafter all his life long, or only to drop it occasionally when very drunk. The youngsters also openly manifested their pleasure, although, as a rule, they try to restrain their feelings in the presence of grown-up people, and with them I became a great favourite.

By-and-by I returned to my foil-making, and gave them fencing lessons, and sometimes invited two or three of the biggest boys to attack me simultaneously, just to show how easily I could disarm and kill them. This practice excited some interest in Kua-kó, who had a little more of curiosity and geniality and less of the put-on dignity of the others, and with him I became most intimate. Fencing with Kua-kó was highly amusing: no sooner was he in position, foil in hand, than all my instructions were thrown to the winds, and he would charge and attack me in his own barbarous manner, with the result that I would send his foil spinning a dozen yards away, while he, struck motionless, would gaze after it in open-mouthed astonishment.

Three weeks had passed by not unpleasantly when, one morning, I took it into my head to walk by myself across that somewhat sterile savannah west of the village and stream, which ended, as I have said, in a long, low, stony ridge. From the village there was nothing to attract the eye in that direction; but I wished to get a better view of that great solitary hill or mountain of Ytaioa, and of the cloud-like summits beyond it in the distance. From the stream the ground rose in a gradual slope, and the highest part of the ridge for which I made was about two miles from the starting-point—a parched brown plain, with nothing growing on it but scattered tussocks of sere hair-like grass.

When I reached the top and could see the country beyond, I was agreeably disappointed at the discovery that the sterile ground extended only about a mile and a quarter on the farther side, and was succeeded by a forest—a very inviting patch of woodland covering five or six square miles, occupying a kind of oblong basin, extending from the foot of Ytaioa on the north to a low range of rocky hills on the south. From the wooded basin long narrow strips of forest ran out in various directions like the arms of an octopus, one pair embracing the slopes of Ytaioa, another much broader belt extending along a valley which cut through the ridge of hills on the south side at right angles, and was lost to sight beyond; far away in the west and south and north distant mountains appeared, not in regular ranges, but in groups or singly, or looking like blue banked-up clouds on the horizon.

Glad at having discovered the existence of this forest so near home, and wondering why my Indian friends had never taken me to it, or ever went out on that side, I set forth with a light heart to explore it for myself, regretting only that I was without a proper weapon for procuring game. The walk from the ridge over the savannah was easy, as the barren, stony ground sloped downward the whole way. The outer part of the wood on my side was very open, composed in most part of dwarf trees that grow on stony soil, and scattered thorny bushes bearing a yellow pea-shaped blossom. Presently I came to thicker wood, where the trees were much taller and in greater variety; and after this came another sterile strip, like that on the edge of the wood, where stone cropped out from the ground and nothing grew except the yellow-flowered thorn bushes. Passing this sterile ribbon, which seemed to extend to a considerable distance north and south, and was fifty to a hundred yards wide, the forest again became dense and the trees large, with much undergrowth in places obstructing the view and making progress difficult.

I spent several hours in this wild paradise which was so much more delightful than the extensive gloomier forests I had so often penetrated in Guayana: for here, if the trees did not attain to such majestic proportions, the variety of vegetable forms was even greater; as far as I went it was nowhere dark under the trees, and the number of lovely parasites everywhere illustrated the kindly influence of light and air. Even where the trees were largest the sunshine penetrated, subdued by the foliage to exquisite greenish-golden tints, filling the wide lower spaces with tender half-lights, and faint blue-and-grey shadows. Lying on my back and gazing up, I felt reluctant to rise and renew my ramble. For what a roof was that above my head! Roof I call it, just as the poets in their poverty sometimes describe the infinite ethereal sky by that word; but it was no more roof-like and hindering to the soaring spirit than the higher clouds that float in changing forms and tints, and like the foliage chasten the intolerable noonday beams. How far above me seemed that leafy cloudland into which I gazed! Nature, we know, first taught the architect to produce by long colonnades the illusion of distance; but the light-excluding roof prevents him from getting the same effect above. Here Nature is unapproachable with her green, airy canopy, a sun-impregnated cloud—cloud above cloud; and though the highest may be unreached by the eye, the beams yet filter through, illuming the wide spaces beneath—chamber succeeded by chamber, each with its own special lights and shadows. Far above me, but not nearly so far as it seemed, the tender gloom of one such chamber or space is traversed now by a golden shaft of light falling through some break in the upper foliage, giving a strange glory to everything it touches —projecting leaves, and beard-like tuft of moss, and snaky bush-rope. And in the most open part of that most open space, suspended on nothing to the eye, the shaft reveals a tangle of shining silver threads— the web of some large tree-spider. These seemingly distant, yet distinctly visible threads, serve to remind me that the human artist is only able to get his horizontal distance by a monotonous reduplication of pillar and arch, placed at regular intervals, and that the least departure from this order would destroy the effect. But Nature produces her effects at random, and seems only to increase the beautiful illusion by that infinite variety of decoration in which she revels, binding tree to tree in a tangle of anaconda-like lianas, and dwindling down from these huge cables to airy webs and hair-like fibres that vibrate to the wind of the passing insect's wing.

Thus in idleness, with such thoughts for company, I spent my time, glad that no human being, savage or civilised, was with me. It was better to be alone to listen to the monkeys that chattered without offending; to watch them occupied with the unserious business of their lives. With that luxuriant tropical nature, its green clouds and illusive aerial spaces, full of mystery, they harmonised well in language, appearance, and motions:—mountebank angels, living their fantastic lives far above earth in a half-way heaven of their own.

I saw more monkeys on that morning than I usually saw in the course of a week's rambling. And other animals were seen; I particularly remember two accouries I startled, that after rushing away a few yards stopped and stood peering back at me as if not knowing whether to regard me as friend or enemy. Birds, too, were strangely abundant; and altogether this struck me as being the richest hunting-ground I had seen, and it astonished me to think that the Indians of the village did not appear to visit it.

On my return in the afternoon I gave an enthusiastic account of my day's ramble, speaking not of the things that had moved my soul, but only of those which move the Guayana Indian's soul—the animal food he craves, and which, one would imagine, Nature would prefer him to do without, so hard he finds it to wrest a sufficiency from her. To my surprise they shook their heads and looked troubled at what I said; and finally, my host informed me that the wood I had been in was a dangerous place; that if they went there to hunt, a great injury would be done to them; and he finished by advising me not to visit it again.

I began to understand from their looks and the old man's vague words that their fear of the wood was superstitious. If dangerous creatures had existed there—tigers, or camoodis, or solitary murderous savages—they would have said so; but when I pressed them with questions they could only repeat that "something bad" existed in the place, that animals were abundant there because no Indian who valued his life dared venture into it. I replied that unless they gave me some more definite information I should certainly go again, and put myself in the way of the danger they feared.

My reckless courage, as they considered it, surprised them; but they had already begun to find out that their superstitions had no effect on me, that I listened to them as to stories invented to amuse a child, and for the moment they made no further attempt to dissuade me.

Next day I returned to the forest of evil report, which had now a new and even greater charm—the fascination of the unknown and the mysterious; still, the warning I had received made me distrustful and cautious at first, for I could not help thinking about it. When we consider how much of their life is passed in the woods, which become as familiar to them as the streets of our native town to us, it seems almost incredible that these savages had a superstitious fear of all forests, fearing them as much, even in the bright light of day, as a nervous child with memory filled with ghost-stories fears a dark room. But, like the child in the dark room, they fear the forest only when alone in it, and for this reason always hunt in couples or parties. What, then, prevented them from visiting this particular wood, which offered so tempting a harvest? The question troubled me not a little; at the same time I was ashamed of the feeling, and fought against it; and in the end I made my way to the same sequestered spot where I had rested so long on my previous visit.

In this place I witnessed a new thing, and had a strange experience. Sitting on the ground in the shade of a large tree, I began to hear a confused noise as of a coming tempest of wind mixed with shrill calls and cries. Nearer and nearer it came, and at last a multitude of birds of many kinds, but mostly small, appeared in sight swarming through the trees, some running on the trunks and larger branches, others flitting through the foliage, and many keeping on the wing, now hovering and now darting this way or that. They were all busily searching for and pursuing the insects, moving on at the same time, and in a very few minutes they had finished examining the trees near me, and were gone; but not satisfied with what I had witnessed, I jumped up and rushed after the flock to keep it in sight. All my caution and all recollection of what the Indians had said was now forgot, so great was my interest in this bird-army; but as they moved on without pause they quickly left me behind, and presently my career was stopped by an impenetrable tangle of bushes, vines, and roots of large trees extending like huge cables along the ground. In the midst of this leafy labyrinth I sat down on a projecting root to cool my blood before attempting to make my way back to my former position. After that tempest of motion and confused noises the silence of the forest seemed very profound; but before I had been resting many moments it was broken by a low strain of exquisite bird-melody, wonderfully pure and expressive, unlike any musical sound I had ever heard before. It seemed to issue from a thick cluster of broad leaves of a creeper only a few yards from where I sat. With my eyes fixed on this green hiding-place I waited with suspended breath for its repetition, wondering whether any civilised being had ever listened to such a strain before. Surely not, I thought, else the fame of so divine a melody would long ago have been noised abroad. I thought of the rialejo, the celebrated organ-bird or flute-bird, and of the various ways in which hearers are affected by it. To some its warbling is like the sound of a beautiful mysterious instrument, while to others it seems like the singing of a blithe-hearted child with a highly melodious voice. I had often heard and listened with delight to the singing of the rialejo in the Guayana forests, but this song, or musical phrase, was utterly unlike it in character. It was purer, more expressive, softer—so low that at a distance of forty yards I could hardly have heard it. But its greatest charm was its resemblance to the human voice—a voice purified and brightened to something almost angelic. Imagine, then, my impatience as I sat there straining my sense, my deep disappointment when it was not repeated; I rose at length very reluctantly and slowly began making my way back; but when I had progressed about thirty yards, again the sweet voice sounded just behind me, and turning quickly I stood still and waited. The same voice, but not the same song—not the same phrase; the notes were different, more varied and rapidly enunciated, as if the singer had been more excited. The blood rushed to my heart as I listened; my nerves tingled with a strange new delight, the rapture produced by such music heightened by a sense of mystery. Before many moments I heard it again, not rapid now, but a soft warbling, lower than at first, infinitely sweet and tender, sinking to lisping sounds that soon ceased to be audible; the whole having lasted as long as a sentence of a dozen words. This seemed the singer's farewell to me, for I waited and listened in vain to hear it repeated; and after getting back to the starting-point I sat for upwards of an hour, still hoping to hear it once more!

The westering sun at length compelled me to quit the wood, but not before I had resolved to return the next morning and seek for the spot where I had met with so enchanting an experience. After crossing the sterile belt I have mentioned within the wood, and just before I came to the open outer edge where the stunted trees and bushes die away on the border of the savannah, what was my delight and astonishment at hearing the mysterious melody once more! It seemed to issue from a clump of bushes close by; but by this time I had come to the conclusion that there was a ventriloquism in this woodland voice which made it impossible for me to determine its exact direction. Of one thing I was, however, now quite convinced, and that was the singer had been following me all the time. Again and again as I stood there listening it sounded, now so faint and apparently far off as to be scarcely audible; then all at once it would ring out bright and clear within a few yards of me, as if the shy little thing had suddenly grown bold; but, far or near, the vocalist remained invisible, and at length the tantalising melody ceased altogether.

❧ 3 ❧

I was not disappointed on my next visit to the forest, nor on several succeeding visits; and this seemed to show that if I was right in believing that these strange, melodious utterances proceeded from one individual, then the bird or being, although still refusing to show itself, was always on the watch for my appearance, and followed me wherever I went. This thought only served to increase my curiosity; I was constantly pondering over the subject, and at last concluded that it would be best to induce one of the Indians to go with me to the wood on the chance of his being able to explain the mystery.

One of the treasures I had managed to preserve in my sojourn with these children of nature, who were always anxious to become possessors of my belongings, was a small prettily fashioned metal match-box, opening with a spring. Remembering that Kua-kó, among others, had looked at this trifle with covetous eyes—the covetous way in which they all looked at it had given it a fictitious value in my own—I tried to bribe him with the offer of it to accompany me to my favourite haunt. The brave young hunter refused again and again; but on each occasion he offered to perform some other service or to give me something in exchange for the box. At last I told him that I would give it to the first person who should accompany me, and fearing that someone would be found valiant enough to win the prize, he at length plucked up a spirit, and on the next day, seeing me going out for a walk, he all at once offered to go with me. He cunningly tried to get the box before starting—his cunning, poor youth! was not very deep. I told him that the forest we were about to visit abounded with plants and birds unlike any I had seen elsewhere, that I wished to learn their names, and everything about them, and that when I had got the required information the box would be his—not sooner. Finally we started, he, as usual, armed with his zabatana, with which, I imagined, he would procure more game than usually fell to his little poisoned arrows. When we reached the wood I could see that he was ill at ease: nothing would persuade him to go into the deeper parts; and even where it was very open and light he was constantly gazing into bushes and shadowy places, as if expecting to see some frightful creature lying in wait for him. This behaviour might have had a disquieting effect on me had I not been thoroughly convinced that his fears were purely superstitious, and that there could be no dangerous animal in a spot I was accustomed to walk in every day. My plan was to ramble about with an unconcerned air, occasionally pointing out an uncommon tree or shrub or vine, or calling his attention to a distant bird cry and asking the bird's name, in the hope that the mysterious voice would make itself heard, and that he would be able to give me some explanation of it. But for upwards of two hours we moved about, hearing nothing except the usual bird voices, and during all that time he never stirred a yard from my side nor made an attempt to capture anything. At length we sat down under a tree, in an open spot close to the border of the wood. He sat down very reluctantly, and seemed more troubled in his mind than ever, keeping his eyes continually roving about, while he listened intently to every sound. The sounds were not few, owing to the abundance of animal and especially of bird life in this favoured spot. I began to question my companion as to some of the cries we heard. There were notes and cries familiar to me as the crowing of the cock—parrot screams and yelping of toucans, the distant wailing calls of maam and duraquara; and shrill laughter-like notes of the large tree-climber as it passed from tree to tree; the quick whistle of cotingas; and strange throbbing and thrilling sounds, as of pigmies beating on metallic drums, of the skulking pitta-thrushes; and with these mingled other notes less well known. One came from the treetops, where it was perpetually wandering amid the foliage—a low note, repeated at intervals of a few seconds, so thin and mournful and full of mystery, that I half expected to hear that it proceeded from the restless ghost of some dead bird. But no; he only said that it was uttered by a "little bird"—too little presumably to have a name. From the foliage of a neighbouring tree came a few tinkling chirps, as of a small mandolin, two or three strings of which had been carelessly struck by the player. He said that it came from a small green frog that lived in trees; and in this way my rude Indian—vexed perhaps at being asked such trivial questions—brushed away the pretty fantasies my mind had woven in the woodland solitude. For I often listened to this tinkling music, and it had suggested the idea that the place was frequented by a tribe of fairy-like troubadour monkeys, and that if I could only be quick-sighted enough I might one day be able to detect the minstrel sitting, in a green tunic perhaps, cross-legged on some high, swaying bough, carelessly touching his mandolin suspended from his neck by a yellow ribbon.

By-and-by a bird came with low, swift flight, its great tail spread open fan-wise, and perched itself on an exposed bough not thirty yards from us. It was all of a chestnut-red colour, long-bodied, in size like a big pigeon: its actions showed that its curiosity had been greatly excited, for it jerked from side to side, eyeing us first with one eye, then the other, while its long tail rose and fell in a measured way.

"Look, Kua-kó," I said in a whisper, "there is a bird for you to kill."

But he only shook his head, still watchful.

"Give me the blow-pipe, then," I said, with a laugh, putting out my hand to take it. But he refused to let me take it, knowing that it would only be an arrow wasted if I attempted to shoot anything.

As I persisted in telling him to kill the bird, he at last bent his lips near me and said in a half-whisper, as if fearful of being overheard, "I can kill nothing here. If I shot at the bird the daughter of the Didi would catch the dart in her hand and throw it back and hit me here," touching his breast just over his heart.

I laughed again, saying to myself, with some amusement, that Kua-kó was not such a bad companion after all—that he was not without imagination. But in spite of my laughter his words roused my interest, and suggested the idea that the voice I was curious about had been heard by the Indians, and was as great a mystery to them as to me; since not being like that of any creature known to them, it would be attributed by their superstitious minds to one of the numerous demons or semi-human monsters inhabiting every forest, stream, and mountain; and fear of it would drive them from the wood. In this case, judging from my companion's words, they had varied the form of the superstition somewhat, inventing a daughter of a water-spirit to be afraid of. My thought was that if their keen, practised eyes had never been able to see this flitting woodland creature with a musical soul, it was not likely that I would succeed in my quest.

I began to question him, but he now appeared less inclined to talk and more frightened than ever, and each time I attempted to speak he imposed silence, with a quick gesture of alarm, while he continued to stare about him with dilated eyes. All at once he sprang to his feet as if overcome with terror, and started running at full speed. His fear infected me, and, springing up, I followed as fast as I could, but he was far ahead of me, running for dear life; and before I had gone forty yards my feet were caught in a creeper trailing along the surface, and I measured my length on the ground. The sudden violent shock almost took away my senses for a moment, but when I jumped up and stared round to see no unspeakable monster—Curupitá or other—rushing on to slay and devour me there and then, I began to feel ashamed of my cowardice; and in the end I turned and walked back to the spot I had just quitted and sat down once more. I even tried to hum a tune, just to prove to myself that I had completely recovered from the panic

caught from the miserable Indian; but it is never possible in such cases to get back one's serenity immediately, and a vague suspicion continued to trouble
me for a time. After sitting there for half an hour
or so, listening to distant bird songs, I began to recover my old confidence, and even to feel inclined to
penetrate farther into the wood. All at once, making
me almost jump, so sudden it was, so much nearer
and louder than I had ever heard it before, the mysterious melody began. Unmistakably it was uttered by
the same being heard on former occasions; but to-day
it was different in character. The utterance was far
more rapid, with fewer silent intervals, and it had
none of the usual tenderness in it, nor ever once sunk
to that low, whisper-like talking, which had seemed
to me as if the spirit of the wind had breathed its
low sighs in syllables and speech. Now it was not
only loud, rapid, and continuous, but, while still musical, there was an incisiveness in it, a sharp ring as of
resentment, which made it strike painfully on the
sense.

The impression of an intelligent unhuman being
addressing me in anger took so firm a hold on my
mind that the old fear returned, and, rising, I began
to walk rapidly away, intending to escape from the
wood. The voice continued violently rating me, as
it seemed to my mind, moving with me, which caused
me to accelerate my steps; and very soon I would have
broken into a run, when its character began to change

again. There were pauses now, intervals of silence, long or short, and after each one the voice came to my ear with a more subdued and dulcet sound—more of that melting, flute-like quality it had possessed at other times; and this softness of tone, coupled with the talking-like form of utterance, gave me the idea of being no longer incensed, addressing me now in a peaceable spirit, reasoning away my unworthy tremors, and imploring me to remain with it in the wood. Strange as this voice without a body was, and always productive of a slightly uncomfortable feeling on account of its mystery, it seemed impossible to doubt that it came to me now in a spirit of pure friendliness; and when I had recovered my composure I found a new delight in listening to it—all the greater because of the fear so lately experienced, and of its seeming intelligence. For the third time I reseated myself on the same spot, and at intervals the voice talked to me there for some time, and to my fancy expressed satisfaction and pleasure at my presence. But later, without losing its friendly tone, it changed again. It seemed to move away and to be thrown back from a considerable distance; and, at long intervals, it would approach me again with a new sound, which I began to interpret as of command, or entreaty. Was it, I asked myself, inviting me to follow? And if I obeyed, to what delightful discoveries or frightful dangers might it lead? My curiosity, together with the belief that the being—I called it being, not bird, now—was friendly to me, overcame all timidity, and I rose and walked at random towards the interior of the wood. Very soon I had no doubt left that the being had desired me to follow; for there was now a new note of gladness in its voice, and it continued near me as I walked, at intervals approaching me so closely as to set me staring into the surrounding shadowy places like poor scared Kua-kó.

On this occasion, too, I began to have a new fancy, for fancy or illusion I was determined to regard it, that some swift-footed being was treading the ground near me; that I occasionally caught the faint rustle of a light footstep, and detected a motion in leaves and fronds and thread-like stems of creepers hanging near the surface, as if some passing body had touched and made them tremble; and once or twice that I even had a glimpse of a grey, misty object moving at no great distance in the deeper shadows.

Led by this wandering tricksy being, I came to a spot where the trees were very large and the damp dark ground almost free from undergrowth; and here the voice ceased to be heard. After patiently waiting and listening for some time I began to look about me with a slight feeling of apprehension. It was still about two hours before sunset; only in this place the shade of the vast trees made a perpetual twilight: moreover, it was strangely silent here, the few bird cries that reached me coming from a long distance. I had flattered myself that the voice had become to some extent intelligible to me; its outburst of anger caused no doubt by my cowardly flight after the Indian; then its recovered friendliness which had induced me to return; and, finally, its desire to be followed. Now that it had led me to this place of shadow and profound silence, and had ceased to speak and to lead, I could not help thinking that this was my goal, that I had been brought to this spot with a purpose, that in this wild and solitary retreat some tremendous adventure was about to befall me.

As the silence continued unbroken there was time to dwell on this thought. I gazed before me and listened intently, scarcely breathing, until the suspense became painful—too painful at last, and I turned and took a step with the idea of going back to the border of the wood, when close by, clear as a silver bell, sounded the voice once more, but only for a moment —two or three syllables in response to my movement, then it was silent again.

Once more I was standing still, as if in obedience to a command, in the same state of suspense; and whether the change was real or only imagined I know not, but the silence every minute grew more profound and the gloom deeper. Imaginary terrors began to assail me. Ancient fables of men allured by beautiful forms and melodious voices to destruction all at once acquired a fearful significance. I recalled some of the Indian beliefs, especially that of the misshapen, man-devouring monster who is said to beguile his victims into the dark forest by mimicking the human voice —the voice sometimes of a woman in distress—or by singing some strange and beautiful melody. I grew almost afraid to look round lest I should catch sight of him stealing towards me on his huge feet with toes pointing backwards, his mouth snarling horribly to display his great green fangs. It was distressing to have such fancies in this wild, solitary spot—hateful to feel their power over me when I knew that they were nothing but fancies and creations of the savage mind. But if these supernatural beings had no existence, there were other monsters, only too real, in these woods which it would be dreadful to encounter alone and unarmed, since against such adversaries a revolver would be as ineffectual as a popgun. Some huge camoodi, able to crush my bones like brittle twigs in its constricting coils, might lurk in these shadows, and approach me stealthily, unseen in its dark colour on the dark ground. Or some jaguar or black tiger might steal towards me, masked by a bush or tree-trunk, to spring upon me unawares. Or worse still, this way might suddenly come a pack of those swift-footed, unspeakably terrible hunting-leopards, from which every living thing in the forest flies with shrieks of consternation or else falls paralysed in their path to be instantly torn to pieces and devoured.

A slight rustling sound in the foliage above me

made me start and cast up my eyes. High up, where a pale gleam of tempered sunlight fell through the leaves, a grotesque human-like face, black as ebony and adorned with a great red beard, appeared staring down upon me. In another moment it was gone. It was only a large araguato, or howling monkey, but I was so unnerved that I could not get rid of the idea that it was something more than a monkey. Once more I moved, and again, the instant I moved my foot, clear, and keen, and imperative, sounded the voice! It was no longer possible to doubt its meaning. It commanded me to stand still—to wait—to watch—to listen! Had it cried "Listen! Do not move!" I could not have understood it better. Trying as the suspense was, I now felt powerless to escape. Something very terrible, I felt convinced, was about to happen, either to destroy or to release me from the spell that held me.

And while I stood thus rooted to the ground, the sweat standing in large drops on my forehead, all at once close to me sounded a cry, fine and clear at first, and rising at the end to a shriek so loud, piercing, and unearthly in character that the blood seemed to freeze in my veins, and a despairing cry to heaven escaped my lips; then, before that long shriek expired, a mighty chorus of thunderous voices burst forth around me; and in this awful tempest of sound I trembled like a leaf; and the leaves on the trees were agitated as if by a high wind, and the earth itself seemed to shake beneath my feet. Indescribably horrible were my sensations at that moment; I was deafened, and would possibly have been maddened had I not, as by a miracle, chanced to see a large araguato on a branch overhead, roaring with open mouth and inflated throat and chest.

It was simply a concert of howling monkeys which had so terrified me! But my extreme fear was not strange in the circumstances; since everything that had led up to the display, the gloom and silence, the period of suspense and my heated imagination, had raised my mind to the highest degree of excitement and expectancy. I had rightly conjectured, no doubt, that my unseen guide had led me to that spot for a purpose; and the purpose had been to set me in the midst of a congregation of araguatos to enable me for the first time fully to appreciate their unparalleled vocal powers. I had always heard them at a distance: here they were gathered in scores, possibly hundreds —the whole araguato population of the forest, I should think—close to me; and it may give some faint conception of the tremendous power and awful character of the sound thus produced by their combined voices when I say that this animal—miscalled "howler" in English—would outroar the mightiest lion that ever woke the echoes of an African wilderness.

This roaring concert, which lasted three or four

minutes, having ended, I lingered a few minutes longer on the spot, and not hearing the voice again, went back to the edge of the wood, and then started on my way back to the village.

❧ 4 ❦

PERHAPS I was not capable of thinking quite coherently on what had just happened until I was once more fairly outside of the forest shadows—out in that clear open daylight, where things seem what they are, and imagination, like a juggler detected and laughed at, hastily takes itself out of the way. As I walked homewards I paused midway on the barren ridge to gaze back on the scene I had left, and then the recent adventure began to take a semi-ludicrous aspect in my mind. All that circumstance of preparation, that mysterious prelude to something unheard of, unimaginable, surpassing all fables ancient and modern, and all tragedies—to end at last in a concert of howling monkeys! Certainly the concert was very grand, indeed one of the most astounding in nature, but still—I sat down on a stone and laughed freely.

The sun was sinking behind the forest, its broad red disc still showing through the topmost leaves, and the higher part of the foliage was of a luminous green, like green flame, throwing off flakes of quivering, fiery light, but lower down the trees were in profound shadow.

I felt very light-hearted while I gazed on this scene; for how pleasant it was just now to think of the strange experience I had passed through—to think that I had come safely out of it, that no human eye had witnessed my weakness, and that the mystery existed still to fascinate me! For, ludicrous as the dénouement now looked, the cause of all, the voice itself, was a thing to marvel at more than ever. That it proceeded from an intelligent being I was firmly convinced; and although too materialistic in my way of thinking to admit for a moment that it was a supernatural being, I still felt that there was something more than I had at first imagined in Kua-kó's speech about a daughter of the Didi. That the Indians knew a great deal about the mysterious voice, and had held it in great fear, seemed evident. But they were savages, with ways that were not mine; and however friendly they might be towards one of a superior race, there was always in their relations with him a low cunning, prompted partly by suspicion, underlying their words and actions. For the white man to put himself mentally on their level is not more impossible than for these aborigines to be perfectly open, as children are, towards the white. Whatever subject the stranger within their gates exhibits an interest in, that they will be reticent about; and their reticence, which conceals itself under easily invented lies or an affected stupidity, invariably increases with his desire for information. It was plain to them that some very unusual interest took me to the wood, consequently I could not expect that they would tell me anything they might know to enlighten me about the matter; and I concluded that Kua-kó's words about the daughter of the Didi, and what she would do if he blew an arrow at a bird, had accidentally escaped him in a moment of excitement. Nothing, therefore, was to be gained by questioning them, or, at all events, by telling them how much the subject attracted me. And I had nothing to fear; my independent investigations had made this much clear to me; the voice might proceed from a very frolicsome and tricksy creature, full of wild fantastic humours, but nothing worse. It was friendly to me, I felt sure; at the same time it might not be friendly towards the Indians; for, on that day, it had made itself heard only after my companion had taken flight; and it had then seemed incensed against me, possibly because the savage had been in my company.

That was the result of my reflections on the day's events, when I returned to my entertainer's roof, and sat down among my friends to refresh myself with stewed fowl and fish from the household pot, into which a hospitable woman invited me with a gesture to dip my fingers.

Kua-kó was lying in his hammock, smoking, I think—certainly not reading. When I entered he lifted his head and stared at me, probably surprised to see me alive, unharmed, and in a placid temper. I laughed at the look, and somewhat disconcerted, he dropped his head down again. After a minute or two I took the metal match-box and tossed it on to his breast. He clutched it, and starting up, stared at me in the utmost astonishment. He could scarcely believe his good fortune; for he had failed to carry out his part of the compact and had resigned himself to the loss of the coveted prize. Jumping down to the floor, he held up the box triumphantly, his joy overcoming the habitual stolid look; while all the others gathered about him, each trying to get the box into his own hands to admire it again, notwithstanding that they had all seen it a dozen times before. But it was Kua-kó's now and not the stranger's, and therefore more nearly their own than formerly, and must look different, more beautiful, with a brighter polish on the metal. And that wonderful enamelled cock on the lid—figured in Paris probably, but just like a cock in Guayana, the pet bird which they no more think of killing and eating than we do our purring pussies and lemon-coloured canaries—must now look more strikingly valiant and cock-like than ever, with its crimson comb and wattles, burnished red hackles, and dark green arching tail-plumes. But Kua-kó, while willing enough to have it admired and praised, would not let it out of his hands, and told them pompously that it was not theirs for them to handle, but his— Kua-kó's—for all time; that he had won it by accompanying me—valorous man that he was!—to that evil wood into which they—timid, inferior creatures that they were!—would never have ventured to set foot. I am not translating his words, but that was what he gave them to understand pretty plainly, to my great amusement.

After the excitement was over, Runi, who had maintained a dignified calm, made some roundabout remarks, apparently with the object of eliciting an account of what I had seen and heard in the forest of evil fame. I replied carelessly that I had seen a great many birds and monkeys—monkeys so tame that I might have procured one if I had had a blow-pipe, in spite of my never having practised shooting with that weapon.

It interested them to hear about the abundance and tameness of the monkeys, although it was scarcely news: but how tame they must have been when I, the stranger not to the manner born—not naked, brown-skinned, lynx-eyed, and noiseless as an owl in his movements—had yet been able to look closely at them! Runi only remarked, apropos of what

I had told him, that they could not go there to hunt; then he asked me if I feared nothing.

"Nothing," I replied carelessly. "The things you fear hurt not the white man, and are no more than this to me," saying which I took up a little white wood-ash in my hand and blew it away with my breath. "And against other enemies I have this," I added, touching my revolver. A brave speech, just after that araguato episode; but I did not make it without blushing—mentally.

He shook his head, and said it was a poor weapon against some enemies; also—truly enough—that it would procure no birds and monkeys for the stew-pot.

Next morning my friend Kua-kó, taking his zaba-tana, invited me to go out with him, and I consented with some misgivings, thinking he had overcome his superstitious fears, and, inflamed by my account of the abundance of game in the forest, intended going there with me. The previous day's experience had made me think that it would be better in the future to go there alone. But I was giving the poor youth more credit than he deserved: it was far from his intention to face the terrible unknown again. We went in a different direction, and tramped for hours through woods where birds were scarce and only of the smaller kinds. Then my guide surprised me a second time by offering to teach me to use the zaba-tana. This, then, was to be my reward for giving him

the box! I readily consented, and with the long
weapon, awkward to carry, in my hand, and imitating
the noiseless movements and cautious, watchful
manner of my companion, I tried to imagine myself
a simple Guayana savage, with no knowledge of that
artificial social state to which I had been born, dependent on my skill and little roll of poison-darts for
a livelihood. By an effort of the will I emptied myself
of my life experience and knowledge—or as much of it
as possible—and thought only of the generations of
my dead imaginary progenitors, who had ranged these
woods back to the dim forgotten years before Columbus; and if the pleasure I had in the fancy was childish,
it made the day pass quickly enough. Kua-kó was
constantly at my elbow to assist and give advice; and
many an arrow I blew from the long tube, and hit
no bird. Heaven knows what I hit, for the arrows
flew away on their wide and wild career to be seen
no more, except a few which my keen-eyed comrade
marked to their destination and managed to recover.
The result of our day's hunting was a couple of birds,
which Kua-kó, not I, shot, and a small opossum his
sharp eyes detected high up a tree, lying coiled up on
an old nest, over the side of which the animal had
incautiously allowed his snaky tail to dangle. The
number of darts I wasted must have been a rather
serious loss to him, but he did not seem troubled at
it, and made no remark.

Next day, to my surprise, he volunteered to give

me a second lesson, and we went out again. On this
occasion he had provided himself with a large bundle
of darts, but—wise man!—they were not poisoned, and
it therefore mattered little whether they were wasted
or not. I believe that on this day I made some little
progress; at all events, my teacher remarked that before long I would be able to hit a bird. This made me
smile and answer that if he could place me within
twenty yards of a bird not smaller than a small man
I might manage to touch it with an arrow.

This speech had a very unexpected and remarkable
effect. He stopped short in his walk, stared at me
wildly, then grinned, and finally burst into a roar of
laughter, which was no bad imitation of the howling
monkey's performance, and smote his naked thighs
with tremendous energy. At length recovering himself, he asked whether a small woman was not the
same as a small man, and being answered in the af-
firmative, went off into a second extravagant roar of
laughter.

Thinking it was easy to tickle him while he continued in this mood, I began making any number of
feeble jokes—feeble, but quite as good as the one
which had provoked such outrageous merriment—for
it amused me to see him acting in this unusual way.
But they all failed of their effect—there was no hitting the bull's-eye a second time; he would only stare
vacantly at me, then grunt like a peccary—not ap-
preciatively—and walk on. Still, at intervals he would

go back to what I said about hitting a very big bird, and roar again, as if this wonderful joke was not easily exhausted.

Again on the third day we were out together practising at the birds—frightening, if not killing them; but before noon, finding that it was his intention to go to a distant spot where he expected to meet with larger game, I left him and returned to the village. The blow-pipe practice had lost its novelty, and I did not care to go on all day and every day with it; more than that, I was anxious after so long an interval to pay a visit to *my* wood, as I began to call it, in the hope of hearing that mysterious melody, which I had grown to love and to miss when even a single day passed without it.

≈ 5 ≈

AFTER making a hasty meal at the house, I started, full of pleasing anticipations, for the wood; for how pleasant a place it was to be in! What a wild beauty and fragrance and melodiousness it possessed above all forests, because of that mystery that drew me to it! And it was mine, truly and absolutely—as much mine as any portion of earth's surface could belong to any man—mine with all its products; the precious woods and fruits and fragrant gums that would never be trafficked away; its wild animals that man would never persecute; nor would any jealous savage dispute my ownership or pretend that it was part of his hunting-ground. As I crossed the savannah I played with this fancy; but when I reached the ridgy eminence, to look down once more on my new domain, the fancy changed to a feeling so keen that it pierced to my heart, and was like pain in its intensity, causing tears to rush to my eyes. And caring not in that solitude to disguise my feelings from myself, and from the wide heaven that looked down and saw me—for this is the sweetest thing that solitude has for us, that we are free in it, and no convention holds us—I dropped on my knees and kissed the stony ground, then casting up my eyes, thanked the Author of my being for the gift of that wild forest, those green mansions where I had found so great a happiness!

Elated with this strain of feeling, I reached the wood not long after noon; but no melodious voice gave me familiar and expected welcome; nor did my invisible companion make itself heard at all on that day, or, at all events, not in its usual bird-like warbling language. But on this day I met with a curious little adventure, and heard something very extraordinary, very mysterious, which I could not avoid connecting in my mind with the unseen warbler that so often followed me in my rambles.

It was an exceedingly bright day, without cloud, but windy, and finding myself in a rather open part of the wood, near its border, where the breeze could be felt, I sat down to rest on the lower part of a large branch, which was half broken, but still remained attached to the trunk of the tree, while resting its terminal twigs on the ground. Just before me, where I sat, grew a low, wide-spreading plant, covered with broad, round, polished leaves; and the roundness, stiffness, and perfectly horizontal position of the upper leaves made them look like a collection of small platforms or round tabletops placed nearly on a level. Through the leaves, to the height of a foot or more above them, a slender dead stem protruded, and from a twig at its summit depended a broken spider's web. A minute dead leaf had become attached to one of the loose threads, and threw its small but distinct shadow on the platform leaves below: and as it trembled and swayed in the current of air the black spot trembled with it or flew swiftly over the bright green surfaces, and was seldom at rest. Now, as I sat looking down on the leaves and the small dancing shadow, scarcely thinking of what I was looking at, I noticed a small spider, with a flat body and short legs, creep cautiously out on to the upper surface of a leaf. Its pale red colour barred with velvet black first drew my attention to it, for it was beautiful to the eye; and presently I discovered that this was no web-spinning, sedentary spider, but a wandering hunter, that captured its prey, like a cat, by stealing on it concealed and making a rush or spring at the last. The moving shadow had attracted it, and, as the sequel showed, was mistaken for a fly running about over the leaves, and flitting from leaf to leaf. Now began a series of wonderful manoeuvres on the spider's part, with the object of circumventing the imaginary fly, which seemed specially designed to meet this special case;

for certainly no insect had ever before behaved in
quite so erratic a manner. Each time the shadow flew
past, the spider ran swiftly in the same direction, hiding itself under the leaves, always trying to get near
without alarming its prey; and then the shadow would
go round and round in a small circle, and some new
strategic move on the part of the hunter would be
called forth. I became deeply interested in this curious scene; I began to wish that the shadow would
remain quiet for a moment or two, so as to give the
the hunter a chance. And at last I had my wish: the
shadow was almost motionless, and the spider moving
towards it, yet seeming not to move, and as it crept
closer I fancied that I could almost see the little
striped body quivering with excitement. Then came
the final scene: swift and straight as an arrow the
hunter shot himself on to the fly-like shadow, then
wriggled round and round, evidently trying to take
hold of his prey with fangs and claws; and finding
nothing under him, he raised the fore part of his body
vertically, as if to stare about him in search of the
delusive fly; but the action may have simply expressed
astonishment. At this moment I was just on the point
of giving free and loud vent to the laughter which
I had been holding in, when, just behind me, as if
from some person who had been watching the scene
over my shoulder and was as much amused as myself
at its termination, sounded a clear trill of merry
laughter. I started up and looked hastily around, but

no living creature was there. The mass of loose foliage I stared into was agitated, as if from a body having just pushed through it. In a moment the leaves and fronds were motionless again; still, I could not be sure that a slight gust of wind had not shaken them. But I was so convinced that I had heard close to me a real human laugh, or sound of some living creature that exactly simulated a laugh, that I carefully searched the ground about me, expecting to find a being of some kind. But I found nothing, and going back to my seat on the hanging branch, I remained seated for a considerable time, at first only listening, then pondering on the mystery of that sweet trill of laughter; and finally I began to wonder whether I, like the spider that chased the shadow, had been deluded, and had seemed to hear a sound that was not a sound.

On the following day I was in the wood again, and after a two or three hours' ramble, during which I heard nothing, thinking it useless to haunt the known spots any longer, I turned southwards and penetrated into a denser part of the forest, where the undergrowth made progress difficult. I was not afraid of losing myself; the sun above and my sense of direction, which was always good, would enable me to return to the starting-point.

In this direction I had been pushing resolutely on for over half an hour, finding it no easy matter to make my way without constantly deviating to this side or that from the course I wished to keep, when I came to a much more open spot. The trees were smaller and scantier here, owing to the rocky nature of the ground, which sloped rather rapidly down; but it was moist and overgrown with mosses, ferns, creepers, and low shrubs, all of the liveliest green. I could not see many yards ahead owing to the bushes and tall fern fronds; but presently I began to hear a low, continuous sound, which, when I had advanced twenty or thirty yards farther, I made out to be the gurgling of running water; and at the same moment I made the discovery that my throat was parched and my palms tingling with heat. I hurried on, promising myself a cool draught, when all at once, above the soft dashing and gurgling of the water, I caught yet another sound—a low, warbling note, or succession of notes, which might have been emitted by a bird. But it startled me nevertheless—bird-like warbling sounds had come to mean so much to me—and pausing, I listened intently. It was not repeated, and finally, treading with the utmost caution so as not to alarm the mysterious vocalist, I crept on until, coming to a greenheart with a quantity of feathery foliage of a shrub growing about its roots, I saw that just beyond the tree the ground was more open still, letting in the sunlight from above, and that the channel of the stream I sought was in this open space, about twenty yards from me, although the water was still hidden from sight. Something else was there, which

I did see; instantly my cautious advance was arrested. I stood gazing with concentrated vision, scarcely daring to breathe lest I should scare it away.

It was a human being—a girl form, reclining on the moss among the ferns and herbage, near the roots of a small tree. One arm was doubled behind her neck for her head to rest upon, while the other arm was held extended before her, the hand raised towards a small brown bird perched on a pendulous twig just beyond its reach. She appeared to be playing with the bird, possibly amusing herself by trying to entice it on to her hand; and the hand appeared to tempt it greatly, for it persistently hopped up and down, turning rapidly about this way and that, flirting its wings and tail, and always appearing just on the point of dropping on to her finger. From my position it was impossible to see her distinctly, yet I dared not move. I could make out that she was small, not above four feet six or seven inches in height, in figure slim, with delicately shaped little hands and feet. Her feet were bare, and her only garment was a slight chemise-shaped dress reaching below her knees, of a whitish-grey colour, with a faint lustre as of a silky material. Her hair was very wonderful; it was loose and abundant, and seemed wavy or curly, falling in a cloud on her shoulders and arms. Dark it appeared, but the precise tint was indeterminable, as was that of her skin, which looked neither brown nor white. Altogether, near to me as she actually was, there was a kind of mistiness in the figure which made it appear somewhat vague and distant, and a greenish grey seemed the prevailing colour. This tint I presently attributed to the effect of the sunlight falling on her through the green foliage; for once, for a moment, she raised herself to reach her finger nearer to the bird, and then a gleam of unsubdued sunlight fell on her hair and arm, and the arm at that moment appeared of a pearly whiteness, and the hair, just where the light touched it, had a strange lustre and play of iridescent colour.

I had not been watching her more than three seconds before the bird, with a sharp, creaking little chirp, flew up and away in sudden alarm; at the same moment she turned and saw me through the light leafy screen. But although catching sight of me thus suddenly, she did not exhibit alarm like the bird; only her eyes, wide open, with a surprised look in them, remained immovably fixed on my face. And then slowly, imperceptibly—for I did not notice the actual movement, so gradual and smooth it was, like the motion of a cloud of mist which changes its form and place, yet to the eye seems not to have moved—she rose to her knees, to her feet, retired, and with face still towards me, and eyes fixed on mine, finally disappeared, going as if she had melted away into the verdure. The leafage was there occupying the precise spot where she had been a moment before—the feathery foliage of an acacia shrub, and stems and broad, arrow-shaped leaves of an aquatic plant, and slim, drooping fern fronds, and they were motionless, and seemed not to have been touched by something passing through them. She had gone, yet I continued still, bent almost double gazing fixedly at the spot where I had last seen her, my mind in a strange condition, possessed by sensations which were keenly felt and yet contradictory. So vivid was the image left on my brain that she still seemed to be actually before my eyes; and she was not there, nor had been, for it was a dream, an illusion, and no such being existed, or could exist, in this gross world: and at the same time I knew that she had been there—that imagination was powerless to conjure up a form so exquisite.

With the mental image I had to be satisfied, for although I remained for some hours at that spot I saw her no more, nor did I hear any familiar melodious sound. For I was now convinced that in this wild solitary girl I had at length discovered the mysterious warbler that so often followed me in the wood. At length, seeing that it was growing late, I took a drink from the stream and slowly and reluctantly made my way out of the forest, and went home.

Early next day I was back in the wood, full of delightful anticipations, and had no sooner got well among the trees than a soft, warbling sound reached my ears; it was like that heard on the previous day just before catching sight of the girl among the ferns. So soon! thought I, elated, and with cautious steps

I proceeded to explore the ground, hoping again to catch her unawares. But I saw nothing; and only after beginning to doubt that I had heard anything unusual, and had sat down to rest on a rock, the sound was repeated, soft and low as before, very near and distinct. Nothing more was heard at this spot, but an hour later, in another place, the same mysterious note sounded near me. During my remaining time in the forest I was served many times in the same way, and still nothing was seen, nor was there any change in the voice.

Only when the day was near its end did I give up my quest, feeling very keenly disappointed. It then struck me that the cause of the elusive creature's behaviour was that she had been piqued at my discovery of her in one of her most secret hiding-places in the heart of the wood, and that it had pleased her to pay me out in this manner.

On the next day there was no change; she was there again, evidently following me, but always invisible, and varied not from that one mocking note of yesterday, which seemed to challenge me to find her a second time. In the end I was vexed, and resolved to be even with her by not visiting the wood for some time. A display of indifference on my part would, I hoped, result in making her less coy in the future.

Next day, firm in my new resolution, I accompanied Kua-kó and two others to a distant spot where they expected that the ripening fruit on a cashew tree would attract a large number of birds. The fruit, however, proved still green, so that we gathered none and killed few birds. Returning together, Kua-kó kept at my side, and by-and-by, falling behind our companions, he complimented me on my good shooting, although, as usual, I had only wasted the arrows I had blown.

"Soon you will be able to hit," he said; "hit a bird as big as a small woman"; and he laughed once more immoderately at the old joke. At last, growing confidential, he said that I would soon possess a zabatana of my own, with arrows in plenty. He was going to make the arrows himself, and his uncle Otawinki, who had a straight eye, would make the tube. I treated it all as a joke, but he solemnly assured me that he meant it.

Next morning he asked me if I was going to the forest of evil fame, and when I replied in the negative seemed surprised and, very much to *my* surprise, evidently disappointed. He even tried to persuade me to go, where before I had been earnestly recommended not to go, until, finding that I would not, he took me with him to hunt in the woods. By-and-by he returned to the same subject: he could not understand why I would not go to that wood, and asked me if I had begun to grow afraid.

"No, not afraid," I replied; "but I know the place well, and am getting tired of it." I had seen everything

in it—birds and beasts—and had heard all its strange
noises.

"Yes, heard," he said, nodding his head knowingly;
"but you have *seen* nothing strange; your eyes are not
good enough yet."

I laughed contemptuously, and answered that I
had seen everything strange the wood contained, including a strange young girl; and I went on to describe
her appearance, and finished by asking if he thought
a white man was frightened at the sight of a young
girl.

What I said astonished him; then he seemed
greatly pleased, and, growing still more confidential
and generous than on the previous day, he said that
I would soon be a most important personage among
them, and greatly distinguish myself. He did not like
it when I laughed at all this, and went on with great
seriousness to speak of the unmade blow-pipe that
would be mine—speaking of it as if it had been something very great, equal to the gift of a large tract of
land, or the governorship of a province, north of the
Orinoco. And by-and-by he spoke of something else
more wonderful even than the promise of a blow-
pipe, with arrows galore, and this was that young sister of his, whose name was Oolava, a maid of about
sixteen, shy and silent and mild-eyed, rather lean and
dirty; not ugly, nor yet prepossessing. And this copper-
coloured little drab of the wilderness he proposed to
bestow in marriage on me! Anxious to pump him, I

managed to control my muscles, and asked him what
authority he—a young nobody, who had not yet risen
to the dignity of buying a wife for himself—could
have to dispose of a sister in this off-hand way? He
replied that there would be no difficulty, that Runi
would give his consent, as would also Otawinki,
Piaké, and other relations; and last, *and* least, according to the matrimonial customs of these latitudes,
Oolava herself would be ready to bestow her person—
queyou, worn fig-leaf wise, necklace of accouri teeth,
and all—on so worthy a suitor as myself. Finally, to
make the prospect still more inviting, he added that it
would not be necessary for me to subject myself to
any voluntary tortures to prove myself a man and
fitted to enter into the purgatorial state of matri-
mony. He was a great deal too considerate, I said,
and, with all the gravity I could command, asked
him what kind of torture he would recommend. For
me—so valorous a person—"no torture," he answered
magnanimously. But he—Kua-kó—had made up his
mind as to the form of torture he meant to inflict
some day on his own person. He would prepare a large
sack and into it put fire-ants—"As many as that!" he
exclaimed triumphantly, stooping and filling his two
hands with loose sand. He would put them in the
sack, and then get into it himself naked, and tie it
tightly round his neck, so as to show to all spectators
that the hellish pain of innumerable venomous stings
in his flesh could be endured without a groan, and

with an unmoved countenance. The poor youth had
not an original mind, since this was one of the com-
monest forms of self-torture among the Guayana
tribes. But the sudden wonderful animation with
which he spoke of it, the fiendish joy that illumined
his usually stolid countenance, sent a sudden disgust
and horror through me. But what a strange inverted
kind of fiendishness is this, which delights at the an-
ticipation of torture inflicted on oneself! And towards
others these savages are mild and peaceable!

No, I could not believe in their mildness; that
was only on the surface, when nothing occurred
to rouse their savage, cruel instincts. I could have
laughed at the whole matter, but the exulting look
on my companion's face had made me sick of the
subject, and I wished not to talk any more about it.

But he would talk still—this fellow whose words,
as a rule, I had to take out of his mouth with a fork,
as we say; and still on the same subject he said that
not one person in the village would expect to see me
torture myself; that after what I would do for them
all—after delivering them from a great evil—nothing
further would be expected of me.

I asked him to explain his meaning; for it now began to appear plain that in everything he had said he
had been leading up to some very important matter.
It would, of course, have been a great mistake to
suppose that my savage was offering me a blow-pipe

and a marketable virgin sister from purely disinterested motives.

In reply he went back to that still unforgotten joke about my being able eventually to hit a bird as big as a small woman with an arrow. Out it all came, when he went on to ask me if that mysterious girl I had seen in the wood was not of a size to suit me as a target when I had got my hand in with a little more practice. That was the great work I was asked to do for them—that shy, mysterious girl with the melodious wild-bird voice was the evil being I was asked to slay with poisoned arrows! This was why he now wished me to go often to the wood, to become more and more familiar with her haunts and habits, to overcome all shyness and suspicion in her; and at the proper moment, when it would be impossible to miss my mark, to plant the fatal arrow! The disgust he had inspired in me before, when gloating over anticipated tortures, was a weak and transient feeling to what I now experienced. I turned on him in a sudden transport of rage, and in a moment would have shattered the blow-pipe I was carrying in my hand on his head, but his astonished look as he turned to face me made me pause, and prevented me from committing so fatal an indiscretion. I could only grind my teeth and struggle to overcome an almost overpowering hatred and wrath. Finally, I flung the tube down and bade him take it, telling him that I would not touch it again if he offered me all the sisters of all the savages in Guayana for wives.

He continued gazing at me mute with astonishment, and prudence suggested that it would be best to conceal as far as possible the violent animosity I had conceived against him. I asked him somewhat scornfully if he believed that I should ever be able to hit anything—bird or human being—with an arrow. "No," I almost shouted, so as to give vent to my feelings in some way, and drawing my revolver, "this is the white man's weapon; but he kills men with it— men who attempt to kill or injure him—but neither with this nor any other weapon does he murder innocent young girls treacherously."

After that we went on in silence for some time; at length he said that the being I had seen in the wood and was not afraid of was no innocent young girl, but a daughter of the Didi, an evil being; and that so long as she continued to inhabit the wood they could not go there to hunt, and even in other woods they constantly went in fear of meeting her. Too much disgusted to talk with him, I went on in silence; and when we reached the stream near the village I threw off my clothes and plunged into the water to cool my anger before going in to the others.

❧ 6 ❧

Thinking about the forest girl while lying awake that night, I came to the conclusion that I had made it sufficiently plain to her how little her capricious behaviour had been relished, and had therefore no need to punish myself more by keeping any longer out of my beloved green mansions. Accordingly, next day, after the heavy rain that fell during the morning hours had ceased, I set forth about noon to visit the wood. Overhead the sky was clear again; but there was no motion in the heavy sultry atmosphere, while dark blue masses of banked-up clouds on the western horizon threatened a fresh downpour later in the day. My mind was, however, now too greatly excited at the prospect of a possible encounter with the forest nymph to allow me to pay any heed to these ominous signs.

I had passed through the first strip of wood, and was in the succeeding stony sterile space, when a gleam of brilliant colour close by on the ground caught my sight. It was a snake lying on the bare earth; had I kept on without noticing it, I should most probably have trodden upon or dangerously near it. Viewing it closely, I found that it was a coral snake, famed as much for its beauty and singularity as for its deadly character. It was about three feet long, and very slim; its ground colour a brilliant vermilion, with broad jet-black rings at equal distances round its body, each black ring or band divided by a narrow yellow strip in the middle. The symmetrical pattern and vividly contrasted colours would have given it the appearance of an artificial snake made by some fanciful artist, but for the gleam of life in its bright coils. Its fixed eyes, too, were living gems, and from the point of its dangerous arrowy head the glistening tongue flicked ceaselessly as I stood a few yards away regarding it.

"I admire you greatly, Sir Serpent," I said, or thought, "but it is dangerous, say the military authorities, to leave an enemy or possible enemy in the rear; the person who does such a thing must be either a bad strategist or a genius, and I am neither."

Retreating a few paces, I found and picked up a stone about as big as a man's hand, and hurled it at the dangerous-looking head with the intention of crushing it; but the stone hit upon the rocky ground a little on one side of the mark, and being soft flew into a hundred small fragments. This roused the creature's anger, and in a moment with raised head he was gliding swiftly towards me. Again I retreated, not so slowly on this occasion: and finding another stone, I raised and was about to launch it when a sharp, ringing cry issued from the bushes growing near, and, quickly following the sound, forth stepped the forest girl; no longer elusive and shy, vaguely seen in the shadowy wood, but boldly challenging attention, exposed to the full power of the meridian sun, which made her appear luminous and rich in colour beyond example. Seeing her thus, all those emotions of fear and abhorrence invariably excited in us by the sight of an active venomous serpent in our path vanished instantly from my mind: I could now only feel astonishment and admiration at the brilliant being as she advanced with swift, easy, undulating motion towards me; or rather towards the serpent, which was now between us, moving more and more slowly as she came nearer. The cause of this sudden wonderful boldness, so unlike her former habit, was unmistakable. She had been watching my approach from some hiding-place among the bushes, ready no doubt to lead me a dance through the wood with her mocking voice, as on previous occasions, when my attack on the serpent caused that outburst of wrath. The torrent of ringing and to me inarticulate sounds in that unknown tongue, her rapid gestures, and above all her wide-open sparkling eyes and face aflame with colour, made it impossible to mistake the nature of her feeling.

In casting about for some term or figure of speech in which to describe the impression produced on me at that moment, I think of *waspish*, and, better still, *avispada*—literally the same word in Spanish, not having precisely the same meaning nor ever applied contemptuously—only to reject both after a moment's reflection. Yet I go back to the image of an irritated wasp as perhaps offering the best illustration; of some large tropical wasp advancing angrily towards me, as I have witnessed a hundred times, not exactly flying, but moving rapidly, half running and half flying, over the ground, with loud and angry buzz, the glistening wings open and agitated; beautiful beyond most animated creatures in its sharp but graceful lines, polished surface, and varied brilliant colouring, and that wrathfulness that fits it so well and seems to give it additional lustre.

Wonder-struck at the sight of her strange beauty and passion, I forgot the advancing snake until she came to a stop at about five yards from me; then to my horror I saw that it was beside her naked feet. Although no longer advancing, the head was still raised high as if to strike; but presently the spirit of anger appeared to die out of it; the lifted head, oscillating a little from side to side, sunk down lower and lower to rest finally on the girl's bare instep; and lying there motionless, the deadly thing had the appearance of a gaily coloured silken garter just dropped from her leg. It was plain to see that she had no fear of it, that she was one of those exceptional persons to be found, it is said, in all countries, who possess some magnetic quality which has a soothing effect on even the most venomous and irritable reptiles.

Following the direction of my eyes, she too glanced down, but did not move her foot; then she made her voice heard again, still loud and sharp, but the anger was not now so pronounced.

"Do not fear, I shall not harm it," I said in the Indian tongue.

She took no notice of my speech, and continued speaking with increasing resentment.

I shook my head, replying that her language was unknown to me. Then by means of signs I tried to make her understand that the creature was safe from further molestation. She pointed indignantly at the stone in my hand, which I had forgotten all about. At once I threw it from me, and instantly there was a change; the resentment had vanished, and a tender radiance lit her face like a smile.

I advanced a little nearer, addressing her once more in the Indian tongue; but my speech was evidently unintelligible to her, as she stood now glancing at the snake lying at her feet, now at me. Again I had recourse to signs and gestures; pointing to the snake, then to the stone I had cast away, I endeavoured to convey to her that in the future I would for her sake be a friend to all venomous reptiles, and that I wished her to have the same kindly feelings towards me as towards these creatures. Whether or not she understood me, she showed no disposition to go into hiding again, and continued silently regarding me with a look that seemed to express pleasure at finding herself at last thus suddenly brought face to face with me. Flattered at this, I gradually drew nearer until at the last I was standing at her side, gazing down with the utmost delight into that face which so greatly surpassed in loveliness all human faces I had ever seen or imagined.

And yet to you, my friend, it probably will not seem that she was so beautiful, since I have, alas! only the words we all use to paint commoner, coarser things, and no means to represent all the exquisite details, all the delicate lights, and shades, and swift changes of colour and expression. Moreover, is it not a fact that the strange or unheard of can never appear beautiful in a mere description, because that which is most novel in it attracts too much attention and is given undue prominence in the picture, and we miss that which would have taken away the effect of strangeness—the perfect balance of the parts and harmony of the whole? For instance, the blue eyes of the northerner would, when first described to the

black-eyed inhabitants of warm regions, seem un-
beautiful and a monstrosity, because they would
vividly see with the mental vision that unheard-of
blueness, but not in the same vivid way the accompanying flesh and hair tints with which it harmonises.

Think, then, less of the picture as I have to paint
it in words than of the feeling its original inspired in
me, when looking closely for the first time on that
rare loveliness, trembling with delight I mentally
cried: "Oh, why has Nature, maker of so many types
and of innumerable individuals of each, given to the
world but one being like this?"

Scarcely had the thought formed itself in my mind
before I dismissed it as utterly incredible. No, this
exquisite being was without doubt one of a distinct
race which had existed in this little-known corner of
the continent for thousands of generations, albeit
now perhaps reduced to a small and dwindling rem-
nant.

Her figure and features were singularly delicate, but
it was her colour that struck me most, which indeed
made her differ from all other human beings. The
colour of the skin would be almost impossible to
describe, so greatly did it vary with every change of
mood—and the moods were many and transient—and
with the angle on which the sunlight touched it, and
the degree of light.

Beneath the trees, at a distance, it had seemed a
somewhat dim white or pale grey; near in the strong

sunshine it was not white, but alabastrian, semi-pellucid, showing an underlying rose-colour; and at any point where the rays fell direct this colour was bright and luminous, as we see in our fingers when held before a strong firelight. But that part of her skin that remained in shadow appeared of a dimmer white, and the underlying colour varied from dim, rosy purple to dim blue. With the skin the colour of the eyes harmonised perfectly. At first, when lit with anger, they had appeared flame-like; now the iris was of a peculiar soft or dim and tender red, a shade sometimes seen in flowers. But only when looked closely at could this delicate hue be discerned, the pupils being large, as in some grey eyes, and the long, dark, shading lashes at a short distance made the whole eye appear dark. Think not, then, of the red flower, exposed to the light and sun in conjunction with the vivid green of the foliage; think only of such a hue in the half-hidden iris, brilliant and moist with the eye's moisture, deep with the eye's depth, glorified by the outward look of a bright, beautiful soul. Most variable of all in colour was the hair, this being due to its extreme fineness and glossiness, and to its elasticity, which made it lie fleecy and loose on head, shoulders, and back; a cloud with a brightness on its surface made by the freer outer hairs, a fit setting and crown for a countenance of such rare, changeful loveliness. In the shade, viewed closely, the general colour appeared a slate, deepening in places to purple; but even in the shade the nimbus of free flossy hairs half veiled the darker tints with a downy pallor; and at a distance of a few yards it gave the whole hair a vague, misty appearance. In the sunlight the colour varied more, looking now dark, sometimes intensely black, now of a light uncertain hue, with a play of iridescent colour on the loose surface, as we see on the glossed plumage of some birds; and at a short distance, with the sun shining full on her head, it sometimes looked white as a noon-day cloud. So changeful was it and ethereal in appearance with its cloud colours, that all other human hair, even of the most beautiful golden shades, pale or red, seemed heavy and dull and dead-looking by comparison.

But more than form and colour and that enchanting variability was the look of intelligence, which at the same time seemed complementary to and one with the all-seeing, all-hearing alertness appearing in her face; the alertness one remarks in a wild creature, even when in repose and fearing nothing; but seldom in man, never perhaps in intellectual or studious man. She was a wild, solitary girl of the woods, and did not understand the language of the country in which I had addressed her. What inner or mind life could such a one have more than that of any wild animal existing in the same conditions? Yet looking at her face it was not possible to doubt its intelligence. This union in her of two opposite qualities which, with us, cannot or do not exist together, although so novel, yet struck me as the girl's principal charm. Why had Nature not done this before—why in all others does the brightness of the mind dim that beautiful physical brightness which the wild animals have? But enough for me that that which no man had ever looked for or hoped to find existed here; that through that unfamiliar lustre of the wild life shone the spiritualising light of mind that made us kin.

These thoughts passed swiftly through my brain as I stood feasting my sight on her bright, piquant face; while she on her part gazed back into my eyes, not only with fearless curiosity, but with a look of recognition and pleasure at the encounter so unmistakably friendly that, encouraged by it, I took her arm in my hand, moving at the same time a little nearer to her. At that moment a swift, startled expression came into her eyes; she glanced down and up again into my face; her lips trembled and slightly parted as she murmured some sorrowful sounds in a tone so low as to be only just audible.

Thinking she had become alarmed and was on the point of escaping out of my hands, and fearing, above all things, to lose sight of her again so soon, I slipped my arm round her slender body to detain her, moving one foot at the same time to balance myself; and at that moment I felt a slight blow and a sharp burning sensation shoot into my leg, so sudden and intense that I dropped my arm, at the same time uttering a cry of pain, and recoiled one or two paces from her. But she stirred not when I released her; her eyes followed my movements; then she glanced down at her feet. I followed her look, and figure to yourself my horror when I saw there the serpent I had so completely forgotten, and which even that sting of sharp pain had not brought back to remembrance! There it lay, a coil of its own tail thrown round one of her ankles, and its head, raised nearly a foot high, swaying slowly from side to side, while the swift forked tongue flickered continuously. Then—only then—I knew what had happened, and at the same time I understood the reason of that sudden look of alarm in her face, the murmuring sounds she had uttered, and the downward startled glance. Her fears had been solely for my safety, and she had warned me! Too late! too late! In moving I had trodden on or touched the serpent with my foot, and it had bitten me just above the ankle. In a few moments I began to realise the horror of my position. "Must I die! must I die! Oh, my God, is there nothing that can save me?" I cried in my heart.

She was still standing motionless in the same place: her eyes wandered back from me to the snake; gradually its swaying head was lowered again, and the coil unwound from her ankle; then it began to move away, slowly at first, and with the head a little raised, then faster, and in the end it glided out of sight. Gone!—

but it had left its venom in my blood—O cursed reptile!

Back from watching its retreat, my eyes returned to her face, now strangely clouded with trouble; her eyes dropped before mine, while the palms of her hands were pressed together, and the fingers clasped and unclasped alternately. How different she seemed now; the brilliant face grown so pallid and vague-looking! But not only because this tragic end to our meeting had pierced her with pain; that cloud in the west had grown up and now covered half the sky with vast lurid masses of vapour, blotting out the sun, and a great gloom had fallen on the earth.

That sudden twilight and a long roll of approaching thunder, reverberating from the hills, increased my anguish and desperation. Death at that moment looked unutterably terrible. The remembrance of all that made life dear pierced me to the core—all that nature was to me, all the pleasures of sense and intellect, the hopes I had cherished—all was revealed to me as by a flash of lightning. Bitterest of all was the thought that I must now bid everlasting farewell to this beautiful being I had found in the solitude—this lustrous daughter of the Didi—just when I had won her from her shyness—that I must go away into the cursed blackness of death, and never know the mystery of her life! It was that which utterly unnerved me, and made my legs tremble under me, and brought great drops of sweat to my forehead, until I thought that the venom was already doing its swift, fatal work in my veins.

With uncertain steps I moved to a stone a yard or two away and sat down upon it. As I did so the hope came to me that this girl, so intimate with nature, might know of some antidote to save me. Touching my leg, and using other signs, I addressed her again in the Indian language.

"The snake has bitten me," I said. "What shall I do? Is there no leaf, no root you know that would save me from death? Help me! help me!" I cried in despair.

My signs she probably understood if not my words, but she made no reply; and still she remained standing motionless, twisting and untwisting her fingers, and regarding me with a look of ineffable grief and compassion.

Alas! It was vain to appeal to her: she knew what had happened, and what the result would most likely be, and pitied, but was powerless to help me. Then it occurred to me that if I could reach the Indian village before the venom overpowered me something might be done to save me. Oh, why had I tarried so long, losing so many precious minutes! Large drops of rain were falling now, and the gloom was deeper, and the thunder almost continuous. With a cry of anguish I started to my feet, and was about to rush away towards the village when a dazzling flash of lightning made me pause for a moment. When it van-

ished I turned a last look on the girl, and her face was
deathly pale, and her hair looked blacker than night;
and as she looked she stretched out her arms towards
me and uttered a low, wailing cry. "Good-bye for
ever!" I murmured, and turning once more from her,
rushed away like one crazed into the wood. But in
my confusion I had probably taken the wrong direction, for instead of coming out in a few minutes into
the open border of the forest, and on to the savannah,
I found myself every moment getting deeper among
the trees. I stood still, perplexed, but could not shake
off the conviction that I had started in the right direction. Eventually I resolved to keep on for a hundred
yards or so, and then, if no opening appeared, to turn
back and retrace my steps. But this was no easy matter. I soon became entangled in a dense undergrowth,
which so confused me that at last I confessed de-
spairingly to myself that for the first time in this wood
I was hopelessly lost. And in what terrible circumstances! At intervals a flash of lightning would throw
a vivid blue glare down into the interior of the wood
and only serve to show that I had lost myself in a
place where even at noon in cloudless weather progress would be most difficult; and now the light would
only last a moment, to be followed by thick gloom;
and I could only tear blindly on, bruising and lacerat-
ing my flesh at every step, falling again and again only
to struggle up and on again, now high above the sur-

face climbing over prostrate trees and branches, now plunged to my middle in a pool or torrent of water.

Hopeless—utterly hopeless seemed all my mad efforts; and at each pause, when I would stand exhausted, gasping for breath, my throbbing heart almost suffocating me, a dull, continuous, teasing pain in my bitten leg served to remind me that I had but a little time left to exist—that by delaying at first I had allowed my only chance of salvation to slip by.

How long a time I spent fighting my way through this dense black wood I know not; perhaps two or three hours, only to me the hours seemed like years of prolonged agony. At last, all at once, I found that I was free of the close undergrowth, and walking on level ground: but it was darker here—darker than the darkest night; and at length, when the lightning came and flared down through the dense roof of foliage overhead, I discovered that I was in a spot that had a strange look, where the trees were very large and grew wide apart, and with no undergrowth to impede progress beneath them. Here, recovering breath, I began to run, and after a while found that I had left the large trees behind me, and was now in a more open place, with small trees and bushes: and this made me hope for a while that I had at last reached the border of the forest. But the hope proved vain; once more I had to force my way through dense undergrowth, and finally emerged on to a slope where it was open, and I could once more see for some distance around me by such light as came through the thick pall of clouds. Trudging on to the summit of the slope, I saw that there was open savannah country beyond, and for a moment rejoiced that I had got free from the forest. A few steps more, and I was standing on the very edge of a bank, a precipice not less than fifty feet deep. I had never seen that bank before, and therefore knew that I could not be on the right side of the forest. But now my only hope was to get completely away from the trees and then to look for the village, and I began following the bank in search of a descent. No break occurred, and presently I was stopped by a dense thicket of bushes. I was about to retrace my steps when I noticed that a tall slender tree growing at the foot of the precipice, its green top not more than a couple of yards below my feet, seemed to offer a means of escape. Nerving myself with the thought that if I got crushed by the fall I should probably escape a lingering and far more painful death, I dropped into the cloud of foliage beneath me and clutched desperately at the twigs as I fell. For a moment I felt myself sustained; but branch after branch gave way beneath my weight, and then I only remember, very dimly, a swift flight through the air before losing consciousness.

❧ 7 ❧

WITH THE RETURN of consciousness, I at first had a vague impression that I was lying somewhere, injured, and incapable of motion; that it was night, and necessary for me to keep my eyes fast shut to prevent them from being blinded by almost continuous vivid flashes of lightning. Injured, and sore all over, but warm and dry—surely dry: nor was it lightning that dazzled, but firelight. I began to notice things little by little. The fire was burning on a clay floor a few feet from where I was lying. Before it, on a log of wood, sat or crouched a human figure. An old man, with chin on breast and hands clasped before his drawn-up knees, only a small portion of his forehead and nose visible to me. An Indian I took him to be, from his coarse, lank, grey hair and dark brown skin. I was in a large hut, falling at the sides to within two feet of the floor: but there were no hammocks in it, nor bows and spears; and no skins, not even under me, for I was lying on straw mats. I could hear the storm still raging outside; the rush and splash of rain, and, at intervals, the distant growl of thunder. There was wind, too; I listened to it sobbing in the trees, and occasionally a puff found its way in, and blew up the white ashes at the old man's feet, and shook the yellow flames like a flag. I remembered now how the storm began, the wild girl, the snake-bite, my violent efforts to find a way out of the wood, and, finally, that leap from the bank where recollection ended. That I had not been killed by the venomous tooth, nor the subsequent fearful fall, seemed like a miracle to me. And in that wild, solitary place, lying insensible, in that awful storm and darkness, I had been found by a fellow-creature— a savage, doubtless, but a good Samaritan all the same—who had rescued me from death! I was bruised all over and did not attempt to move, fearing the pain it would give me; and I had a racking headache; but these seemed trifling discomforts after such adventures and such perils. I felt that I had recovered or was recovering from that venomous bite; that I would live and not die—live to return to my country; and the thought filled my heart to overflowing, and tears of gratitude and happiness rose to my eyes.

At such times a man experiences benevolent feelings, and would willingly bestow some of that overplus of happiness on his fellows to lighten other hearts; and this old man before me, who was probably the instrument of my salvation, began greatly to excite my interest and compassion. For he seemed so poor in his old age and rags, so solitary and dejected as he sat there with knees drawn up, his great, brown, bare feet looking almost black by contrast with the white wood-ashes about them! What could I do for him? What could I say to cheer his spirits in that Indian language, which has few or no words to express kindly feelings? Unable to think of anything better to say, I at length suddenly cried aloud, "Smoke, old man! Why do you not smoke? It is good to smoke."

He gave a mighty start, and, turning, fixed his eyes on me. Then I saw that he was not a pure Indian, for although as brown as old leather, he wore a beard and moustache. A curious face had this old man, which looked as if youth and age had made it a battling ground. His forehead was smooth, except for two parallel lines in the middle running its entire length, dividing it in zones; his arched eyebrows were black as ink, and his small black eyes were bright and cunning, like the eyes of some wild carnivorous animal. In this part of his face youth had held its own, especially in the eyes, which looked young and lively. But lower down age had conquered, scribbling his skin all over with wrinkles, while moustache and beard were white as thistledown.

"Aha, the dead man is alive again!" he exclaimed,

with a chuckling laugh. This in the Indian tongue; then in Spanish he added, "But speak to me in the language you know best, señor; for if you are not a Venezuelan call me an owl."

"And you, old man?" said I.

"Ah, I was right! Why, sir, what I am is plainly written on my face. Surely you do not take me for a pagan! I might be a black man from Africa, or an Englishman, but an Indian—that, no! But a minute ago you had the goodness to invite me to smoke. How, sir, can a poor man smoke who is without tobacco?"

"Without tobacco—in Guayana!"

"Can you believe it? But, sir, do not blame me; if the beast that came one night and destroyed my plants when ripe for cutting had taken pumpkins and sweet potatoes instead, it would have been better for him, if curses have any effect. And the plant grows slowly, sir—it is not an evil weed to come to maturity in a single day. And as for other leaves in the forest, I smoke them, yes; but there is no comfort to the lungs in such smoke."

"My tobacco-pouch was full," I said. "You will find it in my coat, if I did not lose it."

"The saints forbid!" he exclaimed. "Grandchild—Rima, have you got a tobacco-pouch with the other things? Give it to me."

Then I first noticed that another person was in the hut, a slim young girl, who had been seated against

the wall on the other side of the fire, partially hid
by the shadows. She had my leather belt, with the revolver in its case, and my hunting-knife attached, and
the few articles I had had in my pockets, on her lap.
Taking up the pouch, she handed it to him, and he
clutched it with a strange eagerness.

"I will give it back presently, Rima," he said. "Let
me first smoke a cigarette—and then another."

It seemed probable from this that the good old man
had already been casting covetous eyes on my property, and that his granddaughter had taken care of it
for me. But how the silent, demure girl had kept it
from him was a puzzle, so intensely did he seem now
to enjoy it, drawing the smoke vigorously into his
lungs, and after keeping it ten or fifteen seconds there,
letting it fly out again from mouth and nose in blue
jets and clouds. His face softened visibly, he became
more and more genial and loquacious, and asked me
how I came to be in that solitary place. I told him
that I was staying with the Indian Runi, his neighbour.

"But, señor," he said, "if it is not an impertinence,
how is it that a young man of so distinguished an appearance as yourself, a Venezuelan, should be resid-
ing with these children of the devil?"

"You love not your neighbours, then?"

"I know them, sir—how should I love them?" He
was rolling up his second or third cigarette by this
time, and I could not help noticing that he took a

great deal more tobacco than he required in his fingers, and that the surplus on each occasion was conveyed to some secret receptacle among his rags. "Love them, sir! They are infidels, and therefore the good Christian must only hate them. They are thieves—they will steal from you before your very face, so devoid are they of all shame. And also murderers; gladly would they burn this poor thatch above my head, and kill me and my poor grandchild, who shares this solitary life with me, if they had the courage. But they are all arrant cowards, and fear to approach me—fear even to come into this wood. You would laugh to hear what they are afraid of—a child would laugh to hear it!"

"What do they fear?" I said, for his words had excited my interest in a great degree.

"Why, sir, would you believe it? They fear this child—my granddaughter, seated there before you. A poor innocent girl of seventeen summers, a Christian who knows her Catechism, and would not harm the smallest thing that God has made—no, not a fly, which is not regarded on account of its smallness. Why, sir, it is due to her tender heart that you are safely sheltered here, instead of being left out of doors in this tempestuous night."

"To her—to this girl?" I returned in astonishment. "Explain, old man, for I do not know how I was saved."

"To-day, señor, through your own heedlessness you were bitten by a venomous snake."

"Yes, that is true, although I do not know how it came to your knowledge. But why am I not a dead man, then—have you done something to save me from the effects of the poison?"

"Nothing. What could I do so long after you were bitten? When a man is bitten by a snake in a solitary place he is in God's hands. He will live or die as God wills. There is nothing to be done. But surely, sir, you remember that my poor grandchild was with you in the wood when the snake bit you?"

"A girl was there—a strange girl I have seen and heard before when I have walked in the forest. But not this girl—surely not this girl!"

"No other," said he, carefully rolling up another cigarette.

"It is not possible!" I returned.

"Ill would you have fared, sir, had she not been there. For after being bitten, you rushed away into the thickest part of the wood, and went about in a circle like a demented person for Heaven knows how long. But she never left you; she was always close to you—you might have touched her with your hand. And at last some good angel who was watching you, in order to stop your career, made you mad altogether and caused you to jump over a precipice and lose your senses. And you were no sooner on the ground than she was with you—ask me not how *she* got down! And when she had propped you up against the bank she came for me. Fortunately the spot where you had fallen is near—not five hundred yards from the door. And I, on my part, was willing to assist her in saving you; for I knew it was no Indian that had fallen, since she loves not that breed, and they come not here. It was not an easy task, for you weigh, señor; but between us we brought you in."

While he spoke the girl continued sitting in the same listless attitude as when I first observed her, with eyes cast down and hands folded in her lap. Recalling that brilliant being in the wood that had protected the serpent from me, and calmed its rage, I found it hard to believe his words, and still felt a little incredulous.

"Rima—that is your name, is it not?" I said. "Will you come here and stand before me, and let me look closely at you?"

"Si, señor," she meekly answered; and removing the things from her lap she stood up; then, passing behind the old man, came and stood before me, her eyes still bent on the ground—a picture of humility.

She had the figure of the forest girl, but wore now a scanty faded cotton garment, while the loose cloud of hair was confined in two plaits and hung down her back. The face also showed the same delicate lines, but of the brilliant animation and variable colour and expression there appeared no trace. Gazing at her countenance, as she stood there silent, shy, and spiritless before me, the image of her brighter self came vividly to my mind, and I could not recover from the astonishment I felt at such a contrast.

Have you ever observed a humming-bird moving about in an aerial dance among the flowers—a living prismatic gem that changes its colour with every change of position—how in turning it catches the sunshine on its burnished neck and gorget plumes—green and gold and flame-coloured, the beams changing to visible flakes as they fall, dissolving into nothing, to be succeeded by others and yet others? In its exquisite form, its changeful splendour, its swift motions and intervals of aerial suspension, it is a creature of such fairy-like loveliness as to mock all description. And have you seen this same fairy-like creature suddenly perch itself on a twig, in the shade, its misty wings and fanlike tail folded, the iridescent glory vanished, looking like some common dull-plumaged little bird sitting listless in a cage? Just so great was the difference in the girl, as I had seen her in the forest and as she now appeared under the smoky roof in the firelight.

After watching her for some moments I spoke: "Rima, there must be a good deal of strength in that frame of yours, which looks so delicate; will you raise me up a little?"

She went down on one knee, and placing her arms round me assisted me to a sitting posture.

"Thank you, Rima—O misery!" I groaned. "Is there a bone left unbroken in my poor body?"

"Nothing broken," cried the old man, clouds of smoke flying out with his words. "I have examined you well—legs, arms, ribs. For this is how it was, señor. A thorny bush into which you fell saved you from being flattened on the stony ground. But you are bruised, sir, black with bruises; and there are more scratches of thorns on your skin than letters on a written page."

"A long thorn might have entered my brain," I said, "from the way it pains. Feel my forehead, Rima; is it very hot and dry?"

She did as I asked, touching me lightly with her little cool hand. "No, señor, not hot, but warm and moist," she said.

"Thank Heaven for that!" I said. "Poor girl! And you followed me through the wood in all that terrible storm! Ah, if I could lift my bruised arm I would take your hand to kiss it in gratitude for so great a service. I owe you my life, sweet Rima—what shall I do to repay so great a debt?"

The old man chuckled as if amused, but the girl lifted not her eyes nor spoke.

"Tell me, sweet child," I said, "for I cannot realise it yet; was it really you that saved the serpent's life when I would have killed it—did you stand by me in the wood with the serpent lying at your feet?"

"Yes, señor," came her gentle answer.

"And it was you I saw in the wood one day, lying on the ground playing with a small bird?"

"Yes, señor."

"And it was you that followed me so often among the trees, calling to me, yet always hiding so that I could never see you?"

"Yes, señor."

"Oh, this is wonderful!" I exclaimed; whereat the old man chuckled again.

"But tell me this, my sweet girl," I continued. "You never addressed me in Spanish; what strange musical language was it you spoke to me in?"

She shot a timid glance at my face and looked troubled at the question, but made no reply.

"Señor," said the old man, "that is a question which you must excuse my child from answering. Not, sir, from want of will, for she is docile and obedient, though I say it, but there is no answer beyond what I can tell you. And this is, sir, that all creatures, whether man or bird, have the voice that God has given them; and in some the voice is musical and in others not so."

"Very well, old man," said I to myself; "there let the matter rest for the present. But, if I am destined to live and not die, I shall not long remain satisfied with your too simple explanation."

"Rima," I said, "you must be fatigued; it is thoughtless of me to keep you standing here so long."

Her face brightened a little, and bending down she

replied in a low voice, "I am not fatigued, sir. Let me get you something to eat now."

She moved quickly away to the fire, and presently returned with an earthenware dish of roasted pumpkin and sweet potatoes, and kneeling at my side fed me deftly with a small wooden spoon. I did not feel grieved at the absence of meat and the stinging condiments the Indians love, nor did I even remark that there was no salt in the vegetables, so much was I taken up with watching her beautiful delicate face while she ministered to me. The exquisite fragrance of her breath was more to me than the most delicious viands could have been; and it was a delight each time she raised the spoon to my mouth to catch a momentary glimpse of her eyes, which now looked dark as wine when we lift the glass to see the ruby gleam of light within the purple. But she never for a moment laid aside the silent, meek, constrained manner; and when I remember her bursting out in her brilliant wrath on me, pouring forth that torrent of stinging invective in her mysterious language, I was lost in wonder and admiration at the change in her, and at her double personality. Having satisfied my wants she moved quietly away, and raising a straw mat disappeared behind it into her own sleeping-apartment, which was divided off by a partition from the room I was in.

The old man's sleeping-place was a wooden cot or stand on the opposite side of the room, but he was in no hurry to sleep, and after Rima had left us, put a fresh log on the blaze, and lit another cigarette. Heaven knows how many he had smoked by this time. He became very talkative and called to his side his two dogs, which I had not noticed in the room before, for me to see. It amused me to hear their names—Susio and Goloso: Dirty and Greedy. They were surly-looking brutes, with rough yellow hair, and did not win my heart, but according to his account they possessed all the usual canine virtues; and he was still holding forth on the subject when I fell asleep.

⇘ 8 ⇙

WHEN MORNING CAME I was too stiff and sore to move, and not until the following day was I able to creep out to sit in the shade of the trees. My old host, whose name was Nuflo, went off with his dogs, leaving the girl to attend to my wants. Two or three times during the day she appeared, to serve me with food and drink, but she continued silent and constrained in manner as on the first evening of seeing her in the hut.

Late in the afternoon old Nuflo returned, but did not say where he had been; and shortly afterwards Rima reappeared, demure as usual, in her faded cotton dress, her cloud of hair confined in two long plaits. My curiosity was more excited than ever, and I resolved to get to the bottom of the mystery of her life. The girl had not shown herself responsive, but now that Nuflo was back I was treated to as much talk as I cared to hear. He talked of many things, only omitting those which I desired to hear about; but his pet subject appeared to be the divine government of the world—"God's politics"—and its manifest imperfections, or in other words, the manifold abuses which from time to time had been allowed to creep into it. The old man was pious, but like many of his class in my country, he permitted himself to indulge in very free criticisms of the powers above, from the King of Heaven down to the smallest saint whose name figures in the calendar.

"These things, señor," he said, "are not properly managed. Consider my position. Here am I compelled for my sins to inhabit this wilderness with my poor granddaughter——"

"She is not your granddaughter!" I suddenly interrupted, thinking to surprise him into an admission.

But he took his time to answer. "Señor, we are never sure of anything in this world. Not absolutely sure. Thus, it may come to pass that you will one day marry, and that your wife will in due time present you with a son—one that will inherit your fortune and transmit your name to posterity. And yet, sir, in this world, you will never know to a certainty that he is your son."

"Proceed with what you were saying," I returned, with some dignity.

"Here we are," he continued, "compelled to inhabit this land and do not meet with proper protection from the infidel. Now, sir, this is a crying evil, and it is only becoming in one who has the true faith, and is a loyal subject of the All-Powerful, to point out with due humility that He is growing very remiss in His affairs, and is losing a good deal of His prestige. And what, señor, is at the bottom of it? Favouritism. We know that the Supreme cannot Himself be everywhere, attending to each little trike-traka that arises in the world—matters altogether beneath His notice; and that He must, like the President of Venezuela or the Emperor of Brazil, appoint men—angels if you like—to conduct His affairs and watch over each district. And it is manifest that for this country of Guayana the proper person has not been appointed. Every evil is done and there is no remedy, and the Christian has no more consideration shown him than the infidel. Now, señor, in a town near the Orinoco I once saw on a church the archangel Michael, made of stone, and twice as tall as a man, with one foot on a monster shaped like a cayman, but with bat's wings, and a head and neck like a serpent. Into this monster he was thrusting his spear. That is the kind of person that should be sent to rule these latitudes—a person of firmness and resolution, with strength in his wrist. And yet it is probable that this very man—this St. Michael—is hanging about the palace, twirling his thumbs, waiting for an appointment, while other weaker men, and—Heaven forgive me for saying it, not above a bribe, perhaps—are sent out to rule over this province."

On this string he would harp by the hour; it was a lofty subject on which he had pondered much in his solitary life, and he was glad of an opportunity of ventilating his grievance and expounding his views. At first it was a pure pleasure to hear Spanish again, and the old man, albeit ignorant of letters, spoke well; but this, I may say, is a common thing in our country, where the peasant's quickness of intelligence and poetic feeling often compensate for want of instruction. His views also amused me, although they were not novel. But after a while I grew tired of listening, yet I listened still, agreeing with him, and leading him on to let him have his fill of talk, always hoping that he would come at last to speak of personal matters and give me an account of his history and of Rima's origin. But the hope proved vain; not a word to enlighten me would he drop, however cunningly I tempted him.

"So be it," thought I; "but if you are cunning, old man, I shall be cunning too—and patient; for all things come to him who waits."

He was in no hurry to get rid of me. On the contrary, he more than hinted that I would be safer under his roof than with the Indians, at the same time apologising for not giving me meat to eat.

"But why do you not have meat? Never have I seen animals so abundant and tame as in this wood."

Before he could reply Rima, with a jug of water from the spring in her hand, came in: glancing at me he lifted his finger to signify that such a subject must not be discussed in her presence; but as soon as she quitted the room he returned to it.

"Señor," he said, "have you forgotten your adventure with the snake? Know, then, that my grandchild would not live with me for one day longer if I were to lift my hand against any living creature. For us, señor, every day is fast-day—only without the fish. We have maize, pumpkin, cassava, potatoes, and these suffice. And even of these cultivated fruits of the earth she eats but little in the house, preferring certain wild berries and gums, which are more to her taste, and which she picks here and there in her rambles in the wood. And I, sir, loving her as I do, whatever my inclinations may be, shed no blood and eat no flesh."

I looked at him with an incredulous smile.

"And your dogs, old man?"

"My dogs? Sir, they would not pause or turn aside if a coatimundi crossed their path—an animal with a strong odour. As a man is, so is his dog. Have you not seen dogs eating grass, sir, even in Venezuela, where these sentiments do not prevail? And when there is no meat—when meat is forbidden—these sagacious animals accustom themselves to a vegetable diet."

I could not very well tell the old man that he was lying to me—that would have been bad policy—and so I passed it off. "I have no doubt that you are right," I said. "I have heard that there are dogs in China that eat no meat, but are themselves eaten by their owners after being fattened on rice. I should not care to dine on one of your animals, old man."

He looked at them critically and replied, "Certainly they are lean."

"I was thinking less of their leanness than of their smell," I returned. "Their odour when they approach me is not flowery, but resembles that of other dogs which feed on flesh, and have offended my too sensitive nostrils even in the drawing-rooms of Caracas. It is not like the fragrance of cattle when they return from the pasture."

"Every animal," he replied, "gives out that odour which is peculiar to its kind"; an incontrovertible fact which left me nothing to say.

When I had sufficiently recovered the suppleness of my limbs to walk with ease I went for a ramble in the wood, in the hope that Rima would accompany me, and that out among the trees she would cast aside that artificial constraint and shyness which was her manner in the house.

It fell out just as I had expected: she accompanied me in the sense of being always near me, or within earshot, and her manner was now free and unconstrained as I could wish; but little or nothing was gained by the change. She was once more the tantalising, elusive, mysterious creature I had first known through her wandering, melodious voice. The only difference was that the musical, inarticulate sounds were now less often heard, and that she was no longer afraid to show herself to me. This for a short time was enough to make me happy, since no lovelier being was ever looked upon, nor one whose loveliness was less likely to lose its charm through being often seen.

But to keep her near me or always in sight was, I found, impossible: she would be free as the wind, free as the butterfly, going and coming at her wayward will, and losing herself from sight a dozen times every hour. To induce her to walk soberly at my side or sit down and enter into conversation with me seemed about as impracticable as to tame the fiery-hearted little humming-bird that flashes into sight, remains suspended motionless for a few seconds before your face, then, quick as lightning, vanishes again.

At length, feeling convinced that she was most happy when she had me out following her in the wood, that in spite of her bird-like wildness she had a tender, human heart, which was easily moved, I determined to try to draw her closer by means of a little innocent stratagem. Going out in the morning, after calling her several times to no purpose, I began to assume a downcast manner, as if suffering pain or depressed with grief; and at last, finding a convenient exposed root under a tree, on a spot where the ground was dry and strewn with loose yellow sand, I sat down and refused to go any farther. For she always wanted to lead me on and on, and whenever I paused she would return to show herself, or to chide or encourage me in her mysterious language. All her pretty little arts were now practised in vain; with cheek resting on my hand I still sat, my eyes fixed on that patch of yellow sand at my feet, watching how the small particles glinted like diamond dust when the sunlight touched them. A full hour passed in this way, during which I encouraged myself by saying mentally: "This is a contest between us, and the most patient and the strongest of will, which should be the man, must conquer. And if I win on this occasion it will be easier for me in the future—easier to discover those things which I am resolved to know, and the girl must reveal to me, since the old man has proved impracticable."

Meanwhile she came and went and came again; and at last, finding that I was not to be moved, she approached and stood near me. Her face, when I glanced at it, had a somewhat troubled look—both troubled and curious.

"Come here, Rima," I said, "and stay with me for a little while—I cannot follow you now."

She took one or two hesitating steps, then stood still again; and at length, slowly and reluctantly, advanced to within a yard of me. Then I rose from my seat on the root, so as to catch her face better, and placed my hand against the rough bark of the tree.

"Rima," I said, speaking in a low, caressing tone, "will you stay with me here a little while and talk to me, not in your language, but in mine, so that I may understand? Will you listen when I speak to you, and answer me?"

Her lips moved, but made no sound. She seemed strangely disquieted, and shook back her loose hair, and with her small toes moved the sparkling sand at her feet, and once or twice her eyes glanced shyly at my face.

"Rima, you have not answered me," I persisted. "Will you not say 'yes'?"

"Yes."

"Where does your grandfather spend his day when he goes out with his dogs?"

She shook her head slightly, but would not speak.

"Have you no mother, Rima? Do you remember your mother?"

"My mother! My mother!" she exclaimed in a low voice, but with a sudden, wonderful animation. Bending a little nearer she continued: "Oh, she is dead! Her body is in the earth and turned to dust. Like that," and she moved the loose sand with her foot. "Her soul is up there, where the stars and the angels are, grandfather says. But what is that to me? I am here—am I not? I talk to her just the same. Everything I see I point out, and tell her everything. In the daytime—in the woods, when we are together. And at night when I lie down I cross my arms on my breast— so, and say, 'Mother, mother, now you are in my arms; let us go to sleep together.' Sometimes I say,

'Oh, why will you never answer me when I speak and speak?' Mother—mother—mother!"

At the end her voice suddenly rose to a mournful cry, then sank, and at the last repetition of the word died to a low whisper.

"Ah, poor Rima! she is dead and cannot speak to you—cannot hear you! Talk to me, Rima; I am living and can answer."

But now the cloud, which had suddenly lifted from her heart, letting me see for a moment into its mysterious depths—its fancies so childlike and feelings so intense—had fallen again; and my words brought no response, except a return of that troubled look to her face.

"Silent still?" I said. "Talk to me, then, of your mother, Rima. Do you know that you will see her again some day?"

"Yes, when I die. That is what the priest said."

"The priest?"

"Yes, at Voa—do you know? Mother died there when I was small—it is so far away! And there are thirteen houses by the side of the river—just here; and on this other side—trees, trees."

This was important, I thought, and would lead to the very knowledge I wished for; so I pressed her to tell me more about the settlement she had named, and of which I had never heard.

"Everything have I told you," she returned, surprised that I did not know that she had exhausted the subject in those half-dozen words she had spoken.

Obliged to shift my ground, I said at a venture: "Tell me, what do you ask of the Virgin Mother when you kneel before her picture? Your grandfather told me that you had a picture in your little room."

"You know!" flashed out her answer, with something like resentment. "It is all there—in there," waving her hand towards the hut. "Out here in the wood it is all gone—like this," and stooping quickly she raised a little yellow sand on her palm, then let it run away through her fingers.

Thus she illustrated how all the matters she had been taught slipped from her mind when she was out-of-doors, out of sight of the picture. After an interval she added, "Only mother is here—always with me."

"Ah, poor Rima!" I said; "alone without a mother, and only your old grandfather! He is old—what will you do when he dies and flies away to the starry country where your mother is?"

She looked inquiringly at me, then made answer in a low voice, "You are here."

"But when I go away?"

She was silent; and not wishing to dwell on a subject that seemed to pain her, I continued: "Yes, I am here now, but you will not stay with me and talk freely. Will it always be the same if I remain with you? Why are you always so silent in the house, so

cold with your old grandfather? So different—so full of
life, like a bird, when you are alone in the woods?
Rima, speak to me! Am I no more to you than your
old grandfather? Do you not like me to talk to you?"

She appeared strangely disturbed at my words. "Oh,
you are not like him," she suddenly replied. "Sitting
all day on a log by the fire—all day, all day; Goloso and
Susio lying beside him—sleep, sleep. Oh, when I saw
you in the wood I followed you, and talked and
talked; still no answer. Why will you not come when I
call? To me!" Then, mocking my voice, "Rima, Rima!
Come here! Do this! Say that! Rima! Rima! It is
nothing, nothing—it is not you," pointing to my
mouth; and then, as if fearing that her meaning had
not been made clear, suddenly touching my lips with
her finger, "Why do you not answer me?—speak to
me—speak to me, like this!" And turning a little more
towards me, and glancing at me with eyes that had all
at once changed, losing their clouded expression for
one of exquisite tenderness, from her lips came a succession of those mysterious sounds which had first attracted me to her, swift and low and bird-like, yet
with something so much higher and more soul-
penetrating than any bird music. Ah, what feeling
and fancies, what quaint turns of expression, unfamiliar to my mind, were contained in those sweet,
wasted symbols! I could never know—never come to
her when she called, or respond to her spirit. To me
they would always be inarticulate sounds, affecting

me like a tender spiritual music—a language without words, suggesting more than words to the soul.

The mysterious speech died down to a lisping sound, like the faint note of some small bird falling from a cloud of foliage on the topmost bough of a tree; and at the same time that new light passed from her eyes and she half averted her face in a disappointed way.

"Rima," I said at length, a new thought coming to my aid, "it is true that I am not here," touching my lips as she had done, "and that my words are nothing. But look into my eyes, and you will see me there—all, all that is in my heart."

"Oh, I know what I should see there!" she returned quickly.

"What would you see—tell me?"

"There is a little black ball in the middle of your eye; I should see myself in it no bigger than that," and she marked off about an eighth of her little finger-nail. "There is a pool in the wood, and I look down and see myself there. That is better. Just as large as I am—not small and black like a small, small fly." And after saying this a little disdainfully she moved away from my side and out into the sunshine; and then, half turning towards me, and glancing first at my face and then upwards, she raised her hand to call my attention to something there.

Far up, high as the tops of the tallest trees, a great blue-winged butterfly was passing across the open space with loitering flight. In a few moments it was gone over the trees; then she turned once more to me with a little rippling sound of laughter—the first I had heard from her, and called, "Come, come!"

I was glad enough to go with her then; and for the next two hours we rambled together in the wood; that is, together in her way, for though always near she contrived to keep out of my sight most of the time. She was evidently now in a gay, frolicsome temper; again and again, when I looked closely into some wide-spreading bush, or peered behind a tree, when her calling voice had sounded, her rippling laughter would come to me from some other spot. At length, somewhere about the centre of the wood, she led me to an immense mora tree, growing almost isolated, covering with its shade a large space of ground entirely free from undergrowth. At this spot she all at once vanished from my side; and after listening and watching some time in vain I sat down beside the giant trunk to wait for her. Very soon I heard a low, warbling sound which seemed quite near.

"Rima! Rima!" I called, and instantly my call was repeated like an echo. Again and again I called, and still the words flew back to me, and I could not decide whether it was an echo or not. Then I gave up calling; and presently the low, warbling sound was repeated, and I knew that Rima was somewhere near me.

"Rima, where are you?" I called.

"Rima, where are you?" came the answer.

"You are behind the tree."

"You are behind the tree."

"I shall catch you, Rima." And this time, instead of repeating my words, she answered, "Oh, no."

I jumped up and ran round the tree, feeling sure that I should find her. It was about thirty-five or forty feet in circumference; and after going round two or three times I turned and ran the other way, but failing to catch a glimpse of her I at last sat down again.

"Rima, Rima!" sounded the mocking voice as soon as I had sat down. "Where are you, Rima? I shall catch you, Rima! Have you caught Rima?"

"No, I have not caught her. There is no Rima now. She has faded away like a rainbow—like a drop of dew in the sun. I have lost her; I shall go to sleep." And stretching myself out at full length under the tree, I remained quiet for two or three minutes. Then a slight rustling sound was heard, and I looked eagerly round for her. But the sound was overhead and caused by a great avalanche of leaves which began to descend on to me from that vast leafy canopy above.

"Ah, little spider-monkey—little green tree-snake—you are there!" But there was no seeing her in that immense aerial palace hung with dim drapery of green and copper-coloured leaves. But how had she got there? Up the stupendous trunk even a monkey could not have climbed, and there were no lianas dropping to earth from the wide horizontal branches that I could see; but by-and-by, looking farther away, I perceived that on one side the longest lower branches reached and mingled with the shorter boughs of the neighbouring trees. While gazing up I heard her low, rippling laugh, and then caught sight of her as she ran along an exposed horizontal branch, erect on her feet; and my heart stood still with terror, for she was fifty to sixty feet above the ground. In another moment she vanished from sight in a cloud of foliage, and I saw no more of her for about ten minutes, when all at once she appeared at my side once more, having come round the trunk of the mora. Her face had a bright, pleased expression, and showed no trace of fatigue or agitation.

I caught her hand in mine. It was a delicate, shapely little hand, soft as velvet, and warm—a real human hand: only now when I held it did she seem altogether like a human being, and not a mocking spirit of the wood, a daughter of the Didi.

"Do you like me to hold your hand, Rima?"

"Yes," she replied, with indifference.

"Is it I?"

"Yes." This time as if it was small satisfaction to make acquaintance with this purely physical part of me.

Having her so close gave me an opportunity of examining that light sheeny garment she wore always in the woods. It felt soft and satiny to the touch, and there was no seam nor hem in it that I could see, but

it was all in one piece, like the cocoon of the caterpillar. While I was feeling it on her shoulder and
looking narrowly at it, she glanced at me with a mocking laugh in her eyes.

"Is it silk?" I asked. Then, as she remained silent, I
continued, "Where did you get this dress, Rima? Did
you make it yourself? Tell me."

She answered not in words, but in response to my
question a new look came into her face; no longer
restless and full of change in her expression, she was
now as immovable as an alabaster statue; not a silken
hair on her head trembled; her eyes were wide open,
gazing fixedly before her; and when I looked into
them they seemed to see and yet not to see me. They
were like the clear, brilliant eyes of a bird, which reflect as in a miraculous mirror all the visible world
but do not return our look, and seem to see us merely
as one of the thousand small details that make up the
whole picture. Suddenly she darted out her hand like
a flash, making me start at the unexpected motion,
and quickly withdrawing it, held up a finger before
me. From its tip a minute gossamer spider, about
twice the bigness of a pin's head, appeared suspended
from a fine, scarcely visible line three or four inches
long.

"Look!" she exclaimed, with a bright glance at my
face.

The small spider she had captured, anxious to be
free, was falling, falling earthward, but could not

reach the surface. Leaning her shoulder a little forward, she placed the finger-tip against it, but lightly, scarcely touching, and moving continuously, with a motion rapid as that of a fluttering moth's wing; while the spider, still paying out his line, remained suspended, rising and falling slightly at nearly the same distance from the ground. After a few moments she cried, "Drop down, little spider." Her finger's motion ceased, and the minute captive fell, to lose itself on the shaded ground.

"Do you not see?" she said to me, pointing to her shoulder. Just where the finger-tip had touched the garment a round shining spot appeared, looking like a silver coin on the cloth; but on touching it with my finger it seemed part of the original fabric, only whiter and more shiny on the grey ground, on account of the freshness of the web of which it had just been made.

And so all of this curious and pretty performance, which seemed instinctive in its spontaneous quickness and dexterity, was merely intended to show me how she made her garments out of the fine floating lines of small gossamer spiders!

Before I could express my surprise and admiration she cried again, with startling suddenness, "Look!"

A minute shadowy form darted by, appearing like a dim line traced across the deep glossy mora foliage, then on the lighter green foliage farther away. She waved her hand in imitation of its swift, curving flight, then dropping it exclaimed, "Gone—oh, little thing!"

"What was it?" I asked, for it might have been a bird, a bird-like moth, or a bee.

"Did you not see? And you asked me to look into your eyes!"

"Ah, little squirrel Sakawinki, you remind me of that!" I said, passing my arm round her waist and drawing her a little closer. "Look into my eyes now and see if I am blind, and if there is nothing in them except an image of Rima like a small, small fly."

She shook her head and laughed a little mockingly, but made no effort to escape from my arm.

"Would you like me always to do what you wish, Rima—to follow you in the woods when you say 'Come'—to chase you round the tree to catch you, and lie down for you to throw leaves on me, and be glad when you are glad?"

"Oh yes."

"Then let us make a compact. I shall do everything to please you, and you must promise to do everything to please me."

"Tell me."

"Little things, Rima—none so hard as chasing you round a tree. Only to have you stand or sit by me and talk will make me happy. And to begin you must call me by my name—Abel."

"Is that your name? Oh, not your real name! Abel,

Abel—what is that? It says nothing. I have called you by so many names—twenty, thirty—and no answer."

"Have you? But, dearest girl, every person has a name—one name he is called by. Your name, for instance, is Rima, is it not?"

"Rima! only Rima—to you? In the morning, in the evening . . . now in this place and in a little while where know I? . . . in the night when you wake and it is dark, dark, and you see me all the same. Only Rima—oh, how strange!"

"What else, sweet girl? Your grandfather Nuflo calls you Rima."

"Nuflo?" She spoke as if putting a question to herself. "Is that an old man with two dogs that lives somewhere in the wood?" And then, with sudden petulance, "And you ask me to talk to you!"

"Oh, Rima, what can I say to you? Listen——"

"No, no," she exclaimed, quickly turning and putting her fingers on my mouth to stop my speech, while a sudden merry look shone in her eyes. "You shall listen when I speak, and do all I say. And tell me what to do to please you with your eyes—let me look in your eyes that are not blind."

She turned her face more towards me, and with head a little thrown back and inclined to one side, gazing now full into my eyes as I had wished her to do. After a few moments she glanced away to the distant trees. But I could see into those divine orbs, and knew that she was not looking at any particular object. All the ever-varying expressions—inquisitive, petulant, troubled, shy, frolicsome—had now vanished from the still face, and the look was inward and full of a strange, exquisite light, as if some new happiness or hope had touched her spirit.

Sinking my voice to a whisper I said, "Tell me what you have seen in my eyes, Rima?"

She murmured in reply something melodious and inarticulate, then glanced at my face in a questioning way; but only for a moment, then her sweet eyes were again veiled under those drooping lashes.

"Listen, Rima," I said. "Was that humming-bird we saw a little while ago? You are like that, now dark, a shadow in the shadow, seen for an instant, and then—gone, oh, little thing! And now in the sunshine standing still, how beautiful!—a thousand times more beautiful than the humming-bird. Listen, Rima, you are like all beautiful things in the wood—flower, and bird, and butterfly, and green leaf, and frond, and little silky-haired monkey high up in the trees. When I look at you I see them all—all and more, a thousand times, for I see Rima herself. And when I listen to Rima's voice, talking in a language I cannot understand, I hear the wind whispering in the leaves, the gurgling running water, the bee among the flowers, the organ-bird singing far, far away in the shadows of the trees. I hear them all, and more, for I hear Rima. Do you understand me now? Is it I speaking to you— have I answered you—have I come to you?"

She glanced at me again, her lips trembling, her eyes now clouded with some secret trouble. "Yes," she replied in a whisper, and then, "No, it is not you," and after a moment, doubtfully, "Is it you?"

But she did not wait to be answered: in a moment she was gone round the mora; nor would she return again for all my calling.

$$≽ 9 ≼$$

THAT AFTERNOON with Rima in the forest under the
mora tree had proved so delightful that I was eager
for more rambles and talks with her, but the variable
little witch had a great surprise in store for me. All
her wild natural gaiety had unaccountably gone out
of her: when I walked in the shade she was there, but
no longer as the blithe, fantastic being, bright as an
angel, innocent and affectionate as a child, tricksy as
a monkey, that had played at hide-and-seek with me.
She was now my shy, silent attendant, only occasionally visible, and appearing then like the mysterious
maid I had found reclining among the ferns who had
melted away mist-like from sight as I gazed. When I
called she would not now answer as formerly, but in
response would appear in sight as if to assure me that

I had not been forsaken; and after a few moments her grey shadowy form would once more vanish among the trees. The hope that as her confidence increased and she grew accustomed to talk with me she would be brought to reveal the story of her life had to be abandoned, at all events for the present. I must, after all, get my information from Nuflo, or rest in ignorance. The old man was out for the greater part of each day with his dogs, and from these expeditions he brought back nothing that I could see but a few nuts and fruits, some thin bark for his cigarettes, and an occasional handful of haima gum to perfume the hut of an evening. After I had wasted three days in vainly trying to overcome the girl's now inexplicable shyness, I resolved to give for a while my undivided attention to her grandfather to discover, if possible, where he went and how he spent his time.

My new game of hide-and-seek with Nuflo instead of with Rima began on the following morning. He was cunning: so was I. Going out and concealing myself among the bushes, I began to watch the hut. That I could elude Rima's keener eyes I doubted; but that did not trouble me. She was not in harmony with the old man, and would do nothing to defeat my plan. I had not been long in my hiding-place before he came out, followed by his two dogs, and going to some distance from the door he sat down on a log. For some minutes he smoked, then rose, and after looking cautiously round slipped away among the

trees. I saw that he was going off in the direction of
the low range of rocky hills south of the forest. I
knew that the forest did not extend far in that direction, and thinking that I should be able to catch a
sight of him on its borders, I left the bushes and ran
through the trees as fast as I could to get ahead of
him. Coming to where the wood was very open, I
found that a barren plain beyond it, a quarter of a
mile wide, separated it from the range of hills; thinking that the old man might cross this open space I
climbed into a tree to watch. After some time he appeared, walking rapidly among the trees, the dogs at
his heels, but not going towards the open plain; he
had, it seemed, after arriving at the edge of the wood,
changed his direction, and was going west, still keeping in the shelter of the trees. When he had been
gone about five minutes I dropped to the ground and
started in pursuit; once more I caught sight of him
through the trees, and I kept him in sight for about
twenty minutes longer; then he came to a broad strip
of dense wood which extended into and through the
range of hills, and here I quickly lost him. Hoping
still to overtake him, I pushed on, but after struggling
through the underwood for some distance, and finding the forest growing more difficult as I progressed,
I at last gave him up. Turning eastward I got out of
the wood to find myself at the foot of a steep rough
hill, one of the range which the wooded valley cut
through at right angles. It struck me that it would

be a good plan to climb the hill to get a view of the
forest belt in which I had lost the old man; and after
walking a short distance I found a spot which allowed
of an ascent. The summit of the hill was about three
hundred feet above the surrounding level, and did not
take me long to reach; it commanded a fair view, and
I now saw that the belt of wood beneath me extended
right through the range, and on the south side opened
out into an extensive forest. "If that is your destination," thought I, "old fox, your secrets are safe from
me."

It was still early in the day, and a slight breeze
tempered the air and made it cool and pleasant on
the hilltop after my exertions. My scramble through
the wood had fatigued me somewhat, and resolving
to spend some hours on that spot, I looked round
for a comfortable resting-place. I soon found a shady
spot on the west side of an upright block of stone
where I could recline at ease on a bed of lichen. Here,
with shoulders resting against the rock, I sat thinking
of Rima, alone in her wood to-day, with just a tinge
of bitterness in my thoughts which made me hope
that she would miss me as much as I missed her; and
in the end I fell asleep.

When I woke it was past noon, and the sun was
shining directly on me. Standing up to gaze once more
on the prospect, I noticed a small wreath of white
smoke issuing from a spot about the middle of the
forest belt beneath me, and I instantly divined that

Nuflo had made a fire at that place, and I resolved to surprise him in his retreat. When I got down to the base of the hill the smoke could no longer be seen, but I had studied the spot well from above, and had singled out a large clump of trees on the edge of the belt as a starting-point; and after a search of half an hour I succeeded in finding the old man's hiding-place. First I saw smoke again through an opening in the trees, then a small rude hut of sticks and palm-leaves. Approaching cautiously, I peered through a crack and discovered old Nuflo engaged in smoking some meat over a fire, and at the same time grilling some bones on the coals. He had captured a coati-mundi, an animal somewhat larger than a tame tom cat, with a long snout and long ringed tail: one of the dogs was gnawing at the animal's head, and the tail and the feet were also lying on the floor, among the old bones and rubbish that littered it. Stealing round I suddenly presented myself at the opening to his den, when the dogs rose up with a growl and Nuflo instantly leaped to his feet, knife in hand.

"Aha, old man," I cried, with a laugh, "I have found you at one of your vegetarian repasts; and your grass-eating dogs as well!"

He was disconcerted and suspicious, but when I explained that I had seen a smoke while on the hills, where I had gone to search for a curious blue flower which grew in such places, and had made my way to it to discover the cause, he recovered confidence and invited me to join him at his dinner of roast meat.

I was hungry by this time and not sorry to get animal food once more; nevertheless, I ate this meat with some disgust, as it had a rank taste and smell, and it was also unpleasant to have those evil-looking dogs savagely gnawing at the animal's head and feet at the same time.

"You see," said the old hypocrite, wiping the grease from his moustache, "this is what I am compelled to do in order to avoid giving offence. My granddaughter is a strange being, sir, as you have perhaps observed——"

"That reminds me," I interrupted, "that I wish you to relate her history to me. She is, as you say, strange, and has speech and faculties unlike ours, which shows that she comes of a different race."

"No, no, her faculties are not different from ours. They are sharper, that is all. It pleases the All-Powerful to give more to some than to others. Not all the fingers on the hand are alike. You will find a man who will take up a guitar and make it speak, while I——"

"All that I understand," I broke in again. "But her origin, her history—that is what I wish to hear."

"And that, sir, is precisely what I am about to relate. Poor child, she was left on my hands by her sainted mother—my daughter, sir—who perished young. Now her birthplace, where she was taught letters and the Cathechism by the priest, was in an unhealthy situation. It was hot and wet—always wet—a place suited to frogs rather than to human beings. At length, thinking that it would suit the child better —for she was pale and weakly—to live in a drier atmosphere among mountains, I brought her to this district. For this, señor, and for all I have done for her, I look for no reward here, but to that place where my daughter has got her foot; not, sir, on the threshold, as you might think, but well inside. For, after all, it is to the authorities above, in spite of some blots which we see in their administration, that we must look for justice. Frankly, sir, this is the whole story of my granddaughter's origin."

"Ah, yes," I returned, "your story explains why she can call a wild bird to her hand, and touch a venomous serpent with her bare foot and receive no harm."

"Doubtless you are right," said the old dissembler. "Living alone in the wood she had only God's creatures to play and make friends with; and wild animals, I have heard it said, know those who are friendly towards them."

"You treat her friends badly," said I, kicking the long tail of the coatimundi away with my foot, and regretting that I had joined him in his repast.

"Señor, you must consider that we are only what Heaven made us. When all this was formed," he continued, opening his arms wide to indicate the entire creation, "the Person who concerned himself with this matter gave seeds and fruitlets and nectar of flowers for the sustentation of His small birds. But we have not their delicate appetites. The more robust stomach which he gave to man cries out for meat. Do you understand? But of all this, friend, not one word to Rima!"

I laughed scornfully. "Do you think me such a child, old man, as to believe that Rima, that little sprite, does not know that you are an eater of flesh? Rima, who is everywhere in the wood, seeing all things, even if I lift my hand against a serpent, she herself unseen."

"But, sir, if you will pardon my presumption, you are saying too much. She does not come here, and therefore cannot see that I eat meat. In all that wood where she flourishes and sings, where she is in her house and garden, and mistress of the creatures, even of the small butterfly with painted wings, there, sir, I hunt no animal. Nor will my dogs chase any animal there. That is what I meant when I said that if an animal should stumble against their legs, they would lift up their noses and pass on without seeing it. For in that wood there is one law, the law that Rima imposes, and outside of it a different law."

"I am glad that you have told me this," I replied. "The thought that Rima might be near, and, unseen herself, look in upon us feeding with the dogs and, like dogs, on flesh, was one which greatly troubled my mind."

He glanced at me in his usual quick, cunning way.

"Ah, señor, you have that feeling too—after so short a time with us! Consider, then, what it must be for me, unable to nourish myself on gums and fruitlets, and that little sweetness made by wasps out of flowers, when I am compelled to go far away and eat secretly to avoid giving offence."

It was hard, no doubt, but I did not pity him; secretly I could only feel anger against him for refusing to enlighten me, while making such a pretence of openness; and I also felt disgusted with myself for having joined him in his rank repast. But dissimulation was necessary, and so, after conversing a little more on indifferent topics, and thanking him for his hospitality, I left him alone to go on with his smoky task.

On my way back to the lodge, fearing that some taint of Nuflo's evil-smelling den and dinner might still cling to me, I turned aside to where a streamlet in the wood widened and formed a deep pool, to take a plunge in the water. After drying myself in the air, and thoroughly ventilating my garments by shaking and beating them, I found an open, shady spot in the wood and threw myself on the grass to wait for evening before returning to the house. By that time the sweet, warm air would have purified me. Besides, I did not consider that I had sufficiently punished Rima for her treatment of me. She would be anxious for my safety, perhaps even looking for me everywhere in the wood. It was not much to make her suffer one day after she had made me miserable for three; and perhaps when she discovered that I could exist without her society she would begin to treat me less capriciously.

So ran my thoughts as I rested on the warm ground, gazing up into the foliage, green as young grass in the lower, shady parts, and above luminous with the bright sunlight, and full of the murmuring sounds of insect life. My every action, word, thought, had my feeling for Rima as a motive. Why, I began to ask myself, was Rima so much to me? It was easy to answer that question: Because nothing so exquisite had ever been created. All the separate and fragmentary beauty and melody and graceful motion found scattered throughout nature were concentrated and harmoniously combined in her. How various, how luminous, how divine she was! A being for the mind to marvel at, to admire continually, finding some new grace and charm every hour, every moment, to add to the old. And there was, besides, the fascinating mystery surrounding her origin to arouse and keep my interest in her continually active.

That was the easy answer I returned to the question I had asked myself. But I knew that there was another answer—a reason more powerful than the first. And I could no longer thrust it back, or hide its shining face with the dull, leaden mask of mere intellectual curiosity. *Because I loved her;* loved her as

I had never loved before, never could love any other being, with a passion which had caught something of her own brilliance and intensity, making a former passion look dim and commonplace in comparison—a feeling known to everyone, something old and worn out, weariness even to think of.

From these reflections I was roused by the plaintive three-syllabled call of an evening bird—a nightjar common in these woods; and was surprised to find that the sun had set, and the woods already shadowed with the twilight. I started up and began hurriedly walking homewards, thinking of Rima, and was consumed with impatience to see her; and as I drew near to the house, walking along a narrow path which I knew, I suddenly met her face to face. Doubtless she had heard my approach, and instead of shrinking out of the path and allowing me to pass on without seeing her, as she would have done on the previous day, she had sprung forward to meet me. I was struck with wonder at the change in her as she came with a swift, easy motion, like a flying bird, her hands outstretched as if to clasp mine, her lips parted in a radiant, welcoming smile, her eyes sparkling with joy.

I started forward to meet her, but had no sooner touched her hands than her countenance changed, and she shrank back trembling, as if the touch had chilled her warm blood; and moving some feet away, she stood with downcast eyes, pale and sorrowful as she had seemed yesterday. In vain I implored her to tell me the cause of this change and of the trouble she evidently felt; her lips trembled as if with speech, but she made no reply, and only shrank farther away when I attempted to approach her; and at length, moving aside from the path, she was lost to sight in the dusky leafage.

I went on alone, and sat outside for some time, until old Nuflo returned from his hunting; and only after he had gone in and had made the fire burn up did Rima make her appearance, silent and constrained as ever.

❧ 10 ❧

On the following day Rima continued in the same inexplicable humour; and feeling my defeat keenly, I determined once more to try the effect of absence on her, and to remain away on this occasion for a longer period. Like old Nuflo, I was secret in going forth next morning, waiting until the girl was out of the way, then slipping off among the bushes into the deeper wood; and finally quitting its shelter I set out across the savannah towards my old quarters. Great was my surprise on arriving at the village to find no person there. At first I imagined that my disappearance in the forest of evil fame had caused them to abandon their home in a panic; but on looking round I concluded that my friends had only gone on one of their periodical visits to some neighbouring village.

For when these Indians visit their neighbours they do it in a very thorough manner; they all go, taking with them their entire stock of provisions, their cooking utensils, weapons, hammocks, and even their pet animals. Fortunately in this case they had not taken quite everything; my hammock was there, also one small pot, some cassava bread, purple potatoes, and a few ears of maize. I concluded that these had been left for me in the event of my return; also that they had not been gone very many hours, since a log of wood buried under the ashes of the hearth was still alight. Now as their absences from home usually last many days, it was plain that I would have the big naked barn-like house to myself for as long as I thought proper to remain, with little food to eat; but the prospect did not disturb me, and I resolved to amuse myself with music. In vain I hunted for my guitar; the Indians had taken it to delight their friends by twanging its strings. At odd moments during the last day or two I had been composing a simple melody in my brain, fitting it to ancient words; and now, without an instrument to assist me, I began softly singing to myself:

> *Muy mas clara que la luna*
> *Sola una*
> *en el mundo vos nacistes.*

After music I made up the fire and parched an ear of maize for my dinner, and while laboriously crunching the dry hard grain I thanked Heaven for having bestowed on me such good molars. Finally, I slung my hammock in its old corner, and placing myself in it in my favourite oblique position, my hands clasped behind my head, one knee cocked up, the other leg dangling down, I resigned myself to idle thought. I felt very happy. How strange, thought I, with a little self-flattery, that I, accustomed to the agreeable society of intelligent men and charming women, and of books, should find such perfect contentment here! But I congratulated myself too soon. The profound silence began at length to oppress me. It was not like the forest, where one has wild birds for company, where their cries, albeit inarticulate, have a meaning and give a charm to solitude. Even the sight and whispered sounds of green leaves and rushes trembling in the wind have for us something of intelligence and sympathy; but I could not commune with mud walls and an earthen pot. Feeling my loneliness too acutely, I began to regret that I had left Rima, then to feel remorse at the secrecy I had practised. Even now, while I reclined idly in my hammock, she would be roaming the forest in search of me, listening for my footsteps, fearing perhaps that I had met with some accident where there was no person to succour me. It was painful to think of her in this way, of the pain I had doubtless given her by stealing off without a word of warning. Springing to the floor, I flung out of the house and went down to the stream. It was better there, for now the greatest heat of the day was over, and the westering sun began to look large, and red, and rayless through the afternoon haze.

I seated myself on a stone within a yard or two of the limpid water: and now the sight of nature and the warm, vital air and sunshine infected my spirit, and made it possible for me to face the position calmly, even hopefully. The position was this: for some days the idea had been present in my mind, and was now fixed there, that this desert was to be my permanent home. The thought of going back to Caracas, that little Paris in America, with its old-world vices, its idle political passions, its empty round of gaieties, was unendurable. I was changed, and this change—so great, so complete—was proof that the old artificial life had not been and could not be the real one, in harmony with my deeper and truer nature. I deceived myself, you will say, as I have often myself said. I had and I had not. It is too long a question to discuss here; but just then I felt that I had quitted the hot, tainted atmosphere of the ballroom, that the morning air of heaven refreshed and elevated me, and was sweet to breathe. Friends and relations I had who were dear to me; but I could forget them, even as I could forget the splendid dreams which had been mine. And the woman I had loved, and who had perhaps loved me in return—I could forget her too. A daughter of civilisation and of that artificial life, she could never experience such feelings as these and return to nature as I was doing. For women, though within narrow limits more plastic than men, are yet without that larger adaptiveness which can take us back to the sources of life, which they have left eternally behind. Better, far better for both of us that she should wait through the long, slow months, growing sick at heart with hope deferred; that, seeing me no more, she should weep my loss, and be healed at last by time, and find love and happiness again in the old way, in the old place.

And while I thus sat thinking, sadly enough, but not despondingly, of past and present and future, all at once on the warm, still air came the resonant, far-reaching *kling-klang* of the campanero from some leafy summit half a league away. *Kling-klang* fell the sound again, and often again, at intervals, affecting me strangely at that moment, so bell-like, so like the great wide-travelling sounds associated in our minds with Christian worship. And yet so unlike. A bell, yet not made of gross metal dug out of earth, but of an ethereal, sublimer material that floats impalpable and invisible in space—a vital bell suspended on nothing, giving out sounds in harmony with the vastness of blue heaven, the unsullied purity of nature, the glory of the sun, and conveying a mystic, a higher message to the soul than the sounds that surge from tower and belfry.

O mystic bell-bird of the heavenly race of the swallow and dove, the quetzal and the nightingale! When the brutish savage and the brutish white man that slay thee, one for food, the other for the benefit of science, shall have passed away, live still, live to tell thy message to the blameless spiritualised race that shall come after us to possess the earth, not for a thousand years, but for ever; for how much shall thy voice be to our clarified successors when even to my dull, unpurged soul, thou canst speak such high things, and bring it a sense of an impersonal, all-comprising One who is in me and I in him, flesh of his flesh and soul of his soul.

The sounds ceased, but I was still in that exalted mood, and, like a person in a trance, staring fixedly before me into the open wood of scattered dwarf trees on the other side of the stream, when suddenly on the field of vision appeared a grotesque human figure moving towards me. I started violently, aston-ished and a little alarmed, but in a very few moments I recognised the ancient Cla-cla, coming home with a large bundle of dry sticks on her shoulders, bent al-most double under the burden, and still ignorant of my presence. Slowly she came down to the stream, then cautiously made her way over the line of stepping-stones by which it was crossed; and only when within ten yards did the old creature catch sight of me sitting silent and motionless in her path. With a sharp cry of amazement and terror she straightened herself up, the bundle of sticks dropping to the ground, and turned to run from me. That, at all events, seemed her intention, for her body was thrown forward, and her head and arms working like those of a person going at full speed, but her legs seemed paralysed and her feet remained planted on the same spot. I burst out laughing; whereat she twisted her neck until her wrinkled, brown old face appeared over her shoulder staring at me. This made me laugh again, whereupon she straightened herself up once more and turned round to have a good look at me.

"Come, Cla-cla," I cried; "can you not see that I am a living man and no spirit? I thought no one had remained behind to keep me company and give me food. Why are you not with the others?"

"Ah, why!" she returned tragically. And then deliberately turning from me and assuming a most unladylike attitude, she slapped herself vigorously on the small of the back, exclaiming, "Because of my pain here!"

As she continued in that position with her back towards me for some time, I laughed once more and begged her to explain.

Slowly she turned round and advanced cautiously towards me, staring at me all the time. Finally, still eyeing me suspiciously, she related that the others had all gone on a visit to a distant village, she starting with them: that after going some distance a pain had attacked her in her hind quarters, so sudden and acute that it had instantly brought her to a full stop;

and to illustrate how full the stop was she allowed herself to go down, very unnecessarily, with a flop to the ground. But she no sooner touched the ground than up she started to her feet again, with an alarmed look on her owlish face, as if she had sat down on a stinging-needle.

"We thought you were dead," she remarked, still thinking that I might be a ghost after all.

"No, still alive," I said. "And so because you came to the ground with your pain they left you behind! Well, never mind, Cla-cla, we are two now and must try to be happy together."

By this time she had recovered from her fear and began to feel highly pleased at my return, only lamenting that she had no meat to give me. She was anxious to hear my adventures, and the reason of my long absence. I had no wish to gratify her curiosity, with the truth at all events, knowing very well that with regard to the daughter of the Didi her feelings were as purely savage and malignant as those of Kua-kó. But it was necessary to say something, and, fortifying myself with the good old Spanish notion that lies told to the heathen are not recorded, I related that a venomous serpent had bitten me; after which a terrible thunderstorm had surprised me in the forest, and night coming on prevented my escape from it; then, next day, remembering that he who is bitten by a serpent dies, and not wishing to distress my friends with the sight of my dissolution, I elected

to remain, sitting there in the wood, amusing myself
by singing songs and smoking cigarettes; and after
several days and nights had gone by, finding that I
was not going to die after all, and beginning to feel
hungry, I got up and came back.

Old Cla-cla looked very serious, shaking and nodding her head a great deal, muttering to herself;
finally, she gave it as her opinion that nothing ever
would or could kill me; but whether my story had
been believed or not she only knew.

I spent an amusing evening with my old savage
hostess. She had thrown off her ailments, and pleased
at having a companion in her dreary solitude, she was
good-tempered and talkative, and much more inclined
to laugh than when the others were present, when
she was on her dignity.

We sat by the fire, cooking such food as we had,
and talked and smoked; then I sang her songs in
Spanish with that melody of my own:

Muy mas clara que la luna;

and she rewarded me by emitting a barbarous chant
in a shrill, screechy voice; and, finally, starting up, I
danced for her benefit polka, mazurka, and valse,
whistling and singing to my motions.

More than once during the evening she tried to in-
troduce serious subjects, telling me that I must always live with them, learn to shoot the birds and
catch the fishes, and have a wife; and then she would

speak of her granddaughter Oolava, whose virtues it was proper to mention, but whose physical charms needed no description since they had never been concealed. Each time she got on this topic I cut her short, vowing that if I ever married she only should be my wife. She informed me that she was old and past her fruitful period; that not much longer would she make cassava-bread, and blow the fire to a flame with her wheezy old bellows, and talk the men to sleep at night. But I stuck to it that she was young and beautiful, that our descendants would be more numerous than the birds in the forests. I went out to some bushes close by, where I had noticed a passion plant in bloom, and gathering a few splendid scarlet blossoms with their stems and leaves, I brought them in and wove them into a garland for the old dame's head; then I pulled her up, in spite of screams and struggles, and waltzed her wildly to the other end of the room and back again to her seat beside the fire. And as she sat there, panting and grinning with laughter, I knelt before her, and with suitable passionate gestures, declaimed again the old delicate lines sung by Mena before Columbus sailed the seas:

> Muy mas clara que la luna
> Sola una
> en el mundo vos nacistes
> tan gentil, que no vecistes
> ni tuvistes
> competedora ninguna

Desde niñez en la cuna
cobrastes fama, beldad,
con tanta graciosidad,
que vos dotó la fortuna.

Thinking of another all the time! O poor old Clacla, knowing not what the jingle meant nor the secret of my wild happiness, now when I recall you sitting there, your old grey owlish head crowned with scarlet passion flowers, flushed with firelight, against the background of smoke-blackened walls and rafters, how the old undying sorrow comes back to me!

Thus our evening was spent, merrily enough; then we made up the fire with hard wood that would last all night, and went to our hammocks, but wakeful still. The old dame, glad and proud to be on duty once more, religiously went to work to talk me to sleep; but although I called out at intervals to encourage her to go on, I did not attempt to follow the ancient tales she told, which she had imbibed in childhood from other white-headed grandmothers long, long turned to dust. My own brain was busy thinking, thinking now of the woman I had once loved, far away in Venezuela, waiting and weeping and sick with hope deferred; now of Rima, wakeful and listening to the mysterious night-sounds of the forest—listening, listening for my returning footsteps.

Next morning I began to waver in my resolution to remain absent from Rima for some days: and before evening my passion, which I had now ceased to struggle against, coupled with the thought that I had acted unkindly in leaving her, that she would be a prey to anxiety, overcame me, and I was ready to return. The old woman, who had been suspiciously watching my movements, rushed out after me as I left the house, crying out that a storm was brewing, that it was too late to go far, and night would be full of danger. I waved my hand in good-bye, laughingly reminding her that I was proof against all perils. Little she cared what evil might befall me, I thought; but she loved not to be alone; even for her, low down as she was intellectually, the solitary earthen pot had no "mind stuff" in it, and could not be sent to sleep at night with the legends of long ago.

By the time I reached the ridge I had discovered that she had prophesied truly, for now an ominous change had come over nature. A dull grey vapour had overspread the entire western half of the heavens; down, beyond the forest, the sky looked black as ink, and behind this blackness the sun had vanished. It was too late to go back now; I had been too long absent from Rima, and could only hope to reach Nuflo's lodge, wet or dry, before night closed round me in the forest.

For some moments I stood still on the ridge, struck by the somewhat weird aspect of the shadowed scene before me—the long strip of dull uniform green, with here and there a slender palm lifting its feathery crown above the other trees, standing motionless, in

strange relief against the advancing blackness. Then
I set out once more at a run, taking advantage of the
downward slope to get well on my way before the
tempest should burst. As I approached the wood
there came a flash of lightning, pale, but covering
the whole visible sky, followed after a long interval
by a distant roll of thunder, which lasted several
seconds, and ended with a succession of deep throbs.
It was as if Nature herself, in supreme anguish and
abandonment, had cast herself prone on the earth,
and her great heart had throbbed audibly, shaking the
world with its beats. No more thunder followed, but
the rain was coming down heavily now in huge drops
that fell straight through the gloomy, windless air.
In half a minute I was drenched to the skin; but for
a short time the rain seemed an advantage, as the
brightness of the falling water lessened the gloom,
turning the air from dark to lighter grey. This subdued rain-light did not last long: I had not been
twenty minutes in the wood before a second and
greater darkness fell on the earth, accompanied by an
even more copious downpour of water. The sun had
evidently gone down, and the whole sky was now
covered with one thick cloud. Becoming more nervous as the gloom increased, I bent my steps more to
the south, so as to keep near the border and more
open part of the wood. Probably I had already grown
confused before deviating and turned the wrong way,
for instead of finding the forest easier, it grew closer

and more difficult as I advanced. Before many minutes the darkness so increased that I could no longer distinguish objects more than five feet from my eyes. Groping blindly along, I became entangled in a dense undergrowth, and after struggling and stumbling along for some distance in vain endeavours to get through it, I came to a stand at last in sheer despair. All sense of direction was now lost: I was entombed in thick blackness—blackness of night and cloud and rain and of dripping foliage and network of branches bound with bush-ropes and creepers in a wild tangle. I had struggled into a hollow, or hole, as it were, in the midst of that mass of vegetation, where I could stand upright and turn round and round without touching anything; but when I put out my hands they came into contact with vines and bushes. To move from that spot seemed folly; yet how dreadful to remain there standing on the sodden earth, chilled with rain, in that awful blackness in which the only luminous thing one could look to see would be the eyes, shining with their own internal light, of some savage beast of prey. Yet the danger, the intense physical discomfort, and the anguish of looking forward to a whole night spent in that situation, stung my heart less than the thought of Rima's anxiety and of the pain I had carelessly given by secretly leaving her.

It was then, with that pang in my heart, that I was startled by hearing, close by, one of her own low, warbled expressions. There could be no mistake; if the forest had been full of the sounds of animal life and songs of melodious birds, her voice would have been instantly distinguished from all others. How mysterious, how infinitely tender it sounded in that awful blackness!—so musical and exquisitely modulated, so sorrowful, yet piercing my heart with a sudden, unutterable joy.

"Rima! Rima!" I cried. "Speak again. Is it you? Come to me here."

Again that low, warbling sound, or series of sounds, seemingly from a distance of a few yards. I was not disturbed at her not replying in Spanish: she had always spoken it somewhat reluctantly, and only when at my side; but when calling to me from some distance she would return instinctively to her own mysterious language, and call to me as bird calls to bird. I knew that she was inviting me to follow her, but I refused to move.

"Rima," I cried again, "come to me here, for I know not where to step, and cannot move until you are at my side, and I can feel your hand."

There came no response, and after some moments, becoming alarmed, I called to her again.

Then close by me, in a low, trembling voice, she returned, "I am here."

I put out my hand and touched something soft and wet; it was her breast, and moving my hand higher up, I felt her hair, hanging now and streaming with water. She was trembling, and I thought the rain had chilled her.

"Rima—poor child! How wet you are! How strange to meet you in such a place! Tell me, dear Rima, how did you find me?"

"I was waiting—watching—all day. I saw you coming across the savannah, and followed at a distance through the wood."

"And I had treated you so unkindly! Ah, my guardian angel, my light in the darkness, how I hate myself for giving you pain! Tell me, sweet, did you wish me to come back and live with you again?"

She made no reply. Then, running my fingers down her arm, I took her hand in mine. It was hot, like the hand of one in a fever. I raised it to my lips, and then attempted to draw her to me, but she slipped down and out of my arms to my feet. I felt her there, on her knees, with head bowed low. Stooping and putting my arm round her body, I drew her up and held her against my breast, and felt her heart throbbing wildly. With many endearing words I begged her to speak to me; but her only reply was, "Come—come," as she slipped again out of my arms, and holding my hand in hers, guided me through the bushes.

Before long we came to an open path or glade, where the darkness was not so profound; and releasing my hand she began walking rapidly before me, always keeping at such a distance as just enabled me to distinguish her grey, shadowy figure, and with fre-

quent doublings to follow the natural paths and open-
ings which she knew so well. In this way we kept
on nearly to the end, without exchanging a word,
and hearing no sound except the continuous rush
of rain, which to our accustomed ears had ceased to
have the effect of sound, and the various gurgling
noises of innumerable runnels. All at once, as we
came to a more open place, a strip of bright firelight
appeared before us, shining from the half-open door
of Nuflo's lodge. She turned round as much as to say,
"Now you know where you are," then hurried on,
leaving me to follow as best I could.

❧ 11 ❧

THERE WAS a welcome change in the weather when
I rose early next morning; the sky was now without
cloud, and had that purity in its colour and look of
infinite distance seen only when the atmosphere is
free from vapour. The sun had not yet risen, but old
Nuflo was already among the ashes, on his hands
and knees, blowing the embers he had uncovered to
a flame. Then Rima appeared only to pass through
the room with quick light tread to go out of the
door without a word or even a glance at my face.
The old man, after watching at the door for a few
minutes, turned and began eagerly questioning me
about my adventures on the previous evening. In
reply I related to him how the girl had found me in

171

the forest lost and unable to extricate myself from the tangled undergrowth.

He rubbed his hands on his knees and chuckled. "Happy for you, señor," he said, "that my granddaughter regards you with such friendly eyes, otherwise you might have perished before morning. Once she was at your side, no light, whether of sun or moon or lantern, was needed, nor that small instrument which is said to guide a man aright in the desert, even in the darkest night—let him that can believe such a thing!"

"Yes, happy for me," I returned. "I am filled with remorse that it was all through my fault that the poor child was exposed to such weather."

"O señor," he cried airily, "let not that distress you! Rain and wind and hot suns, from which we seek shelter, do not harm her. She takes no cold, and no fever, with or without ague."

After some further conversation I left him to steal away unobserved on his own account, and set out for a ramble in the hope of encountering Rima and winning her to talk to me.

My quest did not succeed: not a glimpse of her delicate shadowy form did I catch among the trees; and not one note from her melodious lips came to gladden me. At noon I returned to the house, where I found food placed ready for me, and knew that she had come there during my absence and had not been forgetful of my wants. "Shall I thank you for this?"

I said. "I ask for heavenly nectar for the sustentation of the higher winged nature in me, and you give me a boiled sweet potato, toasted strips of sun-dried pumpkins, and a handful of parched maize! Rima! Rima! my woodland fairy, my sweet saviour, why do you yet fear me? Is it that love struggles in you with repugnance? Can you discern with clear spiritual eyes the grosser elements in me, and hate them; or has some false imagination made me appear all dark and evil, but too late for your peace, after the sweet sickness of love has infected you?"

But she was not there to answer me, and so after a time I went forth again and seated myself listlessly on the root of an old tree not far from the house. I had sat there a full hour, when all at once Rima appeared at my side. Bending forward she touched my hand, but without glancing at my face; "Come with me," she said, and turning, moved swiftly towards the northern extremity of the forest. She seemed to take it for granted that I would follow, never casting a look behind, nor pausing in her rapid walk; but I was only too glad to obey, and starting up, was quickly after her. She led me by easy ways, familiar to her, with many doublings to escape the undergrowth, never speaking or pausing until we came out from the thick forest, and I found myself for the first time at the foot of the great hill or mountain Ytaioa. Glancing back for a few moments, she waved a hand towards the summit, and then at once began the ascent. Here too it seemed all familiar ground to her. From below the sides had presented an exceedingly rugged appearance—a wild confusion of huge jagged rocks, mixed with a tangled vegetation of trees, bushes, and vines; but following her in all her doublings it became easy enough, although it fatigued me greatly owing to our rapid pace. The hill was conical, but I found that it had a flat top; an oblong or pear-shaped area, almost level, of a soft, crumbling sandstone, with a few blocks and boulders of a harder stone scattered about; and no vegetation, except the grey mountain lichen and a few sere-looking dwarf shrubs.

Here Rima, at a distance of a few yards from me, remained standing still for some minutes, as if to give me time to recover my breath; and I was right glad to sit down on a stone to rest. Finally she walked slowly to the centre of the level area, which was about two acres in extent; rising I followed her, and climbing on to a huge block of stone, began gazing at the wide prospect spread out before me. The day was windless and bright, with only a few white clouds floating at a great height above and casting travelling shadows over that wild, broken country, where forest, marsh, and savannah were only distinguishable by their different colours, like the greys and greens and yellows on a map. At a great distance the circle of the horizon was broken here and there by mountains, but the hills in our neighbourhood were all beneath our feet.

After gazing all round for some minutes, I jumped down from my stand, and leaning against the stone, stood watching the girl, waiting for her to speak. I felt convinced that she had something of the very highest importance (to herself) to communicate, and that only the pressing need of a confidant, not Nuflo, had overcome her shyness of me; and I determined to let her take her own time to say it in her own way. For a while she continued silent, her face averted, but her little movements and the way she clasped and unclasped her fingers showed that she was anxious and her mind working. Suddenly, half turning to me, she began speaking eagerly and rapidly.

"Do you see," she said, waving her hand to indicate the whole circuit of earth, "how large it is? Look!" pointing now to mountains in the west. "Those are the Vahanas—one, two, three—the highest—I can tell you their names—Vahana-Chara, Chumi, Aranoa. Do you see that water? It is a river, called Guaypero. From the hills it comes down, Inaruna is their name, and you can see them over there in the south—far, far." And in this way she went on pointing out and naming all the mountains and rivers within sight. Then she suddenly dropped her hands to her sides, and continued, "That is all. Because we can see no further. But the world is larger than that! Other mountains, other rivers. Have I not told you of Voa, on the River Voa, where I was born, where mother died, where the priest taught me, years, years ago? All that you cannot see, it is so far away—so far."

I did not laugh at her simplicity, nor did I smile or feel any inclination to smile. On the contrary, I only experienced a sympathy so keen that it was like pain, while watching her clouded face, so changeful in its expression, yet in all changes so wistful. I could not yet form any idea as to what she wished to communicate or to discover, but seeing that she paused for a reply I answered, "The world is so large, Rima, that we can only see a very small portion of it from any one spot. Look at this," and with a stick I had used to aid me in my ascent I traced a circle six or seven inches in circumference on the soft stone and in its centre placed a small pebble. "This represents the mountain we are standing on," I continued, touching the pebble; "and this line encircling it encloses all of the earth we can see from the mountaintop. Do you understand?—the line I have traced is the blue line of the horizon beyond which we cannot see. And outside of this little circle is all the flat top of Ytaioa representing the world. Consider, then, how small a portion of the world we can see from this spot!"

"And do you know it all?" she returned excitedly. "All the world?" waving her hand to indicate the little stone plain. "All the mountains, and rivers, and forests—all the people in the world?"

"That would be impossible, Rima; consider how large it is."

"That does not matter. Come, let us go together —we two and grandfather, and see all the world; all the mountains and forests, and know all the people."

"You do not know what you are saying, Rima. You might as well say, 'Come, let us go to the sun and find out everything in it.'"

"It is you who do not know what you are saying," she retorted, with brightening eyes which for a moment glanced full into mine. "We have no wings like birds to fly to the sun. Am I not able to walk on the earth, and run? Can I not swim? Can I not climb every mountain?"

"No, you cannot. You imagine that all the earth is like this little portion you see. But it is not all the same. There are great rivers which you cannot cross by swimming; mountains you cannot climb; forests you cannot penetrate—dark, and inhabited by dangerous beasts, and so vast that all this space your eyes look on is a mere speck of earth in comparison."

She listened excitedly. "Oh, do you know all that?" she cried, with a strangely brightening look; and then half turning from me, she added, with sudden petulance, "Yet only a minute ago you knew nothing of the world—because it is so large! Is anything to be gained by speaking to one who says such contrary things?"

I explained that I had not contradicted myself, that she had not rightly interpreted my words. I knew, I said, something about the principal features of the different countries of the world, as, for instances, the largest mountain ranges, and rivers, and the cities. Also something, but very little, about the tribes of savage men. She heard me with impatience, which made me speak rapidly, in very general terms; and to simplify the matter I made the world stand for the continent we were in. It seemed idle to go beyond that, and her eagerness would not have allowed it.

"Tell me all you know," she said the moment I ceased speaking. "What is there—and there—and there?" pointing in various directions. "Rivers and forests—they are nothing to me. The villages, the tribes, the people everywhere; tell me, for I must know it all."

"It would take long to tell, Rima."

"Because you are so slow. Look how high the sun is! Speak, speak! What is there?" pointing to the north.

"All that country," I said, waving my hands from east to west, "is Guayana; and so large is it that you could go in this direction, or in this, travelling for months, without seeing the end of Guayana. Still it would be Guayana; rivers, rivers, rivers, with forests between, and other forests and rivers beyond. And

savage people, nations and tribes—Guahibo, Aguari-
coto, Ayano, Maco, Piaroa, Quiriquiripo, Tuparito—
shall I name a hundred more? It would be useless,
Rima; they are all savages, and live widely scattered
in the forests, hunting with bow and arrow and the
zabatana. Consider, then, how large Guayana is!"

"Guayana—Guayana! Do I not know all this is
Guayana? But beyond, and beyond, and beyond? Is
there no end to Guayana?"

"Yes; there northwards it ends at the Orinoco, a
mighty river, coming from mighty mountains, compared with which Ytaioa is like a stone on the ground
on which we have sat down to rest. You must know
that Guayana is only a portion, a half, of our country,
Venezuela. Look," I continued, putting my hand
round my shoulder to touch the middle of my back,
"there is a groove running down my spine dividing
my body into equal parts. Thus does the great Orinoco
divide Venezuela, and on one side of it is all Guayana;
and on the other side the countries or provinces
of Cumana, Maturin, Barcelona, Bolivar, Guarico,
Apure, and many others." I then gave a rapid description of the northern half of the country, with
its vast llanos covered with herds in one part, its plan-
tations of coffee, rice, and sugar-cane, in another, and
its chief towns; last of all Caracas, the gay and opu-
lent little Paris in America.

This seemed to weary her; but the moment I
ceased speaking, and before I could well moisten my

dry lips, she demanded to know what came after Caracas—after all Venezuela.

"The ocean—water, water, water," I replied.

"There are no people there—in the water; only fishes," she remarked; then suddenly continued, "Why are you silent—is Venezuela, then, all the world?"

The task I had set myself to perform seemed only at its commencement yet. Thinking how to proceed with it my eyes roved over the level area we were standing on, and it struck me that this little irregular plain, broad at one end, and almost pointed at the other, roughly resembled the South American continent in its form.

"Look, Rima," I began, "here we are on this small pebble—Ytaioa; and this line round it shuts us in— we cannot see beyond. Now let us imagine that we can see beyond—that we can see the whole flat mountain-top; and that, you know, is the whole world. Now listen while I tell you of all the countries, and principal mountains, and rivers, and cities of the world."

The plan I had now fixed on involved a great deal of walking about and some hard work in moving and setting up stones and tracing boundary and other lines; but it gave me pleasure, for Rima was close by all the time, following me from place to place, listening to all I said in silence but with keen interest. At the broad end of the level summit I marked out Venezuela, showing by means of a long line how the

Orinoco divided it, and also marking several of the greater streams flowing into it. I also marked the sites of Caracas and other large towns with stones; and rejoiced that we are not like the Europeans, great city builders, for the stones proved heavy to lift. Then followed Colombia and Ecuador on the west; and, successively, Bolivia, Peru, Chili, ending at last in the south with Patagonia, a cold arid land, bleak and desolate. I marked the littoral cities as we progressed on that side, where earth ends and the Pacific Ocean begins, and infinitude.

Then, in a sudden burst of inspiration, I described the Cordilleras to her—that world-long, stupendous chain; its sea of Titicaca, and wintry, desolate Paramo, where lie the ruins of Tiahuanaco, older than Thebes. I mentioned its principal cities—those small inflamed or festering pimples that attract much attention from appearing on such a body. Quito, called —not in irony, but by its own people—the Splendid and the Magnificent; so high above the earth as to appear but a little way removed from heaven—"de Quito al cielo," as the saying is. But of its sublime history, its kings and conquerors, Haymar Capac the Mighty, and Huascar, and Atahualpa the Unhappy, not one word. Many words—how inadequate!—of the summits, white with everlasting snows, above it—above this navel of the world, above the earth, the ocean, the darkening tempest, the condor's flight. Flame-breathing Cotopaxi, whose wrathful mutterings are audible two hundred leagues away, and Chimborazo, Antisana, Sarata, Illimani, Aconcagua—names of mountains that affect us like the names of gods, implacable Pachacamac and Viracocha, whose everlasting granite thrones they are. At the last I showed her Cuzco, the city of the sun, and the highest dwelling-place of men on earth.

I was carried away by so sublime a theme; and remembering that I had no critical hearer, I gave free reins to fancy, forgetting for the moment that some undiscovered thought or feeling had prompted her questions. And while I spoke of the mountains she hung on my words, following me closely in my walk, her countenance brilliant, her frame quivering with excitement.

There yet remained to be described all that unimaginable space east of the Andes; the rivers—what rivers!—the green plains that are like the sea—the illimitable waste of water where there is no land—and the forest region. The very thought of the Amazonian forest made my spirit droop. If I could have snatched her up and placed her on the dome of Chimborazo she would have looked on an area of ten thousand square miles of earth, so vast is the horizon at that elevation. And possibly her imagination would have been able to clothe it all with an unbroken forest. Yet how small a portion this would be of the stupendous whole—of forest region equal in extent to the whole of Europe! All loveliness, all grace, all majesty are there; but we cannot see, cannot conceive—come away! From this vast stage, to be occupied in the distant future by millions and myriads of beings, like us of upright form, the nations that will be born when all the existing dominant races on the globe and the civilisations they represent have perished as utterly as those who sculptured the stones of old Tiahuanaco—from this theatre of palms prepared for a drama unlike any which the Immortals have yet witnessed—I hurried away; and then slowly conducted her along the Atlantic coast, listening to the thunder of its great waves, and pausing at intervals to survey some maritime city.

Never probably since old Father Noah divided the earth among his sons had so grand a geographical discourse been delivered; and having finished, I sat down, exhausted with my efforts, and mopped my brow, but glad that my huge task was over, and satisfied that I had convinced her of the futility of her wish to see the world for herself.

Her excitement had passed away by now. She was standing a little apart from me, her eyes cast down and thoughtful. At length she approached me and said, waving her hand all round, "What is beyond the mountains over there, beyond the cities on that side—beyond the world?"

"Water, only water. Did I not tell you?" I returned stoutly; for I had, of course, sunk the Isthmus of Panama beneath the sea.

"Water! All round?" she persisted.

"Yes."

"Water, and no beyond? Only water—always water?"

I could no longer adhere to so gross a lie. She was too intelligent, and I loved her too much. Standing up, I pointed to distant mountains and isolated peaks.

"Look at those peaks," I said. "It is like that with the world—this world we are standing on. Beyond that great water that flows all round the world, but far away, so far that it would take months in a big boat to reach them, there are islands, some small, others as large as this world. But, Rima, they are so far away, so impossible to reach, that it is useless to speak or to think of them. They are to us like the sun and moon and stars, to which we cannot fly. And now sit down and rest by my side, for you know everything."

She glanced at me with troubled eyes.

"Nothing do I know—nothing have you told me. Did I not say that mountains and rivers and forests are nothing? Tell me about all the people in the world. Look! there is Cuzco over there, a city like no other in the world—did you not tell me so? Of the people nothing. Are they also different from all others in the world?"

"I will tell you that if you will first answer me one question, Rima."

She drew a little nearer, curious to hear, but was silent.

"Promise that you will answer me," I persisted, and as she continued silent I added, "Shall I not ask you, then?"

"Say," she murmured.

"Why do you wish to know about the people of Cuzco?"

She flashed a look at me, then averted her face. For some moments she stood hesitating, then coming closer, touched me on the shoulder, and said softly, "Turn away, do not look at me."

I obeyed, and bending so close that I felt her warm breath on my neck, she whispered, "Are the people in Cuzco like me? Would they understand me—the things you cannot understand? Do you know?"

Her tremulous voice betrayed her agitation, and her words, I imagined, revealed the motive of her action in bringing me to the summit of Ytaioa, and of her desire to visit and know all the various peoples inhabiting the world. She had begun to realise, after knowing me, her isolation and unlikeness to others, and at the same time to dream that all human beings might not be unlike her and unable to understand her mysterious speech and to enter into her thoughts and feelings.

"I can answer that question, Rima," I said. "Ah no, poor child, there are none there like you—not one, not one. Of all there—priests, soldiers, merchants, workmen, white, black, red, and mixed; men and women, old and young, rich and poor, ugly and beautiful—not one would understand the sweet language you speak."

She said nothing, and glancing round, I discovered that she was walking away, her fingers clasped before her, her eyes cast down, and looking profoundly dejected. Jumping up, I hurried after her. "Listen!" I said, coming to her side. "Do you know that there are others in the world like you who would understand your speech?"

"Oh, do I not! Yes—mother told me. I was young when you died, but, O mother, why did you not tell me more?"

"But where?"

"Oh, do you not think that I would go to them if I knew—that I would ask?"

"Does Nuflo know?"

She shook her head, walking dejectedly along.

"But have you asked him?" I persisted.

"Have I not! Not once—not a hundred times."

Suddenly she paused. "Look," she said, "now we are standing in Guayana again. And over there in Brazil, and up there towards the Cordilleras it is unknown. And there are people there. Come, let us go and seek for my mother's people in that place. With grandfather, but not the dogs; they would frighten the animals and betray us by barking to cruel men who would slay us with poisoned arrows."

"O Rima, can you not understand? It is too far. And your grandfather, poor old man, would die of weariness and hunger and old age in some strange forest."

"Would he die—old grandfather? Then we could cover him up with palm leaves in the forest and leave him. It would not be grandfather; only his body that must turn to dust. He would be away—away where the stars are. We should not die, but go on, and on, and on."

To continue the discussion seemed hopeless. I was silent, thinking of what I had heard—that there were others like her somewhere in that vast green world, so much of it imperfectly known, so many districts never yet explored by white men. True, it was strange that no report of such a race had reached the ears of any traveller; yet here was Rima herself at my side, a living proof that such a race did exist. Nuflo probably knew more than he would say; I had failed, as we have seen, to win the secret from him by fair means, and could not have recourse to foul—the rack and thumbscrew—to wring it from him. To the Indians she was only an object of superstitious fear—a daughter of the Didi—and to them nothing of her origin was known. And she, poor girl, had only a vague remembrance of a few words heard in childhood from her mother, and probably not rightly understood.

While these thoughts had been passing through my mind Rima had been standing silent by, waiting, perhaps, for an answer to her last words. Then stooping, she picked up a small pebble and tossed it three or four yards away.

"Do you see where it fell?" she cried, turning towards me. "That is on the border of Guayana—is it not? Let us go there first."

"Rima, how you distress me! We cannot go there. It is all a savage wilderness, almost unknown to men —a blank on the map——"

"The map?—speak no word that I do not understand."

In a very few words I explained my meaning; even fewer would have sufficed, so quick was her apprehension.

"If it is a blank," she returned quickly, "then you know of nothing to stop us—no river we cannot swim, and no great mountains like those where Quito is."

"But I happen to know, Rima, for it has been related to me by old Indians, that of all places that is the most difficult of access. There is a river there, and although it is not on the map, it would prove more impassable to us than the mighty Orinoco and Amazon. It has vast malarious swamps on its borders, overgrown with dense forest, teeming with savage and venomous animals, so that even the Indians dare not venture near it. And even before the river is reached there is a range of precipitous mountains called by the same name—just here where your pebble fell—the mountains of Riolama——"

Hardly had the name fallen from my lips before a change swift as lightning came over her countenance; all doubt, anxiety, petulance, hope, and despondence, and these in ever-varying degrees, chasing each other like shadows, had vanished, and she was instinct and burning with some new powerful emotion which had flashed into her soul.

"Riolama! Riolama!" she repeated so rapidly and in a tone so sharp that it tingled in the brain. "That is the place I am seeking! There was my mother found —there are her people and mine! Therefore was I called Riolama—that is my name!"

"Rima!" I returned, astonished at her words.

"No, no, no—Riolama. When I was a child, and the priest baptised me, he named me Riolama—the place where my mother was found. But it was long to say, and they called me Rima."

Suddenly she became still, and then cried in a ringing voice:

"And he knew it all along—that old man—he knew that Riolama was near—only there where the pebble fell—that we could go there!"

While speaking she turned towards her home, pointing with raised hand. Her whole appearance now reminded me of that first meeting with her when the serpent bit me; the soft red of her irides shone like fire, her delicate skin seemed to glow with an intense rose-colour, and her frame trembled with her agitation, so that her loose cloud of hair was in motion as if blown through by the wind.

"Traitor! Traitor!" she cried, still looking homewards and using quick, passionate gestures. "It was all known to you, and you deceived me all these years; even to me, Rima, you lied with your lips! Oh, horrible! Was there ever such a scandal known in Guayana? Come, follow me, let us go at once to Riolama." And without so much as casting a glance behind to see whether I followed or no, she hurried away, and in a couple of minutes disappeared from sight over the edge of the flat summit.

"Rima! Rima! Come back and listen to me! Oh, you are mad! Come back! Come back!"

But she would not return or pause and listen; and looking after her I saw her bounding down the rocky slope like some wild, agile creature possessed of padded hoofs and an infallible instinct; and before many minutes she vanished from sight among crags and trees lower down.

"Nuflo, old man," said I, looking out towards his lodge, "are there no shooting pains in those old bones of yours to warn you in time of the tempest about to burst on your head?"

Then I sat down to think.

❧ 12 ❧

To FOLLOW IMPETUOUS, bird-like Rima in her descent of the hill would have been impossible, nor had I any desire to be a witness of old Nuflo's discomfiture at the finish. It was better to leave them to settle their quarrel themselves, while I occupied myself in turning over these fresh facts in my mind to find out how they fitted into the speculative structure I had been building during the last two or three weeks. But it soon struck me that it was getting late, that the sun would be gone in a couple of hours; and at once I began the descent. It was not accomplished without some bruises and a good many scratches. After a cold draught, obtained by putting my lips to a black rock from which the water was trickling, I set out on my walk home, keeping near the western border of the forest for fear of losing myself. I had covered about half the distance from the foot of the hill to Nuflo's lodge when the sun went down. Away on my left the evening uproar of the howling monkeys burst out, and after three or four minutes ceased; the after silence was pierced at intervals by screams of birds going to roost among the trees in the distance, and by many minor sounds close at hand, of small bird, frog, and insect. The western sky was now like amber-coloured flame, and against that immeasurably distant luminous background the near branches and clustered foliage looked black; but on my left hand the vegetation still appeared of a uniform dusky green. In a little while night would drown all colour, and there would be no light but that of the wandering lantern-fly, always unwelcome to the belated walker in a lonely place, since, like the ignis fatuus, it is confusing to the sight and sense of direction.

With increasing anxiety I hastened on, when all at once a low growl issuing from the bushes some yards ahead of me brought me to a stop. In a moment the dogs, Susio and Goloso, rushed out from some hiding-place furiously barking; but they quickly recognised me and slunk back again. Relieved from fear, I walked on for a short distance; then it struck me that the old man must be about somewhere, as the dogs scarcely ever stirred from his side. Turning back I went to the spot where they had appeared to me; and there, after a while, I caught sight of a dim, yellow form, as one of the brutes rose up to look at me. He had been lying on the ground by the side of a wide-spreading bush, dead and dry, but overgrown by a creeping plant which had completely covered its broad, flat top like a piece of tapestry thrown over a table, its slender terminal stems and leaves hanging over the edge like a deep fringe. But the fringe did not reach to the ground, and under the bush, in its dark interior, I caught sight of the other dog; and after gazing in for some time I also discovered a black, recumbent form, which I took to be Nuflo.

"What are you doing there, old man?" I cried. "Where is Rima—have you not seen her? Come out."

Then he stirred himself, slowing creeping out on all fours; and, finally, getting free of the dead twigs and leaves, he stood up and faced me. He had a strange, wild look, his white beard all disordered, moss and dead leaves clinging to it, his eyes staring like an owl's, while his mouth opened and shut, the teeth striking together audibly, like an angry peccary's. After silently glaring at me in this mad way for some moments he burst out: "Cursed be the day when I first saw you, man of Caracas! Cursed be the serpent that bit you and had not sufficient power in its venom to kill! Ha! you come from Ytaioa, where you talked with Rima? And you have now returned to the tiger's den to mock that dangerous animal with the loss of its whelp. Fool, if you did not wish the dogs to feed on your flesh it would have been better if you had taken your evening walk in some other direction."

These raging words did not have the effect of alarming me in the least, nor even of astonishing me very much, albeit up till now the old man had always shown himself suave and respectful. His attack did not seem quite spontaneous. In spite of the wildness of his manner and the violence of his speech, he appeared to be acting a part which he had rehearsed beforehand. I was only angry, and stepping forward I dealt him a very sharp rap with my knuckles on his chest. "Moderate your language, old man," I said; "remember that you are addressing a superior."

"What do you say to me?" he screamed in a shrill, broken voice, accompanying his words with emphatic gestures. "Do you think you are on the pavement of Caracas? Here are no police to protect you—here we are alone in the desert, where names and titles are nothing, standing man to man."

"An old man to a young man," I returned. "And in virtue of my youth I am your superior. Do you wish me to take you by the throat and shake your insolence out of you?"

"What, do you threaten me with violence?" he exclaimed, throwing himself into a hostile attitude. "You, the man I saved, and sheltered, and fed, and treated like a son! Destroyer of my peace, have you not injured me enough? You have stolen my grandchild's heart from me; with a thousand inventions you have driven her mad! My child, my angel, Rima, my saviour! With your lying tongue you have changed her into a demon to persecute me! And you are not satisfied, but must finish your evil work by inflicting blows on my worn body! All, all is lost to me! Take my life if you wish it, for now it is worth nothing, and I desire not to keep it!" And here he threw himself on his knees, and tearing open his old, ragged mantle, presented his naked breast to me. "Shoot! Shoot!" he screeched. "And if you have no weapon take my knife, and plunge it into this sad heart, and let me die!" And drawing his knife from its sheath, he flung it down at my feet.

All this performance only served to increase my anger and contempt; but before I could make any reply I caught sight of a shadowy object at some distance moving towards us—something grey and formless, gliding swift and noiseless, like some great low-flying owl among the trees. It was Rima, and hardly had I seen her before she was with us, facing old Nuflo, her whole frame quivering with passion, her wide-open eyes appearing luminous in that dim light.

"You are here!" she cried in that quick, ringing tone that was almost painful to the sense. "You thought to escape me! To hide yourself from my eyes in the wood! Miserable! Do you not know that I have need of you—that I have not finished with you yet? Do you then wish to be scourged to Riolama with thorny twigs—to be dragged thither by the beard?"

He had been staring open-mouthed at her, still on his knees, and holding his mantle open with his skinny hands. "Rima! Rima! have mercy on me!" he cried out piteously. "Oh, my child, I cannot go to Riolama, it is so far—so far. And I am old and should meet my death. Oh, Rima, child of the woman I saved from death, have you no compassion? I shall die, I shall die!"

"Shall you die? Not until you have shown me the way to Riolama. And when I have seen Riolama with my eyes then you may die, and I shall be glad at your death; and the children and the grand-children and cousins and friends of all the animals you have slain and fed on shall know that you are dead and be glad at your death. For you have deceived me with lies all these years—even me—and are not fit to live! Come now to Riolama; rise instantly, I command you!"

Instead of rising he suddenly put out his hand and snatched up the knife from the ground. "Do you then wish me to die?" he cried. "Shall you be glad at my death? Behold, then I shall slay myself before your eyes. By my own hand, Rima, I am now about to perish, striking this knife into my heart!"

While speaking he waved the knife in a tragic manner over his head, but I made no movement; I was convinced that he had no intention of taking his own life—that he was still acting. Rima, incapable of understanding such a thing, took it differently.

"Oh, you are going to kill yourself!" she cried. "Oh, wicked man, wait until you know what will happen to you after death. All shall now be told to my mother. Hear my words, then kill yourself."

She also now dropped on to her knees, and lifting her clasped hands and fixing her resentful sparkling eyes on the dim blue patch of heaven visible beyond the treetops, began to speak rapidly in clear, vibrating tones. She was praying to her mother in heaven; and while Nuflo listened absorbed, his mouth open, his eyes fixed on her, the hand that clutched the knife dropped to his side. I also heard with the greatest wonder and admiration. For she had been shy and reticent with me, and now, as if oblivious of my presence, she was telling aloud the secrets of her inmost heart.

"O mother, mother, listen to me, to Rima, your beloved child!" she began. "All these years I have been wickedly deceived by grandfather—Nuflo—the old man that found you. Often have I spoken to him of Riolama, where you once were, and your people are, and he denied all knowledge of such a place. Sometimes he said that it was at an immense distance, in a great wilderness full of serpents larger than the trunks of great trees, and of evil spirits and savage men, slayers of all strangers. At other times he affirmed that no such place existed; that it was a tale told by the Indians; such false things did he say to me—to Rima, your child. O mother, can you believe such wickedness?

"Then a stranger, a white man from Venezuela, came into our woods: this is the man that was bitten by a serpent, and his name is Abel: only I do not call him by that name, but by other names, which I have told you. But perhaps you did not listen, or did not hear, for I spoke softly and not as now, on my knees, solemnly. For I must tell you, O mother, that after you died the priest at Voa told me repeatedly that when I prayed, whether to you or to any of the saints, or to the Mother of Heaven, I must speak as he had taught me, if I wished to be heard and understood. And that was most strange, since you had taught me differently; but you were living then, at Voa, and now that you are in Heaven perhaps you know better. Therefore listen to me now, O mother, and let nothing I say escape you.

"When this white man had been for some days with us a strange thing happened to me, which made me different, so that I was no longer Rima, although Rima still—so strange was this thing; and I often went to the pool to look at myself and see the change in me, but nothing different could I see. In the first place it came from his eyes passing into mine, and filling me just as the lightning fills a cloud at sunset: afterwards it was no longer from his eyes only, but it came into me whenever I saw him, even at a distance, when I heard his voice, and most of all when he touched me with his hand. When he is out of my sight I cannot rest until I see him again; and when I see him then I am glad, yet in such fear and trouble that I hide myself from him. O mother, it could not be told; for once when he caught me in his arms and compelled me to speak of it he did not understand; yet there was need to tell it; then it came to me that only to our people could it be told, for they would understand, and reply to me, and tell me what to do in such a case.

"And now, O mother, this is what happened next. I went to grandfather and first begged and then commanded him to take me to Riolama; but he would not obey, nor give attention to what I said, but whenever I spoke to him of it he rose up and hurried from me; and when I followed he flung back a confused and angry reply, saying in the same breath that it was so long since he had been to Riolama that he had forgotten where it was, and that no such place existed. And which of his words were true and which false I knew not: so that it would have been better if he had returned no answer at all; and there was no help to be got from him. And having thus failed, and there being no other person to speak to except this stranger, I determined to go to him, and in his company seek through the whole world for my people. This will surprise you, O mother, because of that fear which came on me in his presence, causing me to hide from his sight; but my wish was so great that for a time it overcame my fear; so that I went to him as he sat alone in the wood, sad because he could not see me, and spoke to him, and led him to the summit of Ytaioa to show me all the countries of the world from the summit. And you must also know that I tremble in his presence, not because I fear him as I fear Indians and cruel men; for he has no evil in him, and is beautiful to look at, and his words are gentle, and his desire is to be always with me, so that he differs from all other men I have seen, just as I differ from all women, except from you only, O sweet mother.

"On the mountain-top he marked out and named all the countries of the world, the great mountains, the rivers, the plains, the forests, the cities; and told me also of the peoples, white and savages, but of our people nothing. And beyond where the world ends there is water, water, water. And when he spoke of that unknown part on the borders of Guayana, on the side of the Cordilleras, he named the mountains of Riolama, and in that way I first found out where my people are. I then left him on Ytaioa, he refusing to follow me, and ran to grandfather and taxed him with his falsehoods; and he, finding I knew all, escaped from me into the woods, where I have now found him once more, talking with the stranger. And now, O mother, seeing himself caught and unable to escape a second time, he has taken up a knife to kill himself, so as not to take me to Riolama; and he is only waiting until I finish speaking to you, for I wish him to know what will happen to him after death. Therefore, O mother, listen well and do what I tell you. When he has killed himself, and has come into that place where you are, see that he does not escape the punishment he merits. Watch well for his coming, for he is full of cunning and deceit, and will endeavour to hide himself from your eyes. When you have recognised him—an old man, brown as an Indian, with a white beard—point him out to the angels, and say, 'This is Nuflo, the bad man that lied to Rima.' Let them take him and singe his wings with fire, so that he may not escape by flying; and afterwards thrust him into some dark cavern under a mountain, and place a great stone that a hundred men could not remove over its mouth, and leave him there alone and in the dark for ever!"

Having ended, she rose quickly from her knees, and at the same moment Nuflo, dropping the knife, cast himself prostrate at her feet.

"Rima—my child, my child, not that!" he cried out in a voice that was broken with terror. He tried to take hold of her feet with his hands, but she shrank from him with aversion; still he kept on crawling after her like a disabled lizard, abjectly imploring her to forgive him, reminding her that he had saved from death the woman whose enmity had now been enlisted against him, and declaring that he would do anything she commanded him, and gladly perish in her service.

It was a pitiable sight, and moving quickly to her side I touched her on the shoulder and asked her to forgive him.

The response came quickly enough. Turning to him once more she said: "I forgive you, grandfather. And now get up and take me to Riolama."

He rose, but only to his knees. "But you have not told *her!*" he said, recovering his natural voice, although still anxious, and jerking a thumb over his shoulder. "Consider, my child, that I am old and shall doubtless perish on the way. What would become of my soul in such a case? For now you have told her everything, and it will not be forgotten."

She regarded him in silence for a few moments, then moving a little way apart, dropped on to her knees again, and with raised hands and eyes fixed on the blue space above, already sprinkled with stars, prayed again.

"O mother, listen to me, for I have something fresh to say to you. Grandfather has not killed himself, but has asked my forgiveness and has promised to obey me. O mother, I have forgiven him, and he will now take me to Riolama, to our people. Therefore, O mother, if he dies on the way to Riolama let nothing be done against him, but remember only that I forgave him at the last; and when he comes into that place where you are, let him be well received, for that is the wish of Rima, your child."

As soon as this second petition was ended she was up again and engaged in an animated discussion with him, urging him to take her without further delay to Riolama; while he, now recovered from his fear, urged that so important an undertaking required a great deal of thought and preparation; that the journey would occupy about twenty days, and unless he set out well provided with food he would starve before accomplishing half the distance; and his death would leave her worse off than before: he concluded by affirming that he could not start in less time than seven or eight days.

For a while I listened with keen interest to this dispute, and at length interposed once more on the old man's side. The poor girl in her petition had unwittingly revealed to me the power I possessed, and it was a pleasing experience to exercise it. Touching her shoulder again, I assured her that seven or eight days was only a reasonable time in which to prepare for so long a journey: she instantly yielded, and after one glance at my face she moved swiftly away into the darker shadows, leaving me alone with the old man.

As we returned together through the now profoundly dark wood I explained to him how the subject of Riolama had first come up during my conversation with Rima, and he then apologised for the violent language he had used to me. This personal question disposed of, he spoke of the pilgrimage before him, and informed me in confidence that he intended preparing a quantity of smoke-dried meat and packing it in a bag, with a layer of cassava bread, dried pumpkin slips, and such innocent trifles to conceal it from Rima's keen sight and delicate nostrils. Finally, he made a long rambling statement, which, I vainly imagined, was intended to lead up to an account of Rima's origin, with something about her people at Riolama; but it led to nothing except an expression of opinion that the girl was afflicted with a maggot in the brain, but that as she had interest with the powers above, especially with her mother, who was now a very important person among the celestials, it was good policy to submit to her wishes. Turning to me, doubtless to wink (only I missed the sign owing to the darkness), he added that it was a fine thing to have a friend at court. With a little gratulatory chuckle he went on to say that for others it was necessary to obey all the ordinances of the Church, to contribute to its support, hear mass, confess from time to time, and receive absolution: consequently those who went out into the wilderness, where there were no churches and no priests to absolve them, did so at the risk of losing their souls. But with him it was different: he expected in the end to escape the fires of purgatory, and go directly in all his uncleanness to heaven—a thing, he remarked,

which happened to very few; and he, Nuflo, was no
saint, and had first become a dweller in the desert,
as a very young man, in order to escape the penalty
of his misdeeds.

I could not resist the temptation of remarking
here that to an unregenerate man the celestial country might turn out a somewhat uncongenial place for
a residence. He replied airily that he had considered
the point and had no fear about the future; that he
was old, and from all he had observed of the methods
of government followed by those who ruled over
earthly affairs from the sky, he had formed a clear
idea of that place, and believed that even among so
many glorified beings he would be able to meet with
those who would prove companionable enough, and
would think no worse of him on account of his little
blemishes.

How he had first got this idea into his brain about
Rima's ability to make things smooth for him after
death I cannot say; probably it was the effect of the
girl's powerful personality and vivid faith acting on
an ignorant and extremely superstitious mind. While
she was making that petition to her mother in heaven
it did not seem in the least ridiculous to me: I had
felt no inclination to smile, even when hearing all
that about the old man's wings being singed to prevent his escape by flying. Her rapt look; the intense
conviction that vibrated in her ringing, passionate
tones; the brilliant scorn with which she, a hater of

bloodshed, one so tender towards all living things, even the meanest, bade him kill himself, and only hear first how her vengeance would pursue his deceitful soul into other worlds; the clearness with which she had related the facts of the case, disclosing the inmost secrets of her heart—all this had had a strange, convincing effect on me. Listening to her I was no longer the enlightened, the creedless man. She herself was so near to the supernatural that it seemed brought near me; indefinable feelings, which had been latent in me, stirred into life, and following the direction of her divine, lustrous eyes, fixed on the blue sky above, I seemed to see there another being like herself, a Rima glorified, leaning her pale, spiritual face to catch the winged words uttered by her child on earth. And even now, while hearing the old man's talk, showing as it did a mind darkened with such gross delusions, I was not yet altogether free from the strange effect of that prayer. Doubtless it was a delusion; her mother was not really there above listening to the girl's voice. Still, in some mysterious way, Rima had become to me, even as to superstitious old Nuflo, a being apart and sacred, and this feeling seemed to mix with my passion, to purify and exalt it and make it infinitely sweet and precious.

After we had been silent for some time I said, "Old man, the result of the grand discussion you have had with Rima is that you have agreed to take her to

Riolama, but about my accompanying you not one word has been spoken by either of you."

He stopped short to stare at me, and although it was too dark to see his face, I felt his astonishment. "Señor!" he exclaimed, "we cannot go without you. Have you not heard my granddaughter's words—that it is only because of you that she is about to undertake this crazy journey? If you are not with us in this thing, then, señor, here we must remain. But what will Rima say to that?"

"Very well, I will go, but only on one condition."

"What is it?" he asked, with a sudden change of tone, which warned me that he was becoming cautious again.

"That you tell me the whole story of Rima's origin, and how you came to be now living with her in this solitary place, and who these people are she wishes to visit at Riolama."

"Ah, señor, it is a long story, and sad. But you shall hear it all. You must hear it, señor, since you are now one of us; and when I am no longer here to protect her then she will be yours. And although you will never be able to do more than old Nuflo for her, perhaps she will be better pleased; and you, señor, better able to exist innocently by her side, without eating flesh, since you will always have that rare flower to delight you. But the story would take long to tell. You shall hear it all as we journey to Riolama. What else will there be to talk about when we are walking that long distance, and when we sit at night by the fire?"

"No, no, old man, I am not to be put off in that way. I must hear it before I start."

But he was determined to reserve the narrative until the journey, and after some further argument I yielded the point.

❧ 13 ❦

THAT EVENING by the fire old Nuflo, lately so miserable, now happy in his delusions, was more than
usually gay and loquacious. He was like a child, who
by timely submission has escaped a threatened severe
punishment. But his lightness of heart was exceeded
by mine; and, with the exception of one other yet
to come, that evening now shines in memory as the
happiest my life has known. For Rima's sweet secret
was known to me; and her very ignorance of the
meaning of the feeling she experienced, which caused
her to fly from me as from an enemy, only served
to make the thought of it more purely delightful.

On this occasion she did not steal away like a timid
mouse to her own apartment, as her custom was, but
remained to give that one evening a special grace,

seated well away from the fire in that same shadowy corner where I had first seen her indoors, when
I had marvelled at her altered appearance.

From that corner she could see my face, with the
firelight full upon it, she herself in shadow, her eyes
veiled by their drooping lashes. Sitting there in vivid
consciousness of my happiness was like draughts of
strong, delicious wine, and its effect was like wine,
imparting such freedom to fancy, such fluency, that
again and again old Nuflo applauded, crying out that
I was a poet, and begging me to put it all into rhyme.
I could not do that to please him, never having acquired the art of improvisation—that idle trick of
making words jingle which men of Nuflo's class in
my country so greatly admire: yet it seemed to me
on that evening that my feelings could be adequately
expressed only in that sublimated language used by
the finest minds in their inspired moments; and, accordingly, I fell to reciting. But not from any modern,
nor from the poets of the last century, nor even from
the greater seventeenth century. I kept to the more
ancient romances and ballads, the sweet old verse
that, whether glad or sorrowful, seems always natural
and spontaneous as the song of a bird, and so simple
that even a child can understand it.

It was late that night before all the romances I
remembered or cared to recite were exhausted, and
not until then did Rima come out of her shaded corner and steal silently away to her sleeping-place.

Although I had resolved to go with them, and had set Nuflo's mind at rest on the point, I was bent on getting the request from Rima's own lips; and the next morning the opportunity of seeing her alone presented itself, after old Nuflo had sneaked off with his dogs. From the moment of his departure I kept a close watch on the house, as one watches a bush in which a bird he wishes to see has concealed itself, and out of which it may dart at any moment and escape unseen.

At length she came forth, and seeing me in the way, would have slipped back into hiding; for, in spite of her boldness on the previous day, she now seemed shyer than ever when I spoke to her.

"Rima," I said, "do you remember where we first talked together under a tree one morning, when you spoke of your mother, telling me that she was dead?"

"Yes."

"I am going now to that spot to wait for you. I must speak to you again in that place about this journey to Riolama." As she kept silent, I added, "Will you promise to come to me there?"

She shook her head, turning half away.

"Have you forgotten our compact, Rima?"

"No," she returned; and then, suddenly coming near, spoke in a low tone, "I will go there to please you, and you must also do as I tell you."

"What do you wish, Rima?"

She came nearer still. "Listen! You must not look

into my eyes, you must not touch me with your hands."

"Sweet Rima, I must hold your hand when I speak with you."

"No, no, no," she murmured, shrinking from me; and finding that it must be as she wished, I reluctantly agreed.

Before I had waited long she appeared at the trysting-place, and stood before me, as on a former occasion, on that same spot of clean yellow sand, clasping and unclasping her fingers, troubled in mind even then. Only now her trouble was different and greater, making her shyer and more reticent.

"Rima, your grandfather is going to take you to Riolama. Do you wish me to go with you?"

"Oh, do you not know that?" she returned, with a swift glance at my face.

"How should I know?"

Her eyes wandered away restlessly. "On Ytaioa you told me a hundred things which I did not know," she replied in a vague way, wishing, perhaps, to imply that with so great a knowledge of geography it was strange I did not know everything, even her most secret thoughts.

"Tell me, why must you go to Riolama?"

"You have heard. To speak to my people."

"What will you say to them? Tell me."

"What you do not understand. How tell you?"

"I understand you when you speak in Spanish."

"Oh, that is not speaking."

"Last night you spoke to your mother in Spanish. Did you not tell her everything?"

"Oh no—not then. When I tell her everything I speak in another way, in a low voice—not on my knees and praying. At night, and in the woods, and when I am alone I tell her. But perhaps she does not hear me; she is not here, but up there—so far! She never answers, but when I speak to my people they will answer me."

Then she turned away as if there was nothing more to be said.

"Is this all I am to hear from you, Rima—these few words?" I exclaimed. "So much did you say to your grandfather, so much to your dead mother, but to me you say so little!"

She turned again, and with eyes cast down replied—

"He deceived me—I had to tell him that, and then to pray to mother. But to you that do not understand, what can I say? Only that you are not like him and all those that I knew at Voa. It is so different—and the same. You are you, and I am I; why is it—do you know?"

"No; yes—I know, but cannot tell you. And if you find your people what will you do—leave me to go to them? Must I go all the way to Riolama only to lose you?"

"Where I am there you must be."

"Why?"

"Do I not see it there?" she returned, with a quick gesture to indicate that it appeared in my face.

"Your sight is keen, Rima—keen as a bird's. Mine is not so keen. Let me look once more into those beautiful wild eyes, then perhaps I shall see in them as much as you see in mine."

"Oh, no, no, not that!" she murmured in distress, drawing away from me; then with a sudden flash of brilliant colour cried—

"Have you forgotten the compact—the promise you made me?"

Her words made me ashamed, and I could not reply. But the shame was as nothing in strength compared to the impulse I felt to clasp her beautiful body in my arms and cover her face with kisses. Sick with desire, I turned away, and sitting on a root of the tree, covered my face with my hands.

She came nearer: I could see her shadow through my fingers; then her face and wistful, compassionate eyes.

"Forgive me, dear Rima," I said, dropping my hands again. "I have tried so hard to please you in everything. Touch my face with your hand—only that, and I will go to Riolama with you, and obey you in all things."

For a while she hesitated, then stepped quickly aside so that I could not see her; but I knew that she had not left me, that she was standing just behind me. And after waiting a moment longer I felt

her fingers touching my skin, softly, trembling over
my cheek as if a soft-winged moth had fluttered
against it; then the slight aerial touch was gone, and
she, too, moth-like, had vanished from my side.

Left alone in the wood I was not happy. That
fluttering, flattering touch of her finger-tips had
been to me like spoken language, and more eloquent
than language, yet the sweet assurance it conveyed
had not given perfect satisfaction; and when I asked
myself why the gladness of the previous evening had
forsaken me—why I was infected with this new sadness when everything promised well for me, I found
that it was because my passion had greatly increased
during the last few hours; even during sleep it had
been growing and could no longer be fed by merely
dwelling in thought on the charms, moral and physical, of its object, and by dreams of future fruition.

I concluded that it would be best for Rima's sake
as well as my own to spend a few of the days, before
setting out on our journey, with my Indian friends,
who would be troubled at my long absence; and, accordingly, next morning I bade good-bye to the old
man, promising to return in three or four days, and
then started without seeing Rima, who had quitted
the house before her usual time. After getting free of
the woods, on casting back my eyes I caught sight of
the girl standing under an isolated tree watching me
with that vague, misty, greenish appearance she so

frequently had when seen in the light shade at a short distance.

"Rima!" I cried, hurrying back to speak to her, but when I reached the spot she had vanished; and after waiting some time, seeing and hearing nothing to indicate that she was near me, I resumed my walk, half thinking that my imagination had deceived me.

I found my Indian friends home again, and was not surprised to observe a distinct change in their manner towards me. I had expected as much; and considering that they must have known very well where and in whose company I had been spending my time, it was not strange. Coming across the savannah that morning I had first begun to think seriously of the risk I was running. But this thought only served to prepare me for a new condition of things; for now to go back and appear before Rima, and thus prove myself to be a person not only capable of forgetting a promise occasionally, but also of a weak, vacillating mind, was not to be thought of for a moment.

I was received—not welcomed—quietly enough: not a question, not a word, concerning my long absence fell from anyone; it was as if a stranger had appeared among them, one about whom they knew nothing, and consequently regarded with suspicion, if not actual hostility. I affected not to notice the change, and dipped my hand uninvited in the pot to satisfy my hunger, and smoked and dozed away the sultry hours in my hammock. Then I got my guitar and

spent the rest of the day over it, tuning it, touching
the strings so softly with my finger-tips that to a
person four yards off the sound must have seemed
like the murmur or buzz of an insect's wings; and
to this scarcely audible accompaniment I murmured
in an equally low tone a new song.

In the evening, when all were gathered under the
roof and I had eaten again, I took up the instrument
once more, furtively watched by all those half-closed
animal eyes, and swept the strings loudly, and sang
aloud. I sang an old simple Spanish melody, to which
I had put words in their own language—a language
with no words not in everyday use, in which it is so
difficult to express feelings out of and above the common. What I had been constructing and practising
all the afternoon *sotto voce* was a kind of ballad, an
extremely simple tale of a poor Indian living alone
with his young family in a season of dearth: how
day after day he ranged the voiceless words to return each evening with nothing but a few withered
sour berries in his hand, to find his lean, large-eyed
wife still nursing the fire that cooked nothing, and his
children crying for food, showing their bones more
plainly through their skins every day; and how, without anything miraculous, anything wonderful, happening, that barrenness passed from earth, and the
garden once more yielded them pumpkin and maize
and manioc, the wild fruits ripened, and the birds
returned, filling the forest with their cries; and so

their long hunger was satisfied, and the children grew sleek, and played and laughed in the sunshine; and the wife, no longer brooding over the empty pot, wove a hammock of silk grass, decorated with blue-and-scarlet feathers of the macaw; and in that new hammock the Indian rested long from his labours, smoking endless cigars.

When I at last concluded with a loud note of joy, a long, involuntary suspiration in the darkening room told me that I had been listened to with profound interest; and, although no word was spoken, though I was still a stranger and under a cloud, it was plain that the experiment had succeeded, and that for the present the danger was averted.

I went to my hammock and slept, but without undressing. Next morning I missed my revolver and found that the holster containing it had been detached from the belt. My knife had not been taken, possibly because it was under me in the hammock while I slept. In answer to my inquiries I was informed that Runi had *borrowed* my weapon to take it with him to the forest, where he had gone to hunt, and that he would return it to me in the evening. I affected to take it in good part, although feeling secretly ill at ease. Later in the day I came to the conclusion that Runi had had it in his mind to murder me, that I had softened him by singing that Indian story, and that by taking possession of the revolver he showed that he now only meant to keep me a prisoner. Subsequent events confirmed me in this suspicion. On his return he explained that he had gone out to seek for game in the woods; and, going without a companion, he had taken my revolver to preserve him from dangers—meaning those of a supernatural kind; and that he had had the misfortune to drop it among the bushes while in pursuit of some animal. I answered hotly that he had not treated me like a friend; that if he had asked me for the weapon it would have been lent to him; that as he had taken it without permission he must pay me for it. After some pondering, he said that when he took it I was sleeping soundly; also, that it would not be lost; he would take me to the place where he had dropped it, when we could search together for it.

He was in appearance more friendly towards me now, even asking me to repeat my last evening's song, and so we had that performance all over again to everybody's satisfaction. But when morning came he was not inclined to go to the woods: there was food enough in the house, and the pistol would not be hurt by lying where it had fallen a day longer. Next day the same excuse; still I disguised my impatience and suspicion of him and waited, singing the ballad for the third time that evening. Then I was conducted to a wood about a league and half away, and we hunted for the lost pistol among the bushes, I with little hope of finding it, while he attended to the bird voices and frequently asked me to stand or lie still when a chance of something offered.

The result of that wasted day was a determination on my part to escape from Runi as soon as possible, although at the risk of making a deadly enemy of him and of being compelled to go on that long journey to Riolama with no better weapon than a hunting-knife. I had noticed, while appearing not to do so, that outside of the house I was followed or watched by one or other of the Indians, so that great circumspection was needed. On the following day I attacked my host once more about the revolver, telling him with well-acted indignation that if not found it must be paid for. I went so far as to give a list of the articles I should require, including a bow and arrows, zabatana, two spears, and other things which I need not specify, to set me up for life as a wild man in the woods of Guayana. I was going to add a wife, but as I had already been offered one it did not appear to be necessary. He seemed a little taken aback at the value I set upon my weapon, and promised to go and look for it again. Then I begged that Kua-kó, in whose sharpness of sight I had great faith, might accompany us. He consented, and named the next day but one for the expedition. Very well, thought I, to-morrow their suspicion will be less, and my opportunity will come; then taking up my rude instrument, I gave them an old Spanish song—

Desde aquel doloroso momento;

but this kind of music had lost its charm for them, and I was asked to give them the ballad they understood so well, in which their interest seemed to increase with every repetition. In spite of anxiety it amused me to see old Cla-cla regarding me fixedly with owlish eyes and lips moving. My tale had no wonderful things in it, like hers of the olden time, which she told only to send her hearers to sleep. Perhaps she had discovered by now that it was the strange honey of melody which made the coarse, common cassava-bread of everyday life in my story so pleasant to the palate. I was quite prepared to receive a proposal to give her music and singing lessons, and to bequeath a guitar to her in my last will and testament. For, in spite of her hoary hair and million wrinkles, she, more than any other savage I had met with, seemed to have taken a draught from Ponce de Leon's undiscovered fountain of eternal youth. Poor old witch!

The following day was the sixth of my absence from Rima, and one of intense anxiety to me, a feeling which I endeavoured to hide by playing with the children, fighting our old comic stick fights, and by strumming noisily on the guitar. In the afternoon, when it was hottest, and all the men who happened to be indoors were lying in their hammocks, I asked Kua-kó to go with me to the stream to bathe. He refused—I had counted on that—and earnestly advised me not to bathe in the pool I was accustomed to, as some little caribe fishes had made their appearance there and would be sure to attack me. I laughed at his idle tale, and taking up my cloak swung out of the door, whistling a lively air. He knew that I always threw my cloak over my head and shoulders as a protection from the sun and stinging flies when coming out of the water, and so his suspicion was not aroused, and I was not followed. The pool was about ten minutes' walk from the house; I arrived at it with palpitating heart, and going round to its end, where the stream was shallow, sat down to rest for a few moments and take a few sips of cool water dipped up in my palm. Presently I rose, crossed the stream, and began running, keeping among the low trees near the bank until a dry gully, which extended for some distance across the savannah, was reached. By following its course the distance to be covered would be considerably increased, but the shorter way would have exposed me to sight and made it more dangerous. I had put forth too much speed at first, and in a short time my exertions, and the hot sun, together with my intense excitement, overcame me. I dared not hope that my flight had not been observed; I imagined that the Indians, unencumbered by any heavy weight, were already close behind me, and ready to launch their deadly spears at my back. With a sob of rage and despair I fell prostrate on my face in the dry bed of the stream, and for two or three minutes remained thus exhausted and unmanned, my heart throbbing so violently that my whole frame was shaken. If my enemies had come on me then disposed to kill me, I could not have lifted a hand in defence of my life. But minutes passed, and they came not. I rose and went on, at a fast walk now, and when the sheltering stream-bed ended, I stooped among the sere dwarfed shrubs scattered about here and there on its southern side; and now creeping and now running, with an occasional pause to rest and look back, I at last reached the dividing ridge at its southern extremity. The rest of the way was over comparatively easy ground, inclining downwards; and with that glad green forest now full in sight, and hope growing stronger every minute in my breast, my knees ceased to tremble, and I ran on again, scarcely pausing until I had touched and lost myself in the welcome shadows.

❧14❦

AH THAT RETURN to the forest where Rima dwelt, after so anxious a day, when the declining sun shone hotly still, and the green woodland shadows were so grateful! The coolness, the sense of security, allayed the fever and excitement I had suffered on the open savannah; I walked leisurely, pausing often to listen to some bird voice or to admire some rare insect or parasitic flower shining starlike in the shade. There was a strangely delightful sensation in me. I likened myself to a child that, startled at something it had seen while out playing in the sun, flies to its mother to feel her caressing hand on its cheek and forget its tremors. And describing what I felt in that way, I was a little ashamed and laughed at myself; nevertheless the feeling was very sweet. At that moment Mother and Nature seemed one and the same thing. As I kept to the more open part of the wood, on its southernmost border, the red flame of the sinking sun was seen at intervals through the deep humid green of the higher foliage. How every object it touched took from it a new wonderful glory! At one spot, high up where the foliage was scanty, and slender bush ropes and moss depended like broken cordage from a dead limb—just there, bathing itself in that glory-giving light, I noticed a fluttering bird, and stood still to watch its antics. Now it would cling, head downwards, to the slender twigs, wings and tail open; then, righting itself, it would flit from waving line to line, dropping lower and lower; and anon soar upwards a distance of twenty feet and alight to recommence the flitting and swaying and dropping towards the earth. It was one of those birds that have a polished plumage, and as it moved this way and that, flirting its feathers, they caught the beams and shone at moments like glass or burnished metal. Suddenly another bird of the same kind dropped down to it as if from the sky, straight and swift as a falling stone; and the first bird sprang up to meet the comer, and after rapidly wheeling round each other for a moment they fled away in company, screaming shrilly through the wood, and were instantly lost to sight, while their jubilant cries came back fainter and fainter at each repetition.

I envied them not their wings: at that moment

earth did not seem fixed and solid beneath me, nor I bound by gravity to it. The faint, floating clouds, the blue infinite heaven itself, seemed not more ethereal and free than I, or the ground I walked on. The low, stony hills on my right hand, of which I caught occasional glimpses through the trees, looking now blue and delicate in the level rays, were no more than the billowy projections on the moving cloud of earth: the trees of unnumbered kinds—great mora, cecropia, and greenheart, bush and fern and suspended lianas, and tall palms balancing their feathery foliage on slender stems—all was but a fantastic mist embroidery covering the surface of that floating cloud on which my feet were set, and which floated with me near the sun.

The red evening flame had vanished from the summits of the trees, the sun was setting, the woods in shadow, when I got to the end of my walk. I did not approach the house on the side of the door, yet by some means those within became aware of my presence, for out they came in a great hurry, Rima leading the way, Nuflo behind her, waving his arms and shouting. But as I drew near the girl dropped behind and stood motionless regarding me, her face pallid and showing strong excitement. I could scarcely remove my eyes from her eloquent countenance: I seemed to read in it relief and gladness mingled with surprise and something like vexation. She was piqued perhaps that I had taken her by surprise, that after much watching for me in the wood I had come through it undetected when she was indoors.

"Happy the eyes that see you!" shouted the old man, laughing boisterously.

"Happy are mine that look on Rima again," I answered. "I have been long absent."

"Long—you may say so," returned Nuflo. "We had given you up. We said that, alarmed at the thought of the journey to Riolama, you had abandoned us."

"*We* said!" exclaimed Rima, her pallid face suddenly flushing. "I spoke differently."

"Yes, I know—I know!" he said airily, waving his hand. "You said that he was in danger, that he was kept against his will from coming. He is present now —let him speak."

"She was right," I said. "Ah, Nuflo, old man, you have lived long, and got much experience, but not insight—not that inner vision that sees farther than the eyes."

"No, not that—I know what you mean," he answered. Then, tossing his hand towards the sky, he added, "The knowledge you speak of comes from there."

The girl had been listening with keen interest, glancing from one to the other. "What!" she spoke suddenly, as if unable to keep silence, "do you think, grandfather, that *she* tells me—when there is danger—

when the rain will cease—when the wind will blow—everything? Do I not ask and listen, lying awake at night? She is always silent, like the stars."

Then, pointing to me with her finger, she finished—

"*He* knows so many things! Who tells them to *him?*"

"But distinguish, Rima. You do not distinguish the great from the little," he answered loftily. "*We* know a thousand things, but they are things that any man with a forehead can learn. The knowledge that comes from the blue is not like that—it is more important and miraculous. Is it not so, señor?" he ended, appealing to me.

"Is it, then, left for me to decide?" said I, addressing the girl.

But though her face was towards me she refused to meet my look and was silent. Silent, but not satisfied: she doubted still, and had perhaps caught something in my tone that strengthened her doubt.

Old Nuflo understood the expression. "Look at me, Rima," he said, drawing himself up. "I am old, and he is young—do I not know best? I have spoken and have decided it."

Still that unconvinced expression, and the face turned expectant to me.

"Am I to decide?" I repeated.

"Who, then?" she said at last, her voice scarcely more than a murmur; yet there was reproach in the tone, as if she had made a long speech and I had tyrannously driven her to it.

"Thus, then, I decide," said I. "To each one of us, as to every kind of animal, even to small birds and insects, and to every kind of plant, there is given something peculiar—a fragrance, a melody, a special instinct, an art, a knowledge, which no other has. And to Rima has been given this quickness of mind and power to divine distant things; it is hers, just as swiftness and grace and changeful, brilliant colour are the humming-bird's; therefore she need not that anyone dwelling in the blue should instruct her."

The old man frowned and shook his head; while she, after one swift, shy glance at my face, and with something like a smile flitting over her delicate lips, turned and re-entered the house.

I felt convinced from that parting look that she had understood me, that my words had in some sort given her relief; for, strong as was her faith in the supernatural, she appeared as ready to escape from it, when a way of escape offered, as from the limp cotton gown and constrained manner worn in the house. The religion and cotton dress were evidently remains of her early training at the settlement of Voa.

Old Nuflo, strange to say, had proved better than his word. Instead of inventing new causes for delay, as I had imagined would be the case, he now informed me that his preparations for the journey were all but complete, that he had only waited for my return to set out.

Rima soon left us in her customary way, and then, talking by the fire, I gave an account of my detention by the Indians and of the loss of my revolver, which I thought very serious.

"You seem to think little of it," I said, observing that he took it very coolly. "Yet I know not how I shall defend myself in case of an attack."

"I have no fear of an attack," he answered. "It seems to me the same thing whether you have a revolver or many revolvers and carbines and swords, or no revolver—no weapon at all. And for a very simple reason. While Rima is with us, so long as we are on her business, we are protected from above. The angels, señor, will watch over us by day and night. What need of weapons, then, except to procure food?"

"Why should not the angels provide us with food also?" said I.

"No, no, that is a different thing," he returned. "That is a small and low thing, a necessity common to all creatures, which all know how to meet. You would not expect an angel to drive away a cloud of mosquitoes, or to remove a bush-tick from your person. No, sir, you may talk of natural gifts, and try to make Rima believe that she is what she is, and knows what she knows, because, like a humming-bird or some plants with a peculiar fragrance, she has been made so. It is wrong, señor, and pardon me for saying it, it ill becomes you to put such fables into her head."

I answered, with a smile, "She herself seems to doubt what you believe."

"But, señor, what can you expect from an ignorant girl like Rima? She knows nothing, or very little, and will not listen to reason. If she would only remain quietly indoors, with her hair braided, and pray and read her Catechism, instead of running about after flowers and birds and butterflies and such unsubstantial things, it would be better for both of us."

"In what way, old man?"

"Why, it is plain that if she would cultivate the acquaintance of the people that surround her—I mean those that come to her from her sainted mother —and are ready to do her bidding in everything, she could make it more safe for us in this place. For example, there is Runi and his people, why should they remain living so near us as to be a constant danger when a pestilence of small-pox or some other fever might easily be sent to kill them off?"

"And have you ever suggested such a thing to your grandchild?"

He looked surprised and grieved at the question. "Yes, many times, señor," he said. "I should have been a poor Christian had I not mentioned it. But when I speak of it she gives me a look and is gone, and I see no more of her all day, and when I see her she refuses even to answer me; so perverse, so foolish is she in her ignorance; for, as you can see for yourself, she has no more sense or concern about what is most important than some little painted fly that flits about all day long without any object."

❧ 15 ❧

THE NEXT DAY we were early at work. Nuflo had already gathered, dried, and conveyed to a place of concealment the greater portion of his garden produce. He was determined to leave nothing to be taken by any wandering party of savages that might call at the house during our absence. He had no fear of a visit from his neighbours; they would not know, he said, that he and Rima were out of the wood. A few large earthen pots, filled with shelled maize, beans, and sun-dried strips of pumpkin, still remained to be disposed of. Taking up one of these vessels and asking me to follow with another, he started off through the wood. We went a distance of five or six hundred yards; then made our way down a very steep incline, close to the border of the forest on the western side;

arrived at the bottom, we followed the bank a little farther, and I then found myself once more at the foot of the precipice over which I had desperately thrown myself on the stormy evening after the snake had bitten me. Nuflo, stealing silently and softly before me through the bushes, had observed a caution and secrecy in approaching this spot resembling that of a wise old hen when she visits her hidden nest to lay an egg. And here was his nest, his most secret treasure-house, which he had probably not revealed even to me without a sharp inward conflict, notwithstanding that our fates were now linked together. The lower portion of the bank was of rock; and in it, about ten or twelve feet above the ground, but easily reached from below, there was a natural cavity large enough to contain all his portable property. Here, besides the food-stuff, he had already stored a quantity of dried tobacco leaf, his rude weapons, cooking utensils, ropes, mats, and other objects. Two or three more journeys were made for the remaining pots, after which we adjusted a slab of sandstone to the opening, which was fortunately narrow, plastered up the crevices with clay, and covered them over with moss to hide all traces of our work.

Towards evening, after we had refreshed ourselves with a long siesta, Nuflo brought out from some other hiding-place two sacks; one weighing about twenty pounds and containing smoke-dried meat, also grease and gum for lighting purposes, and a few other small objects. This was his load; the other sack, which was smaller and contained parched corn and raw beans, was for me to carry.

The old man, cautious in all his movements, always acting as if surrounded by invisible spies, delayed setting out until an hour after dark. Then, skirting the forest on its west side, we left Ytaioa on our right hand, and after travelling over rough, difficult ground, with only the stars to light us, we saw the waning moon rise not long before dawn. Our course had been a north-easterly one at first; now it was due east, with broad, dry savannahs and patches of open forest as far as we could see before us. It was weary walking on that first night, and weary waiting on the first day when we sat in the shade during the long, hot hours, persecuted by small stinging flies; but the days and nights that succeeded were far worse, when the weather became bad with intense heat and frequent heavy falls of rain. The one compensation I had looked for, which would have outweighed all the extreme discomforts we suffered, was denied me. Rima was no more to me or with me now than she had been during those wild days in her native woods, when every bush and bole and tangled creeper or fern-frond had joined in a conspiracy to keep her out of my sight. It is true that at intervals in the daytime she was visible, sometimes within speaking distance, so that I could address a few words to her, but there was no companionship, and we were fellow-travellers only like birds flying independently in the same direction, not so widely separated but that they can occasionally hear and see each other. The pilgrim in the desert is sometimes attended by a bird, and the bird, with its freer motions, will often leave him a league behind and seem lost to him, but only to return and show its form again; for it has never lost sight nor recollection of the traveller toiling slowly over the surface. Rima kept us company in some such wild erratic way as that. A word, a sign from Nuflo was enough for her to know the direction to take; the distant forest or still more distant mountain near which we should have to pass. She would hasten on and be lost to our sight, and when there was a forest in the way she would explore it, resting in the shade and finding her own food; but invariably she was before us at each resting or camping place.

Indian villages were seen during the journey, but only to be avoided: and in like manner, if we caught sight of Indians travelling or camping at a distance, we would alter our course, or conceal ourselves to escape observation. Only on one occasion, two days after setting out, were we compelled to speak with strangers. We were going round a hill, and all at once came face to face with three persons travelling in an opposite direction—two men and a woman, and, by a strange fatality, Rima at that moment happened to be with us. We stood for some time talking to these people, who were evidently surprised at our appearance, and wished to learn who we were; but Nuflo, who spoke their language like one of themselves, was too cunning to give any true answer. They, on their side, told us that they had been to visit a relation at Chani, the name of a river three days ahead of us, and were now returning to their own village at Baila-baila, two days beyond Parahuari. After parting from them Nuflo was much troubled in his mind for the rest of that day. These people, he said, would probably rest at some Parahuari village, where they would be sure to give a description of us, and so it might eventually come to the knowledge of our unneighbourly neighbour Runi that we had left Ytaioa.

Other incidents of our long and wearisome journey need not be related. Sitting under some shady tree during the sultry hours, with Rima only too far out of earshot, or by the nightly fire, the old man told me little by little and with much digression, chiefly on sacred subjects, the strange story of the girl's origin.

About seventeen years back—Nuflo had no sure method to compute time by—when he was already verging on old age, he was one of a company of nine men, living a kind of roving life in the very part of Guayana through which we were now travelling; the others, much younger than himself, were all equally offenders against the laws of Venezuela, and fugitives from justice. Nuflo was the leader of this gang, for it happened that he had passed a great portion of his life outside the pale of civilisation, and could talk

Indian languages, and knew this part of Guayana in-
timately. But according to his own account he was
not in harmony with them. They were bold, desperate
men, whose evil appetites had so far only been
whetted by the crimes they had committed; while he,
with passions worn out, recalling his many bad acts,
and with a vivid conviction of the truth of all he had
been taught in early life—for Nuflo was nothing if
not religious—was now grown timid and desirous
only of making his peace with Heaven. This difference
of disposition made him morose and quarrelsome
with his companions; and they would, he said, have
murdered him without remose if he had not been so
useful to them. Their favourite plan was to hang
about the neighbourhood of some small isolated settlement, keeping a watch on it, and, when most of
the male inhabitants were absent, to swoop down on
it and work their will. Now shortly after one of these
raids it happened that a woman they had carried off,
becoming a burden to them, was flung into a river to
the alligators; but when being dragged down to the
waterside she cast up her eyes, and in a loud voice
cried to God to execute vengeance on her murderers.
Nuflo affirmed that he took no part in this black deed;
nevertheless, the woman's dying appeal to Heaven
preyed on his mind; he feared that it might have
won a hearing, and the "person" eventually commis-
sioned to execute vengeance—after the usual delays,
of course—might act on the principle of the old prov-

erb—*Tell me whom you are with, and I will tell you what you are*—and punish the innocent (himself to wit) along with the guilty. But while thus anxious about his spiritual interests he was not yet prepared to break with his companions. He thought it best to temporise, and succeeded in persuading them that it would be unsafe to attack another Christian settlement for some time to come; that in the interval they might find some pleasure, if no great profit, by turning their attention to the Indians. The infidels, he said, were God's natural enemies and fair game to the Christian. To make a long story short, Nuflo's Christian band, after some successful adventures, met with a reverse which reduced their number from nine to five. Flying from their enemies they sought safety at Riolama, an uninhabited place, where they found it possible to exist for some weeks on game, which was abundant, and wild fruits.

One day at noon, while ascending a mountain at the southern extremity of the Riolama range, in order to get a view of the country beyond from the summit, Nuflo and his companions discovered a cave; and finding it dry, without animal occupants, and with a level floor, they at once determined to make it their dwelling-place for a season. Wood for firing and water were to be had close by; they were also well provided with smoked flesh of a tapir they had slaughtered a day or two before, so that they could afford to rest for a time in so comfortable a shelter. At a short

distance from the cave they made a fire on the rock
to toast some slices of meat for their dinner; and while
thus engaged all at once one of the men uttered a cry
of astonishment, and casting up his eyes Nuflo beheld, standing near and regarding them with surprise
and fear in her wide-open eyes, a woman of a most
wonderful appearance. The one slight garment she
had on was silky and white as the snow on the summit
of some great mountain, but of the snow when the
sinking sun touches and gives it some delicate changing colour which is like fire. Her dark hair was like a
cloud from which her face looked out, and her head
was surrounded by an aureole like that of a saint in a
picture, only more beautiful. For, said Nuflo, a picture is a picture, and the other was a reality, which is
finer. Seeing her he fell on his knees and crossed himself; and all the time her eyes, full of amazement and
shining with such a strange splendour that he could
not meet them, were fixed on him and not on the
others; and he felt that she had come to save his soul,
in danger of perdition owing to his companionship
with men who were at war with God and wholly bad.

But at this moment his comrades, recovering from
their astonishment, sprang to their feet, and the heavenly woman vanished. Just behind where she had
stood, and not twelve yards from them, there was
a huge chasm in the mountain, its jagged precipitous
sides clothed with thorny bushes; the men now cried

out that she had made her escape that way, and down after her they rushed, pell-mell.

Nuflo cried out after them that they had seen a saint and that some horrible thing would befall them if they allowed any evil thought to enter their hearts; but they scoffed at his words, and were soon far down out of hearing, while he, trembling with fear, remained praying to the woman that had appeared to them, and had looked with such strange eyes at him, not to punish him for the sins of the others.

Before long the men returned, disappointed and sullen, for they had failed in their search for the woman; and perhaps Nuflo's warning words had made them give up the chase too soon. At all events, they seemed ill at ease, and made up their minds to abandon the cave: in a short time they left the place to camp that night at a considerable distance from the mountain. But they were not satisfied: they had now recovered from their fear, but not from the excitement of an evil passion; and finally, after comparing notes, they came to the conclusion that they had missed a great prize through Nuflo's cowardice; and when he reproved them they blasphemed all the saints in the calendar and even threatened him with violence. Fearing to remain longer in the company of such godless men, he only waited until they slept, then rose up cautiously, helped himself to most of the provisions, and made his escape, devoutly hoping that after losing their guide they would all speedily perish.

Finding himself alone now and master of his own actions, Nuflo was in terrible distress, for while his heart was in the utmost fear, it yet urged him imperiously to go back to the mountain, to seek again for that sacred being who had appeared to him, and had been driven away by his brutal companions. If he obeyed that inner voice, he would be saved; if he resisted it then there would be no hope for him, and along with those who had cast the woman to the alligators he would be lost eternally. Finally, on the following day, he went back, although not without fear and trembling, and sat down on a stone just where he had sat toasting his tapir meat on the previous day. But he waited in vain, and at length that voice within him, which he had so far obeyed, began urging him to descend into the valley-like chasm down which the woman had escaped from his comrades, and to seek for her there. Accordingly he rose and began cautiously and slowly climbing down over the broken jagged rocks and through a dense mass of thorny bushes and creepers. At the bottom of the chasm a clear, swift stream of water rushed with foam and noise along its rocky bed; but before reaching it, and when it was still twenty yards lower down, he was startled by hearing a low moan among the bushes, and looking about for the cause, he found the wonderful woman—his saviour, as he expressed it. She was not now standing nor able to stand, but half reclining among the rough stones, one foot, which she had sprained in that headlong flight down the ragged slope, wedged immovably between the rocks; and in this painful position she had remained a prisoner since noon on the previous day. She now gazed on her visitor in silent consternation; while he, casting himself prostrate on the ground, implored her forgiveness and begged to know her will. But she made no reply; and at length finding that she was powerless to move, he concluded that, though a saint and one of the beings that men worship, she was also flesh and liable to accidents while sojourning on earth; and perhaps, he thought, that accident which had befallen her had been specially designed by the powers above to prove him. With great labour, and not without causing her much pain, he succeeded in extricating her from her position; and then finding that the injured foot was half crushed and blue and swollen, he took her up in his arms and carried her to the stream. There, making a cup of a broad green leaf, he offered her water, which she drank eagerly; and he also laved her injured foot in the cold stream and bandaged it with fresh aquatic leaves; finally he made her a soft bed of moss and dry grass and placed her on it. That night he spent keeping watch over her, at intervals applying fresh wet leaves to her foot as the old ones became dry and wilted from the heat of the inflammation.

The effect of all he did was that the terror with which she regarded him gradually wore off; and next day, when she seemed to be recovering her strength, he proposed by signs to remove her to the cave higher up, where she would be sheltered in case of rain. She appeared to understand him, and allowed herself to be taken up in his arms, and carried with much labour to the top of the chasm. In the cave he made her a second couch, and tended her assiduously. He made a fire on the floor and kept it burning night and day, and supplied her with water to drink and fresh leaves for her foot. There was little more that he could do. From the choicest and fattest bits of toasted tapir flesh he offered her she turned away with disgust. A little cassava-bread soaked in water she would take, but seemed not to like it. After a time, fearing that she would starve, he took to hunting after wild fruits, edible bulbs and gums, and on these small things she subsisted during the whole time of their sojourn together in the desert.

The woman, although lamed for life, was now so far recovered as to be able to limp about without assistance, and she spent a portion of each day out among the rocks and trees on the mountains. Nuflo at first feared that she would now leave him, but before long he became convinced that she had no such intentions. And yet she was profoundly unhappy. He was accustomed to see her seated on a rock, as if brooding over some secret grief, her head bowed, and great tears falling from half-closed eyes.

From the first he had conceived the idea that she was in the way of becoming a mother at no distant date—an idea which seemed to accord badly with the suppositions as to the nature of this heavenly being he was privileged to minister to and so win salvation; but he was now convinced of its truth, and he imagined that in her condition he had discovered the cause of that sorrow and anxiety which preyed continually on her. By means of that dumb language of signs which enabled them to converse together a little, he made it known to her that at a great distance from the mountains there existed a place where there were beings like herself, women, and mothers of children, who would comfort and tenderly care for her. When she had understood, she seemed pleased and willing to accompany him to that distant place; and so it came to pass that they left their rocky shelter and the mountains of Riolama far behind. But for several days, as they slowly journeyed over the plain, she would pause at intervals in her limping walk to gaze back on those blue summits shedding abundant tears.

Fortunately the village of Voa, on the river of the same name, which was the nearest Christian settlement to Riolama, whither his course was directed, was well known to him; he had lived there in former years, and what was of great advantage, the inhabitants were ignorant of his worst crimes, or, to put it in his own subtle way, of the crimes committed by the men he had acted with. Great was the astonishment and curiosity of the people of Voa when, after many weeks' travelling, Nuflo arrived at last with his companion. But he was not going to tell the truth, nor even the least particle of the truth, to a gaping crowd of inferior persons. For these, ingenious lies: only to the priest he told the whole story, dwelling minutely on all he had done to rescue and protect her; all of which was approved by the holy man, whose first act was to baptise the woman for fear that she was not a Christian. Let it be said to Nuflo's credit that he objected to this ceremony, arguing that she could not be a saint, with an aureole in token of her sainthood, yet stand in need of being baptised by a priest. A priest—he added, with a little chuckle of malicious pleasure—who was often seen drunk, who cheated at cards, and was sometimes suspected of putting poison on his fighting-cock's spur to make sure of the victory! Doubtless the priest had his faults; but he was not without humanity, and for the whole seven years of that unhappy stranger's sojourn at Voa he did everything in his power to make her existence tolerable. Some weeks after arriving she gave birth to a female child, and then the priest insisted on naming it Riolama, in order, he said, to keep in remembrance the strange story of the mother's discovery at that place.

Rima's mother could not be taught to speak either Spanish or Indian; and when she found that the mysterious and melodious sounds that fell from her own lips were understood by none she ceased to utter them, and thereafter preserved an unbroken silence among the people she lived with. But from the presence of others she shrank, as if in disgust or fear, excepting only Nuflo and the priest, whose kindly intentions she appeared to understand and appreciate. So far her life in the village was silent and sorrowful. With her child it was different; and every day that was not wet, taking the little thing by the hand, she would limp painfully out into the forest, and there, sitting on the ground, the two would commune with each other by the hour in their wonderful language.

At length she began to grow perceptibly paler and feebler week by week, day by day, until she could no longer go out into the wood, but sat or reclined, panting for breath in the dull hot room, waiting for death to release her. At the same time little Rima, who had always appeared frail, as if from sympathy now began to fade and look more shadowy, so that it was expected she would not long survive her parent. To the mother death came slowly, but at last it seemed so near that Nuflo and the priest were together at her side waiting to see the end. It was then that little Rima, who had learnt from infancy to speak in Spanish, rose from the couch where her mother had been whispering to her, and began with some difficulty to express what was in the dying woman's mind. Her child, she had said, could not continue alive in that hot wet place, but if taken away to a distance where there were mountains and a cooler air she would revive and grow strong again.

Hearing this, old Nuflo declared that the child should not perish; that he himself would take her away to Parahuari, a distant place where there were mountains and dry plains and open woods; that he would watch over her and care for her there as he had cared for her mother at Riolama.

When the substance of this speech had been made known by Rima to the dying woman, she suddenly rose up from the couch, which she had not risen from for many days, and stood erect on the floor, her wasted face shining with joy. Then Nuflo knew that God's angels had come for her, and put out his arms to save her from falling; and even while he held her that sudden glory went out from her face, now of a dead white like burnt-out ashes; and murmuring something soft and melodious, her spirit passed away.

Once more Nuflo became a wanderer, now with the fragile-looking little Rima for companion, the sacred child who had inherited the position of his intercessor from a sacred mother. The priest, who had probably become infected with Nuflo's superstitions, did not allow them to leave Voa empty-handed, but gave the old man as much calico as would serve to buy hospitality and whatsoever he might require from the Indians for many a day to come.

At Parahuari, where they arrived safely at last, they

lived for some little time at one of the villages. But
the child had an instinctive aversion to all savages,
or possibly the feeling was derived from her mother,
for it had shown itself early at Voa, where she had
refused to learn their language; and this eventually
led Nuflo to go away and live apart from them, in the
forest of Ytaioa, where he made himself a house and
garden. The Indians, however, continued friendly
with him and visited him with frequency. But when
Rima grew up, developing into that mysterious woodland girl I found her, they became suspicious, and in
the end regarded her with dangerously hostile feeling.
She, poor child, detested them because they were incessantly at war with the wild animals she loved, her
companions; and having no fear of them, for she did
not know that they had it in their minds to turn their
little poisonous arrows against herself, she was constantly in the woods frustrating them; and the animals, in league with her, seemed to understand her
note of warning and hid themselves or took to flight
at the approach of danger. At length their hatred and
fear grew to such a degree that they determined to
make away with her, and one day, having matured a
plan, they went to the wood and spread themselves
two and two about it. The couples did not keep together, but moved about or remained concealed at a
distance of forty or fifty yards apart, lest she should
be missed. Two of the savages, armed with blow-
pipes, were near the border of the forest on the side

nearest to the village, and one of them, observing a motion in the foliage of a tree, ran swiftly and cautiously towards it to try and catch a glimpse of the enemy. And as he did see her no doubt, as she was there watching both him and his companions, and blew an arrow at her, but even while in the act of blowing it he was himself struck by a dart that buried itself deep in his flesh just over the heart. He ran some distance with the fatal barbed point in his flesh and met his comrade, who had mistaken him for the girl and shot him. The wounded man threw himself down to die, and dying related that he had fired at the girl sitting up in a tree and that she had caught the arrow in her hand only to hurl it instantly back with such force and precision that it pierced his flesh just over the heart. He had seen it all with his own eyes, and his friend who had accidentally slain him believed his story and repeated it to the others. Rima had seen one Indian shoot the other, and when she told her grandfather he explained to her that it was an accident, but he guessed why the arrow had been fired.

From that day the Indians hunted no more in the wood; and at length one day Nuflo, meeting an Indian who did not know him and with whom he had some talk, heard the strange story of the arrow, and that the mysterious girl who could not be shot was the offspring of an old man and a Didi who had become enamoured of him; that, growing tired of her consort, the Didi had returned to her river, leaving her half-human child to play her malicious pranks in the wood.

This, then, was Nuflo's story, told not in Nuflo's manner, which was infinitely prolix; and think not that it failed to move me—that I failed to bless him for what he had done, in spite of his selfish motives.

≫ 16 ≪

WE WERE EIGHTEEN days travelling to Riolama, on the last two making little progress, on account of continuous rain, which made us miserable beyond description. Fortunately the dogs had found, and Nuflo had succeeded in killing, a great ant-eater, so that we were well supplied with excellent, strength-giving flesh. We were among the Riolama mountains at last, and Rima kept with us, apparently expecting great things. I expected nothing, for reasons to be stated by-and-by. My belief was that the only important thing that could happen to us would be starvation.

The afternoon of the last day was spent in skirting the foot of a very long mountain, crowned at its southern extremity with a huge, rocky mass resembling the head of a stone sphinx above its long, couch-

ant body, and at its highest part about a thousand
feet above the surrounding level. It was late in the
day, raining fast again, yet the old man still toiled on,
contrary to his usual practice, which was to spend
the last daylight hours in gathering firewood and in
constructing a shelter. At length, when we were
nearly under the peak, he began to ascend. The rise
in this place was gentle, and the vegetation, chiefly
composed of dwarf thorn trees rooted in the clefts of
the rock, scarcely impeded our progress; yet Nuflo
moved obliquely, as if he found the ascent difficult,
pausing frequently to take breath and look round
him. Then we came to a deep, ravine-like cleft in the
side of the mountain, which became deeper and narrower above us, but below it broadened out to a valley; its steep sides as we looked down were clothed
with dense, thorny vegetation, and from the bottom
rose to our ears the dull sound of a hidden torrent.
Along the border of this ravine Nuflo began toiling
upwards, and finally brought us out upon a stony
plateau on the mountain-side. Here he paused, and
turning and regarding us with a look as of satisfied
malice in his eyes, remarked that we were at our journey's end, and he trusted that the sight of that barren
mountain-side would compensate us for all the discomforts we had suffered during the last eighteen
days.

I heard him with indifference. I had already recognised the place from his own exact description of it,

and I now saw all that I had looked to see—a big, barren hill. But Rima, what had she expected that her face wore that blank look of surprise and pain? "Is this the place where mother appeared to you?" she suddenly cried. "The very place—this! this!" Then she added, "The cave where you tended her—where is it?"

"Over there," he said, pointing across the plateau, which was partially overgrown with dwarf trees and bushes, and ended at a wall of rock, almost vertical and about forty feet high.

Going to this precipice, we saw no cave until Nuflo had cut away two or three tangled bushes, revealing an opening behind, about half as high and twice as wide as the door of an ordinary dwelling-house.

The next thing was to make a torch, and aided by its light we groped our way in and explored the interior. The cave, we found, was about fifty feet long, narrowing to a mere hole at the extremity; but the anterior portion formed an oblong chamber, very lofty, with a dry floor. Leaving our torch burning, we set to work cutting bushes to supply ourselves with wood enough to last us all night. Nuflo, poor old man, loved a big fire dearly; a big fire and fat meat to eat (the ranker its flavour the better he liked it) were to him the greatest blessings that man could wish for: in me also the prospect of a cheerful blaze put a new heart, and I worked with a will in the rain, which increased in the end to a blinding downpour. By the time I dragged my last load in, Nuflo had got his fire well alight, and was heaping on wood in a most lavish way. "No fear of burning our house down to-night," he remarked, with a chuckle—the first sound of that description he had emitted for a long time.

After we had satisfied our hunger, and had smoked one or two cigarettes, the unaccustomed warmth, and dryness, and the firelight affected us with drowsiness, and I had probably been nodding for some time; but starting at last and opening my eyes, I missed Rima. The old man appeared to be asleep, although still in a sitting posture close to the fire. I rose and hurried out, drawing my cloak close around me to protect me from the rain; but what was my surprise on emerging from the cave to feel a dry, bracing wind in my face and to see the desert spread out for leagues before me in the brilliant white light of a full moon! The rain had apparently long ceased, and only a few thin white clouds appeared moving swiftly over the wide blue expanse of heaven. It was a welcome change, but the shock of surprise and pleasure was instantly succeeded by the maddening fear that Rima was lost to me. She was nowhere in sight beneath, and running to the end of the little plateau to get free of the thorn trees, I turned my eyes towards the summit, and there, at some distance above me, caught sight of her standing motionless and gazing upwards. I quickly made my way to her side, calling to her as I approached; but she only half turned to cast a look at me and did not reply.

"Rima," I said, "why have you come here? Are you actually thinking of climbing the mountain at this hour of the night?"

"Yes—why not?" she returned, moving one or two steps from me.

"Rima—sweet Rima, will you listen to me?"

"Now? Oh, no—why do you ask that? Did I not listen to you in the wood before we started, and you also promised to do what I wished? See, the rain is over and the moon shines brightly. Why should I wait? Perhaps from the summit I shall see my people's country. Are we not near it now?"

"Oh, Rima, what do you expect to see? Listen— you must listen, for I know best. From that summit you would see nothing but a vast dim desert, mountain and forest, mountain and forest, where you might wander for years, or until you perished of hunger, or fever, or were slain by some beast of prey or by savage men; but oh, Rima, never, never, never would you find your people, for they exist not. You have seen the false water of the mirage on the savannah, when the sun shines bright and hot; and if one were to follow it he would at last fall down and perish, with never a cool drop to moisten his parched lips. And your hope, Rima—this hope to find your people which has brought you all the way to Riolama—is a mirage,

a delusion, which will lead to destruction if you will
not abandon it."

She turned to face me with flashing eyes. "You
know best!" she exclaimed. "You know best, and tell
me that! Never until this moment have you spoken
falsely. Oh, why have you said such things to me—
named after this place, Riolama? Am I also like that
false water you speak of—no divine Rima, no sweet
Rima? My mother, had she no mother, no mother's
mother? I remember her, at Voa, before she died, and
this hand seems real—like yours; you have asked to
hold it. But it is not he that speaks to me—not one
that showed me the whole world on Ytaioa. Ah, you
have wrapped yourself in a stolen cloak, only you
have left your old grey beard behind! Go back to the
cave and look for it, and leave me to seek my people
alone!"

Once more, as on that day in the forest when she
prevented me from killing the serpent, and as on the
occasion of her meeting with Nuflo after we had
been together on Ytaioa, she appeared transformed
and instinct with intense resentment—a beautiful human wasp, and every word a sting.

"Rima," I cried, "you are cruelly unjust to say such
words to me. If you know that I have never deceived
you before, give me a little credit now. You are no
delusion—no mirage, but Rima, like no other being
on earth. So perfectly truthful and pure I cannot be,
but rather than mislead you with falsehoods I would

drop down and die on this rock, and lose you and the sweet light that shines on us for ever."

As she listened to my words, spoken with passion, she grew pale and clasped her hands: "What have I said? What have I said?" She spoke in a low voice charged with pain, and all at once she came nearer, and with a low, sobbing cry sank down at my feet, uttering, as on the occasion of finding me lost at night in the forest near her home, tender, sorrowful expressions in her own mysterious language. But before I could take her in my arms she rose again quickly to her feet and moved away a little space from me.

"Oh no, no, it cannot be that you know best!" she began again. "But I know that you have never sought to deceive me. And now, because I falsely accused you, I cannot go there without you"—pointing to the summit—"but must stand still and listen to all you have to say."

"You know, Rima, that your grandfather has now told me your history—how he found your mother at this place, and took her to Voa, where you were born; but of your mother's people he knows nothing, and therefore he can now take you no farther."

"Ah, you think that! He says that now; but he deceived me all these years, and if he lied to me in the past, can he not still lie, affirming that he knows nothing of my people, even as he affirmed that he knew not Riolama?"

"He tells lies and he tells truth, Rima, and one can

be distinguished from the other. He spoke truthfully
at last, and brought us to this place, beyond which he
cannot lead you."

"You are right; I must go alone."

"Not so, Rima, for where you go there we must
go; only you will lead and we follow, believing only
that our quest will end in disappointment, if not in
death."

"Believe that and yet follow! Oh no! Why did he
consent to lead me so far for nothing?"

"Do you forget that you compelled him? You know
what he believes; and he is old and looks with fear
at death, remembering his evil deeds, and is convinced
that only through your intercession and your mother's
he can escape from perdition. Consider, Rima, he
could not refuse, to make you more angry and so deprive himself of his only hope."

My words seemed to trouble her, but very soon she
spoke again with renewed animation. "If my people
exist, why must it be disappointment and perhaps
death? He does not know; but she came to him here
—did she not? The others are not here, but perhaps
not far off. Come, let us go to the summit together to
see from it the desert beneath us—mountain and
forest, mountain and forest. Somewhere there! You
said that I had knowledge of distant things. And
shall I not know which mountain—which forest?"

"Alas! no, Rima; there is a limit to your far-seeing;
and even if that faculty were as great as you imagine

it would avail you nothing, for there is no mountain, no forest, in whose shadow your people dwell."

For a while she was silent, but her eyes and clasping fingers were restless and showed her agitation. She seemed to be searching in the depths of her mind for some argument to oppose to my assertions. Then in a low, almost despondent voice, with something of reproach in it, she said, "Have we come so far to go back again? You were not Nuflo to need my intercession, yet you came too."

"Where you are there I must be—you have said it yourself. Besides, when we started I had some hope of finding your people. Now I know better, having heard Nuflo's story. Now I know that your hope is a vain one."

"Why? Why? Was she not found here—mother? Where, then, are the others?"

"Yes, she was found here, alone. You must remember all the things she spoke to you before she died. Did she ever speak to you of her people—speak of them as if they existed, and would be glad to receive you among them some day?"

"No. Why did she not speak of that? Do you know —can you tell me?"

"I can guess the reason, Rima. It is very sad—so sad that it is hard to tell it. When Nuflo tended her in the cave and was ready to worship her and do everything she wished, and conversed with her by signs, she showed no wish to return to her people. And when

he offered her, in a way she understood, to take her to
a distant place, where she would be among strange beings, among others like Nuflo, she readily consented,
and painfully performed that long journey to Voa.
Would you, Rima, have acted thus—would you have
gone so far away from your beloved people, never to
return, never to hear of them or speak to them again?
Oh no, you could not; nor would she, if her people
had been in existence. But she knew that she had
survived them, that some great calamity had fallen
upon and destroyed them. They were few in number,
perhaps, and surrounded on every side by hostile
tribes, and had no weapons, and made no war. They
had been preserved because they inhabited a place
apart, some deep valley perhaps, guarded on all sides
by lofty mountains and impenetrable forests and
marshes; but at last the cruel savages broke into this
retreat and hunted them down, destroying all except
a few fugitives, who escaped singly like your mother,
and fled away to hide in some distant solitude."

The anxious expression on her face deepened as she
listened to one of anguish and despair; and then,
almost before I concluded, she suddenly lifted her
hands to her head, uttering a low, sobbing cry, and
would have fallen on the rock had I not caught her
quickly in my arms. Once more in my arms—against
my breast, her proper place! But now all that bright
life seemed gone out of her; her head fell on my
shoulder, and there was no motion in her except at

intervals a slight shudder in her frame accompanied by a low, gasping sob. In a little while the sobs ceased, the eyes were closed, the face still and deathly white, and with a terrible anxiety in my heart I carried her down to the cave.

❧ 17 ❧

As I RE-ENTERED the cave with my burden Nuflo sat up and stared at me with a frightened look in his eyes. Throwing my cloak down I placed the girl on it and briefly related what had happened.

He drew near to examine her; then placed his hand on her heart. "Dead!—she is dead!" he exclaimed.

My own anxiety changed to an irrational anger at his words. "Old fool! She has only fainted," I returned. "Get me some water, quick!"

But the water failed to restore her, and my anxiety deepened as I gazed on that white, still face. Oh, why had I told her that sad tragedy I had imagined with so little preparation? Alas! I had succeeded too well in my purpose, killing her vain hope and her at the same moment.

The old man, still bending over her, spoke again. "No, I will not believe that she is dead yet; but, sir, if not dead, then she is dying."

I could have struck him down for his words. "She will die in my arms, then," I exclaimed, thrusting him roughly aside, and lifting her up with the cloak beneath her.

And while I held her thus, her head resting on my arm, and gazed with unutterable anguish into her strangely white face, insanely praying to Heaven to restore her to me, Nuflo fell on his knees before her, and with bowed head, and hands clasped in supplication, began to speak.

"Rima! Grandchild!" he prayed, his quivering voice betraying his agitation. "Do not die just yet: you must not die—not wholly die—until you have heard what I have to say to you. I do not ask you to answer in words—you are past that, and I am not unreasonable. Only, when I finish, make some sign—a sigh, a movement of the eyelid, a twitch of the lips, even in the small corners of the mouth; nothing more than that, just to show that you have heard, and I shall be satisfied. Remember all the years that I have been your protector, and this long journey that I have taken on your account; also all that I did for your sainted mother before she died at Voa, to become one of the most important of those who surround the Queen of Heaven, and who, when they wish for any favour, have only to say half a word to get it. And do not cast in oblivion that at the last I obeyed your wish and brought you safely to Riolama. It is true that in some small things I deceived you; but that must not weigh with you, because it is a small matter and not worthy of mention when you consider the claims I have on you. In your hands, Rima, I leave everything, relying on the promise you made me, and on my services. Only one word of caution remains to be added. Do not let the magnificence of the place you are now about to enter, the new sights and colours, and the noise of shouting, and musical instruments and blowing of trumpets, put these things out of your head. Nor must you begin to think meanly of yourself and be abashed when you find yourself surrounded by saints and angels; for you are not less than they, although it may not seem so at first when you see them in their bright clothes, which, they say, shine like the sun. I cannot ask you to tie a string round your finger: I can only trust to your memory, which was always good, even about the smallest things; and when you are asked, as no doubt you will be, to express a wish, remember before everything to speak of your grandfather, and his claims on you, also on your angelic mother, to whom you will present my humble remembrances."

During this petition, which in other circumstances would have moved me to laughter but now only irritated me, a subtle change seemed to come to the apparently lifeless girl to make me hope. The small hand in mine felt not so icy cold, and though no faintest colour had come to the face, its pallor had lost something of its deathly waxen appearance; and now the compressed lips had relaxed a little and seemed ready to part. I laid my finger-tips on her heart and felt, or imagined that I felt, a faint fluttering; and at last I became convinced that her heart was really beating.

I turned my eyes on the old man, still bending forward, intently watching for the sign he had asked her to make. My anger and disgust at his gross, earthly egoism had vanished. "Let us thank God, old man," I said, the tears of joy half choking my utterance. "She lives—she is recovering from her fit."

He drew back, and on his knees, with bowed head, murmured a prayer of thanks to Heaven.

Together we continued watching her face for half an hour longer, I still holding her in my arms, which could never grow weary of that sweet burden, waiting for other, surer signs of returning life; and she seemed now like one that had fallen into a profound, deathlike sleep which must end in death. Yet when I remembered her face as it had looked an hour ago, I was confirmed in the belief that the progress to recovery, so strangely slow, was yet sure. So slow, so gradual was this passing from death to life that we had hardly ceased to fear when we noticed that the lips were parted, or almost parted, that they were no longer white, and that under her pale, transparent skin a faint, bluish-rosy colour was now visible. And at length, seeing that all danger was past and recovery so slow, old Nuflo withdrew once more to the fireside, and stretching himself out on the sandy floor, soon fell into a deep sleep.

If he had not been lying there before me in the strong light of the glowing embers and dancing flames, I could not have felt more alone with Rima—alone amid those remote mountains, in that secret cavern, with lights and shadows dancing on its grey vault. In that profound silence and solitude the mysterious loveliness of the still face I continued to gaze on, its appearance of life without consciousness, produced a strange feeling in me, hard, perhaps impossible, to describe.

Once, when clambering among the rough rocks, overgrown with forest, among the Queneveta mountains, I came on a single white flower which was new to me, which I have never seen since. After I had looked long at it, and passed on, the image of that perfect flower remained so persistently in my mind that on the following day I went again, in the hope of seeing it still untouched by decay. There was no change; and on this occasion I spent a much longer time looking at it, admiring the marvellous beauty of its form, which seemed so greatly to exceed that of all other flowers. It had thick petals, and at first gave me the idea of an artificial flower, cut by a divinely inspired artist from some unknown precious stone, of the size of a large orange and whiter than milk, and yet, in spite of its opacity, with a crystalline lustre on the surface. Next day I went again, scarcely hoping to find it still unwithered; it was fresh as if only just opened; and after that I went often, sometimes at intervals of several days, and still no faintest sign of any change, the clear, exquisite lines still undimmed, the purity and lustre as I had first seen it. Why, I often asked, does not this mystic forest flower fade and perish like others? That first impression of its artificial appearance had soon left me; it was, indeed, a flower, and, like other flowers, had life and growth, only with that transcendent beauty it had a different kind of life. Unconscious, but higher; perhaps immortal. Thus it would continue to bloom when I had looked my last on it; wind and rain and sunlight would never stain, never tinge, its sacred purity; the savage Indian, though he sees little to admire in a flower, yet seeing this one would veil his face and turn back; even the browsing beast crashing his way through the forest, struck with its strange glory, would swerve aside and pass on without harming it. Afterwards I heard from some Indians, to whom I described it, that the flower I had discovered was called Hata; also that they had a superstition concerning it—a strange belief. They said that only one Hata flower existed in the world; that it bloomed in one spot for the space of a moon; that on the disappearance of the moon in the sky the Hata disappeared from its place, only to reappear blooming in some other spot, sometimes in some distant forest. And they also said that whosoever discovered the Hata flower in the forest would overcome all his enemies and obtain all his desires, and finally outlive other men by many years. But, as I have said, all this I heard afterwards, and my half-superstitious feeling for the flower had grown up independently in my own mind. A feeling like that was in me while I gazed on the face that had no motion, no consciousness in it, and yet had life, a life of so high a kind as to match with its pure, surpassing loveliness. I could almost believe that, like the forest flower, in this state and aspect it would endure for ever; endure and perhaps give of its own immortality to everything around it— to me, holding her in my arms and gazing fixedly on the pale face framed in its cloud of dark, silken hair; to the leaping flames that threw changing lights on the dim stony wall of rock; to old Nuflo and his two yellow dogs stretched out on the floor in eternal, unawakening sleep.

This feeling took such firm possession of my mind that it kept me for a time as motionless as the form I held in my arms. I was only released from its power by noting still further changes in the face I watched, a more distinct advance towards conscious life. The faint colour, which had scarcely been more than a suspicion of colour, had deepened perceptibly; the lids were lifted so as to show a gleam of the crystal orbs beneath; the lips, too, were slightly parted.

And, at last, bending lower down to feel her breath, the beauty and sweetness of those lips could no longer be resisted, and I touched them with mine. Having once tasted their sweetness and fragrance, it was impossible to keep from touching them again and again. She was not conscious—how could she be and not shrink from my caress? Yet there was a suspicion in my mind, and drawing back I gazed into her face once more. A strange new radiance had overspread it. Or was this only an illusive colour thrown on her skin by the red firelight? I shaded her face with my open hand, and saw that her pallor had really gone, that the rosy flame on her cheeks was part of her life. Her lustrous eyes, half open, were gazing into mine. Oh, surely consciousness had returned to her! Had she been sensible of those stolen kisses? Would she now shrink from another caress? Trembling I bent down and touched her lips again, lightly, but lingeringly, and then again, and when I drew back and looked at her face the rosy flame was brighter, and the eyes, more open still, were looking into mine. And gazing with those open, conscious eyes, it seemed to me that at last, at last, the shadow that had rested between us had vanished, that we were united in perfect love and confidence, and that speech was superfluous. And when I spoke it was not without doubt and hesitation: our bliss in those silent moments had been so complete, what could speaking do but make it less!

"My love, my life, my sweet Rima, I know that you will understand me now as you did not before, on that dark night—do you remember it, Rima?—when I held you clasped to my breast in the wood. How it pierced my heart with pain to speak plainly to you as I did on the mountain to-night—to kill the hope that had sustained and brought you so far from home! But now that anguish is over; the shadow has gone out of those beautiful eyes that are looking at me. Is it because loving me, knowing now what love is, knowing, too, how much I love you, that you no longer need to speak to any other living being of such things? To tell it, to show it, to me is now enough—is it not so, Rima? How strange it seemed, at first, when you shrank in fear from me! But, afterwards, when you prayed aloud to your mother, opening all the secrets of your heart, I understood it. In that lonely, isolated life in the wood you had heard nothing of love, of its power over the heart, its infinite sweetness; when it came to you at last it was a new, inexplicable thing, and filled you with misgivings and tumultuous thoughts, so that you feared it and hid yourself from its cause. Such tremors would be felt if it had always been night, with no light except that of the stars and the pale moon, as we saw it a little while ago on the mountain; and, at last, day dawned, and a strange, unheard-of rose and purple flame kindled in the eastern sky, foretelling the coming sun. It would seem beautiful beyond anything that night had shown to you, yet you would tremble, and your heart beat fast at that strange sight; you would wish to fly to those who might be able to tell you its meaning, and whether the sweet things it prophesied would ever really come. That is why you wished to find your people, and came to Riolama to seek them: and when you knew—when I cruelly told you—that they would never be found, then you imagined that that strange feeling in your heart must remain a secret for ever, and you could not endure the thought of your loneliness. If you had not fainted so quickly, then I should have told you what I must tell you now. They are lost, Rima—your people—but I am with you, and know what you feel, even if you have no words to tell it. But what need of words? It shines in your eyes, it burns like a flame in your face; I can feel it in your hands. Do you not also see it in my face—all that I feel for you, the love that makes me happy? For this is love, Rima, the flower and the melody of life, the sweetest thing, the sweet miracle that makes our two souls one."

Still resting in my arms, as if glad to rest there, still gazing into my face, it was clear to me that she understood my every word. And then, with no trace of doubt or fear left, I stooped again, until my lips were on hers; and when I drew back once more, hardly knowing which bliss was greatest—kissing her delicate mouth or gazing into her face—she all at once put her arms about my neck and drew herself up until she sat on my knee.

"Abel—shall I call you Abel now—and always?" she spoke, still with her arms round my neck. "Ah, why did you let me come to Riolama? I would come! I made him come—old grandfather, sleeping there: he does not count, but you—you! After you had heard my story, and knew that it was all for nothing! And all I wished to know was there—in you. Oh, how sweet it is! But a little while ago, what pain! When I stood on the mountain when you talked to me, and I knew that you knew best, and tried and tried not to know. At last I could try no more; they were all dead like mother; I had chased the false water on the savannah. 'Oh, let me die too,' I said, for I could not bear the pain. And afterwards, here, in the cave, I was like one asleep, and when I woke I did not really wake. It was like morning with the light teasing me to open my eyes and look at it. Not yet, dear light; a little while longer, it is so sweet to lie still. But it would not leave me, and stayed teasing me still, like a small shining green fly; until, because it teased me so, I opened my lids just a little. It was not morning, but the fire-light, and I was in your arms, not in my little bed. Your eyes looking, looking into mine. But I could see yours better. I remembered everything then, how you once asked me to look into your eyes. I remembered so many things—oh, so many!"

"How many things did you remember, Rima?"

"Listen, Abel, do you ever lie on the dry moss and look straight up into a tree and count a thousand leaves?"

"No, sweetest, that could not be done, it is so many to count. Do you know how many a thousand are?"

"Oh, do I not! When a humming-bird flies close to my face and stops still in the air, humming like a bee, and then is gone, in that short time I can count a hundred small round bright feathers on its throat. That is only a hundred; a thousand are more, ten times. Looking up I count a thousand leaves; then stop counting, because there are thousands more behind the first, and thousands more, crowded together so that I cannot count them. Lying in your arms, looking up into your face, it was like that; I could not count the things I remembered. In the wood, when you were there, and before; and long, long ago at Voa when I was a child with mother."

"Tell me some of the things you remembered, Rima."

"Yes, one—only one now. When I was a child at Voa mother was very lame—you know that. Whenever we went out, away from the houses, into the forest, walking slowly, slowly, she would sit under a tree while I ran about playing. And every time I came back to her I would find her so pale, so sad, crying— crying. That was when I would hide and come softly back so that she would not hear me coming. 'Oh, mother, why are you crying? Does your lame foot hurt you?' And one day she took me in her arms and told me truly why she cried."

She ceased speaking, but looked at me with a strange new light coming into her eyes.

"Why did she cry, my love?"

"Oh, Abel, can you understand—now—at last!" And putting her lips close to my ear, she began to murmur soft, melodious sounds that told me nothing. Then drawing back her head, she looked again at me, her eyes glistening with tears, her lips half parted with a smile, tender and wistful.

Ah, poor child! in spite of all that had been said, all that had happened, she had returned to the old delusion that I must understand her speech. I could only return her look, sorrowfully and in silence.

Her face became clouded with disappointment, then she spoke again with something of pleading in her tone. "Look, we are not now apart, I hiding in the wood, you seeking, but together, saying the same things. In your language—yours and now mine. But before you came I knew nothing, nothing, for there was only grandfather to talk to. A few words each day, the same words. If yours is mine, mine must be yours. Oh, do you not know that mine is better?"

"Yes, better; but alas! Rima, I can never hope to understand your sweet speech, much less to speak it. The bird that only chirps and twitters can never sing like the organ-bird."

Crying, she hid her face against my neck, murmuring sadly between her sobs, "Never—never!"

How strange it seemed, in that moment of joy, such a passion of tears, such despondent words!

For some minutes I preserved a sorrowful silence, realising for the first time, so far as it was possible to realise such a thing, what my inability to understand her secret language meant to her—that finer language in which alone her swift thoughts and vivid emotions could be expressed. Easily and well as she seemed able to declare herself in my tongue, I could well imagine that to her it would seem like the merest stammering. As she had said to me once when I asked her to speak in Spanish, "That is not speaking." And so long as she could not commune with me in that better language, which reflected her mind, there would not be that perfect union of soul she so passionately desired.

By-and-by, as she grew calmer, I sought to say something that would be consoling to both of us. "Sweetest Rima," I spoke, "it is so sad that I can never hope to talk with you in your way; but a greater love than this that is ours we could never feel, and love will make us happy, unutterably happy, in spite of that one sadness. And perhaps, after a while, you will be able to say all you wish in my language, which is also yours, as you said some time ago. When we are back again in the beloved wood, and talk once more under that tree where we first talked, and under the old mora, where you hid yourself and threw down leaves on me, and where you caught the little spider to show me how you made yourself a dress, you shall speak to me in your own sweet tongue, and then try to say the same things in mine. . . . And in the end, perhaps, you will find that it is not so impossible as you think."

She looked at me, smiling again through her tears, and shook her head a little.

"Remember what I have heard, that before your mother died you were able to tell Nuflo and the priest what her wish was. Can you not, in the same way, tell me why she cried?"

"I can tell you, but it will not be telling you."

"I understand. You can tell the bare facts. I can imagine something more, and the rest I must lose. Tell me, Rima."

Her face became troubled; she glanced away and let her eyes wander round the dim, firelit cavern; then they returned to mine once more.

"Look," she said, "grandfather lying asleep by the fire. So far away from us—oh, so far! But if we were to go out from the cave, and on and on to the great mountains where the city of the sun is, and stood there at last in the midst of great crowds of people, all looking at us, talking to us, it would be just the same. They would be like the trees and rocks and animals—so far! Not with us nor we with them. But we are everywhere alone together, apart—we two. It is love; I know it now, but I did not know it before because I had forgotten what she told me. Do you think I can tell you what she said when I asked her why she cried? Oh no! Only this, she and another were like one, always, apart from the others. Then something came—something came! O Abel, was that the something you told me about on the mountain? And the other was lost for ever, and she was alone in the forests and mountains of the world. Oh, why do we cry for what is lost? Why do we not quickly forget it and feel glad again? Now only do I know what you felt, O sweet mother, when you sat still and cried, while I ran about and played and laughed! O poor mother! Oh, what pain!" And hiding her face against my neck, she sobbed once more.

To my eyes also love and sympathy brought the tears; but in a little while the fond, comforting words I spoke and my caresses recalled her from that sad past to the present; then, lying back as at first, her head resting on my folded cloak, her body partly supported by my encircling arm and partly by the rock we were leaning against, her half-closed eyes turned to mine expressed a tender assured happiness—the chastened gladness of sunshine after rain; a soft delicious languor that was partly passionate with the passion etherealised.

"Tell me, Rima," I said, bending down to her, "in all those troubled days with me in the woods had you no happy moments? Did not something in your heart tell you that it was sweet to love, even before you knew what love meant?"

"Yes; and once—O Abel, do you remember that night, after returning from Ytaioa, when you sat so late talking by the fire—I in the shadow, never stirring, listening, listening; you by the fire with the light on your face, saying so many strange things? I was happy then—oh, how happy! It was black night and raining, and I a plant growing in the dark, feeling the sweet rain-drops falling, falling on my leaves. Oh, it will be morning by-and-by and the sun will shine on my wet leaves; and that made me glad till I trembled with happiness. Then suddenly the lightning would come, so bright, and I would tremble with fear, and wish that it would be dark again. That was when you looked at me sitting in the shadow, and I could not take my eyes away quickly and could not meet yours, so that I trembled with fear."

"And now there is no fear—no shadow; now you are perfectly happy?"

"Oh, so happy! If the way back to the wood was longer, ten times, and if the great mountains, white with snow on their tops, were between, and the great dark forest, and rivers wider than Orinoco, still I would go alone without fear, because you would come after me, to join me in the wood, to be with me at last and always."

"But I should not let you go alone, Rima—your lonely days are over now."

She opened her eyes wider, and looked earnestly into my face. "I must go back alone, Abel," she said. "Before day comes I must leave you. Rest here, with grandfather, for a few days and nights, then follow me."

I heard her with astonishment. "It must not be, Rima," I cried. "What, let you leave me—now you are mine—to go all that distance, through all that wild country where you might lose yourself and perish alone? Oh, do not think of it!"

She listened, regarding me with some slight trouble in her eyes, but smiling a little at the same time. Her small hand moved up my arm and caressed my cheek; then she drew my face down to hers until our lips met. But when I looked at her eyes again I saw that she had not consented to my wish. "Do I not know all the way now," she spoke, "all the mountains, rivers, forests—how should I lose myself? And I must return quickly, not step by step, walking—resting, resting—walking, stopping to cook and eat, stopping to gather firewood, to make a shelter—so many things! Oh, I shall be back in half the time; and I have so much to do."

"What can you have to do, love?—everything can be done when we are in the wood together."

A bright smile with a touch of mockery in it flitted over her face as she replied, "Oh, must I tell you that there are things you cannot do? Look, Abel," and she touched the slight garment she wore, thinner now than at first, and dulled by long exposure to sun and wind and rain.

I could not command her, and seemed powerless to persuade her; but I had not done yet, and proceeded to use every argument I could find to bring her round to my view; and when I finished she put her arms round my neck and drew herself up once more. "O Abel, how happy I shall be!" she said, taking no notice of all I had said. "Think of me alone, days and days, in the wood, waiting for you, working all the time; saying, 'Come quickly, Abel; come slow, Abel. O Abel, how long you are! Oh, do not come until my work is finished!' And when it is finished and you arrive you shall find me, but not at once. First you will seek for me in the house, then in the wood, calling, 'Rima! Rima!' And she will be there, listening, hid in the trees, wishing to be in your arms, wishing for your lips—oh, so glad, yet fearing to show herself. Do you know why? He told you—did he not?—that when he first saw her she was standing before him, all in white—a dress that was like snow on the mountain-tops, when the sun is setting and gives it rose and purple colour. I shall be like that, hidden among the trees, saying, 'Am I different—not like Rima? Will he know me—will he love me just the same?' Oh, do I not know that you will be glad, and love me, and call me beautiful? Listen! Listen!" she suddenly exclaimed, lifting her face.

Among the bushes not far from the cave's mouth a

small bird had broken out in song, a clear, tender melody soon taken up by other birds farther away.

"It will soon be morning," she said, and then clasped her arms about me once more and held me in a long, passionate embrace; then slipping away from my arms and with one swift glance at the sleeping old man, passed out of the cave.

For a few moments I remained sitting, not yet realising that she had left me, so suddenly and swiftly had she passed from my arms and my sight; then, recovering my faculties, I started up and rushed out in hopes of overtaking her.

It was not yet dawn, but there was still some light from the full moon, now somewhere behind the mountains. Running to the verge of the bush-grown plateau, I explored the rocky slope beneath without seeing her form, and then called, "Rima! Rima!"

A soft, warbling sound, uttered by no bird, came up from the shadowy bushes far below; and in that direction I ran on; then pausing called again. The sweet sound was repeated once more, but much lower down now, and so faintly that I scarcely heard it. And when I went on farther, and called again and again, there was no reply, and I knew that she had indeed gone on that long journey alone.

❧ 18 ❧

WHEN NUFLO at length opened his eyes he found me sitting alone and despondent by the fire, just returned from my vain chase. I had been caught in a heavy mist on the mountain-side, and was wet through as well as weighed down by fatigue and drowsiness, consequent upon the previous day's laborious march and my night-long vigil; yet I dared not think of rest. *She* had gone from me, and I could not have prevented it; yet the thought that I had allowed her to slip out of my arms, to go away alone on that long, perilous journey, was as intolerable as if I had consented to it.

Nuflo was at first startled to hear of her sudden departure; but he laughed at my fears, affirming that after having once been over the ground she could not lose herself; that she would be in no danger from the Indians, as she would invariably see them at a distance and avoid them, and that wild beasts, serpents, and other evil creatures would do her no harm. The small amount of food she required to sustain life could be found anywhere; furthermore, her journey would not be interrupted by bad weather, since rain and heat had no effect on her. In the end he seemed pleased that she had left us, saying that with Rima in the wood the house and cultivated patch and hidden provisions and implements would be safe, for no Indian would venture to come where she was. His confidence reassured me, and casting myself down on the sandy floor of the cave, I fell into a deep slumber, which lasted until evening; then I only woke to share a meal with the old man, and sleep again until the following day.

Nuflo was not ready to start yet; he was enamoured of the unaccustomed comforts of a dry sleeping-place and a fire blown about by no wind and into which fell no hissing rain-drops. Not for two days more would he consent to set out on the return journey, and if he could have persuaded me our stay at Rio-lama would have lasted a week.

We had fine weather at starting; but before long it clouded, and then for upwards of a fortnight we had it wet and stormy, which so hindered us that it took us twenty-three days to accomplish the return journey, whereas the journey out had only taken eighteen.

The adventures we met with and the pains we suffered during this long march need not be related. The rain made us miserable, but we suffered more from hunger than from any other cause, and on more than one occasion were reduced to the verge of starvation. Twice we were driven to beg for food at Indian villages, and as we had nothing to give in exchange for it, we got very little. It is possible to buy hospitality from the savage without fish-hooks, nails, and calico; but on this occasion I found myself without that impalpable medium of exchange, which had been so great a help to me on my first journey to Parahuari. Now I was weak and miserable and without cunning. It is true that we could have exchanged the two dogs for cassava-bread and corn, but we should then have been worse off than ever. And in the end the dogs saved us by an occasional capture—an armadillo surprised in the open and seized before it could bury itself in the soil, or an iguana, opossum, or labba, traced by means of their keen sense of smell to its hiding-place. Then Nuflo would rejoice and feast, rewarding them with the skin, bones, and entrails. But at length one of the dogs fell lame, and Nuflo, who was very hungry, made its lameness an excuse for despatching it, which he did apparently without compunction, notwithstanding that the poor brute had served him well in its way. He cut up and smoke-dried the flesh, and the intolerable pangs of hunger compelled me to share the loathsome food with him. We were not only indecent, it seemed to me, but cannibals to feed on the faithful servant that had been our butcher. "But what does it matter?" I argued with myself. "All flesh, clean and unclean, should be, and is, equally abhorrent to me, and killing animals a kind of murder. But now I find myself constrained to do this evil thing that good may come. Only to live I take it now—this hateful strength-giver that will enable me to reach Rima, and the purer, better life that is to be."

During all that time, when we toiled onwards league after league in silence, or sat silent by the nightly fire, I thought of many things; but the past, with which I had definitely broken, was little in my mind. Rima was still the source and centre of all my thoughts; from her they rose, and to her returned. Thinking, hoping, dreaming, sustained me in those dark days and nights of pain and privation. Imagination was the bread that gave me strength, the wine that exhilarated. What sustained old Nuflo's mind I know not. Probably it was like a chrysalis, dormant, independent of sustenance; the bright-winged image to be called at some future time to life by a great shouting of angelic hosts and noises of musical instruments slept secure, coffined in that dull, gross nature.

The old beloved wood once more! Never did his native village in some mountain valley seem more beautiful to the Switzer, returning, war-worn, from long voluntary exile, than did that blue cloud on the horizon—the forest where Rima dwelt, my bride, my beautiful—and towering over it the dark cone of Ytaioa, now seem to my hungry eyes! How near at last—how near! And yet the two or three intervening leagues to be traversed so slowly, step by step—how vast the distance seemed! Even at far Riolama, when I set out on my return, I scarcely seemed so far from my love. This maddening impatience told on my strength, which was small, and hindered me. I could not run nor even walk fast; old Nuflo, slow, and sober, with no flame consuming his heart, was more than my equal in the end, and to keep up with him was all I could do.

At the finish he became silent and cautious, first entering the belt of trees leading away through the low range of hills at the southern extremity of the wood. For a mile or upwards we trudged on in the shade; then I began to recognise familiar ground, the old trees under which I had walked or sat, and knew that a hundred yards farther on there would be a first glimpse of the palm-leaf thatch. Then all weakness forsook me; with a low cry of passionate longing and joy I rushed on ahead; but I strained my eyes in vain for a sight of that sweet shelter: no patch of pale yellow colour appeared amidst the universal verdure of bushes, creepers, and trees—trees beyond trees, trees towering above trees.

For some moments I could not realise it. No, I

had surely made a mistake, the house had not stood on that spot; it would appear in sight a little farther on. I took a few uncertain steps onwards, and then again stood still, my brain reeling, my heart swelling nigh to bursting with anguish. I was still standing motionless, with hand pressed to my breast, when Nuflo overtook me. "Where is it—the house?" I stammered, pointing with my hand. All his stolidity seemed gone now; he was trembling too, his lips silently moving. At length he spoke: "They have come —the children of hell have been here, and have destroyed everything!"

"Rima! What has become of Rima?" I cried; but without replying he walked on, and I followed.

The house, we soon found, had been burnt down. Not a stick remained. Where it had stood a heap of black ashes covered the ground—nothing more. But on looking round we could discover no sign of human beings having recently visited the spot. A rank growth of grass and herbage now covered the once clear space surrounding the site of the dwelling, and the ash heap looked as if it had been lying there for a month at least. As to what had become of Rima the old man could say no word. He sat down on the ground overwhelmed at the calamity: Runi's people had been there, he could not doubt it, and they would come again, and he could only look for death at their hands. The thought that Rima had perished, that she was lost, was unendurable. It could not be! No doubt the

Indians had come and destroyed the house during our absence; but she had returned, and they had gone away again to come no more. She would be somewhere in the forest, perhaps not far off, impatiently waiting our return. The old man stared at me while I spoke; he appeared to be in a kind of stupor, and made no reply: and at last, leaving him still sitting on the ground, I went into the wood to look for Rima.

As I walked there, occasionally stopping to peer into some shadowy glade or opening, and to listen, I was tempted again and again to call the name of her I sought aloud; and still the fear that by so doing I might bring some hidden danger on myself, perhaps on her, made me silent. A strange melancholy rested on the forest, a quietude seldom broken by a distant bird's cry. How, I asked myself, should I ever find her in that wide forest while I moved about in that silent, cautious way? My only hope was that she would find me. It occurred to me that the most likely place to seek her would be some of the old haunts known to us both, where we had talked together. I thought first of the mora tree, where she had hidden herself from me, and thither I directed my steps. About this tree, and within its shade, I lingered for upwards of an hour; and, finally, casting my eyes up into the great dim cloud of green and purple leaves, I softly called, "Rima, Rima, if you have seen me, and have concealed yourself from me in your hiding-place, in mercy answer me—in mercy come down to me now!" But

Rima answered not, nor threw down any red glowing leaves to mock me: only the wind, high up, whispered something low and sorrowful in the foliage; and turning I wandered away at random into the deeper shadows.

By-and-by I was startled by the long, piercing cry of a wild fowl, sounding strangely loud in the silence; and no sooner was the air still again than it struck me that no bird had uttered that cry. The Indian is a good mimic of animal voices, but practice had made me able to distinguish the true from the false bird note. For a minute or so I stood still, at a loss what to do, then moved on again with greater caution, scarcely breathing, straining my sight to pierce the shadowy depths. All at once I gave a great start, for directly before me, on the projecting root in the deeper shade of a tree, sat a dark, motionless human form. I stood still, watching it for some time, not yet knowing that it had seen me, when all doubts were put to flight by the form rising and deliberately advancing—a naked Indian with a zabatana in his hand. As he came up out of the deeper shade I recognised Piaké, the surly elder brother of my friend Kua-kó.

It was a great shock to meet him in the wood, but I had no time to reflect just then. I only remembered that I had deeply offended him and his people, that they probably looked on me as an enemy, and would think little of taking my life. It was too late to attempt to escape by flight; I was spent with my long journey and the many privations I had suffered, while he stood there in his full strength with a deadly weapon in his hand.

Nothing was left but to put a bold face on, greet him in a friendly way, and invent some plausible story to account for my action in secretly leaving the village.

He was now standing still, silently regarding me, and glancing round I saw that he was not alone: at a distance of about forty yards on my right hand two other dusky forms appeared watching me from the deep shade.

"Piaké!" I cried, advancing three or four steps.

"You have returned," he answered, but without moving. "Where from?"

"Riolama."

He shook his head, then asked where it was.

"Twenty days towards the setting sun," I said. As he remained silent I added, "I heard that I could find gold in the mountains there. An old man told me, and we went to look for gold."

"What did you find?"

"Nothing."

"Ah!"

And so our conversation appeared to be at an end. But after a few moments my intense desire to discover whether the savages knew aught of Rima or not made me hazard a question.

"Do you live here in the forest now?" I asked.

He shook his head, and after a while said, "We come to kill animals."

"You are like me now," I returned quickly; "you fear nothing."

He looked distrustfully at me, then came a little nearer and said:

"You are very brave. I should not have gone twenty days' journey with no weapons and only an old man for companion. What weapons did you have?"

I saw that he feared me, and wished to make sure that I had it not in my power to do him some injury. "No weapon except my knife," I replied, with assumed carelessness. With that I raised my cloak so as to let him see for himself, turning my body round before him. "Have you found my pistol?" I added.

He shook his head; but he appeared less suspicious now and came close up to me. "How do you get food? Where are you going?" he asked.

I answered boldly, "Food! I am nearly starving. I am going to the village to see if the women have got any meat in the pot, and to tell Runi all I have done since I left him."

He looked at me keenly, a little surprised at my confidence perhaps, then said that he was also going back and would accompany me. One of the other men now advanced, blow-pipe in hand, to join us, and, leaving the wood, we started to walk across the savannah.

It was hateful to have to recross that savannah

again, to leave the woodland shadows where I had hoped to find Rima; but I was powerless: I was a prisoner once more, the lost captive recovered and not yet pardoned, probably never to be pardoned. Only by means of my own cunning could I be saved, and Nuflo, poor old man, must take his chance.

Again and again as we tramped over the barren ground, and when we climbed the ridge, I was compelled to stand still to recover breath, explaining to Piaké that I had been travelling day and night, with no meat during the last three days, so that I was exhausted. This was an exaggeration, but it was necessary to account in some way for the faintness I experienced during our walk, caused less by fatigue and want of food than by anguish of mind.

At intervals I talked to him, asking after all the other members of the community by name. At last, thinking only of Rima, I asked him if any other person or persons besides his people came to the wood now or lived there.

He said no.

"Once," I said, "there was a daughter of the Didi, a girl you all feared: is she there now?"

He looked at me with suspicion and then shook his head. I dared not press him with more questions; but after an interval he said plainly, "She is not there now."

And I was forced to believe him; for had Rima been in the wood *they* would not have been there.

She was not there, this much I had discovered. Had she, then, lost her way, or perished on that long journey from Riolama? Or had she returned only to fall into the hands of her cruel enemies? My heart was heavy in me; but if these devils in human shape knew more than they had told me, I must, I said, hide my anxiety and wait patiently to find it out, should they spare my life. And if they spared me and had not spared that other sacred life interwoven with mine, the time would come when they would find, too late, that they had taken to their bosom a worse devil than themselves.

❧ 19 ❧

My arrival at the village created some excitement; but I was plainly no longer regarded as a friend or one of the family. Runi was absent, and I looked forward to his return with no little apprehension; he would doubtless decide my fate. Kua-kó was also away. The others sat or stood about the great room, staring at me in silence. I took no notice, but merely asked for food, then for my hammock, which I hung up in the old place, and lying down I fell into a doze. Runi made his appearance at dusk. I rose and greeted him, but he spoke no word, and, until he went to his hammock, sat in sullen silence, ignoring my presence.

On the following day the crisis came. We were once more gathered in the room—all but Kua-kó and another of the men, who had not yet returned from some expedition—and for the space of half an hour not a word was spoken by anyone. Something was expected; even the children were strangely still, and whenever one of the pet birds strayed in at the open door, uttering a little plaintive note, it was chased out again, but without a sound. At length Runi straightened himself on his seat and fixed his eyes on me; then cleared his throat and began a long harangue, delivered in the loud, monotonous sing-song which I knew so well and which meant that the occasion was an important one. And as is usual in such efforts, the same thought and expressions were used again and again, and yet again, with dull, angry insistence. The orator of Guayana to be impressive must be long, however little he may have to say. Strange as it may seem, I listened critically to him, not without a feeling of scorn at his lower intelligence. But I was easier in my mind now. From the very fact of his addressing such a speech to me I was convinced that he wished not to take my life, and would not do so if I could clear myself of suspicion.

I was a white man, he said, they were Indians; nevertheless they had treated me well. They had fed and sheltered me. They had done a great deal for me: they had taught me the use of the zabatana, and had promised to make one for me, asking nothing in return. They had also promised me a wife. How had I treated them? I had deserted them, going away secretly to a distance, leaving them in doubt as to my intentions. How could they tell why I had gone, and where? They had an enemy. Managa was his name; he and his people hated them; I knew that he wished them evil; I knew where to find him, for they had told me. That was what they thought when I suddenly left them. Now I returned to them, saying that I had been to Riolama. He knew where Riolama was, although he had never been there: it was so far. Why did I go to Riolama? It was a bad place. There were Indians there, a few; but they were not good Indians like those of Parahuari, and would kill a white man. *Had* I gone there? Why had I gone there?

He finished at last, and it was my turn to speak, but he had given me plenty of time, and my reply was ready. "I have heard you," I said. "Your words are good words. They are the words of a friend. I am the white man's friend, you say: is he my friend? He went away secretly, saying no word: why did he go without speaking to his friend who had treated him well? Has he been to my enemy Managa? Perhaps he is a friend of my enemy? Where has he been? I must now answer these things, saying true words to my friend. You are an Indian, I am a white man. You do not know all the white man's thoughts. These are the things I wish to tell you. In the white man's country are two kinds of men. There are the rich men, who have all that a man can desire—houses made of stone, full of fine things, fine clothes, fine weapons, fine ornaments; and they have horses, cattle, sheep, dogs

—everything they desire. Because they have gold, for with gold the white man buys everything. The other kind of white men are the poor, who have no gold and cannot buy or have anything: they must work hard for the rich man for the little food he gives them, and a rag to cover their nakedness; and if he gives them shelter they have it; if not they must lie down in the rain out of doors. In my own country, a hundred days from here, I was the son of a great chief, who had much gold, and when he died it was all mine, and I was rich. But I had an enemy, one worse than Managa, for he was rich and had many people. And in a war his people overcame mine, and he took my gold, and all I possessed, making me poor. The Indian kills his enemy, but the white man takes his gold, and that is worse than death. Then I said: I have been a rich man and now I am poor, and must work like a dog for some rich man, for the sake of the little food he will throw me at the end of each day. No, I cannot do it! I will go away and live with the Indians, so that those who have seen me a rich man shall never see me working like a dog for a master, and cry out and mock at me. For the Indians are not like white men: they have no gold; they are not rich and poor; all are alike. One roof covers them from the rain and sun. All have weapons which they make; all kill birds in the forests and catch fish in the rivers; and the women cook the meat and all eat from one pot. And with the Indians, I will be an Indian, and hunt in the forest and eat with them and drink with them. Then I left my country and came here, and lived with you, Runi, and was well treated. And now, why did I go away? This I have now to tell you. After I had been here a certain time I went over there to the forest. You wished me not to go, because of an evil thing, a daughter of the Didi, that lived there; but I feared nothing and went. There I met an old man, who talked to me in the white man's language. He had travelled and seen much, and told me one strange thing. On a mountain at Riolama he told me that he had seen a great lump of gold, as much as a man could carry. And when I heard this I said, 'With the gold I could return to my country, and buy weapons for myself and all my people and go to war with my enemy and deprive him of all his possessions and serve him as he served me.' I asked the old man to take me to Riolama; and when he had consented I went away from here without saying a word, so as not to be prevented. It is far to Riolama, and I had no weapons; but I feared nothing. I said, 'If I must fight I must fight, and if I must be killed I must be killed.' But when I got to Riolama I found no gold. There was only a yellow stone which the old man had mistaken for gold. It was yellow, like gold, but it would buy nothing. Therefore I came back to Parahuari again, to my friend; and if he is angry with me still because I went away without informing him, let him say, 'Go and seek elsewhere for a new friend, for I am your friend no longer.'"

I concluded thus boldly, because I did not wish him to know that I had suspected him of harbouring any sinister designs, or that I looked on our quarrel as a very serious one. When I had finished speaking he emitted a sound which expressed neither approval nor disapproval, but only the fact that he had heard me. But I was satisfied. His expression had undergone a favourable change; it was less grim. After a while he remarked, with a peculiar twitching of the mouth which might have developed into a smile, "The white man will do much to get gold. You walked twenty days to see a yellow stone that would buy nothing." It was fortunate that he took this view of the case, which was flattering to his Indian nature, and perhaps touched his sense of the ludicrous. At all events, he said nothing to discredit my story, to which they had all listened with profound interest.

From that time it seemed to be tacitly agreed to let bygones be bygones; and I could see that as the dangerous feeling that had threatened my life diminished the old pleasure they had once found in my company returned. But my feelings towards them did not change, nor could they while that black and terrible suspicion concerning Rima was in my heart. I talked again freely with them, as if there had been no break in the old friendly relations. If they watched me furtively whenever I went out of doors I affected not to

see it. I set to work to repair my rude guitar, which
had been broken in my absence, and studied to show
them a cheerful countenance. But when alone, or in
my hammock, hidden from their eyes, free to look
into my own heart, then I was conscious that something new and strange had come into my life; that a
new nature, black and implacable, had taken the place
of the old. And sometimes it was hard to conceal this
fury that burnt in me; sometimes I felt an impulse to
spring like a tiger on one of the Indians, to hold him
fast by the throat until the secret I wished to learn
was forced from his lips, then to dash his brains out
against the stone. But they were many, and there was
no choice but to be cautious and patient if I wished
to outwit them with a cunning superior to their own.

Three days after my arrival at the village, Kua-kó
returned with his companion. I greeted him with affected warmth, but was really pleased that he was
back, believing that if the Indians knew anything of
Rima he among them all would be most likely to tell
it.

Kua-kó appeared to have brought some important
news, which he discussed with Runi and the others;
and on the following day I noticed that preparations
for an expedition were in progress. Spears and bows
and arrows were got ready, but not blow-pipes, and
I knew by this that the expedition would not be a
hunting one. Having discovered so much, also that
only four men were going out, I called Kua-kó aside

and begged him to let me go with them. He seemed pleased at the proposal, and at once repeated it to Runi, who considered for a little and then consented.

By-and-by he said, touching his bow, "You cannot fight with our weapons; what will you do if we meet an enemy?"

I smiled and returned that I would not run away. All I wished to show him was that his enemies were my enemies, that I was ready to fight for my friend.

He was pleased at my words, and said no more and gave me no weapons. Next morning, however, when we set out before daylight, I made the discovery that he was carrying my revolver fastened to his waist. He had concealed it carefully under the one simple garment he wore, but it bulged slightly, and so the secret was betrayed. I had never believed that he had lost it, and I was convinced that he took it now with the object of putting it into my hands at the last moment in case of meeting with an enemy.

From the village we travelled in a north-westerly direction, and before noon camped in a grove of dwarf trees, where we remained until the sun was low, then continued our walk through a rather barren country. At night we camped again beside a small stream, only a few inches deep, and after a meal of smoked meat and parched maize prepared to sleep till dawn on the next day.

Sitting by the fire I resolved to make a first attempt to discover from Kua-kó anything concerning Rima

which might be known to him. Instead of lying down
when the others did I remained seated, my guardian
also sitting—no doubt waiting for me to lie down first.
Presently I moved nearer to him and began a conversation in a low voice, anxious not to rouse the attention of the other men.

"Once you said that Oolava would be given to me
for a wife," I began. "Some day I shall want a wife."

He nodded approval, and remarked sententiously
that the desire to possess a wife was common to all
men.

"What has been left to me?" I said despondingly
and spreading out my hands. "My pistol gone, and
did I not give Runi the tinder-box, and the little box
with a cock painted on it to you? I had no return—
not even the blow-pipe. How, then, can I get me a
wife?"

He, like the others—dull-witted savage that he was
—had come to the belief that I was incapable of the
cunning and duplicity they practised. I could not see
a green parrot sitting silent and motionless amidst
the green foliage as they could; I had not their pre-
ternatural keenness of sight: and, in like manner, to
deceive with lies and false seeming was their faculty
and not mine. He fell readily into the trap. My return
to practical subjects pleased him. He bade me hope
that Oolava might yet be mine in spite of my poverty.
It was not always necessary to have things to get a
wife: to be able to maintain her was enough; some

day I would be like one of themselves, able to kill animals and catch fish. Besides, did not Runi wish to keep me with them for other reasons? But he could not keep me wifeless. I could do much: I could sing and make music; I was brave and feared nothing; I could teach the children to fight.

He did not say, however, that I could teach anything to one of his years and attainments.

I protested that he gave me too much praise, that they were just as brave. Did they not show a courage equal to mine by going every day to hunt in that wood which was inhabited by the daughter of the Didi?

I came to this subject with fear and trembling, but he took it quietly. He shook his head, and then all at once began to tell me how they first came to go there to hunt. He said that a few days after I had secretly disappeared, two men and a woman, returning home from a distant place where they had been on a visit to a relation, stopped at the village. These travellers related that two days' journey from Ytaioa they had met three persons travelling in an opposite direction; an old man with a white beard, followed by two yellow dogs, a young man in a big cloak, and a strange-looking girl. Thus it came to be known that I had left the wood with the old man and the daughter of the Didi. It was great news to them, for they did not believe that we had any intention of returning, and at once they began to hunt in the wood, and went there every day, killing birds, monkeys, and other animals in numbers.

His words had begun to excite me greatly, but I studied to appear calm, and only slightly interested, so as to draw him on to say more.

"Then we returned," I said at last. "But only two of us, and not together. I left the old man on the road, and *she* left us in Riolama. She went away from us into the mountains—who knows whither!"

"But she came back!" he returned, with a gleam of devilish satisfaction in his eyes that made the blood run cold in my veins.

It was hard to dissemble still, to tempt him to say something that would madden me! "No, no," I answered, after considering his words. "She feared to return; she went away to hide herself in the great mountains beyond Riolama. She could not come back."

"But she came back!" he persisted, with that triumphant gleam in his eyes once more. Under my cloak my hand had clutched my knife-handle, but I strove hard against the fierce, almost maddening impulse to pluck it out and bury it, quick as lightning, in his accursed throat.

He continued: "Seven days before you returned we saw her in the wood. We were always expecting, watching, always afraid; and when hunting we were three and four together. On that day I and three others saw her. It was in an open place, where the

trees are big and wide apart. We started up and
chased her when she ran from us, but feared to shoot.
And in one moment she climbed up into a small tree,
then, like a monkey, passed from its highest branches
into a big tree. We could not see her there, but she
was there in the big tree, for there was no other tree
near—no way of escape. Three of us sat down to
watch, and the other went back to the village. He was
long gone; we were just going to leave the tree, fearing that she would do us some injury, when he came
back, and with him all the others, men, women, and
children. They brought axes and knives. Then Runi
said, 'Let no one shoot an arrow into the tree thinking
to hit her, for the arrow would be caught in her hand
and thrown back at him. We must burn her in the
tree; there is no way to kill her except by fire.' Then
we went round and round looking up, but could see
nothing; and someone said, She has escaped, flying
like a bird from the tree; but Runi answered that fire
would show. So we cut down the small tree, and
lopped the branches off and heaped them round the
big trunk. Then, at a distance, we cut down ten more
small trees, and afterwards, farther away, ten more,
and then others, and piled them all around, tree
after tree, until the pile reached as far from the trunk
as that," and here he pointed to a bush forty to fifty
yards from where we sat.

The feeling with which I had listened to this recital
had become intolerable. The sweat ran from me in

streams; I shivered like a person in a fit of ague, and clenched my teeth together to prevent them from rattling. "I must drink," I said, cutting him short and rising to my feet. He also rose, but did not follow me, when, with uncertain steps, I made my way to the waterside, which was ten or twelve yards away. Lying prostrate on my chest, I took a long draught of clear cold water, and held my face for a few moments in the current. It sent a chill through me, drying my wet skin, and bracing me for the concluding part of the hideous narrative. Slowly I stepped back to the fireside and sat down again, while he resumed his old place at my side.

"You burnt the tree down," I said. "Finish telling me now and let me sleep—my eyes are heavy."

"Yes. While the men cut and brought trees, the women and children gathered dry stuff in the forest and brought it in their arms and piled it round. Then they set fire to it on all sides, laughing and shouting, 'Burn, burn, daughter of the Didi!' At length all the lower branches of the big tree were on fire, and the trunk was on fire, but above it was still green, and we could see nothing. But the flames went up higher and higher with a great noise; and at last from the top of the tree, out of the green leaves, came a great cry, like the cry of a bird, 'Abel! Abel!' and then looking we saw something fall; through leaves and smoke and flame it fell like a great white bird killed with an arrow and falling to the earth, and fell into the flames beneath. And it was the daughter of the Didi, and she was burnt to ashes like a moth in the flames of a fire, and no one has ever heard or seen her since."

It was well for me that he spoke rapidly, and finished quickly. Even before he had quite concluded I drew my cloak round my face and stretched myself out. And I suppose that he at once followed my example, but I had grown blind and deaf to outward things just then. My heart no longer throbbed violently; it fluttered and seemed to grow feebler and feebler in its action: I remember that there was a dull, rushing sound in my ears, that I gasped for breath, that my life seemed ebbing away. After these horrible sensations had passed, I remained quiet for about half an hour; and during this time the picture of that last act in the hateful tragedy grew more and more distinct and vivid in my mind, until I seemed to be actually gazing on it, that my ears were filled with the hissing and crackling of the fire, the exultant shouts of the savages, and above all the last piercing cry of "Abel! Abel!" from the cloud of burning foliage. I could not endure it longer, and rose at last to my feet. I glanced at Kua-kó lying two or three yards away, and he, like the others, was, or appeared to be, in a deep sleep; he was lying on his back, and his dark firelit face looked as still and unconscious as a face of stone. Now was my chance of escape—if to escape was my wish. Yes; for I now possessed the coveted knowledge, and nothing more was to be gained by keeping with my deadly enemies. And now, most fortunately for me, they had brought me far on the road to that place of the five hills where Managa lived—Managa, whose name had been often in my mind since my return to Parahuari. Glancing away from Kua-kó's still stonelike face, I caught sight of that pale solitary star which Runi had pointed out to me low down in the north-western sky when I had asked him where his enemy lived. In that direction we had been travelling since leaving the village; surely if I walked all night by to-morrow I could reach Managa's hunting-ground, and be safe and think over what I had heard and on what I had to do.

I moved softly away a few steps, then thinking that it would be well to take a spear in my hand, I turned back, and was surprised and startled to notice that Kua-kó had moved in the interval. He had turned over on his side, and his face was now towards me. His eyes appeared closed, but he might be only feigning sleep, and I dared not go back to pick up the spear. After a moment's hesitation I moved on again, and after a second glance back and seeing that he did not stir, I waded cautiously across the stream, walked softly twenty or thirty yards, and then began to run. At intervals I paused to listen for a moment; and presently I heard a pattering sound as of footsteps coming swiftly after me. I instantly concluded that Kua-kó had been awake all the time watching my movements, and that he was now following me. I now put forth my whole speed, and while thus running could distinguish no sound. That he would miss me, for it was very dark, although with a starry sky above, was my only hope; for with no weapon except my knife my chances would be small indeed should he overtake me. Besides, he had no doubt roused the others before starting, and they would be close behind. There were no bushes in that place to hide myself in and let them pass me; and presently, to make matters worse, the character of the soil changed, and I was running over level clayey ground, so white with a salt efflorescence that a dark object moving on it would show conspicuously at a distance. Here I paused to look back and listen, when distinctly came the sound of footsteps, and the next moment I made out the vague form of an Indian advancing at a rapid rate of speed and with his uplifted spear in his hand. In the brief pause I had made he had advanced almost to within hurling distance of me, and turning, I sped on again, throwing off my cloak to ease my flight. The next time I looked back he was still in sight, but not so near; he had stopped to pick up my cloak, which would be his now, and this had given me a slight advantage. I fled on, and had continued running for a distance perhaps of fifty yards when an object rushed past me, tearing through the flesh of my left arm close to the shoulder on its way; and not knowing that I was not badly wounded nor how near my pursuer might be, I turned in desperation to meet him, and saw him not above twenty-five yards away, running towards me with something bright in his hand. It was Kua-kó, and after wounding me with his spear he was about to finish me with his knife. O fortunate young savage, after such a victory, and with that noble blue cloth cloak for trophy and covering, what fame and happiness will be yours! A change swift as lightning had come over me, a sudden exultation. I was wounded, but my right hand was sound and clutched a knife as good as his, and we were on an equality. I waited for him calmly. All weakness, grief, despair had vanished, all feelings except a terrible raging desire to spill his accursed blood; and my brain was clear and my nerves like steel, and I remembered with something like laughter our old amusing encounters with rapiers of wood. Ah, that was only making believe and childish play; this was reality. Could any white man, deprived of his treacherous, far-killing weapon, meet the resolute savage, face to face and foot to foot and equal him with the old primitive weapons? Poor youth, this delusion will cost you dear! It was scarcely an equal contest when he hurled himself against me, with only his savage strength and courage to match my skill; in a few moments he was lying at my feet, pouring out his life blood on that white thirsty plain. From his prostrate form I turned, the wet, red knife in my hand, to meet the others, still thinking that they were on the track and close at hand. Why had he stooped to pick up the cloak if they were not following—if he had not been afraid of losing it? I turned only to receive their spears, to die with my face to them; nor was the thought of death terrible to me; I could die calmly now after killing my first assailant. But had I indeed killed him? I asked, hearing a sound like a groan escape from his lips. Quickly stooping I once more drove my weapon to the hilt in his prostrate form, and when he exhaled a deep sigh, and his frame quivered, and the blood spurted afresh, I experienced a feeling of savage joy. And still no sound of hurrying footsteps came to my listening ears and no vague forms appeared in the darkness. I concluded that he had either left them sleeping or that they had not followed in the right direction. Taking up the cloak, I was about to walk on, when I noticed the spear he had thrown at me lying where it had fallen some yards away, and picking that up also, I went on once more, still keeping the guiding star before me.

❧ 20 ❦

THAT GOOD FIGHT had been to me like a draught of
wine, and made me for a while oblivious of my loss
and of the pain from my wound. But the glow and
feeling of exultation did not last: the lacerated flesh
smarted; I was weak from loss of blood, and oppressed
with sensations of fatigue. If my foes had appeared
on the scene they would have made an easy conquest
of me; but they came not, and I continued to walk on,
slowly and painfully, pausing often to rest.

At last, recovering somewhat from my faint condition, and losing all fear of being overtaken, my sorrow revived in full force, and thought returned to
madden me.

Alas! this bright being, like no other in its divine
brightness, so long in the making, now no more than

a dead leaf, a little dust, lost and forgotten for ever—
O pitiless! O cruel!

But I knew it all before—this law of nature and of
necessity, against which all revolt is idle: often had
the remembrance of it filled me with ineffable melancholy; only now it seemed cruel beyond all cruelty.

Not nature the instrument, not the keen sword
that cuts into the bleeding tissues, but the hand that
wields it—the unseen unknown something, or person, that manifests itself in the horrible workings of
nature.

"Did you know, beloved, at the last, in that intolerable heat, in that moment of supreme anguish,
that *he* is unlistening, unhelpful as the stars, that you
cried not to him? To me was your cry: but your poor,
frail fellow-creature was not there to save, or, failing
that, to cast himself into the flames and perish with
you, hating God."

Thus, in my insufferable pain, I spoke aloud; alone
in that solitary place, a bleeding fugitive in the dark
night, looking up at the stars I cursed the Author of
my being and called on Him to take back the abhorred
gift of life.

Yet, according to my philosophy, how vain it was!
All my bitterness and hatred and defiance were as
empty, as ineffectual, as utterly futile, as are the sup-
plications of the meek worshipper, and no more than
the whisper of a leaf, the light whirr of an insect's
wing. Whether I loved Him who was over all, as when

I thanked Him on my knees for guiding me to where I had heard so sweet and mysterious a melody, or hated and defied Him as now, it all came from Him—love and hate, good and evil.

But I know—I knew then—that in one thing my philosophy was false, that it was not the whole truth; that though my cries did not touch nor come near Him they would yet hurt me; and, just as a prisoner maddened at his unjust fate beats against the stone walls of his cell until he falls back bruised and bleeding to the floor, so did I wilfully bruise my own soul, and knew that those wounds I gave myself would not heal.

Of that night, the beginning of the blackest period of my life, I shall say no more; and over subsequent events I shall pass quickly.

Morning found me at a distance of many miles from the scene of my duel with the Indian, in a broken, hilly country, varied with savannah and open forest. I was well-nigh spent with my long march, and felt that unless food was obtained before many hours my situation would be indeed desperate. With labour I managed to climb to the summit of a hill about three hundred feet high, in order to survey the surrounding country, and found that it was one of a group of five, and conjectured that these were the five hills of Uritay, and that I was in the neighbourhood of Managa's village. Coming down I proceeded to the next hill, which was higher; and before reaching it came to a stream in a narrow valley dividing the hills, and proceeding along its banks in search of a crossing-place, I came full in sight of the settlement sought for. As I approached people were seen moving hurriedly about: and by the time I arrived, walking slowly and painfully, seven or eight men were standing before the village, some with spears in their hands, the women and children behind them, all staring curiously at me. Drawing near I cried out in a somewhat feeble voice that I was seeking for Managa; whereupon a grey-haired man stepped forth, spear in hand, and replied that he was Managa, and demanded to know why I sought him. I told him a part of my story, enough to show that I had a deadly feud with Runi, that I had escaped from him after killing one of his people.

I was taken in and supplied with food; my wound was examined and dressed; and then I was permitted to lie down and sleep, while Managa, with half a dozen of his people, hurriedly started to visit the scene of my fight with Kua-kó, not only to verify my story, but partly also with the hope of meeting Runi. I did not see him again until the next morning, when he informed me that he had found the spot where I had been overtaken, that the dead man had been discovered by the others and carried back towards Parahuari. He had followed the trace for some distance, and he was satisfied that Runi had come thus far in the first place only with the intention of spying on him.

My arrival, and the strange tidings I had brought, had thrown the village into a great commotion; it was evident that from that time Managa lived in constant apprehension of a sudden attack from his old enemy. This gave me great satisfaction; it was my study to keep the feeling alive, and, more than that, to drop continual hints of his enemy's secret murderous purpose, until he was wrought up to a kind of frenzy of mingled fear and rage. And being of a suspicious and somewhat truculent temper, he one day all at once turned on me as the immediate cause of his miserable state, suspecting perhaps that I only wished to make an instrument of him. But I was strangely bold and careless of danger then, and only mocked at his rage, telling him proudly that I feared him not; that Runi, his mortal enemy and mine, feared not him but me; that Runi knew perfectly well where I had taken refuge and would not venture to make his meditated attack while I remained in his village, but would wait for my departure. "Kill me, Managa," I cried, smiting my chest as I stood facing him. "Kill me, and the result will be that he will come upon you unawares and murder you all, as he has resolved to do sooner or later."

After that speech he glared at me in silence, then flung down the spear he had snatched up in his sudden rage and stalked out of the house and into the wood: but before long he was back again seated in his old place, brooding on my words with a face black as night.

It is painful to recall that secret dark chapter of my life—that period of moral insanity. But I wish not to be a hypocrite, conscious or unconscious, to delude myself or another with this plea of insanity. My mind was very clear just then; past and present were clear to me; the future clearest of all: I could measure the extent of my action and speculate on its future effect, and my sense of right or wrong—of individual responsibility—was more vivid than at any other period of my life. Can I even say that I was blinded by passion? Driven, perhaps, but certainly not blinded. For no reaction, or submission, had followed on that furious revolt against the unknown being, personal or not, that is behind nature, in whose existence I believed. I was still in revolt: I would hate Him, and show my hatred by being like Him, as He appears to us reflected in that mirror of Nature. Had He given me good gifts—the sense of right and wrong and sweet humanity? The beautiful sacred flower He had caused to grow in me I would crush ruthlessly; its beauty and fragrance and grace would be dead for ever; there was nothing evil, nothing cruel and contrary to my nature, that I would not be guilty of, glorying in my guilt. This was not the temper of a few days: I remained for close upon two months at Managa's village, never repenting nor desisting in my efforts to induce the Indians to join me in that most barbarous adventure on which my heart was set.

I succeeded in the end: it would have been strange if I had not. The horrible details need not be given. Managa did not wait for his enemy, but fell on him unexpectedly, an hour after nightfall in his own village. If I had really been insane during those two months, if some cloud had been on me, some demoniacal force dragging me on, the cloud and insanity vanished and the constraint was over in one moment, when that hellish enterprise was completed. It was the sight of an old woman, lying where she had been struck down, the fire of the blazing house lighting her wide-open glassy eyes and white hair dabbled in blood, which suddenly, as by a miracle, wrought this change in my brain. For they were all dead at last, old and young, all who had lighted the fire round that great green tree in which Rima had taken refuge, who had danced round the blaze, shouting, "Burn! burn!"

At the moment my glance fell on that prostrate form, I paused and stood still, trembling like a person struck with a sudden pang in the heart, who thinks that his last moment has come to him unawares. After a while I slunk away out of the great circle of firelight into the thick darkness beyond. Instinctively I turned towards the forest across the savannah— my forest again; and fled away from the noise and the sight of flames, never pausing until I found myself within the black shadow of the trees. Into the

deeper blackness of the interior I dared not venture:
on the border I paused to ask myself what I did there
alone in the night time. Sitting down I covered my
face with my hands as if to hide it more effectually
than it could be hidden by night and the forest shadows. What horrible thing—what calamity that frightened my soul to think of, had fallen on me? The
revulsion of feeling, the unspeakable horror, the remorse, was more than I could bear. I started up with
a cry of anguish, and would have slain myself to escape at that moment; but Nature is not always and
utterly cruel, and on this occasion she came to my
aid. Consciousness forsook me, and I lived not again
until the light of early morning was in the east; then
found myself lying on the wet herbage—wet with rain
that had lately fallen. My physical misery was now
so great that it prevented me from dwelling on the
scenes witnessed on the previous evening. Nature was
again merciful in this. I only remembered that it was
necessary to hide myself, in case the Indians should
be still in the neighbourhood and pay the wood a
visit. Slowly and painfully I crept away into the forest,
and there sat for several hours, scarcely thinking at all,
in a half-stupefied condition. At noon the sun shone
out and dried the wood. I felt no hunger, only a vague
sense of bodily misery, and with it the fear that if I
left my hiding-place I might meet some human creature face to face. This fear prevented me from stirring
until the twilight came, when I crept forth and made

my way to the border of the forest, to spend the night there. Whether sleep visited me during the dark hours or not I cannot say: day and night my condition seemed the same; I experienced only a dull sensation of utter misery which seemed in spirit and flesh alike, an inability to think clearly, or for more than a few moments consecutively, about anything. Scenes in which I had been principal actor came and went, as in a dream when the will slumbers: now with devilish ingenuity and persistence I was working on Managa's mind; now standing motionless in the forest listening for that sweet, mysterious melody; now staring aghast at old Cla-cla's wide-open glassy eyes and white hair dabbled in blood; then suddenly, in the cave at Riolama, I was fondly watching the slow return of life and colour to Rima's still face.

When morning came again I felt so weak that a vague fear of sinking down and dying of hunger at last roused me and sent me forth in quest of food. I moved slowly and my eyes were dim to see, but I knew so well where to seek for small morsels—small edible roots and leaf-stalks, berries, and drops of congealed gum—that it would have been strange in that rich forest if I had not been able to discover something to stay my famine. It was little, but it sufficed for the day. Once more Nature was merciful to me; for the diligent seeking among the concealing leaves left no interval for thought; every chance morsel gave a momentary pleasure, and as I prolonged my search my steps grew firmer, the dimness passed from my eyes. I was more forgetful of self, more eager, and like a wild animal with no thought or feeling beyond its immediate wants. Fatigued at the end, I fell asleep as soon as darkness brought my busy rambles to a close, and did not wake until another morning dawned.

My hunger was extreme now. The wailing notes of a pair of small birds, persistently flitting round me, or perched with gaping bills and wings trembling with agitation, served to remind me that it was now breeding-time; also that Rima had taught me to find a small bird's-nest. She found them only to delight her eyes with the sight; but they would be food for me; the crystal and yellow fluid in the gem-like, white or blue or red-speckled shells would help to keep me alive. All day I hunted, listening to every note and cry, watching the motions of every winged thing, and found, besides gums and fruits over a score of nests containing eggs, mostly of small birds, and although the labour was great and the scratches many, I was well satisfied with the result.

A few days later I found a supply of Haima gum, and eagerly began picking it from the tree; not that it could be used, but the thought of the brilliant light it gave was so strong in my mind that mechanically I gathered it all. The possession of this gum, when night closed round me again, produced in me an intense longing for artificial light and warmth. The darkness was harder than ever to endure. I envied the fireflies their natural lights, and ran about in the dusk to capture a few and hold them in the hollow of my two hands, for the sake of their cold, fitful flashes. On the following day I wasted two or three hours trying to get fire in the primitive method with dry wood, but failed, and lost much time, and suffered more than ever from hunger in consequence. Yet there was fire in everything; even when I struck at hard wood with my knife sparks were emitted. If I could only arrest those wonderful heat and light-giving sparks! And all at once, as if I had just lighted upon some new, wonderful truth, it occurred to me that with my steel hunting-knife and a piece of flint fire could be obtained. Immediately I set about preparing tinder with dry moss, rotten wood, and wild cotton; and in a short time I had the wished fire, and heaped wood dry and green on it to make it large. I nursed it well, and spent the night beside it; and it also served to roast some huge white grubs which I had found in the rotten wood of a prostrate trunk. The sight of these great grubs had formerly disgusted me; but they tasted good to me now, and stayed my hunger, and that was all I looked for in my wild forest food.

For a long time an undefined feeling prevented me from going near the site of Nuflo's burnt lodge. I went there at last; and the first thing I did was to go all round the fatal spot, cautiously peering into the rank herbage, as if I feared a lurking serpent; and at length, at some distance from the blackened heap, I discovered a human skeleton and knew it to be Nuflo's. In his day he had been a great armadillo hunter, and these quaint carrion eaters had no doubt revenged themselves by devouring his flesh when they found him dead—killed by the savages.

Having once returned to this spot of many memories, I could not quit it again; while my wild woodland life lasted here must I have my lair, and being here I could not leave that mournful skeleton above ground. With labour I excavated a pit to bury it, careful not to cut or injure a broad-leafed creeper that had begun to spread itself over the spot; and after refilling the hole I drew the long, trailing stems over the mound.

"Sleep well, old man," said I, when my work was done; and these few words, implying neither censure nor praise, was all the burial service that old Nuflo had from me.

I then visited the spot where the old man, assisted by me, had concealed his provisions before starting for Riolama, and was pleased to find that it had not been discovered by the Indians. Besides the store of tobacco-leaf, maize, pumpkin, potatoes, and cassava-bread, and the cooking utensils, I found among other things a chopper—a great acquisition, since with it I would be able to cut down small palms and bamboos to make myself a hut.

The possession of a supply of food left me time

for many things: time in the first place to make my
own conditions; doubtless after them there would be
further progression on the old lines—luxuries added
to necessaries; a healthful, fruitful life of thought and
action combined; and at the last a peaceful, contem-
plative old age.

I cleared away ashes and rubbish, and marked out
the very spot where Rima's separate bower had been
for my habitation, which I intended to make small.
In five days it was finished; then after lighting a fire,
I stretched myself out in my dry bed of moss and
leaves with a feeling that was almost triumphant. Let
the rain now fall in torrents, putting out the firefly's
lamp; let the wind and thunder roar their loudest,
and the lightnings smite the earth with intolerable
light, frightening the poor monkeys in their wet, leafy
habitations, little would I heed it all on my dry bed,
under my dry, palm-leaf thatch, with glorious fire to
keep me company and protect me from my ancient
enemy, Darkness.

From that first sleep under shelter I woke refreshed, and was not driven by the cruel spur of hunger into the wet forest. The wished time had come of
rest from labour, of leisure for thought. Resting here,
just where she had rested, night by night clasping a
visionary mother in her arms, whispering tenderest
words in a visionary ear, I too now clasped her in my
arms—a visionary Rima. How different the nights had
seemed when I was without shelter, before I had re-

discovered fire! How had I endured it? That strange
ghostly gloom of the woods at night-time full of innumerable strange shapes; still and dark, yet with
something seen at times moving amidst them, dark
and vague and strange also—an owl perhaps, or bat,
or great winged moth, or nightjar. Nor had I any
choice then but to listen to the night-sounds of the
forest; and they were various as the day-sounds, and
for every day-sound, from the faintest lisping and
softest trill to the deep boomings and piercing cries,
there was an analogue; always with something mysterious, unreal, in its tone, something proper to the
night. They were ghostly sounds, uttered by the
ghosts of dead animals; they were a hundred different
things by turns, but always with a meaning in them,
which I vainly strove to catch—something to be interpreted only by a sleeping faculty in us, lightly
sleeping, and now, now on the very point of awaking!

Now the gloom and the mystery was shut out; now
I had that which stood in the place of pleasure to me,
and was more than pleasure. It was a mournful rapture to lie awake now, wishing not for sleep and oblivion, hating the thought of daylight that would
come at last to drown and scare away my vision. To
be with Rima again—my lost Rima recovered—mine,
mine at last! No longer the old vexing doubt now—
"You are you and I am I—why is it?"—the question
asked when our souls were near together, like two
raindrops side by side, drawing irresistibly nearer, ever

nearer: for now they had touched and were not two, but one inseparable drop, crystallised beyond change, not to be disintegrated by time, nor shattered by death's blow, nor resolved by any alchemy.

I had other company besides this unfailing vision, and the bright dancing fire that talked to me in its fantastic fire language. It was my custom to secure the door well on retiring: grief had perhaps chilled my blood, for I suffered less from heat than from cold at this period, and the fire seemed grateful all night long; I was also anxious to exclude all small winged and creeping night-wanderers. But to exclude them entirely proved impossible: through a dozen invisible chinks they would find their way to me; also some entered by day to lie concealed until after nightfall. A monstrous hairy hermit spider found an asylum in a dusky corner of the hut, under the thatch, and day after day he was there, all day long, sitting close and motionless; but at dark he invariably disappeared—who knows on what murderous errand! His hue was a deep dead-leaf yellow, with a black and grey pattern, borrowed from some wild cat; and so large was he that his great outspread hairy legs, radiating from the flat disc of his body, would have covered a man's open hand. It was easy to see him in my small interior; often in the night-time my eyes would stray to his corner, never to encounter that strange hairy figure; but daylight failed not to bring him. He troubled me; but now, for Rima's sake, I could slay no living thing except from motives of hunger. I had it in my mind to injure him—to strike off one of his legs, which would not be missed much, as they were many—so as to make him go away and return no more to so inhospitable a place. But courage failed me. He might come stealthily back at night to plunge his long, crooked falces into my throat, poisoning my blood with fever and delirium and black death. So I left him alone, and glanced furtively and fearfully at him, hoping that he had not divined any thoughts; thus we lived on unsocially together. More companionable, but still in an uncomfortable way, were the large crawling, running insects—crickets, beetles, and others. They were shapely and black and polished, and ran about here and there on the floor, just like intelligent little horseless carriages; then they would pause with their immovable eyes fixed on me, seeing, or in some mysterious way divining my presence; their pliant horns waving up and down, like delicate instruments used to test the air. Centipedes and millipedes in dozens came too, and were not welcome. I feared not their venom, but it was a weariness to see them; for they seemed no living things, but the vertebræ of snakes and eels and long slim fishes, dead and desiccated, made to move mechanically over walls and floor by some jugglery. I grew skilful at picking them up with a pair of pliant green twigs, to thrust them forth into the outer darkness.

One night a moth fluttered in and alighted on my

hand as I sat by the fire, causing me to hold my breath as I gazed on it. Its forewings were pale grey, with shadings dark and light written all over in finest characters with some twilight mystery or legend; but the round underwings were clear amber-yellow, veined like a leaf with red and purple veins; a thing of such exquisite chaste beauty that the sight of it gave me a sudden shock of pleasure. Very soon it flew up circling about, and finally lighted on the palm-leaf thatch directly over the fire. The heat, I thought, would soon drive it from the spot; and, rising, I opened the door, so that it might find its way out again into its own cool, dark, flowery world. And standing by the open door I turned and addressed it: "O night-wanderer of the pale, beautiful wings, go forth, and should you by chance meet her somewhere in the shadowy depths, revisiting her old haunts, be my messenger——" Thus much had I spoken, when the frail thing loosened its hold to fall without a flutter, straight and swift, into the white blaze beneath. I sprang forward with a shriek, and stood staring into the fire, my whole frame trembling with a sudden, terrible emotion. Even thus had Rima fallen—fallen from the great height—into the flames that instantly consumed her beautiful flesh and bright spirit! O cruel Nature!

A moth that perished in the flame; an indistinct faint sound; a dream in the night; the semblance of a shadowy form moving mist-like in the twilight gloom of the forest, would suddenly bring back a vivid mem-

ory, the old anguish, to break for a while the calm of
that period. It was calm then after the storm. Nevertheless, my health deteriorated. I ate little and slept
little and grew thin and weak. When I looked down
on the dark, glassy forest pool, where Rima would
look no more to see herself so much better than in the
small mirror of her lover's pupil, it showed me a
gaunt, ragged man with a tangled mass of black hair
falling over his shoulders, the bones of his face showing through the dead-looking, sun-parched skin, the
sunken eyes with a gleam in them that was like insanity.

To see this reflection had a strangely disturbing
effect on me. A torturing voice would whisper in my
ear: "Yes, you are evidently going mad. By-and-by you
will rush howling through the forest, only to drop
down at last and die: and no person will ever find and
bury *your* bones. Old Nuflo was more fortunate in
that he perished first."

"A lying voice!" I retorted in sudden anger. "My
faculties were never keener than now. Not a fruit can
ripen but I find it. If a small bird darts by with a
feather or straw in its bill I mark its flight, and it will
be a lucky bird if I do not find its nest in the end.
Could a savage born in the forest do more? He would
starve where I find food!"

"Ah, yes, there is nothing wonderful in that," answered the voice. "The stranger from a cold country
suffers less from the heat, when days are hottest, than

the Indian who knows no other climate. But mark the result! The stranger dies, while the Indian, sweating and gasping for breath, survives. In like manner the low-minded savage, cut off from all human fellowship, keeps his faculties to the end, while your finer brain proves your ruin."

I cut from a tree a score of long, blunt thorns, tough and black as whalebone, and drove them through a strip of wood in which I had burnt a row of holes to receive them, and made myself a comb, and combed out my long, tangled hair to improve my appearance.

"It is not the tangled condition of your hair," persisted the voice, "but your eyes, so wild and strange in their expression, that show the approach of madness. Make your locks as smooth as you like, and add a garland of those scarlet, star-shaped blossoms hanging from the bush behind you—crown yourself as you crowned old Cla-cla—but the crazed look will remain just the same."

And being no longer able to reply, rage and desperation drove me to an act which only seemed to prove that the hateful voice had prophesied truly. Taking up a stone I hurled it down on the water to shatter the image I saw there, as if it had been no faithful reflection of myself, but a travesty, cunningly made of enamelled clay or some other material, and put there by some malicious enemy to mock me.

➢ 21 ➢

MANY DAYS had passed since the hut was made—how many may not be known, since I notched no stick and knotted no cord—yet never in my rambles in the wood had I seen that desolate ash-heap where the fire had done its work. Nor had I looked for it. On the contrary, my wish was never to see it, and the fear of coming accidentally upon it made me keep to the old familiar paths. But at length, one night, while thinking of Rima's fearful end, it all at once occurred to me that the hated savage, whose blood I had shed on the white savannah, might have only been practising his natural deceit when he told me that most pitiful story. If that were so—if he had been prepared with a fictitious account of her death to meet my questions —then Rima might still exist: lost, perhaps, wandering in some distant place, exposed to perils day and night, and unable to find her way back, but living still! Living! her heart on fire with the hope of reunion with me, cautiously threading her way through the undergrowth of immeasurable forests; spying out the distant villages and hiding herself from the sight of all men, as she knew so well how to hide; studying the outlines of distant mountains, to recognise some familiar landmark at last, and so find her way back to the old wood once more! Even now, while I sat there idly musing, she might be somewhere in the wood—somewhere near me; but after so long an absence full of apprehension, waiting in concealment for what tomorrow's light might show.

I started up and replenished the fire with trembling hands, then set the door open to let the welcoming radiance stream out into the wood. But Rima had done more; going out into the black forest in the pitiless storm, she had found and led me home. Could I do less! I was quickly out in the shadows of the wood. Surely it was more than a mere hope that made my heart beat so wildly! How could a sensation so strangely sudden, so irresistible in its power, possess me unless she was living and near? Can it be, can it be that we shall meet again? To look again into your divine eyes—to hold you again in my arms at last! I so changed—so different! But the old love remains; and of all that has happened in your absence I shall tell you nothing—not one word; all shall be forgotten now—sufferings, madness, crime, remorse! Nothing shall ever vex you again—not Nuflo, who vexed you every day; for he is dead now—murdered, only I shall not say that—and I have decently buried his poor old sinful bones. We alone together in the wood—*our* wood now! The sweet old days again; for I know that you would not have it different, nor would I.

Thus I talked to myself, mad with the thoughts of the joy that would soon be mine; and at intervals I stood still and made the forest echo with my calls. "Rima! Rima!" I called again and again, and waited for some response; and heard only the familiar night-sounds—voices of insect and bird and tinkling tree-frog, and a low murmur in the topmost foliage, moved by some light breath of wind unfelt below. I was drenched with dew, bruised and bleeding from falls in the dark, and from rocks and thorns and rough branches, but had felt nothing: gradually the excitement burned itself out; I was hoarse with shouting and ready to drop down with fatigue, and hope was dead: and at length I crept back to my hut, to cast myself on my grass bed and sink into a dull, miserable, desponding stupor.

But on the following morning I was out once more, determined to search the forest well; since, if no evidence of the great fire Kua-kó had described to me existed, it would still be possible to believe that he had lied to me, and that Rima lived. I searched all day and found nothing; but the area was large, and to search it thoroughly would require several days.

On the third day I discovered the fatal spot, and knew that never again would I behold Rima in the flesh, that my last hope had indeed been a vain one. There could be no mistake: just such an open place as the Indian had pictured to me was here, with giant trees standing apart; while one tree stood killed and blackened by fire, surrounded by a huge heap, sixty or seventy yards across, of prostrate charred tree-trunks and ashes. Here and there slender plants had sprung up through the ashes, and the omnipresent small-leaved creepers were beginning to throw their pale green embroidery over the blackened trunks. I looked long at the vast funeral tree that had a buttressed girth of not less than fifty feet, and rose straight as a ship's mast, with its top about a hundred and fifty feet from the earth. What a distance to fall, through burning leaves and smoke, like a white bird shot dead with a poisoned arrow, swift and straight into that sea of flame below! How cruel imagination was to turn that desolate ash-heap, in spite of feathery foliage and embroidery of creepers, into roaring leaping flames again—to bring those dead savages back, men, women, and children—even the little ones I had played with—to set them yelling around me, "Burn! burn!" Oh, no, this damnable spot must not be her last resting place! If the fire had not utterly consumed her, bones as well as sweet tender flesh, shrivelling her like a frail white-winged moth into the finest white ashes, mixed inseparably with the ashes of stems and leaves innumerable, then whatever remained of her must be conveyed elsewhere to be with me, to mingle with my ashes at last.

Having resolved to sift and examine the entire heap, I at once set about my task. If she had climbed into the central highest branch, and had fallen straight, then she would have dropped into the flames not far from the roots; and so to begin I made a path to the trunk, and when darkness overtook me I had worked all round the tree, in a width of three to four yards, without discovering any remains. At noon on the following day I found the skeleton, or, at all events, the larger bones, rendered so fragile by the fierce heat they had been subjected to, that they fell to pieces when handled. But I was careful—how careful!—to save these last sacred relics, all that was now left of Rima!—kissing each white fragment as I lifted it, and gathering them all in my old frayed cloak, spread out to receive them. And when I had recovered them all, even to the smallest, I took my treasure home.

Another storm had shaken my soul, and had been succeeded by a second calm, which was more complete and promised to be more enduring than the first. But it was no lethargic calm; my brain was more active than ever; and by-and-by it found a work for my hands to do, of such a character as to distinguish me from all other forest hermits, fugitives from their fellows, in that savage land. The calcined bones I had rescued were kept in one of the big, rudely shaped, half-burnt earthen jars, which Nuflo had used for storing grain and other food-stuff. It was of a wood-ash colour; and after I had given up my search for the peculiar fine clay he had used in its manufacture—for it had been in my mind to make a more shapely funeral urn myself—I set to work to ornament its surface. A portion of each day was given to this artistic labour; and when the surface was covered with a pattern of thorny stems, and a trailing creeper with curving leaf and twining tendril, and pendent bud and blossom, I gave it colour. Purples and black only were used, obtained from the juices of some deeply coloured berries; and when a tint, or shade, or line failed to satisfy me I erased it, to do it again; and this so often that I never completed my work. I might, in the proudly modest spirit of the old sculptors, have inscribed on the vase the words, *Abel was doing this.* For was not my ideal beautiful like theirs, and the best that my art could do only an imperfect copy—a rude sketch? A serpent was represented wound round the lower portion of the jar, dull-hued, with a chain of irregular black spots or blotches extending along its body: and if any person had curiously examined these spots he would have discovered that every other one was a rudely shaped letter, and that the letters, by being properly divided, made the following words:—

GREEN MANSIONS

Sin vos y sin dios y mi.

Words that to some might seem wild, even insane in
their extravagance, sung by some ancient forgotten
poet; or possibly the motto of some love-sick knight-
errant, whose passion was consumed to ashes long
centuries ago. But not wild nor insane to me, dwelling
alone on a vast stony plain in everlasting twilight,
where there was no motion, nor any sound; but all
things, even trees, ferns, and grasses, were stone. And
in that place I had sat for many a thousand years,
drawn up and motionless, with stony fingers clasped
round my legs, and forehead resting on my knees;
and there would I sit, unmoving, immovable, for
many a thousand years to come—I, no longer I, in a
universe where *she* was not, and God was not.

The days went by, and to others grouped themselves into weeks and months; to me they were only
days—not Saturday, Sunday, Monday, but nameless.
They were so many and their sum so great, that all
my previous life, all the years I had existed before this
solitary time, now looked like a small island immeasurably far away, scarcely discernible, in the midst of
that endless desolate waste of nameless days.

My stock of provisions had been so long consumed
that I had forgotten the flavour of pulse and maize
and pumpkins and purple and sweet potatoes. For
Nuflo's cultivated patch had been destroyed by the
savages—not a stem, not a root had they left: and I,
like the sorrowful man that broods on his sorrow and

the artist who thinks only of his art, had been improvident, and had consumed the seed without putting a portion into the ground. Only wild food, and too little of that, found with much seeking and got with many hurts. Birds screamed at and scolded me; branches bruised and thorns scratched me; and still worse were the angry clouds of waspish things no bigger than flies. Buzz—buzz! Sting—sting! A serpent's tooth had failed to kill me; little do I care for your small drops of fiery venom so that I get at the spoil—grubs and honey. My white bread and purple wine! Once my soul hungered after knowledge; I took delight in fine thoughts finely expressed; I sought them carefully in printed books: now only this vile bodily hunger, this eager seeking for grubs and honey, and ignoble war with little things!

A bad hunter I proved after larger game. Bird and beast despised my snares, which took me so many waking hours at night to invent, so many daylight hours to make. Once, seeing a troop of monkeys high up in the tall trees, I followed and watched them for a long time, thinking how royally I should feast if by some strange unheard-of accident one were to fall disabled to the ground and be at my mercy. But nothing impossible happened, and I had no meat. What meat did I ever have except an occasional fledgling, killed in its cradle, or a lizard, or small tree-frog detected, in spite of its green colour, among the foliage? I would roast the little green minstrel on the coals. Why not? Why should he live to tinkle on his mandolin and clash his airy cymbals with no appreciative ear to listen? Once I had a different and strange kind of meat; but the starved stomach is not squeamish. I found a serpent coiled up in my way in a small glade, and arming myself with a long stick, I roused him from his siesta, and slew him without mercy. Rima was not there to pluck the rage from my heart and save his evil life. No coral snake this, with slim, tapering body, ringed like a wasp with brilliant colour; but thick and blunt, with lurid scales, blotched with black; also a broad, flat, murderous head, with stony, ice-like, whity-blue eyes, cold enough to freeze a victim's blood in its veins and make it sit still, like some wide-eyed creature carved in stone, waiting for the sharp, inevitable stroke—so swift at last, so long in coming. "O abominable flat head, with icy-cold, human-like, fiend-like eyes, I shall cut you off and throw you away!" And away I flung it, far enough in all conscience; yet I walked home troubled with a fancy that somewhere, somewhere down on the black, wet soil where it had fallen, through all that dense, thorny tangle and millions of screening leaves, the white, lidless, living eyes were following me still, and would always be following me in all my goings and comings and windings about in the forest. And what wonder? For were we not alone together in this dreadful solitude, I and the serpent, eaters of the dust, singled out and cursed above all cattle? *He* would not have bitten me, and I—faithless cannibal!—had murdered him. That cursed fancy would live on, worming itself into every crevice of my mind; the severed head would grow and grow in the night-time to something monstrous at last, the hellish white lidless eyes increasing to the size of two full moons. "Murderer! murderer!" they would say; "first a murderer of your own fellow-creatures—that was a small crime; but God, our enemy, had made them in His image, and he cursed you; and we two were together, alone and apart—you and I, murderer! you and I, murderer!"

I tried to escape the tyrannous fancy by thinking of other things and by making light of it. "The starved, bloodless brain," I said, "has strange thoughts." I fell to studying the dark, thick, blunt body in my hands; I noticed that the livid, rudely blotched, scaly surface showed in some lights a lovely play of prismatic colours. And growing poetical, I said, "When the wild west wind broke up the rainbow on the flying grey cloud and scattered it over the earth, a fragment doubtless fell on this reptile to give it that tender celestial tint. For thus it is Nature loves all her children, and gives to each some beauty, little or much; only to me, her hated stepchild, she gives no beauty, no grace. But stay, am I not wronging her? Did not Rima, beautiful above all things, love me well? said she not that I was beautiful?"

"Ah, yes, that was long ago," spoke the voice that

mocked me by the pool when I combed out my tangled hair. "Long ago, when the soul that looked from your eyes was not the accursed thing it is now. *Now* Rima would start at the sight of them; now she would fly in terror from their insane expression."

O spiteful voice, must you spoil even such appetite as I have for this fork-tongued spotty food? You by day and Rima by night—what shall I do—what shall I do?

For it had now come to this, that the end of each day brought not sleep and dreams, but waking visions. Night by night, from my dry grass bed I beheld Nuflo sitting in his old doubled-up posture, his big brown feet close to the white ashes—sitting silent and miserable. I pitied him; I owed him hospitality; but it seemed intolerable that he should be there. It was better to shut my eyes; for then Rima's arms would be round my neck; the silky mist of her hair against my face, her flowery breath mixing with my breath. What a luminous face was hers! Even with close-shut eyes I could see it vividly, the translucent skin showing the radiant rose beneath, the lustrous eyes, spiritual and passionate, dark as purple wine under their dark lashes. Then my eyes would open wide. No Rima in my arms! But over there, a little way back from the fire, just beyond where old Nuflo had sat brooding a few minutes ago, Rima would be standing, still and pale and unspeakably sad. Why does she come to me from the outside darkness to stand there talking to me, yet never once lifting her mournful eyes to mine? "Do not believe it, Abel; no, that was only a phantom of your brain, the What-I-was that you remember so well. For do you not see that when I come she fades away and is nothing? Not that—do not ask it. I know that I once refused to look into your eyes, and afterwards, in the cave at Riolama, I looked long and was happy—unspeakably happy! But now—oh, you do not know what you ask; you do not know the sorrow that has come into mine; that if you once beheld it for very sorrow you would die. And you must live. But I will wait patiently, and we shall be together in the end, and see each other without disguise. Nothing shall divide us. Only wish not for it soon; think not that death will ease your pain, and seek it not. Austerities? Good works? Prayers? They are not seen; they are not heard, they are less than nothing, and there is no intercession. I did not know it then, but you knew it. Your life was your own; you are not saved nor judged; acquit yourself—undo that which you have done, which Heaven cannot undo—and Heaven will say no word nor will I. You cannot, Abel, you cannot. That which you have done is done, and yours must be the penalty and the sorrow—yours and mine—yours and mine—yours and mine."

This, too, was a phantom, a Rima of the mind, one of the shapes the ever-changing black vapours of remorse and insanity would take; and all her mournful sentences were woven out of my own brain. I was not so crazed as not to know it; only a phantom, an illusion, yet more real than reality—real as my crime and vain remorse and death to come. It was, indeed, Rima returned to tell me that I that loved her had been more cruel to her than her cruelest enemies; for they had but tortured and destroyed her body with fire, while I had cast this shadow on her soul—this sorrow transcending all sorrows, darker than death, immitigable, eternal.

If only I could have faded gradually, painlessly, growing feebler in body and dimmer in my senses each day, to sink at last into sleep! But it could not be. Still the fever in my brain, the mocking voice by day, the phantoms by night; and at last I became convinced that unless I quitted the forest before long, death would come to me in some terrible shape. But in the feeble condition I was now in, and without any provisions, to escape from the neighbourhood of Parahuari was impossible, seeing that it was necessary at starting to avoid the villages where the Indians were of the same tribe as Runi, who would recognise me as the white man who was once his guest and afterwards his implacable enemy. I must wait, and in spite of a weakened body and a mind diseased, struggle still to wrest a scanty subsistence from wild nature.

One day I discovered an old prostrate tree, buried under a thick growth of creeper and fern, the wood of which was nearly or quite rotten, as I proved by thrusting my knife to the haft in it. No doubt it would contain grubs—those huge, white wood-borers which now formed an important item in my diet. On the following day I returned to the spot with a chopper and a bundle of wedges to split the trunk up, but had scarcely commenced operations when an animal, startled at my blows, rushed or rather wriggled from its hiding-place under the dead wood at a distance of a few yards from me. It was a robust, round-headed, short-legged creature, about as big as a good-sized cat, and clothed in a thick, greenish-brown fur. The ground all about was covered with creepers, binding the ferns, bushes, and old dead branches together; and in this confused tangle the animal scrambled and tore with a great show of energy, but really made very little progress; and all at once it flashed into my mind that it was a sloth—a common animal, but rarely seen on the ground—with no tree near to take refuge in. The shock of joy this discovery produced was great enough to unnerve me, and for some moments I stood trembling, hardly able to breathe; then recovering I hastened after it, and stunned it with a blow from my chopper on its round head.

"Poor sloth!" I said as I stood over it. "Poor old lazy-bones! Did Rima ever find you fast asleep in a tree, hugging a branch as if you loved it, and with her little hand pat your round, human-like head; and laugh mockingly at the astonishment in your drowsy, waking eyes; and scold you tenderly for wearing your nails so long, and for being so ugly? Lazy-bones, your death is revenged! O to be out of this wood—away from this sacred place—to be anywhere where killing is not murder!"

Then it came into my mind that I was now in possession of the supply of food which would enable me to quit the wood. A noble capture! As much to me as if a stray, migratory mule had rambled into the wood and found me, and I him. Now I would be my own mule, patient, and long-suffering, and far-going, with naked feet hardened to hoofs, and a pack of provender on my back to make me independent of the dry, bitter grass on the sunburnt savannahs.

Part of that night and the next morning was spent in curing the flesh over a smoky fire of green wood and in manufacturing a rough sack to store it in, for I had resolved to set out on my journey. How safely to convey Rima's treasured ashes was a subject of much thought and anxiety. The clay vessel on which I had expended so much loving, sorrowful labour had to be left, being too large and heavy to carry; eventually I put the fragments into a light sack; and in order to avert suspicion from the people I would meet on the way, above the ashes I packed a layer of roots and bulbs. These I would say contained medicinal properties, known to the white doctors, to whom I would sell them on my arrival at a Christian settlement, and with the money buy myself clothes to start life afresh.

On the morrow I would bid a last farewell to that

forest of many memories. And my journey would be eastwards, over a wild savage land of mountains, rivers, and forests, where every dozen miles would be like a hundred of Europe; but a land inhabited by tribes not unfriendly to the stranger. And perhaps it would be my good fortune to meet with Indians travelling east, who would know the easiest routes; and from time to time some compassionate voyager would let me share his wood-skin, and many leagues would be got over without weariness, until some great river, flowing through British or Dutch Guiana, would be reached; and so on, and on, by slow or swift stages, with little to eat perhaps, with much labour and pain, in hot sun and in storm, to the Atlantic at last, and towns inhabited by Christian men.

In the evening of that day, after completing my preparations, I supped on the remaining portions of the sloth, not suitable for preservation, roasting bits of fat on the coals and boiling the head and bones into a broth; and after swallowing the liquid I crunched the bones and sucked the marrow, feeding like some hungry carnivorous animal.

Glancing at the fragments scattered on the floor, I remembered old Nuflo, and how I had surprised him at his feast of rank coatimundi in his secret retreat. "Nuflo, old neighbour," said I, "how quiet you are under your green coverlet, spangled just now with yellow flowers! It is no sham sleep, old man, I know. If any suspicion of these curious doings, this feast of

flesh on a spot once sacred, could flit like a small
moth into your mouldy hollow skull, you would soon
thrust out your old nose to sniff the savour of roasting
fat once more."

There was in me at that moment an inclination
to laughter: it came to nothing, but affected me
strangely, like an impulse I had not experienced since
boyhood—familiar, yet novel. After the good-night to
my neighbour, I tumbled into my straw and slept
soundly, animal-like. No fancies and phantoms that
night: the lidless, white, implacable eyes of the serpent's severed head were turned to dust at last: no
sudden dream-glare lighted up old Cla-cla's wrinkled
dead face and white, blood-dabbled locks: old Nuflo
stayed beneath his green coverlet; nor did my mournful spirit-bride come to me to make my heart faint
at the thought of immortality.

But when morning dawned again it was bitter to
rise up and go away for ever from that spot where I
had often talked with Rima—the true and the visionary. The sky was cloudless and the forest wet as if
rain had fallen; it was only a heavy dew, and it made
the foliage look pale and hoary in the early light. And
the light grew, and a whispering wind sprang as I
walked through the wood; and the fast-evaporating
moisture was like a bloom on the feathery fronds and
grass and rank herbage; but on the higher foliage it
was like a faint iridescent mist—a glory above the
trees. The everlasting beauty and freshness of nature

was over all again, as I had so often seen it with joy and adoration before grief and dreadful passions had dimmed my vision. And now as I walked, murmuring my last farewell, my eyes grew dim again with the tears that gathered to them.

✺ 22 ✺

Before that well-nigh hopeless journey to the coast was half over I became ill—so ill that anyone who had looked on me might well have imagined that I had come to the end of my pilgrimage. That was what I feared. For days I remained sunk in the deepest despondence; then, in a happy moment, I remembered how, after being bitten by the serpent, when death had seemed near and inevitable, I had madly rushed away through the forest in search of help, and wandered lost for hours in the storm and darkness, and in the end escaped death, probably by means of these frantic exertions. The recollection served to inspire me with a new desperate courage. Bidding good-bye to the Indian village where the fever had smitten me, I set out once more on that apparently hopeless adventure. Hopeless, indeed, it seemed to one in my weak condition. My legs trembled under me when I walked, while hot sun and pelting rain were like flame and stinging ice to my morbidly sensitive skin.

For many days my sufferings were excessive, so that I often wished myself back in that milder purgatory of the forest, from which I had been so anxious to escape. When I try to retrace my route on the map there occurs a break here—a space on the chart where names of rivers and mountains call up no image to my mind, although, in a few cases, they were names I seem to have heard in a troubled dream. The impressions of nature received during that sick period are blurred, or else so coloured and exaggerated by perpetual torturing anxiety, mixed with half-delirious night-fancies, that I can only think of that country as an earthly inferno, where I fought against every imaginable obstacle, alternately sweating and freezing, toiling as no man ever toiled before. Hot and cold, cold and hot, and no medium. Crystal waters; green shadows under coverture of broad, moist leaves; and night with dewy fanning winds—these chilled but did not refresh me; a region in which there was no sweet and pleasant thing; where even the Ita palm and mountain glory and airy epiphyte starring the woodland twilight with pendent blossoms had lost all grace and beauty; where all brilliant colours in earth and heaven were like the unmitigated sun that blinded my sight and burnt my brain. Doubtless I

met with help from the natives, otherwise I do not
see how I could have continued my journey: yet, in
my dim mental picture of that period I see myself
incessantly dogged by hostile savages. They flit like
ghosts through the dark forest; they surround me and
cut off all retreat, until I burst through them, escaping out of their very hands, to fly over some wide,
naked savannah, hearing their shrill, pursuing yells
behind me, and feeling the sting of their poisoned
arrows in my flesh.

This I set down to the workings of remorse in a disordered mind and to clouds of venomous insects perpetually shrilling in my ears and stabbing me with
their small, fiery needles.

Not only was I pursued by phantom savages and
pierced by phantom arrows, but the creations of the
Indian imagination had now become as real to me as
anything in nature. I was persecuted by that superhuman man-eating monster supposed to be the guardian of the forest. In dark, silent places he is lying in
wait for me: hearing my slow, uncertain footsteps he
starts up suddenly in my path, out-yelling the bearded
aguaratos in the trees; and I stand paralysed, my
blood curdled in my veins. His huge, hairy arms are
round me; his foul, hot breath is on my skin; he will
tear my liver out with his great green teeth to satisfy
his raging hunger. Ah, no, he cannot harm me! For
every ravening beast, every cold-blooded, venomous
thing, and even the frightful Curupitá, half brute and

half devil, that shared the forest with her, loved and worshipped Rima, and that mournful burden I carried, her ashes, was a talisman to save me. He has left me, the semi-human monster, uttering such wild, lamentable cries as he hurries away into the deeper, darker woods, that horror changes to grief, and I, too, lament Rima for the first time: a memory of all the mystic, unimaginable grace and loveliness and joy that had vanished smites on my heart with such sudden, intense pain that I cast myself prone on the earth and weep tears that are like drops of blood.

Where, in the rude savage heart of Guiana was this region where the natural obstacles and pain and hunger and thirst and everlasting weariness were terrible enough without the imaginary monsters and legions of phantoms that peopled it, I cannot say. Nor can I conjecture how far I strayed north or south from my course. I only know that marshes that were like Sloughs of Despond, and barren and wet savannahs, were crossed; and forests that seemed infinite in extent and never to be got through; and scores of rivers that boiled round the sharp rocks, threatening to submerge or dash in pieces the frail bark canoe—black and frightful to look on as rivers in hell; and nameless mountain after mountain to be toiled round or toiled over. I may have seen Roraima during that mentally clouded period. I vaguely remember a far-extending gigantic wall of stone that seemed to bar all further progress—a rocky precipice rising to a stupendous height, seen by moonlight, with a huge sinuous rope of white mist suspended from its summit; as if the guardian camoodi of the mountain had been a league-long spectral serpent which was now dropping its coils from the mighty stone table to frighten away the rash intruder.

That spectral moonlight camoodi was one of many serpent fancies that troubled me. There was another, surpassing them all, which attended me many days. When the sun grew hot overhead and the way was over open savannah country I would see something moving on the ground at my side and always keeping abreast of me. A small snake, one or two feet long. No, not a small snake, but a sinuous mark in the pattern on a huge serpent's head, five or six yards long, always moving deliberately at my side. If a cloud came over the sun, or a fresh breeze sprang up, gradually the outline of that awful head would fade and the well-defined pattern would resolve itself into the mottlings on the earth. But if the sun grew more and more hot and dazzling as the day progressed, then the tremendous ophidian head would become increasingly real to my sight, with glistening scales and symmetrical markings; and I would walk carefully not to stumble against or touch it; and when I cast my eyes behind me I could see no end to its great coils extending across the savannah. Even looking back from the summit of a high hill I could see it stretching leagues and leagues away through forests and rivers, across wide plains, valleys and mountains, to lose itself at last in the infinite blue distance.

How or when this monster left me—washed away by cold rains perhaps—I do not know. Probably it only transformed itself into some new shape, its long coils perhaps changing into those endless processions and multitudes of pale-faced people I seem to remember having encountered. In my devious wanderings I must have reached the shores of the undiscovered great White Lake, and passed through the long shining streets of Manoa, the mysterious city in the wilderness. I see myself there, the wide thoroughfare filled from end to end with people, gaily dressed as if for some high festival, all drawing aside to let the wretched pilgrim pass, staring at his fever- and famine-wasted figure, in its strange rags, with its strange burden.

A new Ahasuerus, cursed by inexpiable crime, yet sustained by a great purpose.

But Ahasuerus prayed ever for death to come to him and ran to meet it, while I fought against it with all my little strength. Only at intervals, when the shadows seemed to lift and give me relief, would I pray to Death to spare me yet a little longer; but when the shadows darkened again and hope seemed almost quenched in utter gloom, then I would curse it and defy its power.

Through it all I clung to the belief that my will would conquer, that it would enable me to keep off the great enemy from my worn and suffering body until the wished goal was reached; then only would I cease to fight and let death have its way. There would have been comfort in this belief had it not been for that fevered imagination which corrupted everything that touched me and gave it some new hateful character. For soon enough this conviction that the will would triumph grew to something monstrous, a parent of monstrous fancies. Worst of all, when I felt no actual pain, but only unutterable weariness of body and soul, when feet and legs were numb so that I knew not whether I trod on dry hot rock or in slime, was the fancy that I was already dead, so far as the body was concerned—had perhaps been dead for days —that only the unconquerable will survived to compel the dead flesh to do its work.

Whether it really was will—more potent than the bark of barks and wiser than the physicians—or merely the *vis medicatrix* with which nature helps our weakness even when the will is suspended, that saved me I cannot say; but it is certain that I gradually recovered health, physical and mental, and finally reached the coast comparatively well, although my mind was still in a gloomy, desponding state when I first walked the streets of Georgetown, in rags, half-starved and penniless.

But even when well, long after the discovery that my flesh was not only alive, but that it was of an exceedingly tough quality, the idea born during the darkest period of my pilgrimage, that die I must, persisted in my mind. I had lived through that which would have killed most men—lived only to accomplish the one remaining purpose of my life. Now it was accomplished; the sacred ashes brought so far, with such infinite labour, through so many and such great perils, were safe and would mix with mine at last. There was nothing more in life to make me love it or keep me prisoner in its weary chains. This prospect of near death faded in time; love of life returned, and the earth had recovered its everlasting freshness and beauty: only that feeling about Rima's ashes did not fade or change, and is as strong now as it was then. Say that it is morbid—call it superstition if you like; but there it is, the most powerful motive I have known, always in all things to be taken into account— a philosophy of life to be made to fit it. Or take it as a symbol, since that may come to be one with the thing symbolised. In those darkest days in the forest I had her as a visitor—a Rima of the mind, whose words when she spoke reflected my despair. Yet even then I was not entirely without hope. Heaven itself, she said, could not undo that which I had done; and she also said if I forgave myself Heaven would say no word, nor would she. That is my philosophy still: prayers, austerities, good words—they avail nothing, and there is no intercession, and outside of the soul there is no forgiveness in heaven or earth for sin. Nevertheless there is a way, which every soul can find out for itself—even the most rebellious, the most darkened with crime and tormented by remorse. In that way I have walked; and, self-forgiven and self-absolved, I know that if she were to return once more and appear to me—even here where her ashes are—I know that her divine eyes would no longer refuse to look into mine, since the sorrow which seemed eternal and would have slain me to see would not now be in them.

THE END

By Lawrence Durrell

NOVELS
Monsieur
The Alexandria Quartet:
Justine, Balthazar, Mountolive, Clea
The Revolt of Aphrodite:
Tunc, Nunquam
The Black Book
The Dark Labyrinth

TRAVEL
The Greek Islands
Sicilian Carousel
Bitter Lemons
Reflections on a Marine Venus
Prospero's Cell

POETRY
Collected Poems
Selected Poems
Vega
The Ikons

DRAMA
Sappho

LETTERS AND ESSAYS
Spirit of Place (edited by Alan G. Thomas)
Lawrence Durrell and Henry Miller:
A Private Correspondence

HUMOUR
Stiff Upper Lip
Esprit de Corps
The Best of Antrobus

FOR YOUNG PEOPLE
White Eagles Over Serbia

LIVIA
or
BURIED ALIVE

LAWRENCE DURRELL

THE VIKING PRESS   NEW YORK

For Denis and Nanik de Rougemont

Published in 1979 by The Viking Press
625 Madison Avenue, New York, N.Y. 10022

LIBRARY OF CONGRESS CATALOGING IN PUBLICATION DATA
Durrell, Lawrence.
Livia : or, Buried alive.
I. Title.
PZ3.D9377Li   1979 [PR6007.U76]   823'.9'12   78-20796
ISBN 0-670-43447-7

Second Printing 1979

Printed in the United States of America
Set in Fournier

Contents

"In the name of the Dog the Father, Dog the Son, and Dog the Wholly Ghost, Amen. Here beginneth the second lesson."

━━◆━━

"Between the completely arbitrary and the completely determined perhaps there is a way?"

━━◆━━

"Five colours mixed make people blind."

Chinese Proverb

━━◆━━

A Certain Silence

WHEN THE NEWS OF TU'S DEATH REACHED BLANFORD he was actually living in her house in Sussex, watching the first winter snow fall out of a dark sky, amidst darker woods, which had long since engulfed an ochre sunset. "Actually", because his own version of the event will be slightly different, both for the sake of posterity and also on stylistic grounds. A deep armchair sheltered his back from the draughts which, despite the rippling oak fire burning in the grate, played about the old-fashioned, high-ceilinged room with its tapering musicians' gallery. His crutches lay beside him on the carpet. As he put down the swan-necked telephone he felt the knowledge boom inside him, as if in some great tropical conch – the bang of surf upon white beaches on the other side of the world. She would miss reading (the selfishness of writers!) all the new material he had added to his book – a novel about another novelist called Sutcliffe, who had become almost as real to him and to Tu as he, Blanford, was to himself. He took the handkerchief from his sleeve and dabbed his dry lips – dry from the eternal cigar he needed to bite on when he worked. Then he went swaying to the looking-glass over the bookcase and stared at himself for a good moment. The telephone-bell gave a smart trill and a click – long-distance calls always did this: like the last spurt of blood from an artery. The writer stared on, imagining that he was Tu looking back at him. So this is what she saw, what she had always seen! Eye to eye and mind to mind – this is how it had been with them. He suddenly realised that he was surrounded by the dead woman's books. Underlinings, annotations. She was still here!

He felt his image suddenly refreshed and recreated by her death – the new information was so terrifying, so hard to assimilate. Goodness, there was still so much they had to tell each other – and now all that remained was a mass of severed threads, the loose ends of unfinished conversation. From now on there would be nobody to whom he could really talk. He made a grimace and sighed. Well then, he must lock up all this passionate and enriching conversation in his skull. All morning he had played on the old pipe-organ, glad to find that his memory and his fingers still worked. There is nothing like music in an empty house. Then the telephone-bell. Now the thought of Tu. It is no use really – for once you die you slide into the ground and simply melt. For a while a few personal scraps hang around – like shoes and clothes and unused notepaper with abandoned phone numbers. As if suddenly one had had a hunger for greater simplicity.

Outside children chirped as they skated on the frozen lake. Stones skidded and twanged on the ice. How would his hero Sutcliffe take the news, he wondered? Should he make him whimper in the novel like some ghastly dog? Last night in bed he had read some pages of the Latin poet Tu most loved; it was like sleeping beside her. The phrase came to him: "The steady thudding of the Latin line echoes the thud of her heart. I hear her calm voice uttering the words." There were flies in the room, hatched by the heating. They seemed to be reading Braille. The treble voices outside were marginal. What good were books except to hive off regrets? His back ached all of a sudden – his spine seemed as stiff as a flagpole. He was an ageing war-hero with a spine full of lead.

He wished his own turn would come soon. From now on they could label him "Not Wanted On Voyage" or just "Unaccompanied Luggage" – and sling him into the hold, into the grave. In his mind he gave a great cry of loneliness, but no sound came. It was a shrill galactic cry of a solitary planet whirling through space. Tu had loved walking naked about the house in Italy, she had no sense of misdemeanour, reciting aloud the 16th Psalm. She said once, "It is terrible, but life is on nobody's side."

So the Sutcliffe he invented for his novel *Monsieur* shot himself through the mirror in the early version? "I had to," he explained, pointing to Blanford. "It was him or me." The writer Blanford suddenly felt like an enormously condensed version of a minor epic. Buried alive! The crutches hurt him under the arms. He groaned and swore as he dragged himself about the room.

❦

The consolations of art are precious few. He always had a sneaking fear that what he wrote was too private to reach a reader. Stilted and stunted, the modern product – meagre as spittle or sperm, the result of too rigorous pot-training by his mother who had a thirst for purity. The result was retention of faecal matter – a private prose and verse typical of the modern sphincterine artist. In ordinary life this basic refusal to co-operate with the universe, to surrender, to give, would in its final stage amount to catatonia! In the "acute" wards at Leatherhead they had one twilight catatonic who could be suspended by his coat-collar – suspended by a meat-hook and hung on a bar where he stayed, softly swinging in the foetal position. Like a bat, dreaming his amniotic dreams, lulled in the imaginary mother-fluid. It was all that was left of a once good poet. The whole of his life had been spent in creative constipation, a refusal to give, so now he went on living like this – a life in inverted comas, to coin a pun. Blanford reached out and touched the earlier manuscript of his book *Monsieur*. He had given it to Tu and she had had it

3

bound. He wondered where in his imagination, which was his real life, Sutcliffe might be – he would have liked to talk to him. Last heard of in Oxford, famous for his work on his friend's study of the Templar heresy. Blanford's last communication from him had been a cryptic postcard which said: "An Oxford don can be distinguished among all others by the retractable foreskin."

———◆———

He risked another thought of Tu again and suddenly felt as if he were running a temperature. Breathless, he rose and succeeded in unfastening the French window, to let in a cloud of snowflakes and a rush of cold air. Then, bending his head, he lurched out on to the lawn, watching his breath plume out before him. He rubbed a little snow on his temples with a theatrical gesture. Then he laboriously returned to his fireside seat and his thoughts.

Cade now sidled into the room with the tea things and set them down beside him without a word, his yellow puritanical face set in expressions of fervent concentration such as one only sees on the faces of very stupid but cunning people. He bore in his arms with a kind of meek pride the new orthopaedic waistcoat-brace which had at last arrived from the makers, tailored to size. There was a good hope that this contrivance might allow Blanford one day to throw away his crutches. He gave an exclamation of pleasure while Cade, expressionless as a mandarin, helped him off with the ancient tweed coat he so loved (with its leather-patched elbows) and locked him into the new garment of soft grey rubber and invisible steel. "Stand up, sir," he said at last, and the writer obeyed in smiling wonder; yes, he was free to walk slowly about, to navigate on his own two legs. It was miraculous. But at first he was only allowed to wear it for an hour a day to get his muscles used to its stresses. "A miracle," he said

4

aloud. Cade watched him attentively for a few moments and then, with a nod, turned away to his domestic duties while Blanford, feeling newly born, leaned against the chimney-piece, staring down at his fallen crutches. Cade would never know how much this new invention meant. The valet looked like the lower-class ferret he was. Blanford watched him curiously as he went over the room, emptying the ashtrays and refilling the saucer of water on the radiator, refilling the vase with its hothouse blooms. "Cade," he said, "Constance is dead." Cade nodded expressionlessly. "I know, sir. I was listening on the extension in the hall." That was all. That was Cade all over. His work done, he took himself off with his customary silence and stealth.

> Carbon into diamond
> Sand into pearl.

All process causes pain, and we are part of process. How chimerical the consolations of art against the central horror of death; being sucked down the great sink like an insect, into the *cloaca maxima* of death, the *anus mundi*! Sutcliffe, in writing about him, or rather, he writing about himself in the character of Sutcliffe, under the satirical name of Bloshford in the novel *Monsieur* had said somewhere: "Women to him were simply a commodity. He was not a fool about them; O no! He knew them inside out, or so he thought. That is to say he was worse than a fool."

Was this true of Constance or of Livia her sister, the writer wondered. The blonde girl and the dark. The girl with the velvet conundrum and the girl with beak of the swan?

> Grind grain, press wine,
> Break bread, yours mine,
> Take breath, face death.

Where had he seen these lines underlined by Constance in a book? At that moment the telephone seemed to thrill again, and he knew at once who it was – it could only be his invention Sutcliffe. He must have heard by telepathy the news about Constance (Tu). He realised now that he had been expecting this call all day.

He did not bother to utter the usual Hullo but immediately said to his *confrère*, his *semblable* and *frère:* "You have heard about Tu," and the voice of Sutcliffe, speaking through a heavy cold, and nervous with regret, replied: "My God, Blanford, what is to become of us?"

"We shall go on sitting about regretting our lack of talent; we shall go on trying to convince people. I am as grieved as you are, Robin, and I never thought I would be. I had so often thought of dying that I thought I had the hippogriff under control; yes, but of course like everyone I cheated in my mind by being the first to die. I suppose Constance did the same."

"You made my own life come to a halt when Pia died," said Sutcliffe both reproachfully and gravely, and then blew his nose loudly. "So I set up shop here for a while to completely rewrite Toby's book about the Templars – to apply a bit of gold leaf here and there, to give it such orotundity as befits a fuddled don. But now he is famous and I feel the need for a change, for a new landscape. Tobias has the Chair in History which he coveted. Why not the Sofa? He will live on in a conical dismay, lecturing loudly on the plasticity of pork to the new generation of druggie-thuggies." He chuckled, but mirthlessly. "What about me?" he said. "Have you nothing I could do short of entering the Trappe?" "You are dead, Robin," said Blanford. "Remember the end of *Monsieur?*" "Bring me back then," said Sutcliffe on a heroic note, "and we shall see."

"What happened to the great poem and the *Tu Quoque*

book?" asked Blanford sharply, and Sutcliffe answered: "I was waiting to get over Pia a bit before finishing it. It was cunning of you to make Pia a composite of Constance and Livia, but I never felt I could really achieve the portrait of her simply because I was blinded by love. I wasn't cruel enough. And I wondered about Trash, her black lover. I think your story is better than mine, probably sadder. I don't know. But the death of Tu, of poor Constance, should be celebrated in verse by an Elizabethan."

For some reason this irritated Blanford and he said with asperity, "Well, why not a poem called 'Sutcliffe's Salte Teares upon the tombe of Tu'?"

"Why not?" said his fellow writer, his bondsman, "or perhaps in seventeenth-century style, 'Sutcliffe's Big Boo-Hoo'."

"Poetry," said Blanford on a lower key, talking almost to himself, "which always comes with sadness; poetry, in the jumbo version of the supermarket, enough for a whole family. The economy size. Robby, you can't go on being cheerful in Oxford. Shall I send you to Italy?"

"Another book? Why not?" But Sutcliffe did not sound too sure. "I really think it's your turn to write one – and this time the true story of your love, our love, for Constance and indeed for Livia despite what she did to you, to us, to me. Would it hurt too much if you tried?" Of course it would. Good grief!

Blanford did not answer for a long moment. Then Sutcliffe said, in his old flippant vein: "Last spring I went to Paris with a girl somewhat like Pia-Constance-Livia. The word *archi* had come into vogue as a prefix to almost everything. Our own translation would be *super*, I suppose. Well, everything was *archi* this and *archi* that. I realised that one might describe me as *archicocu*, what? Indeed I went so far as to think of myself as absolutely *archicocuphosphorescent*."

"In a way I did tell the truth about us," said Blanford haltingly. "Livia carried me out of my depth. I had always needed a feather-simple girl; but Livia was only fit to have her tail spliced by a female octoroon. Damn!"

"Aha! but you loved her. We both did. But where you lied was to graft onto her some of the femininity of her sister. You made her a female quaire not a male." After a pause, during which both writers thought furiously about the book which Blanford had called *Monsieur* and Sutcliffe *The Prince of Darkness*, their faltering conversation was resumed. If lonely people have a right to talk to themselves couldn't a lonely author argue with one of his own creations – a fellow-writer, Blanford asked himself.

"A hunt for the larval forms of personality! Livia was, as far as I am concerned – " Sutcliffe gave a groan.

"A powder-monkey in Hell," said Blanford almost shouting with pain, because her beauty had really wounded him, driven him indeed mad with vexation.

"A dry water-hole," agreed Sutcliffe. "Who is Livia, what is she?"

> All our swains commend her.
>
> Perfection's ape, clad in a toga
> And beefed up by the shorter yoga
> A Cuvier of the sexual ploy
> You forged a girl out of a boy.
> You wielded flesh and bones and mind,
> She was attentive, tough but kind,
> Yet unbeknown, behind your back
> She sought the member that you lack.

"Enough, Robin," cried Blanford in a wave of regret and mind-sickness as he thought of the dark head of Livia on the pillow beside him. Sutcliffe laughed sardonically and tormented him with yet another improvisation.

I am loving beyond my means
I am living behind my moans!
O!
Tra la la! Tra la la!
Toi et moi et le chef de gare
Quel bazar, mais quel bazar!

Blanford supposed him to be right; for the story for him
could have begun in Geneva – on a sad Sunday in Geneva. It
was cold; and ill-assorted, straggly and over-gummy were the
bifurcated Swiss under a snow-moon. He closed his eyes the
better to hear the tumultuous chatter of stars, or dining
later at the Bavaria with her face occupying the centre of
his mind, he engulfed the victorious jujubes of mandatory
oysters. Ouf! What prose! *Nabokov, à moi!* In hotels their
lives were wallpapered with sighs. Then tomorrow on the
lake, the white stairways to heaven splashed with a wrinkled
sunshine. "My sister Livia arrives tomorrow from Venice.
She is anxious to meet you."

That was Constance, made for deep attachments as a
cello is made for music – the viol's deepness on certain notes,
in certain moods. It was ages before they had both realised
that the words which passed between them had a certain
specific density; they were registered and understood at a level
somewhere below that of just ordinary speech. The sisters
had just inherited the tumbledown chateau of Tu Duc (hence
the nickname for Constance). It was near the village of
Tubain in the Vaucluse. Not too far from the one city which,
above all others, held for him the greatest number of historic
memories.

Here, Sutcliffe interposed his clumsy presence on
Blanford's train of thought; sniffing and adjusting those
much repaired spectacles of his. "But Livia had what excited
you most – the sexual trigger in the blood; she deserved to be
commemorated in a style which we might call metarealism –

in her aspect of Osiris whose scattered limbs were distributed all over the Mediterranean. Enough of the pornocratic-whimsical, Blanford. For my part I was hunting for a prose line with more body – not paunch, mark you, but body, my boy."

"Remember, Rob," Blanford retorted, "that everything you write about me is deeply suspect – at the best highly arguable. I invented you, after all."

"Or I you, which? The chicken or the egg?"

"The truth of the matter is that we did not really know much about ourselves in those old days; how happy it made one just to squander our youth, lying about in the deep grass eating cherries. The velvet English summers of youth, deep grass, and the clock of cricket balls marking the slow hours of leisure between classes. The distant clapping when some-one struck a ball to the boundary merged with but did not drown the steady drizzle of crickets. We slept in the bosom of an eternal summer.

"Tu once said that nature cured her own fertility imbalances by forcing sterile loves up on – illicit in the biological sense. Of what avail our belief in freewill? For her we were sleepwalkers caught in the current of an irresistible sexuality." He said aloud: "Poor enough consolation for the cowardly Robin Sutcliffe, sitting in that sordid house, drinking his way towards his goal – the leap from the bridge. His Charon was the twisted black woman with the crow's beak, who could procure something for every taste."

"I suppose so," said Rob with a sigh. "The bandages, the whip, the handcuffs – I should have put more of that into the book, instead of leaving it for you. She let her dirty rooms out by the hour. I came there hunting for Pia, just as you came in your turn hunting for Livia and found her in bed with that little hunchback with the pistachio eyes."

Blanford winced; he remembered the cracked bronchial

laugh, gushing out amidst cigarette smoke and coughing. She had said of Livia: *"Une fille qui drague les hommes et saut les gouines."* He had struck her across the face with his string gloves. He said to Sutcliffe sternly: "It is your duty to demonstrate how Livia was tailored down to the sad size of Pia."

"Pia dolorosa," said Sutcliffe. "It would be more than one book, then?"

"Well, squinting round the curves of futurity I saw something like a quincunx of novels set out in a good classical order. Five Q novels written in a highly elliptical quincunxial style invented for the occasion. Though only dependent on one another as echoes might be, they would not be laid end to end in serial order, like dominoes – but simply belong to the same blood group, five panels for which your creaky old *Monsieur* would provide simply a cluster of themes to be reworked in the others. Get busy, Robin!"

"And the relation of form to content?"

"The books would be roped together like climbers on a rockface, but they would all be independent. The relation of the caterpillar to the butterfly, the tadpole to the frog. An organic relation."

Sutcliffe groaned and said: "The old danger is there – a work weighed down with theoretical considerations."

"No. Never. Not on your life. Just a *roman-gigogne*."

"The more desperate the writer the more truthful the music – or so I believed then. Now I don't know. I wonder a great deal about wrongdoing in art, in a way I never did before."

"My dear old Rob, crime gives a wonderful sheen to the skin. The sap rises, the sex blooms in secrecy like some tropical plant. Take an example from me."

All that snowy day Blanford went on talking to his creation, trying to explain himself, to justify his feelings and his thoughts. He was trying to sum it all up – from the point of view of death.

"From the ambush of my disability I watched and noted, hungry for disbelief. I watched my Livia coming and going in the mirror. I watched her walking about Venice from my high balcony, and I saw the woman who was spying on her at my request – for rather a stiff price. Livia was always looking back over her shoulder to see if she was being followed – clever, slender, nervous, and very caryatid, she had won my heart by her effortless sensuality. What a marvellous death-mask that dark face would make – ascetic, heart-shaped and pale. The way the lips and hands trembled when she became passionate.

"My God, what a muddle – it was Constance I really loved. She could have been my second skin. What a strange phrase, 'The rest of my life'. What does it mean? Surely that little rest – the steady diminishing of time – begins at birth? When you discovered you had married a homosexual what did you do, Robin?"

"The foolish fellow put a pistol to his brow."

"Even a writer must be truthful to decay. You burst out laughing first – the predicament was so foolish."

"But worse still, I really loved her, Pia," said Sutcliffe. "It was an unlucky dishonour forced upon me. But have you lived with one? They burn up your oxygen, being maladapted and out of true. They remove the classical pity which love engenders. The sadness which amends. And their beauty is like a spear, Blanford."

"Like a spear, my boy, like a spear."

"In Regent Street, in a sordid pub, a woman I had never regarded as being in any way intuitive listened attentively to my moans and said, 'Someone has wounded you very deeply and for utterly frivolous reasons. You should try to laugh and tell yourself that one is always punished for insincerity.' Damn her eyes!"

"She was right. But she had never seen Livia at bay, with flashing eyes, lying for dear life – you see, she could not bear it really, her inversion. She wouldn't admit it to anyone. With her back to the wall she fenced desperately. Tied to the wheel in the sinking vessel of her self-esteem – as who is not? – she foundered in my arms. I had had her closely watched for a little while when one day ... my servant Cade had to return to England for his mother's funeral and during his absence I moved into the Lutèce on a narrow street; there I sat at evening watching the dusk fall, and the lights spring up over the canals. The street was so narrow that the balconies opposite were almost touching ours, or so it seemed. Three floors up, Lord Galen sat reading the *Financial Times*, full of the sense of his oneliness. I joined him for a cocktail and there, standing on his balcony, I looked across the street and saw the light snap on in a dark room opposite. Two women were just waking from their siesta – yawning and stretching. One rose and came to the balcony to thrust the shutters wide. As she did so the mouse raised her face and her eyes met mine. It was my spy, naked, and behind her in the rumpled bed Livia was drowsing, her fingers on her sex, dreaming – as if fingering a violin one is about to play. Her eyes half-closed, she was presumably riffling through the portfolio of her phantasy life. She had evidently seduced my spy! It was all over in a second. The girl retired, and so did I. Furious and thunderstruck, I said nothing to the old banker, who was particularly worried about the state of copper that day – he had once looked after some of my mother's modest investments for her and was never free from the delicious anal gnawing of money."

Sutcliffe: "So you were crushed with fury, and went

down to the bar; the porter gave you a fat envelope full of marvellous press cuttings, fulsome ones, interviews and pictures. I have always wanted to question you a little about them. For example, you are reported as saying 'I have never sought fame and fortune in my work. I sought happiness.' "

"Yes, I did say that. I thought that."

"And happiness, have you found it?" Sutcliffe put on the adenoidal voice of an interviewer.

"You find it only when you stop looking, Rob."

"And have you?"

"No."

"Why not?"

"Now that would be worth answering but I don't for the life of me know how to."

"I thought not. When you got back to the flat later you played on the little harmonium a whole grisly toccata."

"Yes, the background music for a nervous breakdown. And I reflected on all the psychoanalytic twaddle about our oceanic sexual drives. And in my manly agony I cried out, 'O God, my God, why didst Thou let me marry a Principal Boy?' When Livia slept with me who was she really loving in her imagination, in her phantasy? Who was my rival, the dark lady of the sonnets? And how could I find out? She had carefully masked her batteries. Once set off by the hair-trigger of a simple kiss she turned her face to this veiled form and used me as the *machine à plaisir*."

"And yet she was full of ideals, Livia."

"All ideals are unattainable – that is what makes them worth having. You have to reach for the apple. If you wait until it falls you will be disappointed – you will realise that it is imaginary."

"The apple of gravity, Newton's wish?"

"Exactly. And besides, never forget how much in the dark we all were about our selves, our predilections, our ruling passions. It took a trip to Vienna with Constance to teach us just a very little."

"It resolved nothing, it only unsettled you to know the truth about your sexual predispositions."

"Perhaps; yet knowledge is a sort of exorcism. I am very grateful to Constance, who was the only one among us to read German and thus have direct access to what was being written in Vienna and Zurich; moreover despite the abandoned studies she was already a fine doctor. She explained Livia to me satisfactorily."

"To what avail?"

"To no avail; of course it wasn't enough, it never is, but it enabled me to sympathise with her, to understand many things, like, for example, her deliberate grubbiness at times – the revolt against her femininity, the desire to insult the male. Then always restless, always wanting to be on the move. Several times a day she had to walk down to the village because she had forgotten to buy this or that. It used to puzzle me, it seemed almost deliberate, and of course it was. As Constance said, she was simply a man-at-arms on the look-out for a pick-up! Surely this was valuable, all this information? Eh?"

Sutcliffe deliberated for a moment, and Blanford lit a cigar, saying: "Soon there will be nobody to talk to except you. It is extremely sad – what shall I do for company? You bore me so! It will probably lead to madness."

"We will write a book."

"Of what will it treat?"

"Of the perennity of despair, intractability of language, impenetrability of art, insipidity of human love."

"Livia and Constance, the two faces? Transposed heads!"

"The two faces. You see, Aubrey, the male invert loves his mother, the female hates hers implacably. That is why she won't bear children, or if she does, makes changelings or witches. What we thought we found was that Livia really loved her sister Constance – that is why she set out to marry you, to cut Constance out. She could not bear to think of you coming together."

"But Livia slept with many men."

"Of course, but it was with brave contempt, to prove her own maleness, her masculine superiority. A talented Chartreuse. She would run with her bleeding male scalps and show them to her girl friends. This was a way of advertising her wares. 'Look, this is all men are worth, so easily scalped!' "

"Alas, it was only too true." Sutcliffe fingered the little tonsured part of his own huge cranium where recently the baldness had begun to show through. "After Pia I had to buy a hairpiece," he admitted. "And specially after all this psychoanalytic gibberish. All I learned was that male lesbians are notoriously kind to dogs – but I am not a dog and don't qualify. Another question – was Jesus a lesbian?"

"Cut it out," said Blanford, "I can't bear idle blasphemy."

At this point Sutcliffe sang the little psychoanalytic song he had once made up to celebrate the great men of the science; it went

> Joy, Young and Frenzy,
> Frenzy, Groddeck and Joy.

He broke off and said suddenly: "*Et le bonheur?*"

"Exactly."

"It cannot be impossible to find. It must be knocking about somewhere, just out of sight. Why don't we write a big autobiography? Come on, punish everyone!"

"The last defence! All aboard for the last alibi!"

"What does a man say when his wife leaves him? He cries out in an agony of fury: 'Thrice-triturated gasometers!

Who will burn sugar to this tonsil-snipping tart?' "

"Or seek the consolations of art: the little choking yelp of Desdemona is pleasant to dwell upon."

"Or he will become a widow and in desperation take up with some furry housemaid who will in due course be delivered of some rhubarb-coloured mite."

"The Kismet for novelists with cook-housekeepers. But I have only Cade, and he can't cook. . . ."

The snow went on falling out in the park with its resigned elms full of rooks' nests. Blanford pondered heavily upon human nature and its uncapturable variety while Sutcliffe in his Oxford rooms turned and put a log on the fire. Toby was coming to lunch with a young girl undergraduate. Then he took up the phone once more and said, "The relationship between our books will be incestuous, then, I take it? They will be encysted in each other, not complementary. There would be room for everything, poem, autobiography, short story and so on."

"Yes," said his creator softly. "I suppose you have heard of that peculiar medical phenomenon called the teratoma? It is literally a bag full of unfinished spare parts – nails and hair and half-grown teeth – which is lodged like a benign growth somewhere in a human body. It is removed by surgery. It appears to be part of a twin which at some stage decided to stop growing. . . ."

"A short story lodged in a book?"

"Yes. Do you know at what point Pia began to love you? I bet you don't. It was when you behaved so outrageously at Unesco and fell into the big drum."

"You mean Shakespeare's birthday? They should never have asked me."

"You should never have gone. And then to arrive dead drunk and take your place on the rostrum among the greatest modern poets, all prepared to render homage to the Bard.

And with Toby in the audience cheering and waving a British flag. It was obscene."

"Not entirely," said Sutcliffe, slightly huffed, "it had its moment of truth. Besides, nobody could contravert my twelve commandments*– the indispensable prerequisites for those who wish to make works of art. They were particularly impressive when shouted through a megaphone in a hoarse tormented tone. Why didn't you use them?"

"I will one day when I write the ridiculous scene. You made Ungaretti faint. And then having recited the whole iniquitous catalogue of drivel you fell into the Elizabethan madrigal society's big bassoon, festooned with wires and microphones."

"Rather like Ophelia," said Sutcliffe. "But I stand by my commandments whatever the French say. Let me repeat them to you lest you have forgotten or mislaid them." He cleared his throat energetically and recited them for the benefit of Blanford, who wrote them down in shorthand on the pad at his elbow.

He left a long pause for admiration or applause and then said: "Alas, it ended badly, but it was none of my fault."

There was another longish silence during which Sutcliffe blew his nose in a plaintive sort of way, feeling that he was disapproved of by his mate and pawn. Then he said: "Where will Tu be buried and when?"

"Tonight," said Blanford coolly, with a reserve he was far from feeling. "In the chateau vault, by dispensation, and no ceremony, no flowers. Some lanterns, I suppose, perhaps some torches."

"Will you go down to Tu Duc?"

"Later, when everything is settled and the chateau boarded up for the winter. I love the rain falling over Avignon with all its memories. There is a certain melancholy luxury in

* See Appendix for full text of 12 Commandments.

feeling that everyone has gone, one is completely alone. The place to experience this best of all is on deserted railway stations at night, empty airport lounges, all-night cafés in the town."

Sutcliffe said: "And Livia, who in my own personal life and book turned into Sylvie and went mad? What about her in this context?"

"Livia disappeared, was last heard of on the road to Spain with the old negro pianist. My last news of her was some years ago now, from a girl who had known her; it was in one of those houses which cater to special inclinations – indeed the identical house where you lodged with the old crone. From time to time I passed by just in order to check, because once I had found Livia there, shaking with fatigue or drugs, trembling from head to foot. She said, in a bleary tearful way: "Unless someone takes care of me I am finished." I realised then that I loved her and would never desert her; and all the while a voice inside me was raging and shouting 'Fool!' "

"That was where I hunted for Pia."

"We took her to the kitchen, tottering, and set her down on a stool, imploring her to eat something. The hag buttered some bread. Livia suddenly burst into tears and said, '*J'ai failli t'aimer*,' and the tears ran down her long sweet nose into the plate. Still crying, she began to eat, looking so like a small child in her tearful hunger that I was overwhelmed. I sat there biting my lips and remembering so much that she had told me.

"One day in a dark cinema a woman placed her hand lightly upon her thigh and she felt her whole nature tilt like a galleon in a wind, to run seething through fresh seas. She did not move. She did not speak. She offered no response. Then she got up and walked out of the cinema without looking round. In the vestibule she felt so ill she had to lean her head against the cold tiled wall. A hand touched her sleeve and a voice said, 'Come, let me help you.' And so it began. And as she diminished in my life I started to reinvent her on paper as accurately as I could. Once when she had gone and I was lonely I took another girl from the same establishment to a hotel – purely for the comfort of sleeping with someone who knew her and could talk about her, even though what she had to tell me was wounding. Cynically and with a strong twang to her French this poor creature told me about Livia's exploits in great detail, adding as she did so: 'She gives good value, that one. Among the girls who like it she is known as Moustache.' My dear Rob, my beloved was known as Moustache to her ingles!"

"Perhaps you were wise to make Pia passive rather than active – it gave her a dimension Livia lacked, a pathos."

"But Livia was magnetic, and much harder to paint. I was forever trying to push a bit of femininity back into the lady, like trying to fill a dolly with sawdust, trying to fill an eye with a drip, trying to fill a mind with a prayer. Then she would disappear for a few days, to be brought back by the police dead drunk or else be run to earth in a bar, guttering down, guttering out. You, know, her health was a worry, she was never very strong, and she persistently brutalised it. But her charm! She was irresistible, she smelt of perils and disenchantments. Men could not resist her, and she longed to be able to respond. Yes, she gave herself, but it was only a smear of a woman who responded to the kiss. Affectively she was anaesthetic, her soul was rubberised."

"How funny," said Sutcliffe. "I suppose you discovered the real truth once the wedding-ring was on her finger. It was just like that with Pia, I had all sorts of vague notions that even though she was wild and unstable she was redeemable – a little bit of settled ways and stylised married life . . . I should have known by then how to detect the quaire (feminine version of queer). After all she could neither swim nor dance, and in love she went all anaesthetic but kindly – her kisses were one-dimensional and softer than moths."

"That was not Livia. Her favourite nail varnish was called Sadist Red, and she operated with a violence and zeal of a piglet at dug. A real predator, she liked to wear the fur of wild animals. Lean tomboy of the sexthrust, it was she who impregnated me with her despairing, anodyne, phantasy sensuality."

"Why were you so annoyed about the ring? In my case I felt that Pia had taken an unfair advantage, and wanted to continue in her old style under cover of the status and the stability I offered her. I felt swizzed."

"In my case it was the ring itself – it had belonged to my mother. I had all the tortured and confused impulses of only children, sickly in youth and consequently spoiled. School was torture, other people were torture. She was my only girl, mama, and I remained a *vieux garcon*, a bachelor, until she died when I thought that my loneliness might be less unendurable with a woman about the house. Of course I had had this long love-affair with Constance in between; but she never wished to remarry. Anyway Livia had disappeared somewhere in Asia and in those days it took years before a presumption of death permitted one to dream of divorce. You deformed her a bit in Pia."

"But you are to blame, for making her passive instead of active. Pia, looking so lovely in her white night-dress, obligingly put herself into a state of abstraction to pump out her husband (tenderly, dutifully) but like a collector 'blows' a bird's egg. For the rest, lying warm in bed she played with a masturbatory little curl, and I suppose dreamed about her *fouetteuse*, or her *frotteuse*. Why not? What is cheaper than dreaming? But infantile dreams which recover an early sex life are as feverish as the dreams of an anchorite. Great

Amputator of Egg Bags, save us! The lady was a *station de pompage* merely."

"Childhood, with its gross sexual and psychological damage to the psyche – what a terrible thing to be forced to undergo. No really, Rob, one does not stand a chance!"

"They believed in God. Jesus on pedals! How could they?"

Blanford threw his cigar into the fire and thought with a sudden wave of nostalgic passion of Tu. She rose before his inner eye walking by the lake where they had once and for all staked a claim in each other's minds and bodies; he heard her low voice reading from the book about Nietzsche, whom they had come there to seek.

"What happens," said Sutcliffe thoughtfully, "according to the wiseacres you consulted with so little profit – what happens to the penis is coronation followed by decapitation – the king bowing so low before the ladies that the crown falls off on to the red carpet. Isn't that right?"

Blanford agreed and amplified the statement with a voice full of distaste. "The head lends itself particularly well to the expression of bisexual conflicts, and can cunningly represent both male and female genitalia. Both girls were highly specialised in migraines of great intensity. There are vaginal haemorrhages which can be stopped by the cocaine pad to the inside of the nose. The guillotine, remember, was called *La Vierge*."

"A fig for all this folklore," cried Sutcliffe. "All will end in munch and you know it. The black flag of pure cannibalism will be unfurled. If narcissists (artists) cannot love, what right have they to kick up such a row?"

"You're right."

"*Si on est Dieu pourquoi cochonner?*"

"You're dead right, as they say. What a useful phrase."

Blanford could hear his creation tearing open a bag of potato chips and starting to champ them as he reflected furiously upon these all too alembicated ideas. Blanford thought of his childhood. "An only child is doomed to nostalgia and uncertainty. Nobody will ever guess what it cost me against all my fears and despairs, to teach myself the profession of letters. Solo, solitude, solace ... everything beginning with Sol the father, Sol the Son and Sol the Holy Ghost. She lingered for many years, did my mother, bedridden, suffering from an ill-identified malady which purported to be a heart condition. I think now that it was some grave glandular disturbance – the thymus perhaps. It gave her languor, it gave her a skin like a magnolia; her breasts remained firm and her teeth good to the very end. We lived, she and I, without a father in number twenty-seven Ruskin Road, South Norwood – a gloomy house called The Larches, with arch statuary on the lawn and a fountain which had rusted and would not play. We shared everything, even sleeping – as one might share careers of common silence. Yet I hear her sighs in my dreams now. What a torture it was to pack up my little tuck-box, count my money and set off to school, having assembled my books and kissed mama goodbye. Sterling, the old butler, drove me shakily down to the country – my school was near Arundel – in the ancient Morris. He was a randy old Cockney and he used to say: 'Next week, d'you know what, Master Aubrey? Why, I'm going on a right bender – don't tell your mother because she thinks I'm respectable. In a way she's right, I am. But not on my holidays. I've got a couple of birds right over the pocket in Brixton, and I'm simply thirsting for a bit of knuckle, Master Aubrey, really thirsting.'

"My father had been a scientific don in a minor university; the photographs depicted a large, discordant-looking man with black lace-up boots. I stared and stared at the vague memory-bank of his face but it radiated nothing. 'Come, hand me my pins, my net and my killing bottle, and leave me in peace.' He said that to my mother once who found it inconsiderate. It upset her. The house was full of badly stuffed geese and wildfowl, and in his study was a cabinet containing shelves and shelves of brilliant butterflies all mounted expertly on slabs of cork. I would have to do without all this until the end of term when Christmas came round. Again! The smart toy of the crib, and sex awoken in some little old mistletoe-man with a red peak, at night, in the snow, driving his tinkling harim of reindeer across the snowy roofs.

"Sometimes at night, walking across London, to see scores of silent frozen girls offering their bodies for sale under the blobs of yellow gaslight. Hurrying home to mother with castdown eyes, dying of smothered desires and the all too real fear of syphilis. So my whole life took its direction from there – my mother had rendered me a lamb, ripe for the slaughter; Livia supplied the shears. Cause and effect, my lad, that is why I had to encourage you to have a richer and more robust childhood. Your people were millers, say, from the north country, with a firm fortune and coming of authentic peasant stock. I saw your prototype once, dining beside me in Avignon, and I jotted down in my notebook: 'She is rather frail, but he huge with an egg-shaped cranium and a face which had funny and rather unworldly expressions on it. They smelt of industrious love-making and yawned all through dinner.' "

"Thank you. Was I at school with you?"

"We were both at different schools together."

Sutcliffe answered a ring at the doorbell and then came back to the phone to say briefly: "Toby has arrived. For my part I told everybody that I lived in Ireland in a fairy's armpit. They gave the impression of believing me, I never had trouble like you. Your laughter was a private strategy, mine was whole-hearted."

"I am not so sure," said Blanford thoughtfully, "though it is true that I was loved by a mummy without margins. Result: I wrote tonsured poems in the style of Morris. But I soon came to my senses. The result was not vastly different – we both ran into Livia, but in my case I presented a very simple target, and the motive of course was my unrecognised love for Tu. By the time your turn came you were less vulnerable because of your tough youth and were able to surmount the catastrophe with commendable humour. You at least were able to stand on the Bridge of Sighs and, waving your stick, exclaim aloud: 'Help me, Pia, help me! I am going down by the stern like Laurel and Hardy!' I could never have done that. I was after something else – a cumulus of thought subsumed in one bold metaphor. I had realised something concrete, namely that small art creates a throb, big art a wholesome vertigo. I tried to teach you this in your dealings with the people around you, so that your writing might have pith and irony. But since human consciousness distorts in the act of observing, you and I, seen by a third person, are perverted images of one another. We exchange highly diversified memoranda about the state of our attachment, just like real lovers entering that state which probably never existed. Poets exchanging cowrie shells, not real coin. Unless the images sting you awake. Robin, before you obediently killed yourself, you scribbled in the margins of your unfinished manuscript poem – the *Tu Quoque* – the words, 'Of course like Tiresias I have breasts which see all, and a forked tail in the shape of a lightning conductor. And yes, hooves.' "

Sutcliffe roared with laughter and crunched away at his chips, while in the background Blanford could hear the bearish sounds of Toby clearing his throat and the voice of a girl. He could not imagine her face as he had not yet invented her. That would come, he supposed. O God! Writers! Sutcliffe said: "Toby has been making up an imaginary obituary for you for *The Times* – you know he makes a little cash from working in the graveyard bringing obits up to date. Here's a passage which will please you: 'It is said that when rich he twice refused the thistle.' "

"But the money gave me books and travel and secrecy. And anyway one can't do better than one's best. What more would you like to hear from me if I bring you back to life?"

"About Tu; about Livia; about Hilary the brother and Sam. About the lake, and about Tu Duc and the Avignon of those early days. About us, the real ones."

"Then let me ask you one question," said Blanford sternly. "Just how real do you feel to yourself, Robin Sutcliffe?"

"I have never stopped to think," said his only friend after a pause. "Have you?"

"And you want to know about your own youth? Of course I endowed you with mine, for we are about the same age."

"But different milieux nourished us."

"Yes, but the age was the same, and an age is a state of mind. The twenties – that was purely a state of mind."

"Tell me the details, it will help me to act."

"Very well."

Blanford closed his eyes and let his memory draw him back to the very beginning of the story.

"It was to be their last term at Oxford and Hilary had invited them both to journey with him to Provence for the long vac. Neither he nor Sam had then met his two sisters, Constance and Livia. Indeed, they knew nothing of them at all. But recently, with the death of an old aunt, young

Constance had inherited the little chateau of Tu Duc in the southern Vaucluse, not far from Avignon. The Duchess of Tu, then, was the obvious nickname for her. The children had spent many holidays there once upon a time in their extreme youth; but in her old age the aunt became first eccentric, and then mentally unstable; she turned recluse, locked herself up, and allowed the whole place to fall into ruins around her. The rain and the wind settled down to finish what negligence had begun; the weight of winter snow cracked the black tiles of the roofs and entered the rooms, with their strange scrolled bull's-eye windows. In the rambling, disorderly park, old trees had fallen everywhere, blocking the paths, crushing the summer-house under their weight. The once-tended green plots were now a mass of molehills, while everywhere hares skirmished. They were to live largely on jugged hare that summer!

"Hilary, to do him justice, did not minimise the hardships they might have to face; but the prospect of southern sunlight and good wine was enough to offset any qualms they might have had. And then there was another capital factor – they had both youth and good health. Constance would meet them in Lyon, while Livia would come on later to join them, in her own time. Hilary mentioned Livia's name and frowned affectionately as he did so – as if he found the fact of her existence somehow troubling. His deep family affection for her had a sort of qualified, formalised air, as if he did not wholeheartedly understand her as did Constance. His way of talking gave one the notion that Livia was the wild and unpredictable one, while Constance was the stable and utterly dependable one. This proved to be more or less the case later when they got to know the truth about them – whatever that might mean. But Livia now spent all her time in Germany.

"It was this promise of a wild and somewhat primitive holiday which explained all the heavy camping impedimenta

27

they found stacked up against their arrival in Lyon – they had sent it on in advance. Massive camp-beds and sun-helmets, sleeping-bags, mosquito nets – perfectly ridiculous items which had been invented for safaris in lion-country or for scaling the Indian Himalayas. But none of them knew old Provence at first hand, so perhaps these precautions were excusable.

"Today the world which fathered them is a remote and forgotten one; it was a world wallowing in the wake of one war, trying to gather itself together before plunging irrevo-cably into a second. Their youth had enabled them to escape the trenches – in 1918 they were still just under military age, though Sam nearly managed to join up by a subterfuge; but he was found out and sent back to school; whence, to Oxford where the three, though so different, became inseparable. Hilary was the ringmaster of the little group, for he had more experience than either of the others, and he always led the dance. As a boy he was blond and tall and had ice-blue eyes like a Teuton. Sam was tow-haired and rather massive in his awkward gentle way. I was ... how was I, Aubrey Blanford? Let me see.

"A bit of a slowcoach, I suppose. Sam boxed and Hilary rowed, while all three of us hacked a bit and when possible rode to hounds in a post-Surtees manner.

"I was the least mercuric, the most sedentary of the three, and my poor eyesight made me an indifferent athlete, though I fenced well and even got my blue for it. The post-Wildean twilight of Oxford was no longer a place to cool the mind – the stresses and strains of the war years still weighed on us by proxy, for many of the men who had seen blood and action in 1918 had come back to university to finish studies interrupted by the war. A disturbed and wild crew they were, like foreign barbarians.

"Yes, it is difficult to describe that world, now so

forgotten; its values and habits seem to have retreated into the remotest recesses of time. Do you remember it – a world in awkward transition? The new thing was violent and brash, the old had ankylosed. All that the war had not killed outright lived on in a kind of limbo. Intellectually, let us say, Anatole France and Shaw were at the height of their fame; Proust despite his prizes had not yet won the general public. Henry James versus Wells.

"Was I born old? I never seem to have had a proper youth – mine began at Oxford when I met Hilary. If he was by far the most sophisticated of the three of us it was due to chance. His father had been a diplomat and the children had always travelled with him to his various posts. This stiff old gentleman was something of a stickler for ancient forms, and wherever they went they had tutors and learned the language of the place. Thus Hilary and his sisters became good linguists and thoroughly at home in places which were, to me, semi-mythical – Middle Europe, for example, or the Balkans: Rumania, Russia, Greece, Arabia. . . . It is true that Sam and I spoke laborious French and Italian, with a smidgen of German. But in the case of Hilary he 'possessed' three languages in the French sense of the word, and smattered in four others. All this he turned to good account and took excellent degrees at Oxford. His objective then was archaeology, his hero Evans, and his heart he had set upon exploring the labyrinth at Gortymna which remains unmapped to this day because of its great extent.

"And Sam? I have a picture of him in the back of my mind, lying in the deep grass at the edge of a green cricket-field crunching an apple and chuckling over Wodehouse or Dornford Yates. You must remember that we were overgrown schoolboys then to whom even dull, but raucous London was an excitement, a dream. While Paris was Babylon. Sam's ambitions were simple – all he wanted to do was to climb

Everest single-handed, and on his return rescue a beautiful blonde maiden from a tower where she had been imprisoned by an enchanter, and marry her. Later on he would like to set off on his travels with her disguised as his page and join the Knights of the Round Table. You will see the disastrous effects of Malory on a guileless mind. In my case, I wanted to be a historian – at that time I had really no inclination towards this hollow servitude to ink and paper. I pictured myself doing a definitive book on some aspect of medieval history and winning an Exhibition to Wadham, or something of that nature. As you see the bright one was Hilary, with what he called his 'Minoan tilt' – for his plans and projects opened windows on the world of Europe. Am I right?"

"I suppose so, but it's a bit pedestrian your exposé – it proves that the dull historian is not quite dead in my poor Aubrey. I would have gone about it differently myself."

"Tell me how."

"I should have enumerated other things like school ties, huge woollen scarves, Oxford bags, college blazers, Brough Superiors à la T. E. Lawrence, racing cars with strapped-down bonnets, Lagonda, Bentley, Amilcar. . . . The flappers had come and gone but the vamp was present in force with her cloche hat and cigarette holder."

"I had forgotten all that."

"It is the small things which build the picture."

"London."

"Yes, and the places we frequented in London most of which have disappeared – wiped out one supposes by the bombings?"

"Like the Café de Paris?"

"Yes, and Ciro's and The Blue Peter, The Criterion Bar, Quaglino's, Stone's Chop House, Mannering's Grill, Paton's, The Swan. . . ."

"Good, Robin, and then the night-clubs like The Old

Bag O' Nails, The Blue Lantern, The Black Hole, and Kiki's Place. . . . We simply never slept."

"The music of shows like Funny Face ('Who stole my heart away?'), Charlot, and the divine Hutch smoothing down the big grand piano and singing in his stern unemphatic way 'Life is just a bowl of cherries'."

"Just before dawn Lyons' Corner House, everyone with yellow exhausted faces, whores, undergraduates, all-night watchmen and workers setting off on early jobs. The first newspapers appearing on the icy street. Walking back in the pale nervous rinsed-out dawn, the whole way back across London – over Westminster Bridge and into the baleful suburbs of the capital; perhaps with the memory of some whore in mind, and the ever present worry of a dose. Marry or burn, my boy, marry or burn."

"I did both."

"So did I. So did I."

❖

"And so we come to the misty slip at Lyon where we waited impatiently for Constance and filled in the time by loading all our ludicrous equipment aboard the *Mistral*, a huge flat motor-barge with a capacious hold and enough deck space to take a few passengers. The hold was already battened down and covered with a tarpaulin which gave us a large flat area for lounging and eating; it was not envisaged that we should spend the night on her, but ashore. And then, amidst all these foolish deliberations, the stacking of our gear – you would have thought we were setting off for the Pole – the girl arrived; and with her, suddenly the whole summer too took place – I mean the consciousness of it, the density of its weight. As yet we were only in the mulberry-tree belt of dishevelled Lyon and its sprawling green surroundings. Far from the dustry garrigues as yet, the olive oil, and the anisette. But with Tu one saw what it was: it was sunlight filtered through a summer hat of fine straw onto bronzed shoulders and neck, creating a shadow that was of the darkness of ripe plums. It was ash-blonde hair made rough but silky by too much sun and salt water. It was a neck set perfectly on slender but strong shoulders, it was an eye of periwinkle-blue, which could turn green with the light, an eye full of curiosity and humour. She had cut her foot bathing, and her limp was explained by a bandage. She looked at us without much ardour or interest, I think, but with friendliness because we were her brother's friends. I felt at once that she shared some of his superiority over us – some of what I would call nowadays sophistication. 'Sorry I'm late; it was the train as usual.'

"Our skipper was a grave rotund man, who had the air of a great character actor out of work. His old sea-wolf yachting cap was cocked at a jaunty angle, and his liberality was not in question, for he produced frequent glasses of strong wine and urged them on us as a protection against the inclemency of the weather. What inclemency? The weather was perfectly fine, the old man obviously raving. Nevertheless the full beakers of Côtes du Rhône put us all into a great good humour; Constance sipped from her brother's glass and asked permission to put on shorts which he gravely granted. We winked at one another. The skipper's wife allowed her to make this transformation in the little cabin below which contained a cage bird and some old prints of the days of water haulage on the Rhône – really not so far away in time.

"We were fully loaded for Arles but were waiting for two more passengers who had been delayed. But they were not to detain us for long, and they were profuse in their apologies. One was a lanky, raffish-looking individual with a yellowish complexion and hair all in tufts about his greatcoat collar. He had a kind of shabby air of majesty, but it was only much later, when he advanced to the prow and let fly with an aria from Verdi, of tremendous volume, that we realised we were in the presence of a star from the opera of Marseille. The other was a humble, elderly man with a crown of white hair and the venerable appearance of a beadle. He had a brown old face which was full of character, and he regarded the world around him with an air of slightly impudent amusement. He seemed, however, a man of some real cultivation, not only from his manner but also because he carried under his arm a volume of poems, and actually sported (it is only now in retrospect that I recognise the fact) in his lapel the golden cicada which betokens a member of that famous poetic society the Félibre. Everything about our skipper – his rotundity, his accent, his gestures – seemed to fill this old gentleman with delight. I realise now why, they were both from Avignon, which was also our landfall and from where we hoped to find a carriage to take us to Tubain, if Felix was not at the rendezvous with his spluttering little consular car.

"The hooter gave a hiss and a boom, while drops of steam dribbled down the funnel; we had cast off and were away almost before we knew or felt it. Lying at ease on the spacious deck we saw the sunlit world turn slowly about us, spin faster and faster, and begin to slide away to stern. We swept under a great bridge where the silhouettes of a few onlookers were set against the arc of a sky of utter blue. Constance settled herself among the cushions thoughtfully provided by the gallant old skipper and apparently fell asleep, which gave me a chance to observe her and be struck once again by her beauty, and her resemblance to her brother. The fine blonde hair at her temples was, I thought, finer than the work of silkworms; her sleep was light, she smiled at some happy dream or thought. I would never have dreamed that she was as shy as Hilary, so formidable did her self-possession seem to us poor Englanders, bursting with conventions and the need to worship. Many years later when in a letter I made a reference to this first meeting she wrote on a postcard the one word: 'Shyness'.

"There was no sign of all this in the pose of the calm sleeping girl on the deck. Hilary, if my memory serves, rapidly got on good terms with the old poet and fired questions at him about the places through which we glode so smoothly, over a river suddenly widened by the green junction with the Saône. What I did remember was the droning voice of my geography teacher as he told us its history, softly touching the big wall-map with the black malacca cane which also, in certain contexts, served him to give us the brutal thrashings which were then the order of the day in most schools. They did no harm, I might add, and indeed were really useful as a rough and ready absolution – for one expiated one's sins this way and forgot about them once the blue weals had gone. While those hundred lines or hundred Hail Marys never really did the trick.

"But this first enticing venture towards the south, towards the Mediterranean, has got itself mixed up and superposed upon the many other times when I returned to Tu Duc to spend the summers there. 'The Rhône rises in Lac Léman,' said the droning voice of my geography teacher."

At this point in Blanford's recital Robin Sutcliffe cleared his throat and chuckled and made a noise like someone snuffing. "I bet I can tell what you think of now in that context."

"Carry on. Tell me," said Blanford.

Sutcliffe said: "The Chambre Froide of the central abattoir at Geneva. Of all the extraordinary places to sit and watch the Rhône rise. It was there that Pia took me to tell me that she had met poor Trash. It was a singular place to choose, perhaps more apt than it appears at first sight. The great factory that is the abattoir is built over the lake, remember, and at the back of it there is a little glassed-in restaurant built right over the water, where the personnel of the place take their meals. They call it the birdcage, if I recall right, and it is certainly small. Naturally the prime food is the meat. Trash had found it one day on her wanderings – she had been sent to order a carcase for the old American lady's birthday-party – one which would unite all the queers and queens and quaires of the town. Here among the swinging carcases on their big hooks the butchers in their bloody aprons had a festive air. They found Trash very much to their taste, and after several of the younger ones had refreshed themselves with her they invited her to the canteen for a glass of wine.

"Without this invitation it would have been impossible to find, for the entrance was actually through a huge meat-safe which was usually kept closed. Naturally the place was not open to the general public, it was reserved for the butchers and their friends. But a few people had discovered it and the supervision was lax. Well, I remember sitting over the water listening to this sad recital of Pia's fears and regrets; and all about her love for me which made me blow my nose rather loudly because I was touched, and I felt awfully as if my heart had been broken with a sledge hammer. To be hugged by a boy in a bloodstained apron – Ugh! Of course it was Trash who had been hugged, but now Pia was going to try the same thing under the tuition of the negress. It upset me so much this recital (the foolish girl was asking for my encouragement, for my absolution, repeating that she could not live without me and that I must understand). . . . I got so damned livid with her stupidity in succumbing to the lures of that male succubus with a slit that I rushed out of the place and took a taxi to Trash's hotel with the intention of thrashing her. Luckily she was out and I cooled down as I walked by the lake."

"Lucky is the word," said Blanford, "when I took a dogwhip to Livia for one of her misdemeanours I put her into a transport of sexual delight. Bathed in tears of pain and gratitude she fell to her knees and started licking my shoes. She was my slave now, she told me, utterly my slave. And she kept repeating, 'O why didn't you do it before?' I was disgusted."

"And the abattoir restaurant?"

"If I must disinter Livia's thoughts – it was she, the original of Pia, who took me there – I must record that she adored the smell of blood and fresh water. Indeed everything about new blood delighted her. It reminded her of her first period – she had been so poorly instructed, and was so innocent, that she thought she was bleeding to death like Petronius. And then, of course, the sorrow because it was the first physical proof of the lack of manhood she so coveted inside herself. The tremendous sadness of realising, as she said in her own picturesque phraseology, that she was a boy scout with a vagina. My dear Robin, she did not actually suffer the embrace of bloodstained boys, but she dreamed about it; only in her case the butcher was an elderly man who looked like her father. While we sat over the water and I saw her face suddenly go dead and transform itself into the resolute face of a tough little sailor, something guttered out like a spent candle. My love, like a sick fish, rose to the surface belly upwards. Under the floor of our birdcage the lake-water, narrowed and sluiced by the two banks, gathers speed, as if it could smell Arles already.

"The driving channel was a dark shade of amethyst verging on ultramarine; but right in the middle there was a portion raised like a muscle in a forearm, a green muscle of water which seemed to have more thrust than the great body in which it was embedded. Following the direction of my gaze Livia said: 'You see the green ribbon there? It's the

Rhône setting off on its race for the sea.' I hear her voice, I see the water, and a thousand thoughts throng in my mind. The great rivers of the human sensibility threading the jungles and swamps and forests of lost continents. The big rivers like Nile or Mississippi ferrying their human freight from one world to another. Though short in length our Rhône was one with them as was its cousin the Rhine. . . .

"Livia told me that one night she had been taken by her lover to La Villette where an old kind butcher with the face of her father had, on request, hobbled a cow which was about to be destroyed, and made a swift incision in its throat, like slitting an envelope. He held it by the horns, though the animal felt nothing. But the jet of blood spurted out into the tall wineglasses they proffered. They drank copiously while the old man watched in kindly fashion. Later they had trouble with a policeman for they were both splashed with blood, and it was difficult to explain how they had acquired these smears. But you, Robin, above all will have easily explained Livia's aberrations satisfactorily to yourself by now – didn't you take a degree in Philosophy and Psychology?

"What always bothered me was the question of a stable ego – did such a thing exist? The old notion of such an animal was rather primitive, particularly for novelists with an itch to explain this action or that. Myself, I could hardly write down the name of a character without suddenly being swamped by an ocean of possible attributes, each as valid and as truthful as any other. The human psyche is almost infinitely various – so various that it can afford to be contradictory even as regards itself. How poor is the pathetic little typology of our modern psychology – why, even astrology, however suspect as a science, makes some attempt to encompass the vast multiplicity of purely human attributes. That is why our novels, yours and mine, Robin, are also poor. There were many Livias, some whom I love and will love until my dying day; others fell off me and dried up like dead leeches. Others were just larval forms in the sense of Paracelsus, umbratiles, vampires, ghosts. When she had definitely gone she sent me the taunting telegram which seemed to amuse you.

A little bit of addled Freud
Won't take you far towards the void.

❖

"But the letter to which the thought belonged was written from Gantok and she had headed it, 'On the road to Tibet'. It was long, rambling and inconsequential, and it upset me so much that I destroyed it. But I remember one part in which she wrote: 'You cannot imagine what it is like to find myself in a land where beautiful six-armed Tsungtorma raises her lotus-soft palms.' It was a fair enough criticism of my literary method – why not six-armed psyches? Would it be possible, I wondered, to deal fairly with a multiplicity of attributes and still preserve a semblance of figurative unity in the personage described? I was dreaming of a book which, though multiple, embodied an organic unity. The limbs of Osiris, scattered as they were round the whole known world, were one day united. Out of the egg of futurity stepped that dark and serious girl who was to say one day, with a confident contempt, 'Anyone can see which one of us he loves.' One discovers these things years afterwards, in another context, perhaps even in another country, lying on the beach, pressing warm pebbles against one's cheek. 'What did you do?' I asked Constance. She replied, 'I suddenly realised that I must get free of her, she would always block my light, my growth. I embraced her so hard it drove all the breath from her body.'

"The Livia of that epoch was dark and on the thin side – a contrast to the fairness of her sister. She had beautifully cut cheekbones and eyes of green, while her black soft hair seemed to fly out of the crown of her head and flow down the sides in ringlets reminiscent of Medusa – the snake is quite an appropriate metaphor. Her beauty was not obvious, it came in a sudden kind of revelation. But of course, she slouched, and always had her hands in her pockets, and a cigarette between her lips. We were conventional enough to be shocked by this. But I was dazzled by her brains and her abrasive and articulate way of speech. The voice was deep, and from time to time an expression came into her eyes, a tense fierce expression, and one suddenly saw a man-at-arms peering at one out of a helm. I was too inexperienced to recognise the carapace of her defensive masculinity. But whenever she looked in the direction of Constance, whenever she found us laughing or talking with animation, another more calculating look came into those clever eyes. She could not stand the complicity of our obvious friendship whose warmth at that time was innocent of all ulterior purpose.

"Livia set herself quite deliberately to work upon my obvious inexperience. An easy target. Later when I came to wonder about the shape which events took in the lives of us all I thought that perhaps Livia's role had been less conscious than I had thought; she also was just an instrument registering the electrical impulses set up by a suppressed childhood jealousy. Being wise after the event is one of the specialities of elderly novelists. Quack! Quack! Of course she had no choice, none of us did. It was the peerless beauty and brilliance of the elder sister which magnetised the younger; and I must go on to add, the brother as well. For Hilary, too, formed part of this constellation, and I think that he also found the easy rapport between Tu and myself disquieting, to say the least. But whenever a brother and sister are very close together they naturally fear that marriage, on either side, will wantonly separate them. But Livia was a born conspirator, and once she had decided to prevent anything maturing between Constance and myself she set to work to undermine us – with what success you know only too well; I was captivated by this lizard-swift girl who flattered me in ways which now I would find grossly obvious. But, inhibited as I was then, her praise was manna.

"At that time Tu was taking the first distasteful steps in general medicine, and already had decided not to continue it to the end. The coarse jokes of the students as they handled the fragments of human bodies disgusted her. They betrayed their fear of death thus, the internal shrinking from having to carve up the bodies of drowned, unidentified people, tramps, suicides and the like. Flesh bloated, disfigured, or smashed beyond recognition. And then the smell of formaldehyde following one about the draughty schools! It got into one's clothes, aprons, skirts, white skirts. The loathing was impossible to overcome wholly, though for the present she persevered. Her only inspiration was her anatomy tutor; he was so mad on his subject that his enthusiasm fired her. Once after a particularly bad street accident in Gower Street she saw him pick up a severed arm, wrap it furtively in an evening paper and hurry off to the laboratory which was hard by. Perhaps there was a hope that some less taxing science like chemistry might answer where general medicine and surgery had failed her? She was waiting to see.

"With Livia, alone, swimming in one of the numerous rock pools of the Pont du Gard while the others climbed to the top of the great aqueduct, I discovered another person – not less touching and appealing than her sister, but made of harder and more consistent material. It was very attractive, this down-to-earthness, and even later when I kissed her the lips that met mine seemed deliberately cool and questing and self-possessed. But her fingers were always cold – now I would tend to associate the fact with guilt over treachery; not then. Livia was a dream, impossible to regret, even today."

Sutcliffe cleared his throat and said: "Pia had little of Livia's forthrightness, nor her deep voice. Her own voice was melodious contralto, a fitting instrument on which to play the passive score you wrote for her – and with which I myself don't really agree. I cannot really imagine a Livia in tears. She was always seen walking alone or sitting alone in the middle of the night in deserted cafés, just sitting, staring into her coffee. Her lips were thin when pursed – you forgot to say that; and her eyes had a bitter glimmer. I like that. You fused her uncomfortably with her sister to make Pia, or rather I did, but I was following the hints left by you in the black notebook or the green. Livia had a special little look of smiling contempt when she saw a kitchen; but Constance's face lit up with joy – as if a musician had suddenly come upon a concert-grand in perfect tune."

"I think the trouble is that you are thinking one-dimensionally all the time, like an old-fashioned novelist. You do not seem to be able to envisage a series of books through which the same characters move for all the world as if to illustrate the notion of reincarnation. After all, men and women are polyphonic beings. They know they had previous lives, but they are not sure what they were; all they feel is the weight of their karma, the poetry of previous existences registered in the penumbra of past time."

"How sick I am of the time notions."

"So am I, but the obsession is the age's. We have at any rate come to terms with it, we know that calendar time is a convenience and not a truth. Time is all one sheet – and just as the germs of an illness, say tuberculosis, are there inside one, ready and waiting to be called out by circumstance, so from a temporal point of view are the maggots already in the flesh waiting patiently for the temporal circumstance of death to set them free. Pia into Livia, Livia into Pia, what does it matter? – somewhere in that recess of time they are conscious of each other, of their origins."

"You could go further back still, then?"

"Exactly."

"What are we, then, if not simultaneous artists, 'perishing symmetrically', to borrow the phrase of Madame de Staël?"

"But Livia – even Livia could cry, though you wouldn't believe it. The first time we made love as children was among the rhododendrons at the Pont du Gard, when she was starting to wean me away from my admiration for Tu. Even then she was the expert, the ringmaster, the instigator – and I followed her suit in a sort of daze. It took me dozens of love affairs afterwards to recognise when a lover is sleeping with an imagined phantasy shape, or even with herself. Now I would not be so easily deluded. But then? Yet afterwards she went and laid her head against a tree and gave a small dry sob. It seemed quite private, and was most striking – for even in an exhibition of weakness her self-possession shone through. Before I could place a loving arm over her shoulders the spasm was over and done with. Nor would I have recognised at the time what was an obvious act of contrition – for after all she loved Tu, and hated to do her down. Indeed she loved her all too much to surrender her to me. I only saw all this years afterwards. And reflecting on it, and the possible pity of it, I wondered whether perhaps she had not done me a service in imprisoning me – in preventing me from contracting a love for Tu which could prove premature, ephemeral? If I wasn't experienced enough for Livia surely I was even less so for Tu? Perhaps it is as well to learn to drive on an old, or at least used, car before investing in an expensive new one? I don't really know. But I think it was salutary to have the experience of Livia at that time – though the displacement was at once responsible for other changes, notably in the attitude of Tu herself. I asked her once if she had been in love with me at that early time and she wrote back, 'Yes, I suppose, though I did not know what the word meant then. I was suffering from a sort of undiagnosed pain which was connected with your existence. It took time to master it. It was a case of third-degree burns. But look, I am still alive, happy and breathing.'

"Later, much later, in the flush of her new Viennese science Tu was able to pronounce upon her sister with greater self-confidence – though of course it changed nothing. 'You must treat her with great compassion, for she belongs to the great army of walking wounded in the battle of life. Our mother deserted us, and died far away in another country, never showing the slightest interest in our well-being or even safety during the war. We have a right to a grievance, and a sense of insecurity. Livia was forced to grow a masculine carapace in order to defend herself against life. It is a great nervous strain to keep on subsidising the man in herself. Perhaps she realises it. At any rate nothing can be changed now – she is fixed, like a badly set fracture. It would have to be broken and re-set, and in terms of the human personality this would not be possible. Indeed it would be dangerous to try, specially by analysis. You might overturn her reason.'

"And of course, when I reflected upon Tu herself, I wondered why she did not manifest the same characteristics of a disturbing environmental inheritance. And finally, this is the point at which her new baby science of Freudianism fell apart. If two people share the same environment and circumstances, why would one fall ill and the other not? It is one of the major puzzles and annoyances – for who can doubt the basic accuracy of the diagnosis? I reflected for a long time on the matter without reaching any real conclusion; but the facts were plain, in that Tu was a woman and had the fearlessness of a woman fully conscious of herself. In some strange way she had overcome the hatred for her mother's shade which had had such a crippling effect upon Livia.

"But all this comes long after that sunlit slide under the bridges of Lyon, gathering momentum as the river thickened out and began its headlong descent through a limestone country of such prolix variety that there was not a moment when something new did not catch and fire our attention – it was not only the rosy baked little towns with their castles and battlements which excited one. They were like punctuation marks in a noble poem – a Pindaric Ode, say. It was the consciousness that we were passing out of the north into the Mediterranean; the rich mulberries which had made the silk of Lyon world famous were soon to give place to the more austere decoration of olives, shivering and turning silver in the mistral which followed us down river; a wind of such pure force that if one opened one's mouth it was instantly filled with wind. We were moving from a cuisine based on cream and butter to one more meagre, more austere, based on olive oil and the other fruits of the Athenian tree. We were moving towards the sea – blue bodies of swimmers in the gulf, blue waves drumming the coves and *calenques* of Cassis. We were moving from liqueurs towards the ubiquitous anisette of the south.

"One after another the Rhône bestowed upon us its historic sites and little drunken towns, snuggled among vines, bathed in the insouciance of drowsy days and drowsy silences broken only by the snip-snop of the secateurs among the vines – the holy circumcision which ends the elegiac summers of Provence. The very names were a spur to what imagination and instruction we had – between us we assembled a few shreds of knowledge based on old guide books. Yes, Vienne succeeded desolate Mornas whose very name seemed to echo the sadness of old wars and ruined husbandry; then Vienne with its funny spur – but no trace of the classical splendour recorded in the histories. It must have been the Bournemouth of the ancient world – diplomats retired there from service; the most celebrated among them was Pontius Pilate who spent his quiet retirement there after leaving the Middle East with all its tedious and vexatious problems and stupid agitators. We saluted him in a glass of rosy wine. The river ran through a number of locks and barrages, each with its watchful guardian in his glassed-in perch who took our details before expelling us out of the lock-gates at an altered level, to speed on once more southward.

"As Vienne disappeared round one of the broad curves of the river Hilary looked back at it thoughtfully and said, 'It was there that the Templars were officially abolished.' He spoke as if the event were of momentous significance, but at that time I did not know very much about the Templars – just the broad details of the ancient scandal perpetrated by a King of France and executed by the hooded monsters of the Inquisition. Hilary stood there, gazing back along the water, lost in thought. But now Constance was awake and had succeeded in charming the old Félibre – the Avignon poet; fired by her beauty, and delighted that she knew some French, he proceeded to recite to us, his face creased up like a fine soft handkerchief. It was the first time I had heard Provençal spoken – there seemed to be moss packed between every syllable. Its soft lilt made one think of Gaelic; it echoed the meanderings of the great river with its sudden little tributaries and the occasional mysterious islands of sedge and weeping willow which came up at us out of the distant hazy blue and vine-green. From time to time the lean wolf-like man at the prow practised a trill or a series of sky-shattering head notes, looking round him after each paroxysm, as if for admiration. It was some little time before we were suddenly aware that we were in the presence of a master-alcoholic, an amateur of *pastis*. What matter? He was in tremendous form.

"At one our hampers were unstrapped on the deck and the two French passengers were happy to join us; Hilary had made the purchases in the town before our departure, and with the skill that comes of experience. Never had the delicacies of the French table tasted like this, before or since, washed down as they were with the simple sunlight of a great wine. Never had fresh bread tasted like this. So this was Provence! Cloudless sky, tall planes with their freckled outer skin glimmering like trout in a stream – reflected in the flowing green current. Then weeping willows, like great character actors entangled in their own foliage, and later as we climbed down, lock by lock, towards Valence, the smell of dust, honeysuckle, convolvulus. Objects occupied a place all to themselves; one little donkey – the only donkey in the whole universe, the essence of all donkeys – trotted along a path with its panniers full, raising a plume of dense dust. At Tournon our poet launched into a history of wine – while on the opposite bank glowed like jewels the vines from which came the senior wines like Côte Rôti, St Joseph and so on. We tasted some, we trinked, we came back aboard in fighting form, ready almost to take part in the opera, snatches from which our fellow-passenger continued to sing. The sun burned like a brazier. The skipper's wife opened an umbrella – the mistral had offered us a respite – and settled to her knitting. Round the massive curves of the Rhône we soared, doing almost twenty knots I judged with the current at our backs. At Condrieu an old bent man in a sea captain's hat waved a paper flag at us, evidently recognising one of our number. We all waved back.

"That evening we came up with Valence as dusk fell – our skipper appeared to hate hurrying and we had lost a great deal of time at Tournon. We tramped dazedly ashore, full of the fatigue of sunlight and wine, and found ourselves a grubby billet in a small hotel – Valence was disappointing in spite of its Napoleonic associations, and we turned in very early as the skipper had warned us that the voyage would be resumed very early the next morning.

"But in the cool pearly light of dawn, when we made our way back to the ship we found that the skipper, amidst violent expletives, was trying to counter a mysterious form of engine-trouble which prevented the motors from firing. And here to everyone's astonishment Sam came into his own and after a short and intense examination of their intestines, proffered a diagnosis and a remedy which, being acted upon, set the whole matter to rights in a twinkling. So once more we were sailing down the Rhône spattering the sky with snatches of Verdi, half bemused by the rich verses of Mistral. But we had lost time, we had lost quite a bit of time, and it was late evening before we suddenly rounded a curve of the great river and were treated to a spectacle made more remarkable by a suddenly visible full moon rising in rhetorical splendour over the ramparts of Avignon. High above the city perched the Rocher de Doms – the hanging gardens of this deserted Babylon. It was as if fate had chosen to delay us in order to repay us with its inspiring entry into the city which was later to come to mean so much to us – we did not know any of this then. Now, as I think back, I try to disinter that first impression – the marvellous silhouette of the town magnetically lit by moonlight pouring over it from the direction of the Alpilles. It is still the best way to see it – by water and from afar; and with the historic broken bridge pointing its finger across the river. And the little shrine to St. Nicholas with its bright lamps of benediction for seafaring folk. We had been gliding for nearly an hour among silent islands and deserted channels, watching the bare spars of the Cevennes rise on the night sky. And now suddenly this severe magic. It took much more experience of the town to come to the astonishing conclusion that it was only beautiful in profile – the actual Palaces of the Popes are hideous packing-cases of an uncouth ugliness. Nothing here was built for charm or beauty – everything was sacrificed to the safety of the treasures which these buildings housed. But you must walk about the town to find this out. It is a cathedral to Mammon. It was here our Judeo-Christian culture finally wiped out the rich paganism of the Mediterranean! Here the great god Pan was sent to the gas-chambers of the Popes. Yet seen from a long way off the profile and the promise of the town – they are heartbreaking in their sweetness of line; and by the light of the moon marmoreal in their splendour.

"We had arrived. With a roar we started reversing engines now in order to brake our descent and enable us to moor firm to the shore in that racing river. The boat drummed and throbbed. A small group of gentlemen, all suitably decorated, were waiting for our fellow-passenger on the quay – his name, by the way, he said, was Brunel. They seemed if anything somewhat subdued – they had an air of affectionate sadness as they waited for their friend. Then, as the distance shortened, one of them, a tall and distinguished-looking man in a topcoat, and sporting a beard (much later I was to recognise the poet Peyre from photographs), stepped forward to the gang plank and in a low voice uttered the words: 'He is dead.'

"A mysterious scene to me then – yet I scented that there was something momentous about it, though I could not tell what. Much later I read a modern history of the Félibre, the poets who have been the lifeblood of the region's literature, and discovered the names of that little sad group waiting under the ramparts of the city for Brunel. Their welcoming embraces were long and loving – one felt in them a sort of valedictory quality, perhaps for their dead fellow.

"But behind them in the shadows lurked Felix Chatto with the clumsy old car which would ferry us over the river to the tumbledown mansion which Constance had inherited. Felix, too, had just come down from Oxford and despite his passionate desire to become a banker had succumbed to family pressure and entered the consular service. His uncle, the great Lord Galen, owned a vast property quite near Tubain, while Felix himself was the recently appointed acting consul in Avignon. The two of them were to prove extremely valuable to us in many ways during the period – nearly the whole summer – it took to settle Tu Duc into some semblance of a habitation. No, I exaggerate. The old place was still very sound structurally, though showing signs of neglect which rendered it barely habitable. Water, for example: the pump on the artesian well lacked an essential spare part which (Sam again) had to be more or less re-invented. In the far depths of the grounds was a lily pool full of carp; the tall flukes of the artesian formed a most decorative shape on the evening sky – but though there was plenty of wind, and though the sails turned loyally, no water flowed into the tower, and thence into the kitchen of the old house. We were forced for a few days to resort to buckets drawn from the lily pond, which incidentally afforded us delicious icy swims when these activities made us too hot. The keys fitted the doors, yes, but very approximately: Felix had brought them with him. And it took a while to discover that there was not a lock on the house which had not been put on upside down, and which consequently had to be opened anti-clockwise. Later on we got so used to this factor that one always tried the anti-clockwise turn first in dealing with locks in Provence.

"The first few nights we slept on the terrace by the light of the moon – and began by setting the kitchen to rights in order to cook our meals. A little pony-trap secured our lines of communication with Tubain where we found enough shops to satisfy our modest needs. Here again the resourceful

Sam shamed us all by actually doing some respectable cooking with Constance. The tall shadowy rooms were full of heavy, spiritless furniture, dust-impregnated, and we had to move all this old stuff into the patio to beat the dust out of it and polish it up. The wood floors creaked agreeably but were full of fleas, and called for paraffin-rag treatment. The wallpaper was shredding. On the steep terraces large green lizards, insatiably curious, came out to watch us at work; they were obviously used to being fed and seemed perfectly tame. The cupboards in the bedrooms were full of linen, white with dust, while the big central dining table with its scarlet cloth still had plates and glasses on it – as if a formal party had been suddenly interrupted and the whole company carried off by the devil. In effect the old lady had been taken ill very suddenly, and fortunately for her, during the visit of a friend who was able to find a doctor. She had been taken to a clinic in Avignon, never to return.

" 'How atavistic the sense of possession is,' said Constance. 'I am mad about this house merely because it is mine. Yet it's hideous. I would never have dreamed of buying it. And anyway, I don't believe in possessions. I am ashamed of loving it so much already.'

"We lay in the pond with the cool water up to our necks, chatting among the lilies. She wore her straw hat tilted back. Her hair was wet. Every evening it was like this as long as the moonlight held. Hilary and Sam played chess on the terrace with a little pocket set – Hilary was watching the dinner. We had discovered the local anisette – the *pastis* of the region; surely the most singular of drinks for it coats the palate and utterly alters the taste of a good wine and good food.

"There were owls in the tower, there were swerving, twittering bats in the trees, but as long as the heat of the long grass sent up insects into the evening sky the swallows and martins worked close overhead, swerving in and out like darts, to take the spiring insects in open beaks with a startling judgment and accuracy. One could hear their little beaks click from time to time as they snapped at an insect. And then of course the steady drench, the steady drizzle of cicadas in the great planes and chestnuts of the park. All succumbing and sliding into the silence of the full moon which only the dogs celebrated, together with an occasional nightjar and the plaintive little Athenian owl called the Skops. Coming from the cold north we were continually amazed by the beauty and richness of this land. There was only one old man who worked on the property and he lived far away in the valley; but after the first week he brought up a venerable blind horse and set it to turning about a water wheel, fixed to one of the shallower wells. Mathieu, he was called, and he was very deaf."

◆

Poor Blanford! His reveries had carried him so far afield in the past that he did not notice that the telephone had gone dead. He curtly replaced the receiver, having rung for Cade to clear up the tea things. Then he moved with the stiff precariousness of a doll to the library which they had shared over the years; he had housed his own books here during his travels – Tu had set aside two large bookcases for him to which only he had the key. It was a very long time since he had taken to binding up her letters, unwilling to part with such a testimony of friendship and love so central to his inner life, his development. By now there were a number of slim volumes with brilliant Venetian leather bindings, stamped and tooled with emblems suitable to such an intimate correspondence; the little books were housed in pretty slipcases of expensive leather. He unlocked the bookcase and took out one or two to ruffle in that silent room. She would be, he felt, almost his only reading now that she had "gone". He could grimly follow the vicissitudes of his career through her letters from the first success to the time of the Q novels. Tu had been his oldest and most ardent friend; reading some kindly, ironic passages, he recovered the very timbre of that ever-living voice.

And his own replies? They too were there in her part of the library – an extensive collection of books and manuscripts for he had not been her only friend among the artists. One way and another Constance had known some of the great men of the day. A small pang of jealousy stirred in him with the thought. But it had never occurred to her to bind up his letters, they were in ordinary office folders, as if awaiting a final sorting. Nor were her own somewhat disorderly bookcases locked. He reached down a folder and, opening it, came upon a recent letter addressed to her from the city – sometime last year, it must have been. He had the bad habit of seldom dating his letters. He poked up the fire and sat down with the folder on his knee, trying to read the letter freshly, as if he were Tu, and as if it had just arrived.

"Once again I am here alone in Avignon, walking the deserted streets, full of reminiscences of our many visits, full of thoughts of Tu Duc and yourself. Yes, here I am again in the place where, according to cards set out by my horrible valet Cade, I am due to die by my own hand, sometime during my fifty-ninth year. That still gives me a year or two of clock time; but what Cade speaks of has surely been going on for a long time?

"How shall I explain it to you? For the writer at any rate everything that one might call creatively wrought, brought off, completed aesthetically, comes to you, his reader and his Muse, from the other side of a curtain. From the other side of a hypothetical suicide – ask Sutcliffe! Indeed this is the work of art's point of departure. It need not happen in the flesh to the performer. But it is indispensable to art, if there be any art in the commodity he fathers. Bang!

"Constance, the poet does not choose. The poet does not think of renown, for even the voices which carry the furthest are only the echoes of an anterior, half-forgotten past. The poetic reality of which I speak, and which Sutcliffe might have deployed in his unwritten books, is rather like the schoolchild's definition of a fishing-net as 'a lot of holes tied together with string'. Just as impalpable, yet just as true of our work. Art is only to remind.

"I think, if Cade is right, I shall have enough time to send this project down the slips; afterwards Sutcliffe can flesh it out and fill in the details. Come, let us buy some time for our clocks – a nice juicy slice of time. I must add in all honesty that Sutcliffe is somewhat scared of the idea. When I outlined it he said: 'But Aubrey, this could lead anywhere.' I said: 'Of course. I have freed us both.' The notion of an absolute freedom in the non-deterministic sense alarmed him. As usual he became flippant, to give himself time to reflect. Then he said, 'What would you give me if I wrote a book to prove that the great Blanford is simply the fiction of one of his fictions? Eh?' You know the answer as well as I do, but I could not resist saying it out loud. 'The top prize, Robin Sutcliffe, immortality in the here and now. How would that suit you?' This left him very thoughtful in a somewhat rueful way. He is lazy, he doesn't want to co-operate one little bit. He lacks my driving ambition.

"No, Constance my dear, ours shall be a classical quincunx – a Q; perhaps a *Tu Quoque* will echo throughout it. We will try to refresh poetry and move it more towards the centre of ordinary life.

"Then later, when the blow falls, and I disappear from the scene, it will have to do duty, such as it is, for my *star y-pointed pyramid.* Ever your devoted A."

TWO

Humble Beginnings

BLANFORD NAVIGATED FRETFULLY ABOUT THE HOUSE, talking to himself a little with Constance in mind – there seemed so much still to say to her. His fingers crept along the shelf of her Latin and Greek poets towards the volumes which contained their correspondence. "I know that poets make more boom and slither, but novelists can create personae you loathe or adore." He riffled the coloured pages and then read aloud: "Your notion of Sutcliffe intrigues me. Some detail please. I hope he won't become a provincial Heathcliff."

He had replied, "You ask about Sutcliffe? I cannot tell you for how many years he lay silent, living a larval life in the cocoon of my old black notebook. I did not know what to do with him – though I kept jotting away as directed. It was essential that he should differ greatly from me – so that I could stand off and look at him with a friendly objectivity. He represented my quiddity I suppose – the part which, thanks to you, has converted a black pessimism about life into a belief in cosmic absurdity. He was the me who is sane to the point of outrage. Often I kissed you with his mouth just to see how it felt. He never thanked me."

He sat down with the volume on his knee and stared into the fire once more – into its coiling shapes he read snakes and ladders of fire, a crusader burning on a pyre, a scorpion, a crucifixion.

Yes, a different background. Sutcliffe might get born somewhere north of Loughborough, say, to decent Quaker parents. Millers of grain? He was a scholarship boy who had won an Exhibition to Oxford, and then, like so many others, had found himself thrown upon the slave market of pedagogy. He had edited a few cribs which were badly reviewed by a tiresome clanging professor – and thus lost the chance of a post as a translator. Poverty intervened, and since he had nothing special for which to starve, he accepted the first opening which presented itself. He found himself teaching French and music to schoolgirls at Hymendale, a clergy orphans' establishment, where half the staff was ecclesiastical and half lay. Whence his downfall. For nuns called to dons, dons to nuns, deep to deep, dope to dope. . . . It was really not his fault.

Hymendale was a suburb of Bournemouth, that salubrious south coast resort, which even then was geared to the retirement requirements of professional men and colonial civil servants. Privet hedges, eyes peering from behind curtains, a draughty gentility; silent streets awoken only to the clip clop of the milkman's little van. It was a fine place to develop inner resources – so he told himself grimly as he grimly did his daily walks, twice round the sewage plant and once there and back along the cliffs in the rain. Ah! the eternal rain! Eight hours a week spent with his sallow, skewer-shaped girls with lank hair and torpid intelligences. *Que cosa fare?* He saw himself even then as a rather tragic figure, trapped by fate in this religious treadmill. He played the role to himself for all it was worth, sometimes being overheard laughing aloud – a harsh sardonic bark directed at the greasy teeming sky. The pubs in the place shut early and were full of tobacco smoke, at once acrid and throat-drying. There was one reasonable bookshop, Commin's, as well as a lending library, and of course two cinemas. He buried himself in books, thanking God that he could read enough French to amuse himself. We must imagine a rather large, short-sighted man clad in shapeless tweeds perforated with many a nameless cigarette and pipe hole. He had a stalking walk whose buoyancy suggested an inner exuberance which he was far from feeling. No; he was guilty of over-compensating.

Loneliness led to this passionate self-communing, which in turn led to somewhat eccentric behaviour – at least by the standards of such an establishment. For instance, on Sunday morning, when the class formed up in the quad to draggle to chapel in its desultory Indian file, Sutcliffe (who led the procession in gown and tippet) liked to imagine that he was engaged in other, more romantic activities. Thus one Sunday he would be leading his cricketers out into the field to win the Ashes back from Australia; he snuffled the wind, gazed at the light, sucked his finger boy scout fashion and held it up to determine the direction (before sending in his bowlers). He cleared his throat and made a number of finger signs to invisible umpires, directing the position of the screens ... and so on. On other days he was the leader of an African tribe, clad in nothing but a tiger-skin, and waving a knobkerrie as he walked, chanting under his breath to the rhythm of inaudible drums. He was head of the young hunters and they were going out for lion – nothing less! On other occasions he enacted a priest leading victims of the Terror towards the guillotine. The clatter of the tumbril on the paving stones of Paris were practically audible to the listener. It goes without saying that this intense miming and the strange postures were looked upon by his superiors with misgivings. But they were simply the outward and visible signs of an intense inner life.

There was nobody he could talk to, so he had developed the habit of talking to himself – interminable low monologue of the inner mind. People saw only the outward expression suited to these thoughts which passed in him like shoals of fish. A popping eye, lips pursing, eyebrows going up and down. His nose twitched. Often (he blamed this on the diet of spotted dog and treacle tart) he had piles which divided into three categories, namely Itchers, Bleeders and plain Shouting piles. For his walks he used a shabby old golfing umbrella and vast boots with hooks and eyes. "I was formed by Doctor Arnold," he was wont to tell himself, "whose wife much enjoyed his melancholy long-withdrawing roar." When he was overcome by depression he sometimes went down into the town and for ten shillings and a Devonshire Tea gave Effie a furtive caress, which only increased his sense of despondency and alienation. Effie was a barmaid at The Feathers and a good enough little soul, very modest in her demands upon life. She was indeed sweet but O the cold apple tart between her pale, frog-like legs. He bought her presents because he felt guilty at leading her astray — she was really a good girl and not a whore. She had a marked tendency towards cystitis. But the town, the monotony, the rain and the people can drive you to do anything. One thing about her intrigued him – the way she cocked her little finger over a teacup with such an affectation of gentility.... She did the same in bed as if to confer some of the same sort of gentility upon the love act. He adored this. For some reason not known to science Sutcliffe had the habit of carrying two french letters in the turnups of his broadly cut trousers. They were very expensive these things, and he kept them only for Effie; after use, he washed them out and pegged them up to dry on the mantelpiece of his little room for an hour. They had the word EVERSAFE printed on them. Effie insisted on protection and was affectionately responsive to such little attentions. She liked this man who suffered so often from chilblains and who walked about on his toes with rather a mystified air. She would have dreamed of marrying him perhaps, but he was a gentleman and it would not have done.

His duties entitled him to a little room with a fireplace, with a separate entrance onto the quadrangle – and he always dreamed of enticing some secret woman to visit him. But who? He had a small harmonium of the wheezy sort and a copy of the Forty-eight of Bach, which he played for his own amusement, but not too loud. For the rest he read opera-scores at night, eating an apple the while; occasionally he moved his eyebrows and let out a roar to correspond to a full orchestra unleashing top sound. Vaguely in the back of his mind a project was forming itself; to write a new life of Wagner.

Why not? Sometimes on his walks he saw a point of darkness move indistinctly upon the horizon repeatedly expunged and dimmed and recreated. A ship, forsooth! He waved his umbrella and cheered. All this monotony might be a good aliment for a poet but what if one had no gifts? Sometimes he got so lonely that he could have set his bed on fire.

Sister Rosa must have also suffered from it, perhaps more acutely, for she had come to England from some dusky clime. She was pretty, with a mischievous face, and an octoroon as to complexion. He caught her examining him in chapel, and she gave a dark rosy blush. He smiled at her and she smiled back in a way that suddenly made him feel that for her spring was not far behind. There had been some trouble that day with the Sixth; he had been summoned to the head and asked if he was really "doing" Mallarmé? "Just giving an account of the period," he had replied. The Mother Superior raised a white finger and said, "Mr. Sutcliffe, I know I can count on you not to let anything too French or too suggestive pass. It is a great trust we have put in you in giving you the Sixth. Please guide them in the paths of blamelessness, even if it means *stealing through* the classics rather than doing them in detail."

"Do you mean censoring them?"

"Well, yes, I suppose I do."

"Very well," said Sutcliffe grimly and withdrew. He had already planned a bowdlerised Mallarmé to meet the case. "*Le chien est triste. Hélàs! Il a lu tous les livres*," he wrote on the blackboard in the classroom. It would have to do for today. Surely the English with their love of animals could not complain of *that*? But as he sniffed the air he felt that trouble lay ahead. The pieties of the place argued ill for free thinkers. He was thinking this over when. . . . But this needs a new paragraph.

Poor Sister Rosa, too, was bored to death. Her English was very bad, and it was in the hope of finding someone to speak to her in Congo Pidgin that she had appraised Sutcliffe whom she knew to be teaching French; almost inhaling him with her mind as she raised her neat little muzzle and tip-tilted nose. The inside of her lips were blackish purple, her teeth were small and regular, her smile delicious – or so thought the quivering Master of Arts. Boredom makes strange bedfellows, he could not help remarking, for he knew that all this frantic emotion was a little bit invented. When he closed his eyes he saw her naked on his shabby cot in the alcove, lying back with her eyes closed. Her dark skin tinted like rum, molasses, ginger . . . and so on.

For her part she found it vastly dispiriting to spend hours arranging waxed fruit on the High Altar of the chapel. Nevertheless it gave her access to Sutcliffe's pew which was convenient. At the next service he found a flower on his hassock and a highly suggestive Catholic bookmarker tucked into his hymn-book. The ingenuity of women! Sutcliffe blushed all over with pleasure. It was the work of a second to scribble on the endpapers of the hymn-book the magic words, "How? When? Where?" in French. If he did not add "How much?" it was because he did not want to hurt her feelings by being *too* French. After all, she *was* a bloody nun. Now a short pause supervened, for what reason he could not tell – the designs of nature perhaps, or the feeling that she had gone too far, or something of an administrative order? Hard to tell. Anyway he left another message inviting closer co-operation and tried to fire her by singing very loudly when interpreting hymns whose words ("Nearer My God to Thee", for example) could be taken in more than one way.

At last she yielded – though her handwriting was so inchoate that he had difficulty in making out the words "Tonight. Room 5". Sutcliffe swelled up with desire and pride. That evening he played Bach remorselessly and with keen impatience. He had never been into the nunnery side of the establishment, and while he supposed that they shuffled to bed fairly early he thought it wise to let them get to sleep before starting his own invasion of the premises, EVERSAFE in hand, so to speak. To tell the truth the prospect rather quailed him – wandering about in the gloomy corridors of a nunnery. He waited until midnight before embarking.

He crossed the quad and entered the silent building which showed not a spark of light anywhere. He made brief use of his pocket torch and mounted to the first floor. The numbers were not only battered and almost effaced, they were not in serial order – or so it seemed. But at last he hit upon a room which he took to be numbered correctly, pressed the handle of the door and felt the warm air flow out into the corridor. He stepped into the blackness and stood for a moment to let his eyes accustom themselves to the dark. A figure in a bed stirred and he heard what he took to be a welcoming sigh. "Sister Rosa," he breathed and switched on his little torch.

The Mother Superior gazed at him in terrified silence, with starting eyes; if she had had her teeth in they would have been chattering – but they lay and grinned in a tooth mug beside the bed. Sutcliffe let out an incoherent exclamation of utter panic. Her wig was on a stand by the bed and she wore a nightcap. He was about to turn and run for it when she turned on the light and exclaimed, "Mr. Sutcliffe, what are you doing here?"

It was difficult to explain. He spread his arms and pretended to be sleepwalking; then he awoke with a theatrical start and said, "Where am I?"

It carried no conviction.

As time went on the story changed shape almost as often as it changed hands or tongues; some of this was due to Sutcliffe himself who had the ingrown novelist's habit of embroidering on behalf of novels as yet to be. Thus in one version she produced a pearl-handled revolver and fired a shot through his coat-tails – in fact, he was not wearing a coat. In another equally implausible version she opened wide her arms and legs and cried, "At last you have come to claim me!" thus forcing upon him a distasteful and unholy conjunction of souls and bodies. It was the only way to keep his job.

But what really happened? She cried, "Mr. Sutcliffe, will you leave this room at once!" and this he did with some alacrity. In the morning he was summoned before the board of governors and dismissed with effect from lunchtime – hardly leaving him time to pack before catching the London train. He felt bad about having betrayed Rosa too, for on his way to the station he had a glimpse of her sitting upright between two granite-faced Carthusians in the little black bus of the school which could be converted into a hearse in times of need. Her cheeks were very flushed and her eyes cast down.

Once back in London he returned to the seedy agency which had found him the job and described the circumstances of dismissal to the little Cockney manager whose catarrh and adenoids took turns at interfering with his articulation. He heard Sutcliffe out, shaking his head sadly. "Not very clever," he said more than once. "You know what I should have done? Bicycled to the doctor's and asked for a prescription against sleepwalking." He spread his hands. "Then when the board called me up I would have a watertight excuse." Sutcliffe whistled. "I never thought of that," he said.

"Next time be more wily," said the little man.

"Or less susceptible to female charms."

"Quite."

He turned once more to his sordid register and went through a list of vacancies tracing them with a broken thumbnail.

So the long cultural calvary continued for our hero until (after many humiliations) he rose to glory and affluence by his superior merits. Yet looking back on these episodes in later years he was not displeased with some of his handiwork. When the class, for example, asked him what the last words of Verlaine were he had replied: "Happiness is a little scented pig."

◆

But leaving Sutcliffe to his picaresque early adventures, the thoughts of Aubrey Blanford once more returned to those earliest memories of France, and of Provence. They were wonderfully pristine always – as if only yesterday:

There they were, for example, lying in the pond among the open lilies with the cool lapping water up to their throats, breathing in the silences of the abandoned garden, which, like the house itself, was full of presences which would have been real ghosts if only they had been visible. Doors which opened and shut of their own accord, footsteps on the main staircase at midnight. Voices which whispered names so softly that it was always possible to attribute the noise to the rustle of ivy in the changing wind. With shifts of temperature –

when the heat from the kitchen rose to the first floor – all the cupboards creaked and burst open as if to embrace one. In the dense foliage of the garden there was always a flickering of things just seen out of the corner of the eye. When one turned and looked directly there was nothing. And there was one loose tile on the footpath by the *potager* where every night at dusk one heard a footfall: someone passed and made it click.

Sometimes if you opened the cellar door a black cat flowed out which answered to no name, no blandishment, no caress. It made its way softly through the hall, to disappear by a side door. An animal? Or the ghost of one? It was like a portfolio of sketches of suave postures – something to grace a fashion plate.

A long time later Hilary said that he had once seen a girl in a white evening dress walking by the lily pond reading a letter; what struck him was that the blackbirds gave no sign of seeing a human being and were actually flying through her – or so it appeared. She passed into the trees and took the path to the house; he waited uneasily for her on the balcony but she never appeared. In the afternoons by the little coach-house someone beat the dust out of an invisible carpet. All the silences of the place seemed dense with things just waiting to materialise. A sense of immanence. Constance loved this; at night she was always blowing out the light and sitting in the dark trying to "see". But Livia could not stand it, and after a few days would find an excuse to set off on a camping-trip or spend a few days in neighbouring Avignon where Felix gave her his tiny spare room.

And then the portrait gallery, the three heads! This long gallery was an extension to the house with broad windows running the whole length of it and lit with white panes of toplight; the trees sheltered it from the direct rays of the sun. Now it was empty, for the old lady had sold all her portraits long since – an unremarkable collection by all accounts – and kept only three smoky heads printed in the typical ancestor-style of safe academicians of the last century. And now almost obliterated by corruptions in the pigment. The names too were hardly readable, though one could make out the word Piers on the portrait of the pale young man with a frail and consumptive expression, and the word Sylvie below that of the dark intense girl, who might well have been his sister. The third picture had fared worse and it was literally not possible to tell whether the subject was a man or a woman – only that its colouring was blonde and not dark, its eyes as blue and lucid as Hilary's. All three portraits were draped with black velvet, which created a singular impression on the beholder, who could not help wondering why. Was someone in mourning for them? Did it betoken some special religious gesture – a consecration? Who were they? We were unable to find out. On the back of one picture, written in yellow faded ink was the phrase, "Chateau de Bravedent". To study them one had to draw back their velvet covers with a gold cord.

Felix Chatto, no less intrigued than we, had spent a lot of time and energy trying to find out the meaning of this laconic inscription and the location, if possible, of such a chateau; in vain. "I swear there is no such place in Provence," he added with a sigh, "though of course one day it might surface again as the lost medieval name for a place." We were sitting downstairs then at the oaken kitchen table, having lunch. "And perhaps it is better that way – not to know, I mean, and to go on wondering about them. It would be difficult to invent a romantic enough story to suit that strange trio. And in my view you are wrong about the third person – it is really a woman, not a man. The fingernails are not painted." But of course this proved nothing and he knew it. But then: why the dusty velvet coverings? Were they dead?

Nevertheless the existence of the three and the name of

the apparently non-existent chateau exercised a great influence over the musings of Blanford; they existed as obstinate symbols of something to which the key had been lost. He said to himself sadly, "If only I believed in the novel as a *device* I would incorporate their story in a book which had nothing to do with real life. Bravedent!"

Livia turned her face to him; she had been sucking a coloured sweet they had bought at the village shop. With a swift motion of her tongue she passed it into his mouth and sealed it with a bitter-sweet kiss on the lips. He was lost, Blanford. He found such effortless happiness almost painful.

It was only now, in this backwash of time, and from these heterogeneous documents that he could follow out the slow curve of this *amor fati* – this classic attachment to Livia. When he asked her what her mother was like, for example, it was Constance who replied to him: but at some other time, in another context, for Livia simply looked at him with those dark eyes gone like dead snails and licked her lips as if about to speak, but nothing came. Constance wrote in a letter: "I remember an old, old lady with a piercing blue eye, whose cheeks had subsided for want of teeth and whose ill-fitting false ones did not fulfil the role completely. She had been a poor actress before she married. Now she was mad with regret and forever dwelling on ancient pleasures which had fed that sick vanity. The world of diplomacy – a world of kindly lampreys – provided a delusive background for her needs. Underneath the surface excitements the demon of accidie had her by the hair. She had always been avid for the meretricious, and when her shallow beauty faded everything turned to hate – but chiefly against her children because of their own youthful beauty. Not for her the Great Inkling! Here she was, subsiding into ashes day by day, while we were flowering. Soon she felt herself swelling with pure malevolence, a loathing strong enough to carry, she hoped, even beyond the grave, to blight our lives, to maim our spirits! She complained that her breasts were flaccid because she had nursed us too long, and tried everything then available to plump them out, except surgery. Even that absurd *ventouse* which was supposed to make them firm by suction. We have had to wade though all this powerfully projected hate without quite understanding it – except now, retrospectively. Forgiving it is another thing. Look at Livia!"

He was looking at Livia, at that face which for him spelt an invincible happiness; he was not so much wounded as astonished when the youthful Sam described her eyes like dead fish-eyes and her hair as dandruffy, adding that he could never care for a girl like that. The angle of vision is everything. The poetic vision is manufactured to meet desire. This experience was forming him, and would give him his first short story, which in the long run was what really mattered. But without her and the frightful jolt she gave him he might never have entered the immortality stakes with his first study of the circle she frequented in Paris where she was at this time a professing painter, prone to cubism. His inexperience shielded him from recognising the group of charming if effete personages for what they were – and they were careful not to enlighten him. She lived thus, in happy ambiguity, within this kindly group of homosexual friends whose charm and sensibility were undeniable. As a little band of outlaws they had grouped themselves into postures of social consequence; it was a wise precaution for they were for the most part rather insipid people and they knew it. Their social commerce betrayed a certain fragile uncertainty ... they felt somehow one-dimensional; almost opaque. They telephoned each other several times a day, as if to reassure themselves of each other's existence. They issued bulletins about their health and the state of their art which were like certificates of identity.

Later, when Constance was full (a little too full) of her knowledge, she expressed the cruel paradox of Livia's case more clearly; indeed the total narcissism which is expressed in inversion derives from the sense of abandon by the mother. But crueller still, the sexual drive which alone satisfies it consists of a mock incest precisely with her abandoner. But such a proposition would only have made Livia swear – and the oaths she used turned ugly in her mouth, accompanied as they were by expressions as distasteful as those of a sick bird. A phrase came to mind from the black notebook, where he was trying to lay down a few guide-lines towards a sketch of her character. Looking at Constance with remorse, regret and hate, Livia thought, "There is nothing more enraging than the sight of someone who is unwaveringly, naturally and helplessly good." After all, Constance had her own deceptions to live through, though she was at last able to swallow their absurdity and pretentiousness and write, "Love is the banana-peel that laughter-loving reality leaves on the pavements for men and women to skid on." The thing was that she comprehended and pardoned her sister because she loved her, and for her sake she always hoped against hope that our relations would survive despite the drawbacks. Blanford could not remember just when he made a note in his diary which said, "I fear she lives on tittle-tattle and smoke; I have married a rattle and a snob." But even that was not the worst of the matter; the central feeling of loss was to get denser and richer as bit by bit Livia grew more sure of herself, more careless about hiding matters.

The mind has limits, the body limits; the equation is easily made, the limits quickly reached. It was all my fault, thought Blanford, leaning forward to poke the fire. It was a case of transposed heads. Constance and I were slow to recognise each other. In all this amateur bliss I one day overheard a telephone conversation with Thrush, the little Martinique lover, which made me prick up my ears. In a different voice, one that I had never heard before, she said: "I simply made up my mind to make him marry me." Turning, she saw me at the door, and replaced the receiver. I said nothing and after a while her obvious anxiety died down – I suppose since I offered no comment on this remark. "It was just Thrush," she said, "we are going to the Opera tonight." She knew that I could never stand opera. But just for once I had taken the number of their tickets and had bought myself one in the Gods. I went that evening and easily located the stalls she had reserved; but the seats were occupied by other people whose faces I did not know.

It is only the context which renders such things painful or pleasurable – all that was basically wrong was Blanford's gruesome lack of experience. He knew that now. It was the pliant and lovely Livia's destiny to initiate him – and of course those we initiate we mark for life. "Nature's lay Idiot, I taught thee to f**k," she could have exclaimed as Sutcliffe did on another such occasion; nor would the glancing echo of Donne have been out of keeping. No. But the period of ardour and illusion led on and on for more than a summer – could it perhaps have gone on for a lifetime? – until by an unlucky accident he came upon the letter she had forgotten to hide or destroy and in which everything was made clear. His heart sank with sorrow and disgust; it was not the reaction of a moralist – it was simply that he found the deception cruel and unnecessary. From it all he suddenly developed an exaggerated hate for the little group of neuters – *les handicappés* – and by extension for the Paris he had always found grotesque, but vividly alive and nourishing. How would he stand August now, swollen with the knowledge that he was being run in tandem with some black-hearted Parisienne? He started to write her letters, and to leave them everywhere in the flat. He had moved to a furnished room but still had the key of the flat and used his bookfilled study to work in. He was still raw from the pleasures of her beauty and the excellence of her love-making; there was a poem of that period in which he described her with felicity as "a constellation of fervours". It was published in the *Critic* but he did not show it to her. Thrush, then, was the ringmaster? It was suddenly like being dropped on one's head out of a tree, or diving into an empty swimming pool. With one hand he did some automatic writing in his black notebook. ("The new sexual model will incorporate death somehow as the central experience. The lovers will float to the surface belly upwards, dead from exhaustion.") He wrote an indignant description of his discovery to Constance but did not post it. And years afterwards, in discussing this period of time, he felt glad that he had not, for Constance was busy with profounder matters, and still much hampered by her sexual inexperience. It was this same summer perhaps that she decided to marry Sam – which also called for long and elaborate reflections later on. But in one sense the shock was most salutary for Blanford; he was suddenly able to see all round himself; it was as if he had been living in a dense fog and suddenly it had lifted. It was a real initiation, a real awakening. He suddenly saw, for example, what the two lovers had done to Thrush's husband. He was a pious and swarthy little man, pleasantly coon-coloured and with dense ringlets. It is doubtful that he actually was conscious of what was going on – the notion rested on the edge of his mind like an ominous premonition. He began to feel first an overwhelming lethargy – the affect had started to bleed; the two vampires knew their stuff all right!

But first of all they made him rich and fashionable, a consultant for film stars and bankers, and that sort of animal. They lobbied him decorations of one sort or another, and made sure that he went to all the first nights and cocktail parties. It was about six years since he had last slept with Thrush, though they lived in tender amity; but he began to retire earlier and earlier, gripped by fatigue and the shadow of something like diabetes; until he took to having dinner with the children in the nursery and going straight to bed with them; he yawned more and more and looked vague. Retiring thus from the fray every evening he left the *champs d'honneur* free for the lovers and their doings. Once or twice they talked of finding him a substitute woman – a pretty *repoussoir* like Livia – but he had no energy left for such a project. So thoroughly had they done the work of affect castration that he had gone all anaesthetic. As for Thrush, *animatrice de petit espace* that she was, she kept him soothed and tranquil in his striped pyjamas. In her he had an impresario who had guided him to wealth and social success – should a man ask more? But Blanford could see that this same gloomy fate of Zagreus was going to be his unless he watched out. What to do? As he wrote in one of his letters to Livia, "Of course marriage is an impossible state with all its ups and downs, lapses, temptations, renewals. But the only thing the tattered old contract sets out is that you accord the primacy of your affections to someone, this side idolatry. The cheat was that yours were not free to bestow. It is all that sours me."

He was left with a mountain of scribbled exercise books – an attempted exorcism. But it did little good. It was as futile as founding a society for the abolition of bad weather. Yet the loneliness taught him discipline. There is nothing more beautiful than Method.

About Blanford; before writing the first words of a novel in his Q series he would close his eyes, breathe serenely through his nose, and think of the Pleiades. To him they symbolised the highest form of art – its quiddity of stillness and purity. Nothing could compare with them for noble rigour, for elegance. It was in order to cure this rather

dangerous proclivity that he had invented that mass of
conflicting and contradictory predispositions called Sutcliffe –
a writer who recited the Lord's Prayer, putting a Damn
between every word, before addressing *his* novel.

Blanford took an overdose of sleeping pills and had
horrible dreams in which he was forever helping two nymphs
on with wings they rejected. He imagined them lying together in the sand – Livia's face like an empty playground
waiting for children, her large vague pale brow . . . The long
middle finger which betokened bliss in secret.

Nor was it any solace to think hard thoughts about
Thrush; apart from this unhappy situation he found her
delightful. But he told himself that she opened her mouth so
wide that she resembled a hippo, folding her food into it. As
a matter of fact, even when she laughed her eyes cried
"Help!" He could dimly intuit the terrible jealous insecurity
that ravaged the two quaires – the negative of his own, so to
speak. Once in the rue St.-Honoré when he was waiting for a
massive American businessman (they had the simple authority
of trolleys, comforting), the dentist came up to him in a bar
and got into conversation. They only knew each other by
sight then, and Blanford felt a kind of clinging, pleading
quality in the encounter – as if he were hoping to find some
solution to his case in a talk with Blanford. But they were ill
matched for an exchange of consolations. He told himself that
Thrush had a vicious, thirsty little French face; but it wasn't
true and he knew it. He felt as if his brains had cooled and
dripped into his socks. He could have written an ode called
"A Castrate's Tears beneath the Shears" – but the tone was
wrong and he delegated this to Sutcliffe who would come
along in good time with his own brand of snivel. And then,
on top of it all, to be unfair to poor Paris which all of a sudden
became loathsome to him. He noticed now the dirty hair,
cheaply dyed, and never kept up from meanness – so many

brassy blondes with black partings. And in August the refusal to shave armpits. . . . The town smelt like one large smoking armpit. Acrid as the lather of dancers. And then the selection of sexual provender – perversions worthy of wood-lice. Well, he had come there for infamy in the first place, so what the hell had he got to complain about? He would die, like Sutcliffe, in the arms of some lesbian drum-major, dreaming nostalgically of hot buttered toast between normal thigh and thigh. Indeed he would go further and become a Catholic and enact the funky deathbed scene – the spider on the ceiling and the shadow of a priest and a notary. . . . It wouldn't do, said the voice of Constance, and he knew that it wouldn't. Eheu!

Under the shock of this misadventure Blanford suddenly found that he could read people's minds, and a sudden shyness assailed him; he found now that he lowered his eyes when faced with newcomers – the better to listen to the sound of their voices. It was the voice he was reading so unerringly. People thought that he had become unusually shy of a sudden. (In some lower-middle-class bedroom Sutcliffe heard his tinny wife say, *"Chéri, as tu apporté ton Cadeau Universel?"* And he replied, *"Oui chérie, le-voilà."*

The Consul Awake

THE PRO-CONSUL WAS RULED BY THE DEMON OF INSOMNIA, the royal illness; lying with his eyes fast shut in his little cage of a villa with its creaky bed, old chest of drawers and flawed mirror – lying there suspended in his own anxiety as if in a cloudy solution of some acid – he saw the sombre thoughts passing in flights across the screens of his consciousness. The hours weighed like centuries on his heart. Memories rose up from different periods of his life, crowding the foreground of his mind, contending for attention. They had no shape, no order, but they were vivid and exhausting – at once silky and prickly as thistles. Each night provided an anthology of sensations betokening only hopelessness and helplessness; this handsome and quite cultivated young man who dreamed of nothing so much as a post in the Bank of England (the excellence of his degrees justified such a hope) had been unwittingly sold into slavery by a mother who adored him with all the passion that centres about only children. How had this all come about? He knew only too well. "For you it's *diplomacy*," said his uncle, Lord Galen, one day, conducting the full orchestra of his self-esteem. His opinion was never asked and he was too weak to resist the little corsair who had become his mother's lover after the death of Felix's father. The boy had been weak and irresolute enough, the man was even more so. So here he found himself in a minor consular post in Avignon – a pro-consul of the career, if you please, but paid a mere pittance for his services. Yes, here he was, half dead with boredom and self-disdain.

The Office had not even had the decency to declare the post an honorary one – which would perhaps have forced

Galen to make him an allowance. He was paid like a solicitor's clerk. He was only allowed a part-time consular clerk to keep his petty cash and type the few despatches he ever wrote. There was nothing to report and if there were any British subjects in Avignon they had never shown their faces. The villa was buried deep in dust-gathering oleanders and poinsettias. If only his mother could see him now – a Crown Servant! He gave a croak of sardonic laughter and turned on his side. Yet she must be proud of him. A flood of unformulated wishes and hopes, suddenly floating into view, directed his memory to a picture which made him always catch his breath in pain, as if he had run a thorn under his fingernail. He opened his eyes and saw her sitting withered up in her wheelchair. Looking at the dusty electric bulb hanging naked from the ceiling he went over his history for the thousandth time. His father had died when he was very small; years later his mother had conducted a long and decorous affair with his brother, the dashing Galen (extremely discreet, extremely ambiguous) until the increasing paralysis confined her to this steel trolley, pushed by a gloved attendant dressed in a billy-cock hat and a long grey dustcoat. Felix could hear the munching of its slim tyres on the gravels of gardens in Felixstowe, Harrogate, Bournemouth. When her illness grew too severe she had been too proud to continue her affair with Galen – she could not bear to see herself as a drag on him or on his career. He accepted this decision with guilty relief, though he vowed that she would want for nothing. He kept in touch through her doctors, though he did not write directly any more – he had always had a superstitious hatred of ink and paper. He had been taught that things written down can turn against one in the courts, that was the root of the feeling. But even had he written she could not have answered for she could no longer hold a pen; and as for speech, her own was slurred and indistinct. Her jaw hung down sideways, there were problems with saliva. Deeply shocked by her own condition, the dark eyes blazed with a sort of agonised astonishment. Her attendant was called Wade. In his billy-cock hat he wore the feather of a cock-pheasant. He was now far closer to her than either her son or her lover. She was impatient for only one thing now – to die and get it over with. . . . Wade read the Bible to her for two hours every night.

Felix groaned and rolled over in bed, turning his face to the ghastly wallpaper with its raucous coaching print. He breathed deeply and tried to hurl himself into sleep as if from a high cliff – but in vain, for other shallower thoughts swarmed about him as the fleas swarmed in his bed, despite the Keating's Powder. This time it was exasperating memories of the official pinpricks he had incurred in trying to obtain a new Union Jack to fly from the mast which had been so insecurely fixed to the first-floor balcony of the villa. During the usual Pentecost celebrations, which were closed by a triumphal gallop-past of the Carmargue *gardiens*, some fool had discharged a gun in the air – *un feu de joie* – and the charge had spattered the sacred flag with smallshot, so that now it looked like a relic left over from Fontenoy. Felix simply could not fly such a tattered object any longer and, having described the circumstances, invited London to replace it. But nothing doing. An immense and most acrimonious correspondence had developed around this imperial symbol; the Office insisted that the culprit should be found and sued for his sins, and lastly forced to replace the object; failing that, said the Office of Works (Embassy Furnishings Dept.), the flag might have to be paid for out of Felix's own pocket – a suggestion which drove him mad with rage. Back and forth went these acid letters on headed paper. London was adamant. The culprit must be found. Felix smiled grimly as he recalled the leather-jawed horseman whose racing steed had struck a bouquet of sparks from the cobbles as it went. The man indeed who had so narrowly missed him, for he had been standing on the balcony at the time to watch the procession. A foot to the right and there would have been a consular vacancy which the Crown Agents would have been happy to advertise in *The Times*. He had even felt the wind of the discharge, and smelt the cordite of a badly dosed home-made charge. And the flag?

And the flag! Should he, he wondered, try to get it "invisibly mended"? There was a new shop in the town which promised such an amenity. But an absurd sense of shame held him back. Would it not seem queer for a shabby consul to sneak about the town with a tattered Union Jack, trying to get it repaired on the cheap? Yes. On the other hand if he flew it as it was just to spite the Office there was a risk that some consular nark from Marseille might see it and report adversely on him. He sighed and turned again, turning his back on these futile exchanges, so to speak. And so then Galen had quietly replaced his father, had taken command of everything, school-fees, death-duties, house-rents, etc. In fact he had actually become his father, and as such infallible. He pronounced shortly and crisply on everything now; his will was done, rather like the Almighty's. The overwhelmed and frightened child could do nothing but obey. Galen had, as a matter of fact, demanded worship, but all Felix could supply was a silent obedience to the little man with the plentiful gold teeth which winked and danced in the firelight as he outlined the splendid life which the Foreign Service held in store for the boy.

So here was Felix listening to the sullen twang of the mistral as it poured across the town, dragging at shutter fastenings and making his flagless flagpole vibrate like a jew's harp. The consular shield below it had also taken a few pellets but the damage was not extensive. It merely looked as if some hungry British subject had taken a desperate bite out of it in self-defence. "Whatever you do, Mr. Chatto," the Foreign Secretary had admonished him before handing him his letters of credence and appointment, "never let yourself become cynical while you are in Crown Service. There will be many vexations, I know; you will need all your self-control but try and rise above them. Sincerely." Well, if he had been in a laughing mood he might have managed a feeble cackle. Indeed his shoulders moved in a simulated spasm but in fact his face still wore the pale, dazed expression of a sinus case which aspirin could not relieve. He could smell the dust being blown in from the garden – dust and mimosa. In the spaces between assaults the wind died away to nothing and left a blank in the air into which seeped fragments of ordinary sound like the bells of St. Agricole. The theatre would be emptying into the square by now and despite the foul wind the cafés would awake for a spectral moment; it was too chill to do more than hug the counters and bars and drink "*le grog*". It was early yet, all too early. Like sufferers from sinus and migraine he was used to seeing the dark nights unroll before him in a ribbon of desolation.

But his real calvary began well after midnight when he rose, made himself a pot of vervain *tisane* and slowly dressed, pausing for long intervals to gaze into the bathroom mirror or stand in bemused silence before the cupboard mirror gazing at his own reflection in it, watching himself dress slowly, knot his old school tie, draw on his shabby college blazer with the blazoned pocket. Who was this familiar shadow? He felt completely disembodied as he looked, as he confronted his own anxious, unfamiliar face. He drew on his black felt hat, stuffed his wallet into his breast pocket; then he stayed in the sitting room gazing at the print hanging over the chimney – a pastoral scene of goats and cypresses. With one half of his mind he heard the throbbing of the wind and registered its diminution with something like satisfaction. Perhaps in another twenty minutes it might sink away into one of its sudden calms. He would pause awhile before setting off on one of his all-too-frequent night walks round the town which he had come to regard as the most melancholy in the whole world. Its eminence, its history, its monuments – the whole thing drove him wild with boredom; mentally he let out shriek after shriek of hysteria, though of course his lips did not move and his consular face remained impassive, as befitted a Crown Servant.

Yes, the wind was subsiding slowly; a clock chimed somewhere and there was the long slow moan of a barge from the river like some haunted cow. He licked his finger and traced the dust upon the mantelpiece. The little hunchback maid who came in for an hour of dusting every morning was fighting in vain against the ill-fitting shutters. As for food, Felix arranged his own light meals, or crossed the square to the little penurious café called Chez Jules where they made sandwiches or an occasional hot dish filled with chili and pimento. He threw open the door of the office and stood for a while gazing down at his own imagined ghost – he saw himself writing a despatch about the flag. What furniture, what entrancing ugliness! He enumerated it all as he sipped his tea and stirred a loose tile with the toe of his suede shoe. There was a mouse-hole in the wall which he had stopped with a pellet of paper manufactured from a particularly exasperating and stupid despatch from head office. It had assuaged his feelings and had apparently discouraged the mouse – though God knows what such a poor creature might expect to find here to eat. Books? He was welcome to the consular library. Felix had a small suitcase of private books under his bed, mostly poetry. But now he was looking at the shallow office bookcase with its reference books which were apparently all that a consul ever needed in order to remain efficient. The F.O. List with its supplements made quite good reading. It soothed him to discover the where-abouts of long-lost London colleagues. When he wanted to gloat he looked up some fearful bore like Pater and read (his lips moved as he did so) the small paragraph which recited all his early posts, sinking in gradual diminuendo towards the fatal posting. Consular Agent, Aden. He could hardly forbear to let out a cheer, so much had he disliked Pater while he was being "run in" in the London office. Then there was Sopwith too – another victory of good sense. He had been posted to Rangoon. On the whole then, Avignon might not seem so bad. But he had no money to get to Nice or Paris, and Galen would never have lent him the large slow Hispano which coasted everywhere with its goggled negro chauffeur – trailing long plumes of white dust across the vernal olive groves. What else was there for a decent self-respecting mouse to feed on? *Consular Duties* in six volumes? A volume of consular stamps and some faded ink-rollers which thumped out a splayed crown if properly inked. *Wagner's Basic International Law* – a huge and incompre-hensible compilation. *The British Subject Abroad*, a guide for Residents. Skeat's *English Usage*. *The Consular Register*. *The Shorter Oxford*. All this to keep his despatches in good trim. There were also a few grammars and detective stories. The whole thing was pretty shabby and anyone having a look around would realise (he told himself) that Chatto was very poor, and that Lord Galen was either quite oblivious of the fact or wanted to keep him so. As for pro-consuls in posts as remote as these, they were hardly paid at all, and certainly never got accorded consular *frais*, expense accounts, which they might disburse in the pursuit of pleasure. Moreover Felix had no private income, so that his mind was always pinched by the thought of overspending. Even when people found him agreeable and invited him out to functions he was apt to decline for fear that he would never be able to invite them back. Nothing gives one that hunted look like poverty; and there is no poverty like having to swallow the backwash of extravagantly rich relations, who cannot help patronising you, however much they may try not to. And on such an exiguous budget, in a remote place, everything became a terror – the necessary doctor's visit, an operation, a false tooth, broken spectacles, a winter overcoat. All these possibilities gnawed at his mind, depleting his self-confidence, poisoning the springs of his happiness.

Well then, night after night, as he lay in the coarse sheets, he went over these factors in a trance of sleepless misery; his history seemed to stretch like an unbroken ribbon of distress and anxiety right back to the father's death and his sad schooldays. (His reports always said something like "Could do better if day-dreamed less".) His only refuge had been books; and now he was beginning to take a faked interest in Catholicism because it made one friends and took up time. He felt that unless he could find himself fully occupied the weight of his present boredom and anguish might unseat his reason and lead him towards what was then known as "a brain fever". He whispered, "Oh God, not that," under his breath when the thought came into his mind. Someone to talk to, for the love of God! When he received a note from Blanford telling him of the summer to be spent near Avignon, tears came into his eyes and he gave an involuntary dry sob of pure relief.

In these long night-silences he felt rather like the town itself – all past and no recognisable present. Did Galen know about them coming down – he did not know if Blanford was an acquaintance of the old man. How could one tell? Galen never even bothered to signal his frequent absences and returns – he spent several months a year in the tumbledown chateau which he was too mean, Felix supposed, to restore.

He moved about all over Europe following the threads of the cobweb he had spun with his fortune, playing the game of banking and politics. Everywhere he was accompanied by Max, his negro valet-chauffeur, who in certain lights looked dark violet; and the dumb (literally) male secretary whom Galen had deliberately chosen for himself, saying with a laugh that he knew how to give orders and get them obeyed. A secretary did not need a voice, a nod would suffice.

It should be noted also that where Galen went Wombat went too, seated on a mouldering green velvet cushion with a monogrammed crown printed on it as befitted the animal's pedigree, for Wombat was the imperial cat of this strange, rather sad, motherless household. Max, who loved the thing, carried it everywhere most ceremoniously, as if he were a chamberlain carrying the royal chamberpot of a King. Wombat was half blind and dying of asthma, and if offered the slightest attention or civility like an outstretched hand or a friendly sound, would react unamiably by opening its throat to hiss, and rearing up in anger. When Galen had had a drink or two in the evening he used often to wax sentimental and inform Max that the cat was his only friend; everyone else loved him for his money. With Wombat it was real love. But when he reached out his hand the animal spread its throat and reared like a cobra opening its hood as it hissed – thus avoiding the old man's caress.

No, he had little enough thought for Felix, though every Christmas he received a penny Christmas card of the Woolworth type featuring holly and a robin. It was always signed by Galen but the envelope was made out in the secretary's awkward hand. In summer, then, it was dust and wind and noise, and Keating's Powder and ceremonial processions of scruffy nuns and priests; in winter it was frost and ice and the river swollen to three times its mean summer levels. *Le cafard*, in fact, in its most exaggerated form.

Perambulatory paranoia, they would one day christen his case, of that he was sure.

He had set Blanford's postcard up on his desk as a talisman; he leaned over to read it anew now curbing his impatience by breathing slowly several times. Then he locked up his petty-cash box with its sheets of stamps and the six blank passports in the little wall-safe. He stepped out into the garden of the house, drawing the door to behind him with a soft click. How he hated that door with its ill-fitting lock. It was a glass door with a feverish design executed in squares of cathedral glass; when the sunlight fell upon it it produced extraordinary colour effects on the face of anyone crossing the hall to open it. The features became suddenly the colour of a blood-orange; then, in sharp succession, blue, green and livid yellow. Such theatrical changes often gave the unwary caller a start.

He turned up his coat-collar and, placing his cane under his arm, drew on gloves as he began the slow martyrdom of his night march across the town.

The westering moon drooped towards the battlements and as he turned the dark corner by the abattoir which rang all night to the sound of flushing waters like a public urinal he saw the familiar little lamplighter trotting along ahead of him with his shepherd's crook with which he turned off the street-lights – for only a few corners of the town had been able to afford the new clean electric lighting. He reflected with a selfish pang that he would be sorry when the whole town went electric because the little lamplighters not only marked the hour for him (the lights were turned off at two) but also afforded him a kind of welcome night-company on his walks. He skirted the smoky grey battlements with their crenellations. By now perhaps even the gipsies would have retired to their tents and caravans – they kept up the latest in the town, as far as he could judge; he followed the little lamplighter who padded along ahead of him making almost no sound, and only pausing to put out a lamp with his little crook. It was like someone beheading flowers one after the other; the violet night rushed in at once with its graphic shadows. At the rue St.-Charles he mentally said goodnight to his familiar and turned sharp right towards the Porte St.-Charles which here pierced the massive walls of the town. One emerged upon the apron, so to speak, of the bastion – a dusty *terrain vague* punctuated with tall planes whose leaves had begun to turn green. Here were great areas of shadow and few lights – a fitting place for the enactment of mischief, a corner made for throat-slitting, settling of accounts and active whoring. The gipsies had not been slow to find it and to settle on it – in defiance of the law which from time to time ordered them to leave. In vain. But now their fires had burned low and they had taken to their caravans where frail night-lights burned behind curtains. A point or two of lights could also be seen in the tents and the makeshift shelters where they lay, piled together for warmth like a litter of cats. Felix half envied and half feared them, and as he heard his own dry footfalls change in tone as they passed between the ramps of the tall gate his hand always strayed involuntarily to the electric torch in his pocket, though as yet he had never had occasion to use it in an emergency.

Yes, their fires had burned down to the embers and even their few donkeys and dogs appeared to slumber. But from one of the smaller tents a girl, awakened by his echoing footfalls, arose, seeming to materialise from the very ground, and sidled towards him whining for alms. Yes, she sidled yawning towards him like a pretty kitten, stretching out her slender arms. She could not have been much over sixteen and she was dressed as vividly as a pierrot in her patchwork quilt of bright rags. He felt a whirl of desire overcome him as he saw her beautiful face, so full of the sexual conceit of her people. He felt almost like fainting. Hereabouts the stout ravelins made whole barrows of dark blue shadow – an impenetrable darkness safe from prying eyes. Why did he not simply beckon her into one of these pools of black and sink his consular talons into that lithe and swarthy flesh? She would surely follow him at the mere promise of gold?

Ah! There was the rub – gold! How much would she want for her caresses? He did not know. Anyway he knew that he had not the courage to do such a thing; he would have had to undo the constraints of his whole upbringing. A giant despondency seized him as he waved away the tempting creature. He hurried past her, feeling her predatory fingers brush his sleeve. She was barefoot, and moved soundlessly. Why didn't she hit him with something and then rape him sublimely while he lay insensible – then at least he would not feel guilty about so natural an act? But what about the dose which would almost inevitably follow such an act? It would be very expensive to cure a dose here, as well as unbearably painful. It was a subject on which he could speak with feeling as he had once accompanied a panicky under-graduate friend to the Lock Hospital in Greek Street. The poor boy was expiating a twenty-first birthday party spent at The Old Bag O'Nails in the usual way. Felix out of sympathy accompanied his friend to his first few drastic "treatments": he watched these agonising sessions with fear and repugnance. The background, too, was daunting – the long marble-walled latrines hushing with water, the rows of high white enemas and their long slim tubes. . . . Could this really be the only cure for this foul disease? First the bowel filled and refilled with permanganate (Condy's Fluid) which the patient was encouraged to piss away with whatever force he could command. Then he must submit to the cleaning and scraping of the sensitive mucus surfaces inside the urethra where the infection lay. The surgeon inserted a small catheter shaped like a steel umbrella in the organ and gradually opened it in umbrella fashion, to distend the member. This was supposed to break down and detach the infected parts so that they could be ejected and discharged. It was agony for the patient. Once seen, never forgotten.

And the mere thought of these sessions lent wings to him now, strengthening his resolve to repulse the girl. He quickened his pace and turned away down towards the pretty little railway station with its dark palms. The girl showed some disposition to insist but was soon overtaken by yawns and contented herself by spitting in his wake as she turned aside to regain the tents. The last train had gone out, the first of the new day was still far off. From somewhere among the dark quays came the sharp clanging of milk churns being man-hauled and stacked in the dark sheds against the arrival of the morning milk carts. The refreshment room was also closed at this hour but one naked bulb burned on in it and through the frosted glass he could see the old peasant and his wife washing glasses and teapots and sweeping the flags with tattered straw brooms. He would have liked to drink a grog but they would not open to him until the first train of the day shook the silent station with its clatter and squeals. The *fiacres* still stood outside the main entrance under the clock whose hands had pointed to two-twenty for the last three months. Would it never be mended? The drivers were wrapped in old blankets like effigies, the horses appeared to be asleep standing.

Porte St.-Roche, Porte St.-Charles, Porte de la République – the last led directly to the heart of the town, the throbbing little square around which everything of social consequence was grouped – the Mairie, the handsome old Theatre, the Monument des Morts with its disgraceful but delightful tin cartoon of symbolic lions and the flag-waving Marianne. . . . How well he had come to know it all; he was no longer a hesitant tourist, inspirited by the romance of its history, but one of the forty thousand residents now, his spirit almost embalmed in the boredom of its silences, its frowning churches, its shuttered shops and cafés. The horrifying thing was that this sort of life corresponded most favourably to the best posting available to a young consul, apart from working in a great capital or a town as big as Marseille or Lyon or Rome. After years of expiating his sins like this in places like this he might aspire to the rank of Consul General, though still resting debarred from the mainstream of career diplomacy – for the "real" diplomats were a chosen race, a trade union, a closed circle.

Turning his back to the station he addressed himself to the second massive Porte de la République and entered the inside of the bastions. In the summer he often took the opposite direction and walked over the suspension bridge to the island; but this was rather a sinister place and pitch dark, and he had no stomach to be set upon by footpads. Besides, with the present wind and temperature he could, by taking this anti-clockwise walk, shelter within the walls from the worst inclemencies of the weather. He moved towards the little chapel of the Grey Penitents set incongruously upon its dark canal with the stout wooden waterwheels forever turning with their slopping and swishing sound. From St. Magnagnen one ducked into the terrifying little rue Bon Martinet (the name struck a chord always, though the exact association escaped him for the moment: later Blanford supplied the missing fragment of the puzzle). It was so narrow and dark that one's shoulders brushed the wall on either side and when one passed a dark doorway one prayed that there might be nobody waiting for one in it with a knife or a rope. This emerged – you could see the light at the end of the tunnel – directly upon the canals; this part of the town was the domain of the tanners and dyers, and the paddlewheels,

which would have driven a decent-sized steamboat, turned
night and day though the actual trade had fallen largely into
desuetude.

Here the darkness was like wet velvet; he paused, as
always, at the entrance of the chapel and recited the inscription over the entrance to himself in a whisper. Mostly he took
out his torch hereabouts to read such things. This was the
Grey Penitents – the Black ones were situated in a further
corner of the town. He pushed the door and it squeaked open
upon blackness. Sometimes he sat for a moment in one of the
pews. There was an electric bell in the wall with the name of
a priest – a duty-priest, so to speak, always ready to take
confession if summoned. One night he had "disgraced
himself", as he would have put it if he had been describing
it to someone else. In an access of misery he had entered the
church with some intention of praying; but when he found
himself in the pew facing the cold repugnant statue which
was to act as a focus for this novel set of emotions his spirit
strangled within him, he became choked. He felt as if the
centre was sliding out of his mind. He understood what the
phrase "wrestling with the dark angel" meant. But in his
case it felt more like the slimy tentacles of Laocoön which
closed around him and from which he could not disengage
himself. There was nobody in the place, the silence echoed
to his deep panting. At last, overwhelmed by these stresses, he
crossed the aisle and pressed the bell. Underneath it there
was a card with the name of the duty-priest typed on it –
Menard. Then he stood aghast at what he had done. The
sepulchral sound of the bell died slowly away in the further
entrails of the building, awakening nobody, arousing no
answering sound. He stood there feeling now as foolish and
as irresponsible as before he had felt anguished. Ringing for a
priest at two o'clock in the morning – it was a scandal! And
yet, surely if the religious crisis were a truthful one, a serious

one, no priest could complain of the hour – any more than a doctor complain of a night call by a patient *in extremis?* But no, he felt a guilty fool for importuning the church at this time of day. Yet silence was all that his frantic ring had elicited. He stood there with head cocked on one side. In the dark street outside two cats started their macabre love-wails. Where could he be, the priest? He felt stupid, blameworthy, undeserving of consideration since he himself had shown so little. Turning, he ran to the door and opened it onto the dark causeway with its swishing canal and impassive paddle-wheels turning. Then he closed the door of the chapel silently and leaned his head against its oaken panels, as if to cool his feverish forehead with the cold touch of the wood. As he did so he heard the shuffle of footsteps entering the chapel and the clicking of the confessional wicket. A priest had, after all, answered his summons. The thought panicked him anew and turning, he hurried away into the darkness leaving priest and chapel to their darkness and silence. What a bad show this was! It took him an effort to confess it, not to the priest, but to Blanford who later joined him on these night marches, when they were hunting for traces of Livia. It was here too that Blanford untangled the associative strands which made rue Bon Martinet so evocative. The Marquis de Sade!

"It has one thing, this town, for me. The huge span of human aspiration and human weakness are symbolised by two figures from its bestiary, so to speak. I mean Petrarch's Laura who invented the perfect romantic love and the Marquis de Sade who carried it right back into its despairing infancy with the whip. What a couple of guardian angels!"

Felix pushed on doggedly now towards the next bastion, the frowning Porte Thiers where he started to cut diagonally across the sleeping town. Once or twice he passed signs of life, like an old man on a bicycle who passed him riding so slowly that it seemed as if his journey had begun a long time ago – back in the Pleistocene era perhaps. His bicycle bobbed and bounced upon the uneven cobbles and flags of the street, but quite soundlessly. The old man himself looked neither to right nor left – was he perhaps asleep? Then he coughed sharply and Felix nearly jumped out of his skin. The little wooded Place Bon Pasteur slumbered among its dense planes under which the nearby inhabitants had parked their prams and bicycles and carts which would soon be pressed into service when the market opened. From the end of the street he caught a glimpse of a frail light shining in the cavernous tin shed which housed the three trams. At five their squeals would awaken the toughest sleepers in the town – for they traversed the whole length of it. It was all the towns-people had in the way of public transport – the two large and shaky motor buses were a recent innovation and given over to tourism; they slumbered outside the Hotel Crillon and at ten would carry their fares off to inspect Aigues Mortes and the Carmargue. There was a shadowy figure with a storm-lantern moving among the slumbering trams with an oil-can, servicing them for their daily work. Dawn was as yet a premonition in a clear mistral sky prickling with stars – a mere lightening of the sky at the furthest edges of futurity; but it was like a faint chord struck somewhere far away that echoed here, for the bird colonies in the dense foliage of the trees which sheltered the beautiful old market had started to stir and stretch and converse. In the Clinique Bosque he saw a faint bud of flame under a coffee-urn – an alcohol lamp. In the Banque Foix a night watchman stirred and clanked open massive bolts to let in the two shapeless old ladies – the office cleaners. Somewhere in a nearby street an invisible whistler executed a phrase from a popular tango, and then broke off, as if in embarrassment.

This was the hour when Quatrefages at last fell asleep

in the Princes Hotel, with the lights still burning on – he could not bear the dark. What would Felix have done without the *thought* of poor Quatrefages, the knowledge that poor Quatrefages was alone among the forty thousand souls, awake all night as he himself was? The warmth of this thought made his wanderings somehow possible; the lean youth was a sort of symbolic companion for the consul, a poor scholar who was also, like himself, a serf to Lord Galen. Quatrefages looked like some sleepy raven in his rusty black *tablier* which he wore over his clothes when he worked; on this work-apron he wiped his pen with its steel nib during his pauses; his hand was a copyist's Italian cursive, as beautiful as Arabic script or a Chinese ideogram. Though why Galen should retain the services of this poor scholar to decipher and copy medieval documents, was for a time something of a puzzle. . . .

The dark, famished-looking youth had had quite a chequered history before he found himself here, immured in an ill-lit bedroom of the Princes Hotel, working with the savage concentration of a slave on the projects which Lord Galen had proposed for him. His story began with the Church – he had once been a sexton and then a curate of the Church, but a scandal accompanied by the poisonous gossip of a small village had unseated him – he had been defrocked unjustly, or so he felt. His ardent religious faith died in him there and then and was replaced by an overwhelming sensation of loss – as if the whole outer darkness which lay outside the narrow field of the doctrine had rushed in and taken possession of his soul. "Possession" is not inapt as a thought – for he now became convinced that God could not exist and that atheism was the only honourable philosophy for a logical person like himself. He had wasted his whole youth in mumbo-jumbo. In the grip of this despairing belief – for it did not render him happy, this train of thought – he turned his attention to evil with the same single-mindedness as he

had once devoted to an orthodox goodness. The path led
downwards by obscure stages towards symbolic mathematics,
enigmas, emblems and the shadowy reaches of alchemy and
astrology. On the way he discovered orthodox mathematics
and became, to his own surprise, a very able performer. It
was an accident, but a fruitful one, that had resulted in him
being co-opted into the department of Lord Galen's business
which was called "Trendings"; here a group of four young
mathematicians analysed graphs of prediction as to their
future movements up and down the scale. It was over these
large and pretty graphs that Galen pored at night, wondering
whether to sell or to buy. His little band of statisticians
provided him with a rough guide to the disposition of his
markets, and while they were not infallible there was quite a
large element of correctness, in what they found. Here
Quatrefages found himself in congenial surroundings; he
was well treated, relatively speaking. As he was afraid of the
dark and could not sleep until dawn, for the most part he
elected to do his work at night. He would sit over the old
teak drawing-boards in the uninspiring offices of the firm,
his long pointed nose slanted towards his papers. He looked
like some sleepy raven; his nails were bitten down to the quick,
his fingers always a bit inky, his trousers frayed where the
bicycle clips went. His small black mouse eyes were full of a
sullen brilliance and impatience. His dry cough and eternal
light fever spoke of tuberculosis; indeed his whole physiog-
nomy was that of the old traditional *poitrinaire*, and he had
once been placed in a sanatorium where they had collapsed a
lung to let it mend. In vain.

But the tell-tale coughing, which sometimes doubled
him up and brought tears to his eyes, did not affect the
determined steadiness of his work, despite the aching boredom
of the matter he had been set to analyse. Always at the end
of his night prowl the young consul made a short detour in

order to stand for a moment below the lighted window; to breathe in, so to speak, some of the spectral courage and anxiety of his uncle's bondsman. At such a moment his divided feelings about his uncle – hatred and affection and amusement – rose and subsided within him like a sea. Yes, he hated him; no, for how could one? Like everyone with a silly side Galen was endearing. Every afternoon he boxed with the violet negro for a couple of rounds, puffing and blowing and wiping his nose in his glove like a professional. His partner had once been a real professional and he moved round the ring (which had been set up in the garden) as lazily as a moth, fully aware that he must not hit his boss – for Galen would have died on the spot. So they moved in a strange ballet, the dark boxer grazing the ropes with his back. He wore lace-up kid shoes and a much decorated belt whose medals gleamed richly. From time to time he sent out an exhibition punch – a shadow-punch so to speak – which stopped just short of his rival's small chin. Galen's answering blows might have been aimed at the moon, they were so inaccurate. The negro moved aside, but just once in a while, took a flick upon his violet forehead and gave a deep grunt of admiration.

How beautiful Max was to watch! The negro can do nothing which does not aspire towards dancing. Even his exaggerated shuffle round the ring with the hint of gorilla-like menace – the whole thing was light as air, volatile, buoyant and undeliberate; one felt it was almost as arbitrary as the flutterings of a cabbage-white among the flowers. Yet there was science in it even though the arms hung limp as empty sleeves. Suddenly this classical punch would evolve itself like a bee-sting. Max whistled to himself, little mauve tunes, blues. From time to time he breathed a word of advice to his partner, "You gotta breathe with yo bones, sah," he might say, and shaking his head add, "sure damn thing." And

92

Galen would obediently try to breathe with his bones. After two rounds, speechless and puffing, the old man turned to whoever was watching (most often it was poor Felix) and said: "You see? It's the secret of my iron constitution."

Galen would rise very early in the morning and have himself driven to the main station to see the first train go out towards Paris; he had done this all his life, wherever he might be. Trains were an obsession. The intoxication of the platforms smelling of coal and oil, the bustle and clamour of passengers and porters loading baggage and freight – the whole indescribable chaos and order of the operation never failed to thrill him to the bone. And the farewells! A whole life, a whole human situation is illustrated in the farewells of lovers, friends, married couples, children, dogs. The clang of closing doors, the kisses, the shrill whistles, the red flag, and the steady champ of the engines belching white plumes into the blue sky – it brought him to tears still. It was perhaps by one of those cruel paradoxes in which fate delights that the railway had become connected to the sole tragedy of Galen's life – the inexplicable disappearance of his adolescent daughter. He had spent a fortune trying to trace her or at least to solve the mystery of her disappearance. One supposes that this sort of thing happens every day – to judge by the press, which comments on it for a while and then forgets it. Fifteen schoolgirls accompanied by two nuns from the Sacred Heart Convent took. a Sunday excursion train to London from Sidcote. When they arrived at Waterloo one girl was missing – Galen's daughter. It may be imagined what measures were taken to explain this extraordinary fact. Had she fallen from the train? No; had she absconded? The train was a through train. Her fellow pupils said that about half-way to London she absented herself to go to the lavatory. She never reappeared. Galen was beside himself with horror and incredulity. Every field of enquiry was pursued with all the ferocious relentlessness of a father almost beside himself. It was years ago now, but the memory was still fresh, his room was full of her photographs and hand-painted Christmas cards. He wept unaffectedly when speaking of her. One day in London he unburdened himself to his clerk Quatrefages, who was then buried deep in his alchemical studies. In some vague way Galen hoped, by revealing the degree of his own emotional weakness and commitment towards the memory of his child, to move the boy and win a little sympathy from him – he was such a taciturn creature with his bitten nails. To his surprise Quatrefages produced a ring on a pendulum and asked for a scale map of London and Surrey – so that his divining machine would plot the course of that fatal journey and perhaps offer a solution.

Galen watched with fascination as it swung to and fro in the lean hand of the clerk. Finally Quatrefages said, with a note of finality, "She was not on that train, the children were told to say she was. The nuns were lying to excuse their inattention; at the station she was taken by a gipsy." Galen reeled with hope and delight. So she might still be alive, then? After all, through the whole course of Victorian fiction the gipsies were always responsible for the disappearance of children, and often of grown-ups also. "Is she still alive?" he asked in a paroxysm of anxiety, "if so where should I look?" But Quatrefages did not know – or so he said. The truth was he did not want to go too far, as he was making all this up in order to secure a bit of a hold on this funny, aggressive little man. He had found a way. Soon Galen was dropping in for chats, and ineluctably the subject would drift towards his great obsession – the whereabouts of Sabine. He initiated an elaborate study of all the gipsy tribes, a sort of star map of their movements across Europe, and sent his agents hunting equipped with photos. At the yearly world gathering of gipsy legions his agents were waiting for their caravans to arrive from all over Europe at the Saintes Maries de la Mer. He began to find superior qualities in the French clerk – the boy became precious simply because one day he might find the missing clue to the child's whereabouts. As their intimacy grew he offered him a new sort of secret job – one he would not have confided to just anyone. Quatrefages, stupid as it may sound, was now hunting for buried treasure, nothing less, in the tangled mass of documentation which surrounds the Templars and their heresy.

Sometimes Felix stood for a while in the little square beneath the inspiring square of yellow light where once a gallows had stood, and mentally hanged himself; in the pale moonlight his body swung to and fro in the wind, softly creaking and clanking in its chains. A felon of laziness and cowardice if ever there was one. Ineffectual, too. As for Quatrefages, for all his apparent youthful inexperience and all his pretensions to esoteric knowledge, he had kept a fine French sense of proportion where self-interest was concerned. Happily. It was largely through him that Felix had obtained the part-time use of the little Morris automobile, a blessing they shared in amiable enough fashion. The clerk had asked Galen for some form of transport to enable him to travel about Provence, examining ancient sites and ruins and consulting scholars. He used the machine a fair amount, but for the rest of the time it belonged to the Consulate and undertook other duties. Felix drove himself vaguely about the delectable countryside, swollen with his sense of loneliness, and trying to render it endurable by investigating the grand dishes and finer wines of the area; for though Avignon was not Lyon in richness and variety where cuisine was concerned, nevertheless much remained to marvel at in the realm of country cooking. Even in its poorest corners France seemed quite inexhaustible to one raised on ordinary English fare.

Yet the sense of vacuum persisted, and the healthy sleep to which a youth of his age might claim a right, resisted; hence the night patrols in a city where after dark so little life seemed to exist. The few bedraggled and furtive ladies of the night were amiable but hardly appetising; they packed up at two, with the latest *café dansant*. Only the gipsies had colour and movement, and the courage which he himself lacked. Seekers of a late night out were perforce obliged to "go to the gipsies" and risk a police sweep and an ignominious appearance in court. And then the other question ... Felix shook his head. Wandering among the stray cats feasting on fish-heads and vegetable garbage from the over-turned dustbins outside the "Mireille" he pondered on the fate of consuls, and saw with hungry misgiving the manic moon in her slow dejected fall towards the lightening skyline. He yawned. Somewhere he had read that dogs denied sleep for more than four days automatically died. And consuls? He yawned again, this time from the soles of his feet.

Consummatum est. It was nearly over now. In the darkness ahead he heard the sweet whisper of the great underground ovens of the bakery with its cracked sign *"Pain du Jour"* at street level. The shop was open though still in darkness. The sleeping woman sat wrapped in her black shawl like a rook. The clink of the bell woke her and she sat up to serve him. The little cubicle smelt heavenly – with the rack beginning to fill up with loaves and croissants, with *fougasses* and doughnuts and *brioches*. Felix walked slowly home inhaling the two croissants in their slip of tissue paper. The wind had dropped as it always did at dawn. He pushed open the rusty garden gate and let himself into the musty little house, greeting its familiar smell with a renewed spasm of depression. God, even the palm tree in the garden was dusty – while as for a hideous aspidistra on the balcony the maid would have to wipe it leaf by leaf with a damp cloth, as usual.

He went to the kitchen and made some coffee. On the floor in the corner lay a wooden crate he had cracked open; it bore the insignia of the Crown Agents, Gabbitas and Speed. He had ordered it to be sent on to him when leaving London. No sooner said than done, for the Crown Agents had been constituted to offer solace and comfort to diplomatic exiles with their combination tuckbox and gift-parcel deliveries. His was the smallest and most modest order of this kind – two whisky, two gin, two white sparkling Spanish wine and two Bass. That was all for the liquid solace; but there was quite a range of kitchen commodities which might be more welcome in Africa, say, than in Europe; but Abroad was simply Abroad for the Crown Agents: with a capital letter, too, as in Hell. You could also give these damned parcels to your fellow diplomats at Christmas if you wished – it saved time and thought. In the Service they were known as "consolation prizes" – consoling one against the horrors of foreign residence, among the lesser breeds of the Kipling kind, or simply among backward European states like France with its froglegs and polluted water.

Some of the tins like Plum Jam he had already extracted. On the kitchen table stood a tin of Bumpsted's Bloater Paste beside a bottle of Gentleman's Relish and Mainwearing's Pickle Mix. The consul sat down and stared hard at these sterling products. Imperial Anchovies, Angostura Bitters. Pork and Beans, Imperial size. Lea and Perrin's Sauce ... A profound homesickness overcame him. He had seized in passing the postcard from Blanford with all its exciting promises for the coming summer; but their arrival was some way off as yet. He poured himself a large cup of coffee and hunted for milk in his little ice box which was by now iceless and dank. The milk smelt suspect. However ... the sun was coming up; he had defeated another night. Today was his day with the Morris. He started to unpack the crate and put the pots in the cupboard, arranging them like a fussy old maid so that their names were facing forward. Then a sudden impulse overcame him and he did something he should never have done; he smeared bloater paste on his croissant and ate it with a groan. It was delicious.

There would be plenty of time for a couple of hours of sleep before the maid knocked, but lest he should oversleep by any chance he retrieved the little alarm clock by his bed and, rewinding it, set it for eleven. Then he undressed and climbed yawning into his virgin bed, turning off all the lights save the small bedside lamp, for he proposed to "read himself to sleep" as usual; and the book most suitable for this exercise was *The Foreign Service Guide to Residence Abroad*. It had a blue cover with the royal arms, rather like an outsize passport, and the text had not been revised for forty years owing to a mistakenly large first printing. Together with a Bible and a Book of Common Prayer, it was the statutory going-away present accorded to young officers on their first posting abroad. The hints and instructions contained in it had a wonderfully soothing effect on insomniac consuls. Take the chapter called "Hints to Travellers":

> Officers should take soft caps for sleeping, in a travelling bag; soft shoes to replace boots, a "housewife", a couple of good mauds, a bottle of bovril, a small spirit lamp, a bottle of spirits with cups and saucers, spoons and biscuits. Also a stout sponge bag with two wet sponges in it, a soft towel, a face flannel, a brush and comb. The pillows should be made to roll up tightly and are best made of thistledown and dandelion-down. A travelling ulster with loose fronts is very useful as one can undo the clothes beneath; it should have deep pockets. Always carry an extra pair of gloves. Always take a small book of soap leaves with a small handbag; thus hands can be comfortably washed with one leaf. With a wet sponge and a soap leaf the dusty and tired traveller can always

freshen up his face and hands. It is a good wrinkle to carry an Etna spirit lamp, also a tin of mustard leaves, a medicine glass, sticking plaster, a water bottle, and a flask of good brandy in case of sudden or obstinate illness en route.

On and on went this soothing and comforting rigmarole; across the sleepy vision of the consul passed a long, an endless, line of kindly, colourless yet courageous men in pith helmets followed by their baggage, bulging with brandy flasks and Etna spirit lamps. Now he had joined the long senseless safari – forever deprived of watching the ebb and flow of copper shares on the pretty coloured charts of Quatrefages. And what the devil was "a couple of good mauds"? He would give anything to know. But now sleep had definitely come to claim him: the book dropped from his hand to the carpet and with an involuntary gesture which had become mechanical one hand went out to switch off the little bedside lamp. Felix slept a surprisingly deep and healthy sleep which would be broken by the alarm just ten minutes before the maid arrived to set his little house to rights.

The trams had started squealing and with them came the battering of bells that had once irritated Rabelais so; but he heard nothing.

FOUR

Summer Sunlight

B UT AT LONG LAST THE SUMMER, HIGH SUMMER, WAS upon them, with the promised arrival of the four firstcomers to the old manor house. Felix was in such a fever of excitement that on the expected day he hardly dared to quit the landing stage over the green swift water for fear of missing them when they stepped ashore. He walked distractedly about in the wind, talking to himself and ordering numerous coffees in the little Bistro de la Navigation hard by the river, with its one-eyed sailor host.

There was quite a group of people waiting there, on the *qui vive* for the premonitory whiff of sound from the ship's hooter as it rounded the last bend – as much an accolade to the view of Avignon from the water as a triumphal signal of arrival. In the meantime he had been busy on their behalf; he had visited the house a number of times already, sometimes by car or bicycle, and indeed once on foot; and while he could not get into it until he obtained the keys from Bechet the notary, he had a picnic or two in the dilapidated garden and the herb *potager*, now run hopelessly to seed and weed. Sitting under one of the tall pines, inhaling their sharp odour, he ate his six sandwiches and drank his red wine, dreaming of the excellent company he would enjoy once they arrived. Nor was he wrong – their arrival and their gaiety exceeded all expectation; he was to find himself adopted at once, and the manor of Tu Duc was to become a second home. They were to spend many an evening together sitting round the old kitchen table playing twenty-one; and he even once succeeded in inveigling Quatrefages to accompany him for a dinner, which rendered the boy less morose: the little clerk even expanded enough to show them a series of bewildering card tricks. But the chief factor in his happiness was without doubt the absence of Lord Galen, for the old man had decided to take his liver to Baden-Baden for a cure and had disappeared leaving no word as to when he would return. It was marvellous. The consulate remained closed almost permanently, while Quatrefages downed tools, left his Crusader maps pinned to the walls of his room, and embarked on a series of probably unsavoury adventures in the gipsy section of the town – the quarter known as Les Balances.

Livia appeared, fresh from Munich.

And with her a new element entered the camp, for the icy serenity of the girl, and the hard cutting edge of her character, made an immediate impression on them all – but of course mostly upon the too susceptible Blanford. Yet Felix too in his own fashion was enslaved, for she teased him into a sort of sisterly relationship which tightened his heart-strings with a youthful passion. He could refuse her nothing; even when she asked for the use of the spare room, a sort of glorified alcove, at the consulate (for she was too independent not to find Tu Duc oppressive) he could only limply agree while his spirit performed cartwheels at the thought, and Blanford turned pale. Blanford turned pale.

But despite all the dazzling variety and pleasure of that first summer encounter, more important elements were to form themselves which hinted at future developments and subtly transforming predispositions to come. Sam and Hilary, the inseparables, were the chief inciters to adventure and travel; only when Livia appeared did Hilary seem to take on a new constraint, his ice-blue eyes became evasive and thoughtful as he watched both Felix and Blanford foundering like ships in a gale. Constance and Sam somehow remained in a friendly comradely relationship – something not difficult for a knight-errant born to endure. Sam was not made of flesh and blood, but of flesh and books. And in the blonde, smiling Constance he had found a worshipful lady who only lacked a tower to get locked into. . . . All this, of course, has to be interpreted backwards – for while events are being lived they travel too fast for easy evaluation. Blanford noticed many things which his inexperience could not interpret. In part he reproduced all these errors in Sutcliffe to record some of the surprise they gave him when at last the truth (what truth?) dawned. One day Livia burned Hilary's wrist with her cigarette and he smacked her – and in a trice they were tearing at each other's hair like savages. Well, brothers and sisters. . . .

They had found a hunchback maid who came from the village every day; she had worked long as a *serveuse* in a brothel, so they learned afterwards. The experience had given her insight into the ways of men – she read a bedroom when she entered it, as one reads a book. She interpreted the whole scene like a sleuth, the disordered pillows and blankets, all had something to tell her. She often smiled to herself. One day Blanford, passing the door, saw her pick up a pillow and inhale it deeply. Then she shook her head and smiled. Turning she saw him and said in her hoarse way, "Mademoiselle Livia!" Yes, but it was the bed of Hilary that she was making. Things do not strike you at the time; ages later Livia bit his hand with her white teeth and he suddenly remembered the incident. And with it the kind of strained attention with which Hilary heard him say at the end of that summer: "Hilary, what would you say if I asked Livia to marry me one day?" The hard blue eyes narrowed, and then flared into rather factitious congratulatory warmth; he squeezed his friend's shoulder, however, until it hurt, but he actually said nothing. Later when they were having lunch he said, out of the blue, "I think you should make sure, Aubrey." And Blanford knew at once that he was thinking of Livia. It takes

years to evaluate such tiny glimpses into the multiple mean-
ings of any single human action. As Sutcliffe one day said to
him in one of his notebooks: "Right girl, old boy, but wrong
sex. Hard luck!" At another moment in another notebook the
poor old novelist had jotted down the remark: "My mother's
sterile affect was cocked like a trigger to fire me into the arms
of Livia, or of one of her tribe." Then another thing, another
glimpse – for Livia had now spent several days, or groups of
days, lodging in the box-room of the consulate – with its
clumsy cupboard in which Felix had found a place for a small
wardrobe. When Blanford, at the end of the summer, said
to Felix, "I am going to propose to Livia when we leave here,"
he received a strange wondering look from the youth –
which he rather condescendingly interpreted as jealousy.
Several thousand light years afterwards when Blanford was
recording the strange manoeuvres of his double Sutcliffe,
he met Felix by accident on a rainy platform in Paris, as he
was just setting off for the south; and now Felix told him
what that lost and forlorn glance portended. He did not
repeat the scathing estimate of her character by Quatrefages,
who at that time spent one afternoon a week devilling at the
Consulate, keeping the petty-cash box in order. This report
on her was quite gratuitous and spontaneous on the part of
the little clerk and somewhat shook Felix by its terseness.
Yet ... he himself had strayed into his guest's room while
the maid was cleaning it and had seen, hanging up in the
shabby cupboard, some articles of male wear which aroused
his curiosity. And there was no doubt that late in the evening
she often disappeared in the direction of the gipsy encamp-
ment. Why not? She was young and adventurous and may
well have felt the need of a male disguise. Indeed Felix said
as much, on a note of mild indignation, to the little clerk; but
the latter shook his head and said laconically: "I know. I
myself frequent the *gitanes*." And this too was true. Mind you

(as Blanford told himself) it did not matter – he would not, for anything in the world, have renounced an experience which had literally scorched him awake, precipitated him from raw youth into adulthood. In a sense this was the worst part of it; somewhere, in some dim corner of himself, he must have perversely enjoyed the kind of suffering she was to inflict on him. When he said as much to Felix, the latter warmly praised his loyalty and generosity, which naturally disgusted our hero. "O God, Felix," he said in anguish, "it's not that. I'm trapped. I can do no other. I am fuming with impotent rage."

But he was not the only one to be grateful to the girl; Felix was hardly less so, for Livia, by joining him more than once on his night walk, had performed a miracle – she had made him fall in love with this small and dismal city. *Venite adoremus* said the chipped gold sign above the chapel of the Grey Penitents, almost as if the church had divined his mood, his abandonment to his love for this mysterious and eccentric girl. She sat so docilely hand in hand with him in the silent pews, listening to the thresh and swash of the paddles revolving. She said, whispering, "Go on and pray, if you wish. I have never been able to." But his shyness constrained him and he felt himself blush in the darkness. Nor would he have changed his position for anything, for the feel of her rough little hand in his was bliss. How marvellous, how romantic it all seemed, and how beautiful she was, this Livia who talked about painting and seemed to know everything about the history of the place which had for him been up to now an echoing prison. As for the gipsy side of her character – why, she had been the most brilliant student of the Slade School in the years when the influence of Augustus John was at its height; all students worth anything ached to become Carmen. One night when she disappeared he ran into her by chance in the eastern sector of the town, and she was walking arm in arm with a gipsy girl; behind the couple, as if offering protection or surveillance, came a couple of lean gipsies leading a mule. They were shabby as pariahs, and had a brilliant scavenging gleam in the eye – as if they had just done a successful robbery. Livia dressed in tattered pants and was bare of foot – another passion of hers was to walk about barefoot. That summer she cut her foot on a piece of tin and the wound turned septic; this immobilised her for a while and she accepted the ministrations of Felix with brusque good grace. In the evenings the gipsy girl hung about the consulate quarter, but she always made off when Felix appeared.

Only with Quatrefages nothing worked; Livia and he simply hated each other, and hardly bothered to hide the fact. Later they came to an interesting compromise, for the little clerk blackmailed her into co-operating with him in one of the numerous enterprises of Lord Galen – one which also concerned the gipsies.

What had happened was this: the gipsies had taken up a second headquarters in the corner of the town known as Les Balances, where a number of disreputable and tumble-down houses offered them precarious shelter. Prompted by a hint from Quatrefages, they had removed the heavy stone flags of the floors and started to dig down beneath these shacks, to arrive at a layer of civilisation much anterior to the Papal period of the town. Amphoras, grave headstones, armour, domestic remains, tessellated pavements, they had made one of the richer archaeological finds of the period; and all this material was surreptitiously placed in sacks and sent up to Galen's chateau by mule. Livia, details of whose doings among the gipsies had come to the ears of Quatrefages, was content to lend her good offices to these ventures rather than have him tell anyone about her own tenebrous adventures; and indeed was responsible for securing one or two of the larger pieces which might have been salted away by the band who were vaguely aware that someone was making a larger profit than they were from these finds.

But for Felix the real felicity of that first summer was not merely the marvellous evenings spent at Tu Duc, it was to walk half the night with this dark girl with her haughty face and bare feet; her thin body was erect as a wand, and she seemed to feel absolutely no fear in the darkest corners of the town – some of which made the flesh of poor Felix creep; like the terrifying rue Londe for example with its one gas lamp set askew in a wall so mossy and so dribbling with damp that it exuded a death-chill. Here the shadowy doorways were set in such a way as to afford perfect cover for a footpad. Obviously she felt nothing of all this, for she did not cease her quiet conversation as they travelled down it – perforce in Indian file to avoid the contact of their shoulders with the rotting walls. One thing she had determined to find – a famous Avignon shawl such as her mother had had as a young girl. Alas, these fine kashmirs were no longer made in the old town.

But it was Livia who made him sit and listen to the wakening birds in little squares like that of Le Bon Pasteur, or the Square des Corps Saints with its ragged plashing fountain; or Saint Didier, set slightly at an angle to the rest of the universe, but not the less evocative. And with these night rambles the whole harmony of the Mediterranean south swept over him, filling his consciousness with gorgeous impressions of star-sprinkled nights in the old town – the six of them seated under a tree in front of some old bistro like The Bird, drinking the milky anisette called *pastis* and waiting for the moon to rise over the munched-looking battlements of the city. Once Livia managed to procure them horses from the gipsies and they rode across to the Pont du Gard, to picnic and camp the night on the steep hillsides, overlooking the jade-green Gardon as it swirled its way to the sea. Sometimes, too, Blanford invited himself into town for a consular walk with them both, much to the chagrin of Felix, who looked quite crestfallen when his friend appeared on the scene. But Blanford was as much subject to the magnetism of Livia as Felix was – he simply could not resist forcing himself upon them, though he inwardly cursed his lack of tact. Yet it was Livia who seemed glad, and who indeed seemed to favour him quite unequivocally over Felix. The crestfallen consul was forced to witness, with exquisite pangs of jealousy, the two of them walking tenderly arm in arm, while he followed wistfully after them in his college blazer, uttering fearful imprecations under his breath. Nobody took any of this with high seriousness – it was simply youth, it was simply the spirit of an intoxicating summer felicity among the olives and cherries of Aramon, of Foulkes, of Montfavet or Sorgues. Often, looking back on this halcyon period, Blanford had the sudden vision of them all, standing upon the iron bridge at the Fountain of Vaucluse, gazing down into the trout-curdled water and listening to the roar of the spring as it burst from the mountain's throat and swept down past them, thick with loitering fish.

But if ever in the years to come Blanford might feel the need to account for the enigma of this fierce attachment to Livia there was one scene which quite certainly he knew would rise in his memory to explain everything. Once when Felix was away for a few days Livia gave him a rendezvous at the little Museum in the centre of the town – at four-thirty in the morning; punctually a sleepy Blanford turned up to find the barefooted girl waiting for him at the dark portals of the place with a swarthy gipsy. Dawn was just breaking. The gipsy had a massive pistol-key in his hand which fitted the lock; the tall doors swung back with a hushing noise and ushered them into the red cobbled courtyard; and as they did so they heard the inhuman shrieks which came from the interior garden with its tall dewy plane trees. It was the crying of peacocks on the lawn. They passed through tall glass doors to reach this interior courtyard which exhaled a strange sort of peace in that early light of day. The taciturn gipsy took his leave, having confided his key to the girl. Together they loitered through the galleries with their massive water paintings of the Italian school – lakes and viaducts and avenues depicting imaginary landscapes during the four seasons of the year. Portraits of great ladies and forgotten dignitaries stared urgently at them in the gloom. Then they came to the Graeco-Roman section and after it to a small glass-roofed room with manuscripts and documents galore.

Livia, who seemed to know the place by heart, opened the cases one by one and showed the bemused Blanford medieval documents which mentioned the marriage of Petrarch's sweetheart, and hard by, some pages of handwriting torn from the letters of the Marquis de Sade. It was strange in that silent dawn to hold the white paper in his fingers and read some lines etched in a now rusted ink. He had forgotten that both the libertine and the Muse were called Sade, and were from the same family. . . . Now Livia was at his side, then in his arms; she closed the precious cases and led him back to the cool lawn where they sat side by side on a bench trying to feed the peacocks with scraps of stale sandwich which he had had the forethought to bring with him. "Soon I shall be going back to Germany," the girl said, "and you won't see me until the next long vac – unless you come with me; but I know you can't as yet. Such wonderful things are going to happen there, Aubrey; it's bursting with hope, the whole country. A new philosophy is being built which will give the new Germany the creative leadership of Europe once more." It sounded rather puzzling, but Blanford was politically quite ignorant. He had heard vague rumours of unrest and revisionism in Germany – a reaction against the Versailles treaty. But the whole subject was a bore, and he presumed that some new government would bury all these extravagances once and for all. Besides, a new war was unthinkable and specially for such trivial reasons. . . . This is why Livia intrigued him with her romantic talk. So, more to humour her – for he adored the flushed cheeks and the joined hands which showed her enthusiasm – than from real interest he said: "What was the old world, then?" Livia shook a lock of hair impatiently out of her eyes and said: "It died in 1832, with the death of Goethe; the old world of humanism and liberalism and faith. He exemplified it; and its epitaph was pronounced by Napoleon after he met Goethe; it was an unwilling tribute to the world which the French Revolution was then destroying. '*Voilà un homme,*' said Boney, himself a child of the Directory, and the harbinger of the Leninised Jewish coolie-culture of today. With the death of Goethe the new world was born, and under the aegis of Judeo-Christian materialism it transformed itself into the great labour camp that it is. In every field – art, politics, economics – the Jew came to the forefront and dominated the scene. Only Germany wants to replace this ethos with a new one, an Aryan one, which will offer renewed scope for the old values as exemplified by Goethe's world; for he was the last universal man of the Renaissance. Why should we not go back to that?" Blanford did not see quite how; but her sweet enthusiasm was so warming, and the tang of her kiss so unmanning that he found himself nodding agreement. Livia's new world sounded like the Hesperides – as a matter of fact any new world which had a Livia in it elicited his instant support. He said: "I love you, Livia dear. Tell me more about it, it sounds just what we need to escape from all this fervent dullness." And Livia went on outlining this marvellous intellectual adventure with heart-breaking idealism and naivety. When he mentioned Constance she cried: "I can't bear her devotion to all the Jewish brokers of psychoanalysis, to the Rabbinate of Vienna. It's dead, that whole thing. Its barren mechanism betrays its origins in logical positivism." Blanford was far out of his depth here – he knew very little about these factors and personalities. Livia went on in torrential fashion: "Long before these barren Jewish evaluations of the human psyche, the Ancient Greeks evolved their own, more fruitful, more poetical and just as reasonable. For instance, before that bunch of thugs who ruled Olympus there were others like Uranus who ruled the earth and was castrated by Chronos. Those severed genitals were thrown still frothing and writhing into the sea, and the foam they generated gave birth to Aphrodite. Which world do you prefer? Which seems the more fruitful?" Blanford could only repeat, whispering in that small stag's ear the stupid words, "I love you and I agree."

She touched his face – the haptic sense – and the poor fellow was mesmerised; he was in love, and so full of glory and distress that he could have accepted anything without query provided Livia was part of it.

Here on this moist fresh grass they lay, with their arms under each other's heads, staring up into the clear warm sky with its rising sunlight and light musical clouds – herald of another perfect day. It would soon be time to slip quietly away, locking the doors behind them, and make their sleepy way back to Tu Duc through the olive groves turning to silver in the breeze. The kisses of her hard little mouth with its thin lips, sometimes cut in expressions of smiling contempt or reserve, held a world of promises for him. She had promised to spend her last few nights in his room. "I shall be back in Paris again in three months if you want me," she added, and Blanford began actively, resolutely, planning ways and means to accept this marvellous invitation. Gazing into the *camera lucida* of the eye's screen he saw a vastly enlarged version of Livia, one which filled the whole sky, hovering over them both like some ancient Greek goddess. It seemed a fearful thing to have to share this marvellous creature with the others – but there was nothing to be done for the terms of reference dictated that they should do almost everything together. As their departure began to shape itself into a fact – at first the summer seemed endless and their return to the north a figment – it became imperative to go on as many excursions as possible, to see as much of the country as possible before the fatal day dawned. Constance was staying on in Provence to try and fix up Tu Duc a little against future habitation; Sam and Hilary and Blanford were to affront their final examinations before selecting a profession. The centre of gravity was slowly shifting. At dawn, unable to sleep, and heading for the lily pond for a dip, Blanford came upon the two sisters naked upon the flagged path, walking with sleepy silence towards the same objective in the dusky bloom of daybreak. Slim and tall, with their upright carriage and hieratic style they looked like a couple of young Graces who had slipped out of the pantheon and into the workaday world of men, seeking an adventure. Blanford turned aside and waited until he heard the ripple of water; then he too joined them, sliding soundlessly into the pool like a trout. So the three sat quietly breathing among the lotus flowers, waiting for the sun to rise among the trees.

It was like a dream – the wet stone heads of the sisters, like statues come to life; the dense packages of silence moving about the garden suddenly drilled by a short burst of bird-song. "Perils and absences sharpen desire," says the ancient Greek poet. In all the richness of this perfect summer Blanford felt the pang of the partings to come – vertigo of a desire which must for the time being rest unrequited. Her wet hair made her look shaven; her pretty ears stood out pointed from her head, like gnomes at prayer. From the sunny balcony where breakfast waited they could see the swifts stooping and darting; how beautifully the birds combined with gravity to give life to this wilderness of garden which Constance had sworn never to have tidied and formalised. It was full of treasures like old fruit trees still bearing, strawberry patches, and a bare dry section of holm-oak – a stand of elderly trees – which had a truffle bed beneath.

Days had begun to melt and fuse together in the heat of Provence, their impressions of heat and water and light absolutely forbade them to keep a mental chronology of their journeys, jogging about the gorges of the Gardon in the old pony-cart, or taking the little toy train down to the sea to spend a night on the beach and attend a cockade-snatching bullfight at dusty Lunel. Ah! the little pocket train, which plodded down to the flat Carmargue, to take them to the Grau du Roi. It had such a merry holiday air; the carriages were so bright – red for the first class, yellow for the second, and green for the third. All with the legend PLM modestly painted on them. The long waits in tiny silent stations where the guard sometimes braked to a walking pace so that he could loiter in a field beside the track and gather a few leeks. When you were dying of thirst how good the fresh water from the pump at Aimargues tasted; it was really intended for the engine, but once the machine had drunk its fill it was the turn of the passengers. Once Hilary even used it as a shower while they were waiting for the connection which was to carry them down to the Saintes. In the dry heats of summer the odours of the sand and the sea came up to them from the beaches – and from the inland maquis that of thyme and rosemary bruised by the flocks of sheep. Sometimes they sat in a siding and let a train pass through from Nîmes which was full of the little black Carmargue bulls used in the cockade

fights. Small stations on the roads to paradise, signal boxes at
the end of the world; they would return after these excursions
dazed with the sun and sea. And then in the evening Blanford
would hear the sweet voice of Livia intoning the AUM of
yoga as she sat in the green thicket behind the tower, re-
charging her body, re-oxygenating her brain. Remembering
a phrase from another life, "The heart of flesh in the breast is
not the *vagra* heart; like an inverted lotus the valves of the
flesh heart open by day and close by night during sleep."

The sleep of the south had invaded also their love-
making, giving it a tonality, a resonance of its own; with
Livia it was simple and rather brutal. He would never forget
how she cried out "Ha" as she felt the premonition of the
orgasm approaching; it was the cry of the Japanese swords-
man before the shock of his stroke. And then, so extreme was
the proof that she lay in his arms as if her back were broken.

Eating their picnic lunch among the brown rocks above
the Pont du Gard, watching the eagles wheel and stoop, they
all – as if by sudden consent – felt their minds drawn towards
the thought of the impending future with the inevitable
imperatives which choice would force upon them. Blanford
was perhaps the luckiest for he would inherit a modest income
which he would have no difficulty in supplementing by
academic work – or so he thought. The brown-skinned
Sam was less self-assured as he mused. "I shan't have a
private income, and with the little intelligence I have inherited I don't suppose I could get anything sensational in
the way of a job. To tell the truth the Army seems the
likeliest *pis aller* – though I am not very militant." He had
been an active member of the Oxford Officers Training
Corps and could with luck get a commission in a line regi-
ment. Constance rested her arm lightly in the crook of his
brown arm and smiled up at him, confident and at ease.
There was no stress in their loving, while between Livia and

Blanford there was a kind of premonitory hopelessness; they were in that limbo where destiny, like an undischarged bankrupt, waited for them. They had gone too far to retreat now even if they had wished.

Hilary said: "I am going to surprise and perhaps pain you. I have been seriously tempted by the Catholic faith. I have the notion of really taking it up – if that is the word. I thought after next term to go into a retreat and receive instruction in it. I can easily do a little tutoring for a living. Then we'll see if the thing is lasting or wears out." He smiled round at the others, feeling suddenly abashed and unsure of himself; once these sentiments had been uttered aloud they seemed far less substantial and enriching than they had been before. He climbed down to his favourite diving plinth, above the river, poised, and suddenly fell like a swift to furrow the jade water far below. Sam sighed and rose to follow, followed by Blanford. Suddenly, by this brief conversation, the future had materialised before their eyes.

Blanford had brought a pretty little ring which he hoped to give to Livia, but the act seemed somehow embarrassing and confusing; he had not sufficient courage to indulge in definitive declarations – the only kind which would approximate to what he felt. And Livia needed none; she stared at him, smiling her hard little smile, holding her hand in his. They would meet again in Paris! Ah! in the cafés of that great epoch one arrived, distraught with love, and called for ink and paper, envelopes and stamps, while a concerned waiter, having supplied them, rushed for a *cassis*. Thus were great love-letters born – they would be sent by *pneumatique* and a helmeted motor cyclist would deliver them, like Mercury himself, within the hour.

Blanford decided to send her the ring by post when she had returned to Paris. On the last evening but one they went for a short walk together among the olive groves and Livia surprised him by saying: "I always think of you as a writer, Aubrey; people who keep copious diaries like you always have – they are really writers." She had noted his habit of scribbling in a school exercise book nearly every night before he got into bed. It was a self-indulgence he had, like most lonely people, permitted himself from early adolescence. And it was here, unwittingly, that Sutcliffe got born. Once at school one of his diaries had been pilfered from his locker and a teasing youth read out some passages aloud to a circle of laughing and taunting schoolmates. It was fearfully humiliating; and to guard against a repetition of such a torture Blanford had attributed his thoughts and ideas to an imaginary author called S. He also firmly lettered in the title "Commonplace Book", and put a few genuine quotations into it, to suggest that he was simply copying out things which struck him from the books he read. But slowly and insidiously S began to take shape as a person, a flippant and desperate person, a splintered man, destined for authorship with all its woes and splendours. To him he attached the name of the greatest cricketer of the day – also rather defensively; Sutcliffe was, in the cricket world, a household name. Yet over the years he was fleshed out by quotations which suggested the soliloquies of a lonely and hunted intellectual, a marginal man; Blanford took refuge in him, so to speak, from a world which seemed to him quite insensitive to intellectual matters, in fact calamitously philistine. Later when the great man actually emerged on paper and started his adventurous life of sins and puns Blanford was to adapt a hymn for his use, the first line of which was "Nearer My Goad to Thee." But this was much later. Now he simply looked into the eyes of Livia and replied steadily: "I don't think I could be imaginative enough, I'm too donnish I think."

But she was right.

And looking at her, watching her smiling at him, a

simple thought came into his mind, namely how marvellous not to be blind! Livia said: "Who is this S you are always quoting?" So she had been reading his exercise books behind his back! He answered "Schopenhauer" without a flicker of expression. But in the back of his mind was already looming a large fleshy man with pink knees pressed together, penis *en trompe-l'oeil* as he might say, whirling dumb-bells before an open window. The original Sutcliffe who was to keep his emotions in a high state of chaos; one of those novelists all out of shape from too frequent childbearing. Perhaps he was a poet? Yes, he wrote verses. Some had been published in *Isis*. He would send some to Livia in order to bolster her faith in him as a creative person. She had taught him several yoga *asanas* and now every morning he obediently performed them while he thought of her sitting somewhere out among the olives beyond the tower in the lotus pose which seemed to cost her no effort at all, intoning the Aum; or lying in the corpse posture, snuffing out her whole will and body, and by her meditation "swallowing the sky". He was rather afraid that all this was very much a fad, though he admitted to feeling better after it.

It was by these strange byways and unfrequented paths that years later he was able to track down that corpulent soak, that ignoble ape, Sutcliffe, whose vulpine quivering nose reddened at the approach of whisky, and whose shaggy body rejoiced to feel the warm thrust of alcohol in the nerves. Where did this extraordinary *alter ego* come from? He was never to discover.

Livia was looking at him curiously – a snake with a trigger in its tongue, a cat with afterthoughts. . . .

And now Felix Chatto came up the drive on a derelict bicycle and brought them an invitation from Lord Galen; it was for a farewell dinner before he took his own departure for Berlin. It would be agony to squeeze their swollen feet into socks and shoes, to unearth shirts and ties. . . . But they could not refuse the old man. Anyway it would be a good training for their return to the city after this bemusing Provençal holiday.

FIVE

Lord Galen Dines

WHEN I WAS A BOY", SAID LORD GALEN WITH A massive simplicity, "I read a book called *The Romance of Steam* and I have never forgotten it. It had a red and gold cover with an engine on it and it began, "The steam-engine is a mighty power for Good." Nobody could tell if he were joking or not. He fell into a muse and pulled his upper lip. Max the chauffeur, now transformed into something between a major-domo and an Italian admiral by a costume specially created for him, diligently carved the roast chickens in their chafing dishes before serving them. His black dress-trousers had a broad gold piping, and in the lapels of his dress coat he carried the insignia of a *sommelier* – a master of Cellars. It was he who had trundled up to fetch five young people in the Hispano, and they had been very grateful for the lift, for the walk was a long and dusty one from Tu Duc.

The house Galen owned and occupied sporadically throughout the year was as characteristic as the old man himself – it had been built quite recently by a Greek armaments king with whom he had business dealings; one old tower was all that was left of the original chateau which had stood on the site. All the rest had been rased to clear the ground for the modern villa – architecture of calamitous joviality – which, however, stood in handsome shady gardens. "Nothing old-fashioned does for me," said the old man forcibly; adding, "I have never drunk life through a straw, you know." Jutting out his chin.

The original name of the house had been "The Acropolis", but Lord Galen, with characteristic Jewish modesty,

had renamed it "Balmoral"; the large painted board which
announced the fact always gave Felix Chatto a twinge of
horror as he turned into the drive – his taste had been
educated to a very high pitch of refinement. The inside of
the house also caused him pain by its exuberance; it was the
kind of house that a successful but ignorant actress might
order in Cairo. Masses of marquetry and leather and cretonne;
the salon was raised on pillars so convoluted and painted
that they resembled barbers' poles of the old style. It was
wonderfully modern and slightly profligate in atmosphere.
And on this particular evening they found a new visitor
present who seemed to belong to it, to be most appropriate
to the satin and damascene and scarlet leather. They had
none of them met the Prince before, nor even heard of him;
but it soon transpired that though he was an Egyptian prince
of the blood he was also a business associate of old Galen.
His presence lent a singular and appropriate touch to all this
oriental décor for he wore dove-grey clothes, and dove-grey
London spats over tiny boots polished like mirrors. His
grey waistcoat sported pearl buttons, and he wore a stock
which set off to admiration a lean and aquiline face which
was almost as grey as the rest of him. In his lapel he wore a
gold squirrel, on his finger a scarab ring.

Lord Galen performed the presentation with just the
slightest trace of unction, adding afterwards, "Prince Hassad
is an old business associate of mine." The Prince seemed
extraordinarily meek, he ducked shyly as he shook hands;
his hands were small, bird-like, twiggy, and he seemed glad
to reclaim them after every action. Beside him on a chair lay a
richly chased fly-whisk and a gorgeous fez with gold tassels
of great lustre; the green band indicated not only his royal
antecedents but also the fact that he had made the traditional
pilgrimage to Mecca. At first blush it seemed that what was
striking about him rested on the fact that his dress was exotic,

his person foreign. But within a few moments the impression changed; they felt they were in the presence of some sort of oriental saint who sat so modestly but vividly before them, his face bowed, looking shyly up under his brows as he gazed from face to young face. His English was almost perfect, his French without a trace of a foreign accent or intonation. If ever the fact was commented upon the Prince was apt to say, smiling: "I learned both languages young. There is nothing else to do in the Royal harem but study."

"Champagne," said Galen with a lordly wave and there was a suggestive popping among the rock plants in the winter garden where the dumb secretary presided over a cocktail cabinet; and what a treat it was in all that summer thirst! The Prince sipped a glass and placed it beside him on the table; he was much reassured by the fact that they all talked French as well as English.

Constance, of course, won his immediate attention and admiration by her smiling good sense and swift French; it was to her that he chiefly addressed himself in order to explain himself and expound his habits to all of them – aware perhaps that he must seem a story-tale figure in the French country-side. "I am travelling north into Germany in my carriage, and Lord Galen is coming with me to transact some business on behalf of Egypt." Galen looked rather doubtful about this; he had offered to drive north in his elegant car, but the Prince had quietly insisted on the huge state landau with its four horses – a desperately slow method of getting about. He had also expressed a somewhat alarming wish, namely to visit a cathedral or two on the way north – a sentiment that Lord Galen found slightly morbid. But the little Prince was proposing to enjoy himself as a deeply civilised oriental should do when abroad, and there was nothing for it but to fall in with his wishes. But at night, in bed, Lord Galen gave a groan when he thought of their slow progress across

Europe in this royal contraption. At the moment it reposed in his garage where the two uniformed black Saidhis were currying the horses and watering them.

Needless to say, the Prince made an instant hit with the inhabitants of Tu Duc, though hardly less markedly with Chatto and the taciturn Quatrefages who had put on a tie for the occasion and whose flushed face suggested that he had perhaps had a drink or two to stimulate his courage for such a frightening occasion. Perhaps the Prince sensed this, for he at once paid the boy some special attentions, questioning him softly in his patrician French, and soon the clerk was quite at ease and sufficiently self-confident to venture on talking in an English which was not bad despite his marked accent. So the exchange of politenesses proceeded until Max with a grunt announced that they could come to table if they wished. The Prince put down his gold-tipped cigarette and asked permission to wash his hands; his body-servant, a tall Nubian clad in the scarlet sash of the royal *kavass*, helped him, holding the towels for him to wipe his hands on, and then sprinkling the royal fingers with scent at the end of the operation. The Prince dabbled some scent on his face also. Then he came modestly to table, where they all stood and waited for him; Lord Galen placed him between the two sisters which seemed to please him very much as he instantly engaged Constance once more in small talk.

From the kitchen came the clatter and chatter of the three young farm women who had been conscripted for this fête by the secretary; he himself took his meals apart in the study. "Every year", said Lord Galen happily, "I have this little beano as a farewell treat before leaving France. But it's the first time I have welcomed the Prince to my table." He beamed round him while Prince Hassad with his shy smile made a little self-deprecating *moue* of the lips, as if the allusion embarrassed him. "I am glad to be here," he said, and added:

"particularly because of the work you are doing on your romantic project, in which I find it very hard to believe. We Egyptians are very suspicious people."

"Quite right. Quite right," said Galen with approval, "but our little project is not all fancy, you know. We have certain definite lines of enquiry laid down. This treasure is not a will o' the wisp, eh Quatrefages?"

The Prince shook his head doubtfully. "As an investment?" he murmured, almost under his breath. He motioned to his servant, who had taken up his traditional food-taster's position behind his chair, to leave. It was as if he did not wish for an eavesdropper in the room in case the conversation became confidential. He looked prudently round the table and said: "Perhaps after dinner I could be given some facts about your search. Then I will be able to judge." Then, turning aside with a more definite air, he asked Livia to tell him what monuments he should see in the vicinity, and in her usual forceful way she offered to be his guide if he should so wish, at which he looked hesitant but grateful. "There is so much to see," said Lord Galen with a regretful sigh, "but I never seem to have the chance." The grotesque cat of the household which lay on its velvet cushion in the corner of the room gave a croak. It had smelt the chicken. Lord Galen regally cut a piece from his own portion and had it despatched to her by Max who got a serpentine hiss for his efforts. For such a frail-looking man the Prince was surprisingly adroit with knife and fork, and was soon deeply involved with second helpings and vegetables which he forked on to his side-plate, preferring to eat in the French fashion – to enjoy meat and vegetables separately. Nor did he neglect his glass of Tavel, which he held up to the light with a professional expression of appreciation, to admire its topaz glow. "Though a Moslem," he confided in his host, "I am anything but a fanatic. But I never overdo things in case my wife catches me." He gave a small sweet chuckle and lowered his eyes again.

"Of course," said Lord Galen soothingly, "to drink a little – it's all harmless jollity." Quatrefages had been taciturn and talkative by turns, had been flushed and pale also; Felix knew him well enough to decipher these indications. They betrayed that he had been drinking absinthe again; it made him fiery and apathetic by turns. Now he produced his little pendulum from his vest pocket and allowed it to swing over his glass of wine for a moment. Everyone watched him with interest, as if he were about to do a conjuring trick. But no. After a moment of intense study he put away his divining instrument and drained his glass, giving an involuntary belch as he did so. They all smiled indulgently but he gazed about him with a bloodshot eye and made a sign for Max to refill his glass, which the butler did, but not without an anxious glance in the direction of his boss.

Lord Galen was talking, however, and had not noticed this small diversion. He was talking about the pleasures of Germany, of the pleasant journey they were soon to enjoy together. "Pleasant and I hope profitable," he added. "The brothers Krupp will come in their special train into Austria and we shall become good friends, yes, very good friends." An emotional man, he felt the tears of friendship rising to his eyes. It was to be a most meaningful meeting, he assured the Prince. The Nubians would get what they wanted cheap because of his other interests. Felix whispered an aside to Blanford: "He doesn't seem to know what is going on over there." If Quatrefages divined by the pendulum, Felix divined by the stock pages of the *Financial Times*. The sinister drift of events in Germany had been an object of his concerned study for some time; why, even the Foreign Office Intels had been showing diplomatic unease about the situation – and here was Galen blithely chatting about financial speculations and business interests for all the world as if the country was stable and productive, and in a fit state to welcome foreign investment.

Normally Felix would have said nothing but now his curiosity got the better of him and he said: "I personally don't at all like what appears to be going on there. I am surprised that the situation has not alarmed you." Lord Galen bridled and said: "Situation?" And this gave Felix the chance to give a brief and rather succinct outline of the state of affairs in Germany and the possible issues. To all this Lord Galen listened with a condescending smile, but attentively; he rolled bits of bread in his side-plate and popped them into his mouth. But he politely heard his nephew out, and seemed no whit abashed by the nods and murmured agreement of the old Prince who seemed at least as well informed as Felix if not quite as anxious as the consul. In fact he was delighted at this diversion which he had been too polite to initiate, but which might clear up a lot of points which were still obscure to him. He glanced from one face to the other, trying to divine whether Lord Galen, under his somewhat ineffable air of serenity, was not playing a game with him – a game of investor's poker, so to speak.

But Livia, too, seemed to be on the side of Felix, for she too nodded agreement to the propositions which he put forward. When at last the question of Jewry came up Lord Galen had had enough of his nephew's presumptuous exposition and he held up his hand in a kind but firm way. "Everything you say sounds true, but I can assure you, Felix, that I know the contrary – I know because I have been there, and I have seen with my own eyes. You will imagine when first the press started these rumours about anti-Semitism that I took note, and indeed I felt a vague alarm. As a Manchester man I could not ignore it." For some reason he disliked and avoided the word "Jew" – perhaps because of old schoolboy associations? He preferred to use the circumlocution "Manchester

man"; it sounded almost as if one were a member of
an Oxford college. He repeated on a lower note, and more
impressively: "As a Manchester man I could not ignore it. I
was both personally and financially concerned, as you might
say. So what did I do? Why, I went into the whole thing, I
went over myself and investigated the state of the country
and nature of the opposition to the government. Now, if I
had had the slightest doubt, would I have invited you to come
from Egypt? All the way from Egypt, eh? An old friend, eh?"
There was a long pause in the conversation during which he
and the Prince beamed at one another. But Felix shook his
head and Livia stared at Galen with profound curiosity – was
he just ill-informed, or just pretending in order to deceive the
Prince?

Lord Galen was deceiving nobody but himself. "I went
so far as to see the leader of the National Socialists himself.
I spent a whole weekend with him in face-to-face discussion
about his plans and sentiments." He looked round triumphantly and paused.

Then he lowered his voice and went on: "It was not
possible to distrust the assurances of such a man; his sincerity
was absolutely convincing. Mark you, he was no hotheaded
youth but a mature man who had been through the whole
war as an ordinary sergeant. He had seen the whole thing
from the inside. He spoke most movingly and simply of the
sufferings of his country, and of the political indignities the
Allies had forced upon it. His only desire was to redress these
wrongs and live at peace with the world. He gave me the
most explicit outline of his policies and convictions – it was
really heart-warming, I was touched almost to tears. We had
been really very hard on the Germans. He was right to feel a
certain mild resentment about the fact. But his whole attitude
was grave and measured and his views long deliberated. And
this is where I was first able to question him closely about the

alleged anti-Semitism of his party. There was no doubt that the man was sincere – his whole face and manner betrayed it. He knew, he said, that nobody could pull the wool over my eyes, and that I was free to judge as best I may, but for his part he could guarantee that the whole press campaign was false, and had been stage-managed by political opponents. His party were even thinking of creating a second Jewish state, more stable than mandated Palestine, somewhere in the East. He spoke with passion and conviction – and if ever I trusted a man I trusted him. He showed me a long memorandum prepared by the party department of demography about a Jewish state of ten million souls and asked me what I thought of it. You can imagine my excitement. It was the dream of the race to have a place of their own. It was most reassuring to feel that a modern political leader could think along these lines. He said with a smile: 'You see, Lord Galen, in some ways we are more Zionist than the Zionists.' I found him very splendid indeed."

Galen gazed round at the company whose expressions varied from polite incomprehension to incredulity. Felix listened to his uncle with startled astonishment, Livia with a sort of tremulous doubt – was he roasting the Prince? The rest of them neither knew very much nor cared whether these views were true or false; only the Prince seemed delighted by this brief exposition, and not unfamiliar with its details. His clever grey face was like a silk handkerchief, folding itself into smiles. He said with an air of elation: "And the contracts, P.G. eh?" Lord Galen nodded.

"I was coming to that," he said; "it was right at the end of our talks that we discussed the financial situation of his party. It was, to say the least, precarious, for he was facing powerful vested interests who wished to see other leaders take the helm of state. If he did not get into power what would become of his dreams of founding a small Jewish state? This is what made me think. I sounded him out on the whole question of foreign investment and he told me that he would offer substantial concessions in the future against present aid. In the light of all that had gone before I felt that the situation held out great promise for myself and my associates. Nevertheless, I never act hastily, and I once more went over the whole ground. It was clear to me that this was the chance of a lifetime – to offer a massive contribution to party funds which would be paid for later by wholesale business concessions. I consulted everyone – naturally some were highly doubtful of my good sense, or of his good faith. But my arguments prevailed, and pretty soon we hope he will get in, largely thanks to us; meanwhile, the document which we spent half the night discussing was signed solemnly by us both in the presence of witnesses. I brought it down tonight to show everyone."

He inserted his fingers in a cardboard tube and eased out a scroll which he unrolled and held up before them. It was typewritten and the seal looked expensive with its wax eagle. But it was too far for anyone to read the text, and after a brief exposure of it to the company, he prudently replaced it, smiling the while at the memory of his astuteness. The Prince made as if to clap his hands in appreciation of his host's business acumen.

Livia said she was feeling unwell, and rose with her napkin to her lips; it was nothing, she said, she wanted a breath of fresh air, that was all. They all rose from their chairs to register concern, but were ordered to remain seated, while Constance said: "It's nothing, but I'll go with her," and the two girls made their way out of the house on to the warm green lawns where Livia sank on her knees and then lay fully down and began to turn slowly from side to side. At first it seemed like some sort of paroxysm but in fact it was only an attack of laughter so strong that she was forced to cram her fist between her teeth as she laughed, rolling back and forth. Her sister squatted beside her and watched her with smiling curiosity, waiting patiently until the laughter died away into exhaustion. Livia produced a small pocket handkerchief and mopped up her eyes. "The old fool is giving them money," she said, still a trifle tremulously. "How they must be laughing." She rose now, sighing, and allowed Constance to dust her down. "I thought I would explode at table," said Livia, "and be forced to explain my laughter. Sorry for the diversion. But it's the joke of the year."

Constance knew little and cared nothing about all these problems, so she held her peace; but she linked arms with her sister and together the two women re-entered the dining-room once more where the Prince was just saying: "I also have a car to carry my luggage – but it is a lorry really because I travel with so much luggage." He sighed. In fact, as they later found, the auxiliary vehicle was a very large removers' van – the kind known as a pantechnicon. It carried, apart from the Prince's personal belongings, a crew of three servants. At the moment it was drawn up outside his hotel in Avignon, watched over by a kindly policeman; the Egyptian Embassy had signalled the authorities that the Prince was travelling in France.

The French customs had already been dazzled by the extraordinary contents of the van; all the Prince's boxes were made of rare wood and covered outside with coloured silk and inlaid with metal filigree. There was a royal coffin worthy of Tutankhamun. Expensive bridge tables. Enough plate and cutlery to give a banquet for thirty people. When later he showed them these wonders, which included four of his favourite hawks in case he might be in the mood for hawking, he was good enough to explain that what might seem rather superfluous to them was really very necessary for an Egyptian prince, because one never knew. One never really knew. But all this transpired a little while later when their acquaintance with the Prince had ripened. For the moment they sat at table still, but now over brandy and cigars, while Galen cracked walnuts vividly and chatted knowledge-ably on the subject of investments. The Prince drank off quite healthy swigs of cognac for a man who looked so slender. "Of the other matter – your buried treasure – we will speak later!" His tone was bantering, amused, which somewhat nettled Quatrefages, who glared at him.

The clerk was rather suffused now with drink and his mood was, from the point of view of an outside observer, fretful and precarious. Felix eyed him with curiosity and affection and wondered whether he was going to break out into an impassioned speech about the treasure. As a matter of fact the French boy, always a bit touchy, resented the Prince's smiling scepticism about the seriousness of the work they were doing; why, he wondered, did not Lord Galen insist upon it and say something in defence of it? But he sat mildly rolling bread balls and thinking while the weight of the Prince's scepticism grew and grew.

At last Galen said: "The tradition is a long one and it's been hunted for by many people; a lot of money has gone down the drain hunting for it, so far in vain. More than one consortium of interests has tried its hand. But it is only recently that some documents have come to light which might pin-point the *place*. There is no doubt that there was a treasure and that it disappeared during the trials of the Templars for heresy. After all, the Templars were the bankers of kings with enormous fortunes in their care. In the docu-ments of the trials which are being deciphered and printed in Toulouse it is clear that the burning question for the investigators who tortured them was financial rather than ecclesiastical. Where had the treasure gone? The questions of heresy were all very well – the Inquisition looked into that very thoroughly; but what the Chancellor of Philippe le Bel wanted to know was where the hell they had put the boodle. This is why the trials were so long drawn out; they could have popped off the whole lot of the Templars in a few months. Why did they hang about? They were hoping for a lead which would guide them to the treasure. That was the only thing that obsessed the King – for the state was bankrupt."

He paused and turned to his clerk for confirmation and support. But Quatrefages glared at his plate in a brown study. The Prince was unsmiling now; he had suddenly remembered the stories of buried treasure which figured so largely in Egyptian folklore and the idea appealed to him. His doubts began to be qualified by the reflection that if there were nothing to the story but hot air surely it would not have attracted the attention of a renowned business baron with a reputation for flair and strong dealing? But he realised that he had offended Quatrefages by his bantering tone and he made amends now, reaching out to touch him on the wrist in an apologetic way which quite won the boy's heart and put him once more into a very good humour. *"C'est vrai,"* he said to the smiling old man, "it is true; we have some very precious indications. It is probably a crypt now covered in grass. Part of a chateau or a chapel or a monastery. The sign was an orchard of olives planted like this. . . ." He drew an envelope from his pocket and with his fountain pen sketched a quincunx of trees.

"I think", said Galen, "the thing would be for you to visit Quatrefages' little office at the hotel and see how he is tackling the matter. It's great detective work. The scent has led us as far as Avignon or its immediate surroundings. We are going through the records of the chateaux and chapels in the immediate vicinity of the town; there are plenty of them, as you may imagine, because of its importance as a religious centre during the period when the Popes made it their headquarters. But there's hope; o yes, we have hope. That little affair with King John gave me confidence in my own private intuition. You remember? That also looked foolish, but we won through, didn't we?"

It was perfectly true. Chatting one day to a young Oxford historian at a reception, Galen had been intrigued by a remark dropped at random; the subject of treasure had come up – heaven knows in what context – and the young don enumerated several examples of buried treasure from his history studies. Among them, and one which he found perhaps the most curious, was the loss of King John's treasure in the Wash. One would have thought that that at least was traceable; the depth of the channel was negligible and clearly marked. The local movement of tides and sand bars at the ford was extremely limited. Yet despite the efforts of several generations of treasure-seekers nothing had ever come to light. The treasure itself was the most important ever to be lost in England – almost priceless indeed. This stray remark was enough to fire the admiration of Lord Galen who had always fancied himself as a sort of poet of the commercial instinct. He made a note in his little red morocco notebook and called a meeting.

He knew, of course, that in law all treasure trove belongs to the Crown which has the right, but not the obligation, to reward the finder with a bounty. Lord Galen felt that if he could secure a government promise to reward him to the tune of fifteen per cent for anything he might find, the project might prove to be worth his while. The Prime Minister was a personal friend and was coming to dinner with him the following week. He took the opportunity to explore the situation. He was given a fair wind. Dealing at such a high level with such matters one does not ask for guarantees or formal contracts. He would, he said, be content with an exchange of letters serving as a declaration of intent. Of course it was a risk. The project was a costly one and might end in failure. The Government had nothing to lose. The upshot of the matter was that he was able to attract finance for the project and indulge his sense of romance by having the Wash surveyed from the air and inviting engineers to devise the sort of machinery necessary first to locate, then to raise, the buried treasure. It had taken over two years, but had at last been successful. Lord Galen became as famous in Fleet Street as he was in the City. The profits were extremely handsome.

"I agree," said the Prince on a note of contriteness. "It was fully justified by the outcome, and a lesson to sceptics." Galen accepted the accolade gracefully, nodding his personal agreement with the remark. "That is why I thought of you, my dear Prince, when we embarked upon this little venture – which is perhaps a trifle more risky even than old King John. Many more people have tried to locate what we are hunting for – and there is always a chance that someone might have found it and kept the matter secret in order not to surrender it to the French Government. But I have made exactly identical arrangements with the Government here, and have reserved a fine meaningful percentage for my shareholders. The rest is a matter of science, of luck, and the flair of Quatrefages who will bring you up to date on what we have so far found."

Quatrefages looked steadily at the Prince and nodded gravely. "We will speak," he said on a note of confirmation. And the Prince stroked his hand once more with a warmly oriental gesture, saying: "Of course; we understand each other, no?"

At which the conversation once more became general and the contingent of guests from Tu Duc began to feel a faint disposition to yawn despite the earliness of the hour. The candles had burnt down and begun to drip. Max docked them and changed some for new. "I think", said Felix, "we should consult the clock and perhaps start moving off in good order." But a sudden loneliness assailed Lord Galen at the thought of spending the night alone with his asthmatic cat. His voice became quite quavery and pleading as he said: "O do not go so early. Let us have a last stirrup-cup on the terrace. After all who knows when we shall meet again?" Blanford felt the words entangle the muscles of his throat as he looked at Livia across the table. She smiled at him with a slow affectionate expression, but he was so deeply sunk in his own conjectures that he did not respond. How brown she had become – almost the colour of a gipsy! All of a sudden he too was assailed by a fearful sense of anguish and disenchantment – later he would recognise this as premonitory; but an irrational and boundless fear of what might come to pass for them all, and in particular for himself and Livia who inhabited so temporarily this little enclave of passionate feeling in the immensity of a hostile world. The darkness inside was now (for they were on the terrace) matched by the darkness without.

They sat over new whiskies and coffees to accustom themselves to the faint glimmer of stars. Occasional fireflies snatched in the deep grass of the lawns which that year had not been mowed. The faint wind had turned a point or two northwards and brought with it a welcome and refreshing chill which towards dawn would cause (Felix noted this) a heavy dew upon the leaves and window-panes. "It's beautiful," said Lord Galen with an unwonted warmth of feeling as he gestured towards the star-scattered darkness where the dense mists turned and shifted, now hiding, now revealing the vibrating depths of the Provençal night sky. They heard Max yawning his violet yawns within as he disencumbered the table; each time he passed the stricken Wombat it snapped blindly at his ankles.

Lord Galen contemplated the long empty reaches of insomnia which awaited him as a condemned man might think of an age of servitude ahead. He had started taking sleeping pills which guaranteed him some rest but was depressed to notice that he needed increased doses to maintain the equilibrium. It was the time of night when the thought of his daughter echoed and ached within him with a dull neuralgic insistence, poisoning his peace of mind. Sometimes after midnight he rang for his secretary and bade him produce the chessmen. They would sit silently hunched over a game until the first pale streaks of dawn woke the birds in the park. Sometimes he took a stroll in the icy dew, his footfalls silenced by the deep grass. It was rare that he could return to his bed on such occasions. He hung around until five-thirty when he heard the alarm go off in Max's room. Pretty soon the yawning black man would come and give him breakfast in the kitchen – waffles and maple syrup. Galen ate hungrily. By then he had already despatched his yawning secretary to his room. Soon it would be time to dip down the dusty hill into the town and watch the first passenger train set off for Paris. . . .

Rehearsing all this in his mind he felt the weariness and spleen assail him anew. "I suppose you all want to go to bed," he said at last, rather bitterly. "I can see you yawning and stretching, Felix – not very polite." Felix sprang to attention, metaphorically speaking, and blushed his apologies. He too was quailing at the thought of the night which confronted him; this temporary sleepiness would serve to get him to bed all right, but after an hour or two he would find himself switched on like a light and unable to prevent himself rising to make coffee, and at last, to walk the silent town. They smiled now at each other but the weariness engendered by their thoughts suffused the air, and at last the Prince, fearing that people could not leave before a prince of the blood took his leave, called in soft Arabic for his landau. The tall major-domo was standing just inside the drawing-room, and relayed the message in a low voice. There was a long period of confused noise and at last the travel-apparatus of the Prince rumbled round the house and came to rest before the flight of marble stairs where the restless horses struck sparks from the cobbles with their hooves and whinnied softly. *Noblesse oblige.*

The Prince accepted his fez and fly-whisk from the hands of his servant and then turned smiling to take his leave. "Well, if you young people will forgive me...." he said, pressing their hands for a second in his. "I will expect you all to a drink tomorrow in my hotel at seven." He did not wait for a formal acceptance, but turned to embrace his host in the French fashion, giving him a dab on the cheek with his lips. He smelt aromatic, he smelt of camphor like a mummy – so thought Lord Galen as he returned the accolade. Now the Prince climbed into his coach and turning back said: "Can I give anyone a lift? Surely Mr. Chatto? Quatrefages, no?" They accepted his offer in order to spare Max an extra detour. As they stepped into the landau and sat down beside the Prince he remarked rather unexpectedly: "I feel like a bit of fun tonight, to be sure."

They rumbled off into the darkness and the Prince began a long and animated conversation with his staff in guttural Arabic. He seemed to be asking them for information about something. Then, aware perhaps that it was somewhat impolite to talk in a language the others did not understand, he ventured on an explanation directed largely at Quatrefages. "I am asking them to take us to a good house – surely there must be a nice *pouf* in Avignon?" Felix choked with astonishment but Quatrefages acted as if he had foreseen such a departure and chuckled as he slapped the Prince on the knee in a manner as familiar as it seemed to the dismayed consul downright vulgar. "Of course, of course," said the clerk with a gesture towards the night sky, as if invoking all its starlit bounty upon the head of the grinning Prince.

Felix found that something distasteful had entered the expression of the Prince; those grave, sweet expressions, those silent modesties, had given place to a new set of facial looks – a trifle perky and monkey-like. He looked elated and full of zest; it seemed as if his intentions and desires had become a trifle debased, a trifle vulgar. "You aren't taking him to a brothel?" he said *sotto voce* to Quatrefages, who himself had changed but in a milder degree. He looked slightly tipsy and insolent. "Indeed I am," he said in an airy way, "the old darling is a Gypp and needs a cleanser. He will absolutely love Riquiqui. I will hand him over to old Riquiqui and see what she can provide." Felix looked miserable and alarmed. The Prince was talking Arabic again, heedless of them. "If he catches something," said Felix, "my uncle will never forgive you. Anyway I shan't go; it's too risky. If my uncle thought . . ." Quatrefages said simply but trenchantly "F**k your uncle."

The advice, Felix felt, was apposite and chimed with his own feelings. But it was all too easily said. Moreover he was not at all sure how the sentiment could be implemented. It was partly his cursed uncle and partly the dignity of the Foreign Office which nagged him. He sighed under the importunity of these ideas and set his mind firmly against this frivolous excursion, stifling all his regrets. Actually he would have given anything for an evening of good fellowship and a touch of profligacy. Ah well! The coach went stumbling and swaying through the dark olive glades to where at the outer edges of the darkness the lights of the city gleamed; from the quarter of the gipsies there came a thin plume of wood-smoke. It was still early. Owls whistled in the secret trees. The faint rumour of the city gradually evolved itself from their own noise of creaking coachwork, jingling harness and clattering horseflesh. The Prince was in a great good humour as he sat with an arm thrown round the shoulders of Quatrefages. He was occasionally slipping into his elegant French now as a concession to his companion. "I have a few small oddities of conduct", he said thoughtfully, "which are not unusual for a man of my age. Do you think they will understand?" Quatrefages gave a reassuring grin as he answered. "At Riquiqui they are used to everything, they cater for everything. And as they are frequented by the chief of police they are very much *à l'abri*." Reassured, the Prince beamed and squeezed his knee.

Felix had never been to Riquiqui's sordid establishment except with Blanford – and that for no questionable purpose. Once they had hunted for Livia during a night walk and the gipsies had directed them to try Riquiqui. The sordid surroundings and the darkness did not commend themselves to the two young men; and the personage of Riquiqui herself inspired the worst misgivings. She had opened a cautious inch in response to their tapping upon the rotten oak door. The little side street in which the house stood was pitch dark, and smelt of blocked drains and dead rats. The houses immediately to right and left of Riquiqui's had fallen down or been knocked down; their foundations gaped. Weeds sprouted everywhere. Blanford professed to find the place sinister but romantic – but of course he was lying. Felix was plainly nervous.

Riquiqui had enormous breasts bulging out of the top of a sort of sack dress, divided at the waist by a primeval drawstring. She had a wall-eye which gave her the air of looking over your shoulder while she spoke to you – which they found disconcerting. Moreover, lupus had ravaged her impure face – a burst of purple efflorescence covered one side of it. She tried to present her clear side rather too obviously, but from time to time she was forced to turn and present the diseased profile with its great splash of suffused blood vessels turning to crimson-lake and purple. A faint candle illumined the scene – the gaunt stairs behind her. She could give them no indication of Livia's whereabouts though she seemed to know, from their explanations, the person they were speaking about, for she nodded a great deal and said, "Not today" repeatedly, which suggested, at any rate, Livia was in the habit of calling in at this disreputable establishment. Curiously enough the information, far from depressing Blanford, elated him; he admired the insouciant and courageous way Livia went her own way, busied herself with her own affairs, without expecting their protective company. But Felix found this attitude inconsequent, even compromising.

But tonight, he told himself, there was to be no such excursion for the consul. Pleading a slight headache he had himself dropped off at the station; there was still time to sit and relax at the buffet over a coffee – after the bustle and conversation of a party he loved to spend a few moments alone, thinking his own modest thoughts. A train had pulled out for the north; the engine gave a whiff or two, as if it were calling back over its shoulder. The little *fiacres* stood anchored in the monotony of their function as train-waiters. Later when he set out on his walk he might feed the horses a sugar-lump or two if he felt lonely; this would lead to a conversation with the sleepy drivers.

But for the moment he had had his fill of conversation. The Prince had rumbled off into the darkness with his coach. From the neighbouring livery-stables came the noise of horses coughing and stamping. A bell trilled and wires hummed. Avignon was beginning to settle down for the night – that long painful stretch of time which must somehow be affronted. Felix yawned – yes, it was all very well, but would it last? He paid for his coffee and sauntered across under the frowning darkness of the Porte St.-Charles. It would not take him long to return. Then he would undress and go to bed doggedly; yes, doggedly. But as he neared the villa his nerves gave a jump for there was the figure of a man sitting on his front door-step smoking and waiting for him. It was a mere silhouette; he could not at first make out his identity.

For a moment he hesitated timorously, and then, cursing himself for a coward, advanced with a deliberate *sang-froid* to reach the garden gate. "There you are!" cried Blanford cheerfully. "I wondered if the Prince had taken you off on a binge." Felix recounted his journey home in the coach and Blanford chuckled. He said, "I suddenly decided not to go to bed; we got Max to drop us off and walked the quarter of a mile home – it's not far, after all." Felix opened the front door and entered the musty little villa. "I wondered if you would be walking tonight," said Blanford; and suddenly Felix seemed to sense the loneliness and misgiving behind the words. "Is there anything wrong?" he asked unexpectedly and Blanford shook his head. "No, it's just the end of this perfect holiday and one doesn't want to waste the time on sleep. I went home dutifully with the others but couldn't get to sleep, so I headed for town."

Yes, there was something lame about this long explanation. Felix put a kettle to boil and prepared to make some coffee. Then the explanation of Blanford's tone struck him forcibly and made everything clear. Livia had disappeared, and he had suddenly missed her and decided jealously to come and see if she were with Felix! It was true. Blanford could not help it – though he cursed himself roundly for butting in. He was propelled, as indeed Felix was, by a quite uncontrollable jealousy, which came and went in spasms, and which both struggled to surmount by reminding themselves that they should really be above such feelings. It was no good.

Thinking of all this, Felix poured out the dreadful Camp coffee which was made of liquid chicory and smiled acidly upon his friend as he said (unable to disguise the tone of quiet malice in his voice): "I suppose it's Livia again?"

"Yes," said Blanford surrendering reluctantly to the truth, "it's Livia."

Felix was suddenly furiously contemptuous of this spoilsport friend of his. His pent-up feelings broke loose. "And just suppose that she wanted to be alone with me, to walk with me?" Blanford nodded humbly and said: "I know. I thought of that, Felix. I am most awfully sorry. I just couldn't resist coming here. I felt I had to find her. I am so sorry, I know you care for her too. But I have asked her to marry me later on. . . ." His voice trailed away into silence while his friend sat opposite trying to convey his disapproval and annoyance by small reproving gestures. As a matter of fact, at a deeper level than all this superficial annoyance, he felt a certain misgiving about Livia as a suitable person to marry. To love and if possible lie with – yes. "Marriage", he said sharply, "is quite another affair." Blanford detested the curate's tone in which Felix uttered this sentiment. "Yes," he said, becoming rather acid in his turn, "it happens to be my affair at the moment. That's why I took the liberty of coming. But if my presence upsets you I can take myself off. You only have to say." Felix was on the horns of a dilemma here; for if he were alone and sleepless later on he would welcome company; but if Livia was driven off by the presence of Aubrey . . . it would be far better if he went home now. Which solution was the better? He went into the bedroom to consult his little clock. The hour was pretty advanced now, and the likelihood of Livia coming rather remote. He returned to the disconsolate Blanford and said: "Were you thinking of a walk, then?"

Blanford shook his head and said: "Only as far as

Riquiqui's to see if I can pick up her trail. It's a lovely night."

It was a lovely night! The words echoed in the skull of Felix as he apportioned the last of the coffee and decided that he would not go to bed, he would after all walk. Moreover he now sensed that behind Blanford's tone of voice lurked an anxiety, a fear almost of the gloomy and ramshackle quarter of the town which he proposed to visit in search of the girl. He couldn't resist a slight touch of malice in his own voice as he said: "I suppose you'd want to go to Riquiqui's alone?" Blanford looked up at him and said, somewhat humbly, "On the contrary. I'd welcome company. You know that that whole section of the town scares me a bit – it's so disreputable with its bordels and gipsies."

This went some way towards mollifying Felix who betook himself to the bedroom where he changed out of his formal suit into something lighter, and topped it by his college blazer and a silk scarf. Through the half-open door he caught a glimpse of the glorified alcove which served as the so-called spare room where Livia sometimes lodged. The little cupboard stood there with its door ajar; he had already shown Blanford the male kit hanging up in there. He himself had never seen her in full disguise, though once or twice she had worn trousers to wander about the town. Blanford had made no comment – no comment whatsoever. What did he think? Felix could not say. For his part he found the whole question of marriage unreal – despite the magnetism of her beauty to which he was as much bound as Blanford. But there was something else which had qualified his passion. It was something he remembered with a certain shame – it was not in his nature to spy on people; yet, one evening, in a sudden fit of curiosity and without any conscious premeditation, he had walked into her room, opened the wardrobe and felt in the pockets of her brown cheap suit for all the world as if he knew that he would find something there – which indeed he did. It was a slip of paper torn from an exercise book – a love letter no less, but written in arch, lisping style, as if by an adolescent girl.

"*Ma p'tite Livvie je t'aime,*" and so on in this vein, but riddled with misspellings and turns of phrase which suggested an uneducated and very youthful author. Felix examined the hand with the magnifying glass which was always on his desk, and decided that it was not the writing of a gipsy but of a schoolgirl. But his investigations went no further and after a moment of hesitation he replaced the note where he had found it and went whistling light-heartedly back to his office, glad in spite of himself that his rival was being betrayed. From time to time he frowned, however, and tried to banish the uncharitable and unfriendly feeling – for he was a good-hearted boy who believed in friendship like the rest of us. Yet it kept coming back. Sometimes, walking beside Blanford he repeated the words in his mind, "*Ma p'tite Livvie je t'aime*", almost letting them come to the surface and find utterance. It was very vicious, this sort of behaviour, and he did not approve of it; but he could not help it.

They finished their coffee and Felix put the cups and saucers into the sink in his usual somewhat fussy way. Blanford waited for him, smoking thoughtfully with an air of profound preoccupation touched with sadness. A curious polarity of feelings had beset him – somewhere in the deepest part of himself he was actually glad that Livia was going, that they were to be separated for a time. It would take a weight off his mind, as the saying goes; he had indeed become a little impatient with himself, with the extent of his complete immersion in this unexpected infatuation for a girl who, more often than not, seemed hardly to know he was there, so remotely distant did she seem from all thought of him. The force of this attachment had somewhat exhausted him, and he knew for certain that it had prevented him from enjoying

Provence as deeply as he might have done. Loving – was there some sort of limitation inherent in it? This was the first time he had ever asked himself the question plainly. But the answer eluded him.

"*Avanti*," said Felix, who out of boredom had started to study Italian; and together the two young men crossed the withered garden and advanced among the criss-cross of tenebrous streets and alleys which led them towards Les Balances, that desolate and ruined quarter sloping down towards the rustling Rhône. "I don't suppose she really gives a damn about me," said Blanford unexpectedly, throwing his cigarette onto the pavement and stamping it out with petulance. He was dying for Felix to contradict him, to come out with some reassuring remark, but Felix was not going to pander to his mood. "I suppose not," he said composedly, looking into the deep velvety sky, smiling to himself. Blanford could have strangled him for his composure there and then. He made up his mind to find Livia if they had to walk all night; and when he found her to pick a quarrel with her, to try and make that dry little lizard of a girl cry. Then they would make it up and . . . here he lost himself in pleasant reveries. But what if she had returned home and was snug in his bed while they were wandering about like a couple of fools? It was amazing how his spirits soared optimistically at one thought and then sagged earthwards at its successor. Somewhere at the bottom end of this keyboard – among the bass notes – there lurked migraine and the ancient neurasthenia. They waited for him. He always carried a couple of loose aspirins in his pocket. He took one now, swallowing it easily. *Absit omen.* "It is not easy, I have never been in love before. And whores scare me a bit."

Felix took on a man-of-the-world tone as he said: "O pouf! I regard them simply as a disagreeable necessity in a puritan age."

"I once got clap after a bump supper," said Blanford gloomily, "and it wasn't at all gay. It took ages to get itself cured."

Felix felt an unexpected wave of admiration for his friend; so he had suffered in some subterranean lavatory decorated by horrific posters depicting all the possible ravages of sexual intercourse indulged in without a rubber sheath? The man was a hero after all! "It must have been dreadful," he said with a suddenly alerted wave of sympathy and Blanford nodded, not without pride. "It was, Felix."

They had started downhill, sloping along a set of streets which straggled from the height of the Hotel de Ville to the actual medieval walls which alone prevented them from seeing the scurrying sweeps of the Rhône. A glimpse of Villeneuve on its great promontory – that was all; and a coffin-like darkness in whose soft shifting exhalations of mist prickled a star or two. Felix had brought a torch, but used it sparingly in the deserted streets. The noise of their footsteps sounded lonely and disembodied in the night. The municipal lighting hereabouts was haphazard and sporadic. The last two streets they crossed to reach Riquiqui were in dense darkness; the pavements had melted away, and occasional cobble-stones lay about ready to trip them up. The quarter was an undrained one and smelt accordingly. Riquiqui's establishment stood at an angle in a *cul de sac* and its doors opened into the street. Bundles of old rubbish lay about – broken chairs, bits of marble, sheets of tin, lead pipes and refuse. It stood, the house, like the last remaining molar in a diseased jaw; on either side there was a weed-infested waste land with the remains of low walls. A window gave out into this gloom with a yellow and baleful light. But the hallway of the house seemed to be in darkness, to judge by the blind fanlight over the door.

There was no sign of the coach either – which Blanford

had christened "The Prince's Pumpkin" – but this could
have been dismissed and sent away to the livery stables where
its horses were lodged. Or perhaps they had gone to some
other establishment of the same category – though there
were not many in the town which enjoyed the reputation and
indeed the official protection of Riquiqui, for she also lodged
people and operated (if such a thing can be believed) as a
foster mother to waifs and strays. But she nevertheless
remained in a somewhat ambiguous position as one who kept
a house of ill-fame and was a friend to the gipsies; they called
her "angel maker" for the children confided to her care were
unwanted ones and would soon – so the popular gossip went
– be on their way to heaven to join the angels. The very fact
of her existence was explained by her payment of bribes, in
cash and in kind, which was at least plausible; for she was
fairly openly frequented by minor officials and the lower
echelons of the police force. The two young men trod the
streets of this raffish quarter with a certain native circumspection, though Felix once or twice whistled under his breath
as if to register confidence.

At last they stopped before the door of Riquiqui and
Blanford advanced to tap upon it with timorous knuckles.
It was not much in the way of a summons and it evoked
neither light nor voices in response. They waited for a while
in a downcast manner. Then Felix picked up a brick from the
gutter and made a more reasonable attempt at a knock – he
didn't like making a noise in the street at this time of night.
Supposing that nearby windows were thrown up and exasperated voices urged them to go to hell? They would
scamper away like rabbits. But no windows were raised, no
voices admonished them; worst of all there was no sound
from behind the unyielding front door of the brothel. An
exasperated Blanford tried a couple of kicks, but this was not
much use either as he was wearing tennis-shoes. They waited

and then knocked again, without the slightest result. The silence drained back into the darkness. The only movement was the stirring of large birds in the ragged storks' nests on the battlements. Somewhere – not really so far, but sounding as if it were situated at the other end of the known world – the Jacquemart struck an hour, though they were not quite certain which hour. "Not a sound," breathed poor Blanford with a sigh of despair. "There must be someone there."

Reluctantly they started to move away when Felix had a brainwave; his torch played among the rubbish heaps which filled the abandoned ruin at one side of the brothel. There were some oil drums in the corner and they gave him an idea. He rolled one over the mossy surface and placed it against the wall under the lighted window, mounting it very slowly, with a thousand precautions; for he did not wish to fall among the foundations and break his back. At last he levelled off, and, holding onto the wall, craned his neck towards the light. "It's a lavatory," he said in a low voice. "They've left the light on and the door open." Then he drew a deep breath and said: "Jesus! There they are! Just look at our old Prince!"

Blanford, consumed with curiosity, hurried to take possession of his own olive oil drum and was soon standing up against the wall beside Felix, gazing into the lavatory and, through it, into the relatively well-lighted hallway leading to an inner courtyard full of divans and potted plants of somewhat decayed aspect. And sure enough there was the Prince, spread out on a sofa, and perfectly at ease; while Quatrefages, clad only in a shirt and red socks, sat by his side sipping whisky and talking with the greatest animation. It took a moment or two to register the more piquant details of this scene which had all the air of taking place in some small theatre – it looked a bit unreal.

The Prince had divested himself of everything that covered the top half of his grey little body; he sat, so to speak,

clad only in his heavy paps, and had a sort of chinless gran-
deur. His nether half was clad in lightweight Jaeger combinations which stretched to the ankle and through the fly-slit of
which depended the royal member with its innocent pink tip.
Quatrefages also presented a somewhat equivocal appearance,
being clad only in a shirt and socks. He was clearly engaged
in a long explanation or exhortation addressed to Riquiqui
who stood almost out of range and half in shadow – so that
it seemed that the clerk was talking with animation to two
outsize breasts bulging out of a dirty shift. Beside them stood
a puzzled female dwarf with a hideously rouged face as if
ready for the circus; she was clad in white organdie with a
marriage veil. Moreover, she was jingling with trinkets and
had obviously been dressed against a very special occasion.
As a matter of fact she had been specially dressed for the
Prince, but now his companion was expressing the Prince's
discontent with her, and indeed his general discomfiture,
presumably because of her age. Yes, it was not hard to follow
the train of the argument. The dwarf was too old and too big
to appeal to the Prince. But they were being polite about it
and the horrible little creature bobbed her agreement and
dipped lovingly into a big box of Turkish Delight which the
Prince had pushed towards her. She had huge, discoloured
teeth like rotting dice.

As for Riquiqui she appeared to be at her wits' end to
meet the unusual demand. Languidly the little man extended
a hand and indicated that what he desired was much smaller,
very much smaller. He lent weight to his argument with
flowery little gestures which indicated clearly that there was
no question of ill-feeling or bad humour involved. He was
asking, not commanding. His tone was civilised and equable.
He proffered the box of loucoumi and Riquiqui in her turn
dug out a cube of Turkish Delight and wolfed it, licking the
powder off her talons, before dusting her shift to remove the

last traces of it. Then she held up her finger as one who sees daylight at last and bustled off, leaving them to their whisky. The misshapen little phantom of pleasure followed her, ripping off her bridal veil with an abrupt gesture like an actor quitting a wig as he left the stage.

Left alone, the two occupants of the centre of the stage – the suggestion of intimate theatre was irresistible because of the severely framed scene and the brilliantly stagey lighting – reloaded their glasses and conversed in low tones. The clerk was flushed and jovial-looking in his somewhat unclean shirt. The Prince in his long combinations looked quite regal still in an attenuated sort of way. He scratched his small decoration and exuded amiability. They had not long to wait, for at last Riquiqui burst in, flushed with success, hand in hand with two little girls dressed in a manner appropriate to a First Communion. Their faces were heavily rouged, which gave them the appearance of wearing painted masks through which they peered with unafraid but puzzled wonder. She paused, the huge woman, for dramatic effect as she entered, presenting her charges boldly but hesitantly. *Eureka*! She had remembered the existence of a couple of "angels", no doubt.

The result was a foregone conclusion. The Prince's radiant features expressed his delight and relief; he looked like a small boy who was turning cartwheels from sheer elation. Quatrefages folded his arms after setting down his glass and beamed upon the lady while the Prince extended his hands to take hers and move them half-way to his lips in a simulated kiss of congratulation. The two little children stood mumchance, but with a kindly air. They were sucking sweets. The Prince stood up and embraced them warmly; then he waved his arms and muttered something in Arabic and his major-domo (who must have been waiting in the shadows, the wings, so to speak) entered the lighted stage leading two large and beautifully groomed Afghan hounds on a gold leash.

The Prince clapped his hands in ecstasy and gave a little crow of laughter; he beamed round on the assembled company. Clearly everything was in order now. The next stage. . . .

Riquiqui threw open a side door which gave on to a bedroom of the house which had been decorated in the most extravagant fashion; a vast damascened bed lay under a lozenge-shaped pier-glass. It was covered in a gold cloth, and the shelf above it was full of children's dolls clad in folklore costumes. The walls themselves were draped with scarlet shawls and the whole context suggested a scene from *The Phantom of the Opera.* The little manikins looked as if they were the shrunken bodies of real children which had been patiently and fastidiously pickled before being dressed as harlequins, Arlésiennes, Catalans and Basques. Into this décor she ushered the Prince, now amiably holding the hands of the two children. The dogs, now off the leash, followed at his heels like well-drilled servants who knew their duty. The stage-set was so piquant and the actors so unaware that they were being observed that the two eavesdroppers almost forgot to feel the anxious disgust which had started to seize them.

But it was at this moment that Quatrefages entered the lavatory right under their noses and closed the door on this equivocal spectacle. He sat himself down on the throne and proceeded to more primitive business. They soon could hear his grunts and sighs right under their chins. It was quite a dilemma – they did not wish to be discovered in this spying posture. And they were suddenly aware of the precariousness of their station, for they could not simply jump down and run away. In the darkness one could have broken an ankle. So they stayed on, mentally swearing at the wretched clerk, and hoping that he would soon finish and restore them the lighted stage and the grotesque Egyptian. On the other hand, they could hardly pass the rest of the night standing up there on the oil drums watching the sexual evolutions of this Mecca-blessed libertine. A wild indecision reigned which matched their general situation; neither spoke because neither could think.

No doubt their frustration and gradually mounting discomfort would have sooner or later forced them to take a decision, but fate determined otherwise, for Quatrefages completed his business to his own satisfaction and pulled the chain; and as if by the same token the door was thrown open and the brightly lit stage once more revealed to them. There was a slight change of disposition – the door of the inner room was almost closed and even by craning the neck it would not have been possible to see with any clarity exactly what the Prince and his livestock were up to. Riquiqui was sitting down in a manner so relaxed as to suggest the puncture of an inner tube; and she was profiting by the absence of the Prince to renew her attack on the box of gummy sweets.

The little hunchback crossed the stage – now nude – and seated herself at what appeared to be a small upright piano covered in coloured shawls. She began to pick out monotonous little tunes on it with one finger. Quatrefages firmly retrieved his drink and spread himself over a divan with a relaxed and gluttonous air. The conversation flagged. There were a few indistinct sounds from the direction of the Prince's room but nothing very concrete that might be interpreted. The whole atmosphere had become now slack and humdrum, lacking in great interest, and Blanford began to find his toes going to sleep. It was clearly time to get down and go home. He was about to express this thought to his friend when there was a sudden irruption onto the little stage which all at once reinjected vitality into the drama, brought everything alive again.

The major-domo burst clucking and chattering into the room once more (apparently through the front door, for they heard the bolts shriek) and demanded the presence of his master at once. When he was advised to be patient his voice jumped a whole octave and his hysteria mounted to the ceiling. Greatly daring (so they thought) he threw open the door of the bedroom and revealed a scene of almost domestic tranquillity – the Prince on the bed surrounded by children and dogs and himself wearing a communion veil at which the children were both laughing heartily. He shot up indignantly, forgetting to remove the veil, and let fly a stream of Arabic oaths at the head of his servant, who, however, continued to babble and gesticulate. Apparently the gravity of what he had to relate alone justified this intrusion. After a moment of wild rage the truth dawned on the Prince and he sat up to listen to what the excited man was actually saying. Whatever he at last began to comprehend had an altogether electrifying effect upon him for he leaped out of bed with commendable agility and dashed into the next room, heading for the direction of the front door and crying in a high bird-like tone and in the English of Cairo, "They have pinched the bloody coach."

Such was the excitement of the two men, such was the velocity of their movements, that everyone took fire, everyone was sucked into the procession in spite of themselves, whirled into the drama by the sheer momentum of the Prince's dramatic dash. The two young men balanced on the oil drums outside also gave way to a wave of panic as they realised that the whole of this sudden surge led towards the open street, where they might be discovered in this ignominious posture. They jumped down and by the beam of the torch picked their way through the shattered detritus of the old foundation walls.

But the Prince and his servant, with the trajectory of comets, had rushed into the street, and as if quite mesmerised, so had the rest of them – Riquiqui, Quatrefages, the little naked dwarf, the dogs and the communicating children. They all stood gazing about them in a daze of wonder and confusion and anger, for the coach, which had apparently been standing before the front door, had disappeared. The Prince stamped his naked foot on the pavement with a gesture of febrile vexation, while his servant, as if to make quite sure, ran to the corner of the street and quested about generally like a gun-dog trying for a scent. Then he came back shaking his head and muttering. The Prince gazed around him, his regard travelling from face to face as if for sympathy. "Who could have done it—" he said, and Riquiqui, who had shown less surprise and consternation than the others, replied, "It's the gipsies. Leave it to me. Tomorrow I will find them."

The company was so absorbed in this little drama that they greeted the appearance of Felix and Blanford in an almost absent-minded way, hardly greeting them; but when they brought evidence to suggest that the coach had been stolen some good time ago (for it had not been there when they arrived) they managed to kindle a little interest. They were, after all, potential clients – so thought the little dwarf, who tried to link her arm in that of Felix, to his pained horror. "I will call the police," said the Prince in a sudden burst of childish petulance. "I will telephone to Farouk." It carried little conviction, for there he was with his little member protruding from his long woollen combinations.

Quatrefages, after a moment of reflection, led him muttering back into the house of pleasure and this time Blanford and Felix followed them in order to have a drink and to reassure themselves about the absence of Livia. Quatrefages, overcome by a sudden pudicity, became aware of his naked condition and hunted for his trousers before pouring out more whisky; the Prince retired haughtily to the inner room with his dogs and children and banged the door, leaving instructions that he was not to be disturbed for at least an hour. Blanford sipped his drink and heard the tinny piano tinkle. He felt suddenly terribly sleepy. Quatrefages said with a malicious grin: "Livia has gone to the gipsies."

So she had been there that evening, and had given them the slip as usual! Felix could not repress a slightly malicious side-glance at his fellow sufferer; but Blanford looked more angry than sad. He was telling himself that this would have to stop – this infatuation would have to be brought to an end. "It leads nowhere," he said aloud, talking to himself. At last the real truth of the matter had dawned on him – but like every glimpse of truth it was only fleeting and provisional. With the other half of his mind, so to speak, he was still lamed by his inner vision of her, of her sullen magnetism, of those expiring kisses which had ignited their minds. He did not care for the sardonic remarks of the clerk nor the cynical looks of Felix – the matter was too important, went too far into the gulfs of hopeless sentiment, of bewitchment, for the others to appreciate it.

He hugged his mood to himself, ignoring the rest of them, treasuring every little stab of pleasure or pain which it brought. What did it matter what Livia was or what she did? A strange metaphor came into his mind which expressed the exact nature of this attachment – a metaphor which centuries later Sutcliffe would use when he tried to define his gross attachment to the pale wraith Pia, who was a diluted version of the girl Constance, Livia's sister. But in his present mind it was Livia who provoked this thought which one would have had to be an alchemist to understand. What he loved in her was her "water" – as of a precious stone. It is after all what is really loved in a woman – not the sheath of matter which covers her – but her "signature". In the middle of all the chatter and movement of the brothel he found himself brooding upon this fact in all its singularity and wishing for a scrap of paper on which to jot it down. He would have liked to incorporate it into his diary but he knew that by the morrow he would have forgotten it.

Suddenly an enormous lassitude had taken hold of him. "I want to go home," he said yawning, and to his surprise Felix pronounced himself of the same disposition. Blanford felt so lonely he could have gone out into the dark street and waved vigorously to imaginary people. Quatrefages said he would come too – "*J'ai tiré mon petit coup*," he said modestly. And the Prince? Why, he was to be left; the major-domo would see him safely home to the Imperial where he had taken up his headquarters. Already a substitute pumpkin-coach in the shape of a town *fiacre* had been summoned and stood at the door. But the night was no longer young, and the three young men felt sallow and spent. So they set off across the town on foot, finding some refreshment in the dark coolness which was full of the scent of lemons and mandarines and honeysuckle. Felix would be the first home, then the clerk; Blanford wanted to sit somewhere and watch the dawn come up, to let his thought of Livia ripen like some huge gourd. The pain was in the pleasure – a novelty for him, he realised.

The night had waited for them – a great paunch of silence upon which the ordinary sounds of the city hardly impinged. Somewhere an ambulance raced with its tingling alarm; there was something vengeful in the peals of its bell, he thought, as it hurried back triumphantly to the hospital with its trophy of maimed flesh. They heard its signals diminishing as it dived through the outer ramparts towards the suburbs. Felix yawned. Blanford, sunk himself, felt the whole weight of his unexpressed narcissism heavy inside him, like dough or wax, waiting to be kneaded into some sort of significant shape – by what? – but he did not as yet dare to think of himself as an artist. It was like a blind boil which could not discharge itself except in insomnia or in those sudden dispositions towards tears when some great music stirred him, or the glance of light on some ripe landscape pierced him. For others these vague intimations of beatitude, these realisations of beauty were enough in themselves simply to enjoy. But he came of that obstinate and unbalanced tribe which longed to do something about them – to realise and recreate them in a form less poignantly transitory than that vouchsafed by reality. What was to be *done?* That was always his thought, and he fretted inside himself at the notion that there was nothing, that he could do nothing, there was nothing to be done.

A brief wind ran the whole length of the street and turned a corner, disappearing in a gusty whirl of dead leaves, pouring itself into the throat of the invisible river whose slitherings and strivings they could hear as they approached it. When the sun came a thousand leafing planes would mirror themselves in its greenish waters. Here at last was the Consulate. The pavements were still warm and, because they had been washed with water and Javel, gave off the smell of incense. Felix too felt the gnawings of a nostalgic sadness. "I am sorry you will soon be gone," he said, but comforted himself with the thought that after such a summer he had happy enough memories stored against the winter with the rains and snows it would bring to the city. "I must ask for some leave," he went on, enlivening his thought with the prospect of meeting the others somewhere, perhaps in London. But Blanford's thoughts were of a graver cast – for there was to be no more Oxford after this term. Life was spreading its wings. What was to become of him? He would have enough money to live on – but what would that serve if he had no passionate aptitudes which he might fulfil? Tinker, Tailor, Soldier, Sailor ... what was he to do with his life? He had shown Livia the two little lyrics in the University magazine and he thought that she had looked at him with a new respect; but this was probably imagined. As for the poems they were quite nice pastiche, without an ounce of real feelings in them. Could she not see that? He sighed aloud as he walked. Quatrefages also seemed to be touched, through his fatigue, by the prevailing nostalgia. He gazed at the dark sky and shook himself like a wet mastiff. "Life is only once," he said unexpectedly. Felix now turned yawning into the gateway of the Consulate. "Remember the car is mine tomorrow," he told the clerk who shrugged his shoulders with indifference. Felix paused inside the front door for a moment to listen to their receding footfalls on the dark pavements. Soon the lamplighter would emerge to gather his blossoms of light, shy as a squirrel. Soon he would be alone again in this oppressive city which could only be enjoyed if seen through the eyes of Livia. In spite of his yawns he made the effort to clean his teeth before subsiding into his bed – for he was rather proud of their evenness. He told his sleepy reflection sternly: "I shall not cry myself to sleep because there are no golf courses on the moon." It was a declaration of faith, in a manner of speaking.

The two others walked silently side by side, each absorbed in his thoughts: but as they began to near the little square where Quatrefages' garish window shone out of the dark mass of the darker hotel, their steps began to lag. Despite the fatigue the clerk was reluctant to part with his companion. Truth to tell he was of a timorous nature and was always afraid to return late and alone to his room for fear of finding someone or something waiting for him. He imagined perhaps a very old tramp, sitting in the armchair waiting patiently for his return; or a blind man with a white stick and a great white dog. They would have come to propose some sort of compact with the Devil. He frowned and shook his head at his own stupidity; yet he wondered at the same time what excuse he could give which might persuade Blanford to mount the stairs with him and enter his room – just to reassure him so that he could now turn off the light and get some sleep.

It seemed absurd to propose yet another drink but that is what he heard himself doing, and to his great delight Blanford, who seemed in some obscure way to have divined his feelings, accepted the invitation. The clerk could not believe his luck. His dejected walk became all at once buoyant and nervous, his lassitude slipped from him. As a matter of fact Blanford was always intrigued by a glimpse of this extraordinary office whose walls were covered with death charts of the Templars, each with his date of execution. In the corner lay an unmade bed and a side-table covered with the impedimenta of the insomniac in the shape of bottles of pills and tinctures of opium, packs of cigarettes, and a cluster of books on alchemy and related topics, all bearing the marker of the Calvet Museum.

A pile of children's exercise books were propped up on the mantelshelf. A white chamberpot stood under the bed decorated by a cluster of roses in bloom. The whole centre of the room was taken up with the sort of trestle tables with angle lamps such as an architect might set up to draw a project in detail – or else perhaps the kind of tables upon which a paperhanger might set out his wallpapers before brushing the glue on to them. There was a small alcove in which stood a crucifix together with a bottle of whisky and several small mineral water bottles. The room smelt damply musty. It was situated on the blind side of the street and never got any light. It was heavy with dust and the little lavatory-douche was in a dreadful mess – towels covered in hair cream and, strangely, lipstick. The drains stank. Everywhere cigarettes had burnt out and left a dark burn – even on the wash basin. One wondered how there had never been a fire there. Quatrefages poured out a warmish drink and dragged out an uncomfortable chair for his guest to sit upon.

But Blanford preferred to stand and examine the charts on the wall with their suggestive datings, and the now lively Quatrefages followed his gaze with an air of pride. "We are down to the last of them," he said, "and we know for certain that they had managed to hide the treasure where neither Philippe nor his Chancellor Nogaret, who conducted the persecution, could lay their hands on it. This is why things dragged on so. The Templars would confess to anything but they would not divulge the hiding place. From other documents, some pretty enigmatic, we know that five of the knights were in the secret. But we don't as yet know which. But we have some clues to go on which seem pretty definite." He paused to drain his glass and cough loudly. Blanford, whose curiosity had got the better of him, asked a few questions and then suddenly and perhaps rather rudely said: "Livia told me that she thought you had discovered the place, the vault, the chapel or whatever, and that there was nothing in it. That the treasure had been pinched ages ago. . . . ."

The change in Quatrefages was as sudden as it was marked; his sallow complexion had become strained and laboured. He sat down on the bed and croaked out an oath: "Livia knows nothing," he said, "nothing. The gipsies tell one all sorts of things, but it is false. I have not found the place as yet. But of course Provence is full of ruined chapels and empty vaults destroyed during the various religious upheavals. But nothing that so far corresponds with the evidence of an orchard – the 'Verger de Saint Louis' – where the plane trees were set in a quincunx like an ancient Greek temple grove. No, as yet we have not found the place."

Blanford felt all of a sudden apologetic for having made this intrusion – the more so because he suddenly felt that Quatrefages was probably lying to him. Or was it Livia? At any rate none of this was his business, and he had no intention of making the little clerk feel that he was not to be counted upon, or that his word was not believed. "I am sorry," he said, "it was not my business and I should not have repeated gossip."

Nevertheless, whatever the truth of the matter was, the agitation of Quatrefages seemed somehow excessive, and Blanford could not help speculating upon this fragment of gossip which had slipped from Livia's lips quite casually, seemingly without malice or premeditation. "When we do discover it," said the clerk, his eyes glittering malevolently in his nervous paleness of feature, "that will be the day to rejoice." Blanford turned away to the great wall charts of the dead Templars and as he did so the dawn broke softly in the open street below. Its faint tinges of yellow and rose coloured the walls of that sordid room, almost like some signal from a past full of mystery and significance.

The dead names glowed like jewels, like embers still breathing in the pale ashes of the past. The names slowly recited themselves in his mind, each with its hush of death and silence cradling it. Dead cavaliers of the piebald standard! Raynier de Larchant, Reynaud de Tremblay, Pierre de Tortville, Jacques de Molay, Hugues de Pairaud, Jean du Tour, Geoffroy de Gonneville, Jean Taillefer, Jean L'Anglais, Baudoin de Saint-Just. Inhabitants now of history, destroyed by blind circumstance, by the zeal and cupidity of the lawless ages. "One wonders what they were guilty of," he said aloud, more to himself than to anyone. His eyes traversed the great names again, lingering over them, savouring the mystery and sadness of their premature deaths by starvation, torture, or the burning pyres of the Inquisition. It was a riddle which would never be read, an enigma which still intrigued and baffled new generations of historians.

Quatrefages sat on the edge of the bed leaning forward and concentrating – as if he were trying to follow Blanford's train of thought, to read his mind. His face was flushed now, the fever had come back; and he was full of drink and beginning to feel it. "What were they guilty of?" he repeated aloud in a sharp cracked voice, so curiously at variance with his natural tone that Blanford turned curiously upon him and said: "Well, what?" But it was now clear that Quatrefages was very drunk indeed; he stood up and swayed and began to snivel. "The greatest heresy the world has ever known," he said in an exalted way; he clenched his fists and raised them on high, for all the world as if he himself were standing on a high pyre, feeling the flames rising around his feet, and testifying to the truth of a belief which ran counter to the whole structure of an age's thoughts.

Blanford watched him burning and crying there for a moment, and then reached out a tentative hand, as if to soothe or console him against so much excessive feeling. He felt also a little guilty – as if his idle remark had somehow provoked this orgiastic recital. Quatrefages was now a-tremble with emotion. He was like a wire through which passed a current of a voltage almost too powerful to bear. "You don't know the truth," he said incoherently and his lips began to wobble as he spoke, his tears to choke him.

Blanford was able to glimpse now the zealot who lived underneath the external guise of the young man – the carapace of industry and probity and politeness which made up the outer man. But now it was as if a switch had been thrown, first by the drink and then by Livia's remark – the image of a dam came into his mind, or one of those *écluses* on the Rhône through which their barge had slid. The current had pushed down all the debris of Quatrefages' solitary and secret life – sitting there agonising over long-dead knights, and trying by guile and science to pick their pockets. "We are like grave-robbers in the pay of Galen," he cried with a bitter vehemence, still standing in his theatrical attitude of human sacrifice. "They have reduced the whole thing to a vulgar matter of *fric*, of booty. They have missed the whole point of this tremendous apostasy. Blanford, *écoutez*!" He took his companion by the shoulders and shook him so violently that his drink was nearly upset and he was just able to set it down and free his elbow in time.

Quatrefages sank back on to his bed and plunged his chin moodily into his fists. "That is what is killing me," he said in a lower key, suppressing the drama in his voice a little; "the ignominiousness of what we are doing, and my own part in it." Blanford's reactions to this sort of outburst were typically Christian public-schoolboy; he felt shy, alarmed and overwhelmed. He cursed himself for having unwittingly provoked this storm. He did not want to witness Quatrefages' self-recriminations and breast-beatings. If he so much disapproved of what he was doing why did he not re-sign? It was easy to simplify matters thus – he knew that. But he suppressed a sigh as he sat down, prepared to let the clerk talk himself out. "I began in good economic faith, and then I began to get more and more curious about the Templars – not about their fortune but about the nature of their heresy. To defy the reign of matter as they did, to outface the ruling devil – that was what intrigued me. Yes, they quietly built up an almost unassailable temporal power – they were the bankers of the age. And these great constructions were their banks, their prisons."

He waved an arm vaguely in the direction of the Papal Palaces on their elevation above the river, now doubtless turning rose also, petal by petal, spire by spire. "The knights were systematically destroyed by the hooded anonymous butchers of the Inquisition in order to secure the succession of what they now knew was evil – the pre-eminence of matter and will in the world. They were the instruments of Old Nick himself who was not going to have his throne shaken by this superb refusal of the knights; he was not going to submit without a struggle. The death wish against the life wish – God, you know, is only an alibi in all this, only a cover-story. The real battle between the negative and positive forces was joined here – and all Europe in the coming ages was at stake." He paused and licked his dry lips. Then, draining his glass in a wobbly way, he said, almost in a whisper, "They lost, and we lost with them."

The two of them stared at one another for a moment and then Quatrefages gave a hopeless little chuckle and put his head on one side and, half closing his eyes – like a bird putting its head under its wing – said: "I know why you look at me like that. You are saying to yourself that it is preposterous to feel so strongly about a mere historical event. You are right. But we are living out the fateful destiny of European man which was decided then – right here in Avignon. We are taking part in this materialist funeral of living man. Yes, they were suppressed and deafening clouds of propaganda were pumped out over them to obscure the real issues and blacken their names. They were accused of every kind of sorcery, whereas the only conjuring they indulged in was the flat refusal to continue living the great lie of civilisation as it was then ordered. Of course it had to be kept secret, for it was heresy, in the strict terms of the epoch."

He fell silent at last. Blanford stared at the great wall maps: among them was a series of architectural studies of the various Temples and their disposition. He was, he concluded, in the presence of a harmless young maniac who had allowed his head to be turned by the bogus speculations of the popular mysticism which was at the moment all too fashionable. The Rosy Cross, the dimensions of the Great Pyramid, Madame Blavatsky. . . . He knew the line of country fairly well and indeed had read quite a few books about these matters – but without being swept off his feet by what he regarded as enjoyable fantasies. "What does it *matter* if there is a treasure or not?" cried Quatrefages passionately, waking up temporarily to resume his theme. Bang! "To add a little more *fric* to Galen's fortune? But I think there is no treasure; I think Philippe Le Bel got it all. I have not mentioned this to anyone because I am not absolutely sure – but our search for the quincunx of trees concerns another sort of treasure. That is what I really believe. But who can I talk to about it? Nobody! Nobody!"

Again he banged his fist upon the bed until the springs twanged. The whole confused details of his own apostasy, his own refusal of the body of Christ, the cannibal totem, rose up to choke him with a sense of his unworthiness, his insufficiency. He let out a groan. Blanford said rather primly, "I do understand a little bit. You mean the Philosopher's Stone, don't you?" But the clerk was plunged in his reveries and only nodded abstractedly, as if he were listening to some distant music too absorbing to allow him to shift his attention to what Blanford was saying. "But that is not the sort of treasure one finds in the ground, like a crock of gold containing a liquid rainbow . . . is it?" The question was useless and deserved for answer the silence it got. Quatrefages now whispered something to himself, quietly and confidently, nodding his head sagely and with resignation. Then he sank sideways on to the pillows, cradling his heavy head in his hands as if it were a Roman bust, and fell asleep. Blanford watched him for a while with curiosity and sympathy; his mind seemed to burn with such pathetic intensity in his lean body. Now, sleeping there, with his long nose aimed at the pillow, he looked touchingly defenceless. His wrists were so very thin. As the light had already been turned off there was nothing left but to tiptoe from the room and down the creaking staircase.

He paused to whisper a word to the sleepy night-porter who was putting his improvised bed to rights. Then down to the icy river and the bridge which steered away from the wakening city to the wide green hills beyond. He set out in a new burst of energy to walk back to Tu Duc. Everything on that joyful morning seemed to gleam like a new coin – a newly minted currency of vivid impressions. He felt words stirring inside his mind, like some long-hibernating species which a tardy spring had wakened only now, struck by the romance of the green swirling river and the cypress-punctuated hills he was approaching. To really appreciate a place or time – to extract the poignant essence of it – one should see it in the light of a departure, a leavetaking. It was the sense of farewell in things which impregnated them with this phantom of nostalgia so important for the young artist.

He felt the lure of language stirring in him, like a muscle stretching itself, cramped from long disuse. He did not know how to contain nor what to do with all this happiness. He approached the sleeping house across the unkempt lawns, cutting the dew with every step and feeling the moisture soak into his tennis shoes. A black cat sat on the mat by the kitchen garden – just like in his first nursery-book. But more wonderful still; from the rumple of bedclothes which hid the secret form of the naked Livia he could only pick out one slender hand with its long fingers relaxed and extended – one finger yellow with tobacco stains. He stripped and crawled in beside the sleep-sodden half-drugged nymph and, glad that she slept on, set himself to studying every feature of that slender expressive face with its striking alignment of bones and planes.

He tried to pierce with his eyes the very real bewitchment which transformed it; he realised that what he saw was not Livia but his own transfigured version of her – the reflection of his love. Beside the bed was the little box with the cheap wedding ring he had bought in Lunel from an old Jewish lady in a booth which sold lottery tickets and betting slips. He slipped it softly onto her unresisting finger and, like the unwise mooncalf he was, kissed it. He made love to her at her whispered request, though she neither opened her eyes nor in any way altered the disposition of her body; he moved her about as she lay there, quite limp, rather like one of those articulated "lay figures" that artists and dressmakers use.

Their united spirits seemed to wash down the long river together, entangled in one another, and then far away out to sea – the deep sea of a new sleep. But in order to leave her undisturbed he took a blanket to the balcony and curled up on the stones in the vanishing dew, his sleepy head pillowed upon a damp towel. In the half-sleep of fatigue the whole gorgeous gallery of Provençal images unwound inside his mind as if on a giant spool. There were so many memories he did not know what to do with them. He heard Livia stir and, turning on his elbow, gazed through the open balcony door. Yes, she was sleepily awake and sitting up in bed; but he was not prepared for what he saw now. She was gazing at her ring-finger with a curious expression of horror he had never seen on her face before. It was the expression of some- one who suddenly finds a scorpion on the lapel of a jacket they are wearing. Her lips all but cried out: "Who would have done this?" and with a gesture which combined anger with repulsion she snatched off the ring and flung it with all her might into the corner of the room.

He heard its sour tinkle as it bounced about on the floor. It was quite a shock – something went dead and cold inside him as he took in this involuntary gesture of rejection. He too sat up now, to watch her sink back with a sigh into her bed and draw the covers over her head as she foundered into a deeper sleep. The ring! Blanford reflected on these mysteries and on the independence of Livia as he crossed the wakening garden and plunged into the icy waters of the lily pond; what did it mean? It was Livia who had entertained his callow addresses and his suggestions about marriage. She had shown no distaste for such a thought before. But here she was standing beside the pond, poised for a dive. "What has changed?" he asked her quietly, rather painfully, though he did not know what he might have to fear in her answer. "I was not ready for it," she said. "Not yet. Perhaps I shall never be. We'll see."

But then to make up for this disturbing hesitation she launched herself into the water and came swirling into his arms to kiss and embrace him anew, her body glittering like a fish in a net. So their peace was restored and their solidarity of feeling – yet in the heart of the matter Blanford felt the prick of sadness, of some unachieved intimacy which lay between them like a shadow. "I missed you everywhere, gipsies, Riquiqui's, Felix, Quatrefages. . ." He smiled at her but he all of a sudden seemed to wake up with a jolt and tell himself: "She lies as simply as she breathes – about everything." Later he hunted for the ring but it had gone. She had reclaimed it, then? He did not ask her.

SIX

Talking Back

THE LONG SERPENTINE THOUGHT, AFTER SO MANY parentheses, came at last to rest in his silent mind. A very long silence fell, which seemed to both of them as if it might prolong itself unto eternity. "Hullo!" cried Sutcliffe twice, on a note of almost childish anxiety. (Ghosts always get alarmed when they are not in full manifestation – when they are off duty, so to speak – for it seems to them that they are in danger of ceasing to exist.) Yes. Suppose, I mean, that Blanford forgot to think of *him*! What then? It would be the end! And Blanford himself was, at that moment, bowed under the same thought, for he knew that once the ghosts, which together go to make up the collective memory, cease to care . . . why, one goes out like a light. Ask any artist! For a moment he was quite tongue-tied, he could not answer; in his imagination he had let the old-fashioned receiver fall upon the arm of his chair as he gazed into the fire with frigid intensity, for he had seen the face of Constance there, and it was curling up with the flames, it was disappearing. Sutcliffe could hear his uneven, heavy breathing. "For God's sake," he cried, "why don't you say something, Aubrey?"

But a sudden sense of helpless inadequacy had over-whelmed the writer as he wondered how to compress and condense into a few pages all the events and impressions of that short period which had come so abruptly to an end with the outbreak of the war. This brief glimpse of Constance had suddenly revived it all. It had been so extraordinarily rich, so bursting with promise; then abruptly the whole period had sunk out of sight, into the dark night of Nazi Europe. But what was he saying? For almost a whole year the war had actually been declared, though nobody had moved. The French lurked among their block-houses, wondering at the extraordinary paralysis which had gripped the whole of Europe. Meanwhile the life of Paris and London appeared to continue unchanged – the postal services were normal, for example, the telephone worked, the skies were as yet empty of planes. Yes, a few greasy-looking barrage balloons had appeared above the Thames. Somewhere, in some dim and amorphous region of the group-mind, feverish preparations were being made to forge a weapon which might contain the launching thrust of the German forces. But somehow nobody could believe in it. In all the soft paralysis there was a luxurious hopelessness, a valedictory sensation of the doom which must overtake the great capitals, one by one. Bye-bye to Paris and Rome, to Athens and Madrid. . . . One had a wild desire to revisit them quickly for a moment, to feel their living pulse before it was stilled forever. But even this was late in the day, after the formal declarations had been made. Yet for months, even years, before one could see some sort of war coming, see the horizon darkening. They had lived with this thing and knew that there was nothing to be done.

Tiny incidents, mere crumbs, remained still in Blanford's memories of that epoch, as if they had been simply markers to point the direction of the prevailing wind, the death-wind. How he had lent Sam the money to buy himself a uniform, while down in Provence Constance waited for him, for Sam, with a calm and smiling solicitude which so expertly masked the depth of her feelings. It was no time to decide to marry, but that is what they had done, and walking into his room at Tu Duc she came upon him awkwardly examining his fancy dress in the mirror with an air of rapturous astonishment. She did not actually weep but he put her head on his shoulders and began to laugh at his foolish expression. Meanwhile he said to himself, aloud, in the mirror:

"If she doesn't love me in this get-up she never bloody will."
The trousers had to be altered, the waistcoat set more snugly.
And here Felix came to the rescue and found a tailor in
Avignon. Sam had only a few days' leave before returning
to Oxford and the war. It was not entirely in bantering terms
that he said: "I was really worried about being unemployable,
and now look at this excellent job, so well paid. And bags of
promotion, too, if one is energetic." This was on the platform waiting for the train to Paris. Blanford saw Constance
turn away to hide her emotion and he engaged his friend in
banter to hide his own. The whole world was breaking up
under them like some old raft. It was deplorable to be so
callow, so undemonstrative.

Yet there were certain modifying certainties, among
them the general belief that the Germans would never
penetrate the Maginot Line whatever their bombers might
do to the cities. If there was war, even a long war, France
would remain geographically intact, so that some sort of
civilian life would go on until it ended. The famous Line
was to France what the Channel had always been for the
British. In the back of everyone's consciousness there must
have been obstinate archaic memories left over from 1914,
stalemates on the Somme, and so on. Nobody thought
about mobility, even later when it was clear that things had
gone well beyond compromise. What then? Felix had received
orders to stand by and aid the evacuation of British subjects
should the storm break – and then to hand over his Consulate
to the Swiss. And here came a remarkable and most welcome
discovery. The three of them – Hilary and his two sisters –
were of dual nationality and would claim Swiss citizenship.
Their clever old fox of a father had had them all born in
Geneva. Neither Sam nor Blanford, however, could claim
such an immunity from action, while for his part the latter
wondered whether he should not declare for conscientious

objection. Felix offered him all the necessary documentation but he was gripped by conflicting uncertainties. The fate of the Jews had become clear, and while one could be against war in general one could not really turn one's back on this one, when such terrible issues were at stake. Yet for the time he did nothing.

And then somewhere in the middle of all this period comes a spell in Paris with Livia, a spell which ended in that fatuous marriage anchored by a wedding ring which was never to be worn. A disorderly, roughcast sort of student existence in the fourteenth arrondissement. A Livia who was always busy and preoccupied though he never found out what she was doing. But she was out at all hours in all weathers, and she talked in her sleep and drank absinthe with disquieting application. The little rented flat was a shabby enough place, but there was a table at which he could write so that one basic need was satisfied, though at this time he wrote mostly long letters. Yet stirring deep in the jungle he could hear the rustle of those animal doubts which came creeping upon him. He began to wonder what he had indeed done. At times when she was drunk her laughter was so extravagant as to be insulting. At times he caught glimpses of unusual expressions on that pale face – hate, malevolence, disdain. It made him feel fearful and sad, as if some vital piece of information was missing – the presence of a shadow which stood forever between them. There was. She had become so much thinner that her looks had changed. The head of the cicada had become narrower, the face an adder's.

Then his mother's health began to falter and flicker and he was called back to her bedside where he gazed long and earnestly into that once familiar face, now pained to see that the long illness had altered all its stresses, composed it in new planes and lines, as if to copy on the outer skin the

fearful loneliness and despair of the inner mind. She had
things to tell him about her small fortune, and she had
discovered that she could not trust Cade, the valet. He opened
her letters and in general kept a spying eye out over her
affairs. She had longed to give him notice but in all his other
duties he was so perfect and so dependable that she had not
dared. In this, as in all other things, she was lucidity itself,
and even when she sank back into a last deep coma he did
not think that she would die – indeed the doctor warned
him that she might linger on a long time yet, so strong was
her heart. Nevertheless he spent that day at her bedside,
holding that frail hand in which the pulse continued to beat
like that of a captive sparrow. In these long silences his
mind went about its business slowly and densely. He
wondered much about Livia and about his own future. His
mother was leaving him a small marginal income, as well as
the London house which could be let. There was also a small
cottage on a farm outside Cairo where his father had spent
many summers pursuing his entomological passion with
silent assiduity. This was a mere shack, though, and there
was hardly any land around it. Nevertheless, it was like a
window open upon another country.

Another problem: if she should by any chance wake,
ought he to tell her that he was married to Livia, or was it
better to keep the whole matter a secret? Already there was a
sneaking premonition that he had embarked upon something
which might become a capital misadventure. Sitting in that
grey light of a suburban nightfall, trying mentally to align
her ticking wrist with the ticking of the grandfather-clock
in the hall, he wondered a little bleakly what would come of
it all. In a sense it was good to have the war to think about –
for it dwarfed purely human schemes, and one could shelve
them temporarily. And yet he did not think there would be a
war, despite all the signs; history was like some lump of

viscid porridge sliding slowly down a sink, but with such an infinite slowness! Their gestures, their hopes and schemes, seemed to be somehow insubstantial, chimerical. Meanwhile the frenzy of Paris was still teaching, and he realised how pregnant were the lessons he had learned in this all too brief residence there – the capital of the European nervous system. So many valuable acquisitions: how total freedom did not spell licence, nor gastronomy gluttony, nor passion brutality.

—◇—

The old streets down at the fag-end of the rue St.-Jacques which smelt of piss and stale cooking were the mere folklore of life lived in a relatively waterless capital where the women did not shave under their arms, and preferred stale scent to soapy bath water. In summer the smell of armpits in the cafés was enough to drive one mad. Yet everywhere the river winds cradled the velvet city and one could walk all night under a canopy of stars worthy of grand opera – the brilliant glitter of outer space impacting upon the shimmering brilliance of a world of hot light.

Appropriately enough she had given him a rendezvous (for the marriage) at the old Sphinx, opposite the Gare Montparnasse, where the respectable exterior – a family café, where families up from the country came to eat an ice and wait for their train – masked a charming bordel with a high gallery and several spotless cubicles. A simple bead curtain separated the two establishments, but such was the pleasant naturalness of things in the Paris of that day, that often the girls, dressed only in coloured sarongs and with the traditional napkin over the arm like waiters ("no spots upon the counterpane, please") came out to meet friends and even play a game of chequers with elderly clients whom time had ferried lightly into *impuissance*. "How marvellous," she said when she came, "if you could take all this with you to smoky

Euston." He had told her about his mother, that she was dying; he would leave immediately after the ceremony, which was performed by a very deaf consul and duly entered in the Consular Registers. The Minister then offered them the traditional glass of champagne under the tactless portrait of an idealised Wellington. He was a kind old man but he could not keep his horrified gaze off the dirty feet of Livia in her sandals. Later, much later, when Blanford asked Livia why she had done it at all she replied with a contemptuous laugh: "It seemed so unimportant; so I made you a present of something you wanted."

All this and much more passed through his mind as he sat holding the wrist of his dying mother – a flight of impressions like a brilliant surge of tropical fish across the dim aquarium of his student life. On the other side of the curtain of adolescence was a Paris full of bountiful surprises – a Paris where all the whores had started to take German lessons. The teachers of the German Institute were overwhelmed with requests for classes! A Paris where nobody shaved under the arms. At the Sphinx where he went rather sedately to play *belotte* and drink (with a timid air) an absinthe, which he hated, he had met a charming friend of his new wife, a negress of great beauty with a smile from here to there, and hands which roved into any pocket that presented itself. Livia found her "killing", and derived such amusement from her Martinique French that he was forced to enjoy her as well. Curiously enough she did shave under the arms, though she said the girls in general did not because a swatch of hair excited the customer and was good for business. He was extremely frightened of these unexpected revelations of turpitude, but it was after all romantic and he was in the rapt middle of Proust, and France was after all ... what exactly? He had never been in such an extraordinary ambiance before, a sort of ferment of freedom and treachery, of love and obscenity, of febrility and distress. A life which was so rich in possibilities reduced one to silence.

Nor for that matter had he ever been really in love before, whatever that might mean. The brilliant little taxis which flashed about the town like shooting stars were their favourite transport. Whenever they rushed off the macadam on to a cobbled thoroughfare the kisses of lovers in the back began to hobble and shake as if with an extra passionate emphasis conferred by the *pavé*. And quite apart from the greater beauties of this most beautiful of cities they were made freemasons of the company of its lovers, holding hands dutifully on the Pont des Arts, sitting heart joined to heart at the Closerie des Lilas or the rumbling Dôme. Floods of new books and ideas swamped them. He read relentlessly to keep abreast in quiet cafés and parks. It was the epoch of puzzling Gertrude Stein, Picasso, and the earlier convulsions of the American giants like Fitzgerald and Miller. He was sufficiently mature, however, to reflect that Europe was fast reaching the end of the genito-urinary phase in its literature – and he recognised the approaching impotence it signalled. Soon sex as a subject would be ventilated completely. "Even the act is dying", he allowed Sutcliffe to note, "and will soon become as charmless as badminton. For a little while the cinema may conserve it as a token act – as involuntary as a sneeze or a hiccough: a token rape, while the indifferent victim gnaws an apple." He added: "The future is more visible from France than anywhere because the French push everything to extremes. An audio-judeo-visual age is being born – the Mouton Rothschild epoch where the pre-eminence of Jewish thought is everywhere apparent, which explains the jealousy of the Germans."

Standing at night on a quiet bridge with the whole of reflected heaven flowing beneath them, silent, rapt. "One day you will despise me," she said, talking as if to herself.

One star was ticking over the lemon water. He said to himself: "Pity and she don't match and never will." And here he was – most inappropriate of men, a writer, watching from the abolished tower of his male self-esteem refunding his youth into these silences with this dangerous girl. "In two months' time I am going away, perhaps for good," he said, but he didn't take it seriously, just as he didn't really take the war seriously. Sutcliffe chided him from Geneva where he had landed a temporary job tutoring. "It's all very well to sit up there in your private Pisgah," he said, "but kindly note that Pisgah is the Hebrew word for an outdoor shithouse. It was here that old Moses quietly, while shifting the load of guilt, in the posture of Rodin's *Thinker*, *thunk*. My last words on leaving the school were as follows: 'The school will get no more half holidays unless secret practices cease and a new detachment is born, say a detachment of dragoons, firing off maroons.'" He went on after a pause, "But when I left, after my scandal, such is a frailty of the female organism that there was an outbreak of mumps, chiefly among the nuns."

But in spite of the confusion of this period Blanford was thinking, he was looking around him and taking stock as well as taking notes in his little student's *calepin*. Like: "The old seem to be praying for a war to carry off the young; the young are soliciting a plague to carry off the old. Fortune's maggot, I nestle in the plenitude of my watchful indifference."

She was his, and yet she was not really completely present. Reality, fine as a skin on milk, was called into question the whole time by this disturbance of focus aided by alcohol or tobacco or other unspecified drugs. Shaving himself in the bathroom mirror he realised that he had been pretending to be sane all his life. Now, even while kissing her he did not know which state of mind to assume. To overhear a thought thinking itself, to eavesdrop on a whisper of a truth formulating itself – this was his new state of mind. He began a book – the whole thing seemed to write itself. It was the purest automatic writing. It was a vignette of life in the country somewhere – a country which he himself had never seen. It was overwritten and shapeless so he destroyed it. Yet something important had happened to him – on the mystical plane, though that seems a rather pompous way of speaking about the intervention of "reality prime" into his scheme of things. (He tried saying "I love you" in several ways, in several keys, at several speeds, just to try and imagine what it was she heard when he did.) But what he realised was that from that moment onwards nothing he did was frivolous. It could be bad or good or even just inadequate or indifferent but it would be fraught with his own personal meaning, it would have his fingerprints on it. When he dared to say as much to Sutcliffe, his bondsman groaned aloud: "I see it all," he declared, "another novel written by the automatic pilot," and when Blanford looked at himself in the mirror he could see that in fact his expression was a trifle portentous – swollen, as if he had a gumboil. His self-esteem had boiled over.

Anyway, would there be time? They were pushed by the anxieties of the age to try and drink in everything before the war swallowed it up – that meant Edith Piaf looking like a cracked plate and singing like a cracked dove. "*Mon coeur y bat!*" That meant the new cinema – which had by now forfeited its chances of becoming more than a minor art by the invention of sound-track. It meant piles of saucers growing up under one's drinks at the Dôme while voices spoke of Spengler and the thirteenth law of thermodynamics. ... God! it was good to be alive, but it was an agony also, and he felt it all the more when the slow measured rhythm of England replaced the throbbing Paris rush. He managed a brief visit to Oxford to see friends and collect belongings, and found it strange and secretive and tongue-tied – "theological dons in their Common Rooms dancing round the *filoque*," as Sutcliffe was to put it. For his part the great man had started to do yoga by the lake. "Come," he said in magisterial fashion, "sharpen your intuitions in the cobra pose."

Blanford did nothing of the kind. His thought-glands were too soaked in alcohol, his mouth tasted itself through a coat of fur. He was happy in a distressing sort of way, dwelling in the great shadow of happy fornication with this buccaneer, this bird of paradise. "I am young and handsome," he told Sutcliffe, "and self-possessed as a cervical smear. I want to enjoy myself before age sets in and I suddenly go blue as cheese with a heart condition. . . ."

Publishers, he pretended to himself, were bursting their braces with desire to receive a new masterpiece, and here he was destroying everything he wrote as fast as he wrote it. In a friend's studio here was a grand piano on which from time to time he would practise. He played Schubert for her until she wept, and then innocently fell asleep, chin on paws like a Persian cat, a catspaw. Self-pity engenders oxygen and she was very sad to be sad. He started to write the memoirs of The Superfluous Man, but found he lacked the art. A pelican, he was trying to drink a little blood from his own breast.

> The tirra lirra of the public purse,
> The piggy bank whose use we learned from Nurse;
> The affect cannot hoard its wild regrets
> Except as dark repressions in cold sweats.

"I see you have a poetic turn?" said the patronising Sutcliffe. "I too dabble, and before leaving England I tried my hand at everything, even Sapphics which have never been done well since Campion. Listen!

"Deliciously sapped by the swish of thy swansdown chemise
I perch on a porch in Belgravia pansexually pooped."

It was full of false quantities and not at all a real Sapphic,
but what was the point of arguing with Sutcliffe? It was clear
that he was pained and lonely, and probably had toothache
as well. He struck a chord, a sad diminished seventh, to wake
the sleeper but she slept on.

> If pianos could polish themselves
> They would be turned to cats;
> In mirrors of self-esteem efface their lust
> Licking their likenesses to dust.

Suddenly Constance appeared in Paris and strangely
enough with her the war became suddenly real – as if she
herself had declared it. She was very much thinner and yet
calmer, and she had had what she declared was a momentous
series of meetings with Freud in Vienna. She had attended a
conference of psychs at which he had presided and they
had taken a fancy to each other. Other meetings followed
and the result was that now she was a wholly submitted pupil
of the old man whom she now vehemently declared to be the
foremost thinker in Europe.

"Here! Wait a moment!" said Blanford, shocked by so
uncompromising a hero-worship, and of course she laughed.
It was obvious to her that he, in common with nearly all
so-called intellectuals of that epoch, understood next to
nothing of the modest provisional theses of the old professor.
How to make it clear? She took him by the shoulders with an
affectionately admonishing air and said: "From now on it
has become impossible for anyone to write *Hamlet* again,
do you see?" He did not see, did not wish to see much beyond
the dancing points of her bright eyes and the grand flush
of colour with which she announced that she was meeting
Sam secretly that evening, and they were going to get

married before the war broke out. "It will be a long sad stalemate of years perhaps," she said. "They will never get through the Line and we will never have the force to go after them. Meanwhile, lots of bombing and short rations and stalemate." It was of course the general view, hence the strange kind of stagnation in which they lived. But she had other fish to fry as well for she suddenly changed her expression from gladness to bitter gloom. "Where is Livia?" she asked with a kind of waspish sharpness. How should he know? Nobody could keep track of Livia's movements; sometimes in desperation he left her little notes on the notice-board of the Café Dôme for she turned up there from time to time.

Constance paused for a long moment with her chin on her breast, thinking; then, as if coming to a decision, she said: "All right, well, I shall tell you then. In Vienna I saw a German newsreel of some great Nazi rally in Bavaria – there she was, plumb in the centre of things, dressed in a German uniform."

The news was electrifying and numbing at the same time. What could it mean? "Are you sure?" he said weakly. Constance nodded and said: "Never surer. She was full in the camera for about ten seconds, singing and giving the salute. She looked out of her mind. I am terrified for her."

Blanford did not know what to say, so acute was his shame. "She has never confided in me," was all he could think of in the way of self-defence. But even at this late stage the full extent of the tragedy which was slowly being enacted in Germany failed to register – its impact skilfully dulled by false propaganda and censorship to which they were as yet unaccustomed. They walked a little together in the Luxembourg, mostly in silence, trying to shape some sort of true perspective for their future lives – but only vague prospects and qualified hopes stretched away from them into ... what? But at least Constance was sure of her basic direction. She had joined the Red Cross on the medical side, and with her Swiss passport proposed to be of some use in the crisis to come. Sam had a fortnight before rejoining his unit in Britain. Tonight, after getting married, they would take the old train from the Gare de Lyon, and spend a brief honeymoon in Tu Duc. She asked: "Why don't you two come for a few days? Hilary can't, he is still in his Scottish seminary." But he sensed that it would not have done. They parted with warmth, and on his side with a pang of vague and imprecise regret, as if he feared that their friendship might be qualified by his marriage. It was silly of course. The old certain stability of things had melted into something new – a sort of state of limbo. And in the midst of all this, glowing like a precious stone, was the memory of Provence and all it had held for them on this first rich encounter with it. The richness was overwhelming, and in his own dreams he returned again and again to the old house lying so secretively among the tall trees, in a silence orchestrated only by the wind and the ripple of river which passed through the garden.

As they parted she said in a sudden little flurry of agonised feeling: "Do you think I am doing the wrong thing? I wouldn't like to hurt Sam." He shook his head but he felt the shock of her words. The question meant that, in fact, she *was* doing the wrong thing, and that somewhere in her inner consciousness she knew it. But what made him feel ashamed was his own sudden feeling of elation as he recognised the fact. He felt it was horrible and quite un-pardonable. He would seek absolution in thinking up some extravagant present for her in London.

Cremation is a clean and unemphatic way of disposing, not only of your dead, but also of your thoughts about death and any fears and misgivings they might engender. The rain melted down over everything, a soft blue rain which pearled down the windows of the old respectable Daimler they had hired for himself and Cade, the only two mourners. The coffin looked small and very light. It lobbed slightly as the hearse gathered way. He had been extravagant about the flowers because he knew she had loved flowers, yet an obstinate parallel thought crossed his mind as he wrote out the cheque, namely: "I never received a moment's affection from either side of the blanket." He felt aware of some sort of emotional attrition, of a withering away inside himself – a kind of poverty of affect which art and literature might only pretend to redress. Perhaps later, in middle life . . . yes, but would there be a middle life, with all this war business going on? To his surprise he bought a new car on an impulse and paid for driving-lessons. He retained Cade's services for a year, but offered him an extended leave to revisit his family in the north. When all this was over he would drive down to Provence and wait there for history to declare itself.

The crematorium was a gaunt-looking place, of an architecture so frivolous that it resembled an abandoned Casino in Southern Italy. The plume of smoke which rose from behind the main building flapped upwards into the rain and then flattened out across the fields of concrete which surrounded the place. The whole area was tastefully laid out with gardens full of daffodils and other Wordsworthian aids to memory. But there was quite a waiting list of bodies for cremation and they were a few moments early. They were set down to wait, and optionally pray if they wished, in a small ante-chapel which did duty as a waiting-room. The suburban church architecture of the chapel was of glacial coldness and infernal ugliness. The altar with its cheap cathedral-glass saints wallowing in the crepuscular gloom shed a dreadful Sunday School light upon them. On the wall in the corner there was what the cricketer in Blanford recognised as a score board such as every school buys for its

cricket field. Instead of a score however there was the pro-
gramme of the day neatly indicated in detachable lettering.
Theirs was to be preceded by three other cremations – those
of Mrs. Humble, Mrs. Godbone and Mrs. Lamb; then came
Evelyn Blanford. They must wait their turn? Cade ostenta-
tiously prayed and the chief mute sycophantically followed
suit. He was a Dickensian caricature of fruitless respectability
in his old and scruffy top hat and withered tail-coat. His
cuffs were dirty and had been arranged rather impres-
sionistically with the help of nail scissors. He was wheezy
with asthma and false devoutness. Blanford closed his eyes
and breathed deeply through his gills, praying that this might
soon be over. It was astonishing how deeply upset he found
himself to be – he would not have suspected this wave of
intense sorrow and loneliness.

The officiating clergyman was a robust and pink young
man with a touch of bustle about him, as if he were anxious
to get through the work of the day as soon as possible. But
he was very detached and otherworldly as well, and one
might have supposed him to be cremating some headhunters
from darkest Borneo rather than respectable suburban
matrons from fondest Folkestone. Blanford felt rather put
out by his offhand manner and the hint of cockney in his
speech which made Holy Writ read like an advertisement for
Glaxo. But at last the session wound to its end and Blanford
was suddenly aware that throughout the length of the
service his mother had been slowly sinking into the ground
before their eyes: the coffin slowly sinking down the trap
into the operational part of the concern. The young man
achieved perfect timing, for the last word of his peroration
coincided with the muffled clap of the doors closing, after
having launched the coffin onto the rails of a subterranean
railway. They heard it whirring off down the chute. The
machinery was a trifle squeaky. Then followed a long

silence during which the mute turned to them and said, "Of course you'll be wanting an urn, sir?" "Of course," said Cade sternly. "*Two* urns!"

The man tiptoed off after saying: "I will meet you outside at the car." The parson shook a pale pork-like hand and took his leave. They were free. Blanford was wild with relief and regret. And yet speechless as an anchorite.

They had not long to wait outside the chapel before the beadle-like mute stalked round the corner of the building, holding in his arms two grotesque *bonbonnières* a little larger than the traditional Easter egg, which he distributed with an air of conscientious commiseration. Cade almost snatched at his, and to Blanford's surprise, actually beamed with pleasure, as if he were receiving a gift which brought the greatest joy. Then he caught the curious eye of his master upon him and scowled his way back into his normal taciturnity. Blanford felt a fool sitting in the back of the Daimler with an urn in his lap, and as soon as he could he placed it gingerly on the nearest mantelpiece. Ashes to ashes, dust to dust. . . .

But he was aware that a deep fault had opened in the ground under his feet – the past was now separated from the future by it. The taste of this new freedom was unnerving, as was the knowledge that if he chose to live modestly on what he had inherited he need not seek employment. A life of quiet travel and introspection seemed to sketch itself upon the horizons – yes, but with Livia? Yes, but with a war? History with the slow fuses of calamity smouldering away . . . He had selected a modest hotel from which he started to take long afternoon walks in the rain, passing more often than not the gates of the school where Sutcliffe taught and read music so many moons later. Once he even went into the close and sneaked a glance into the chapel which would so often echo with the great man's voice. On the white cliffs mewed up by seagulls with the voices of sick kittens he felt the (valedictory?) rain pouring off the peak of his hat, the shoulders of his coat. Is there only one sort of death for us all, or does each death partake of the ... valency, so to speak, of the life it replaces? It would be marvellous to know. Suddenly there came into his memory the dark intense face of Quatrefages saying: "I believe Eliphas Levi when he says that the devil is God's ruins. If you embark on the path to sainthood and fail to achieve your goal you are condemned to become a demon."

Suddenly Tu Duc rose up in his mind's eye and vibrated with an almost unbearable longing; it had all been too brief. What he must try and do, he suddenly thought, is to drive down there and await the war in the seclusion of that little village of Tubain. If he was called up, well and good. (He was still envisaging a 1914-type war.) Yes, he would leave this week and see what Livia thought of the notion – would she come too? If they had to start a married life together surely that would be the most propitious way and the right place to do so? From the window of his bedroom, which gave out onto the recreation ground of the local school, he could stand and watch the boys during "break" and marvel at the unchanging habits of schoolboys through the years. Their habit of buying a tin of condensed milk and punching a hole in it – the sweetened version. This they would suck like monkeys all day long. The older Victorian versions of sweets were still on the market – like the Sherbet Dab, which made you dream you were in bed with the Queen of Sheba. It was rather expensive. Other boys bought an orange and screwed a sugar lump into its skin. This wound could be also sucked with pleasure. Most magical of all was the Gob Stopper, almost the size of a golf ball, which shed successive coats of colour as one sucked. . . . His own schooldays seemed half a century away. He often stood there in a muse until dusk fell, and then darkness, while once in a while the moon, "in her exaltation" as the astrologers say, rose to remind him that such worldly musings meant nothing to the hostile universe without. Even war meant nothing? Yes. He would write poems in invisible ink, then, and post them to himself. Was he then *doomed* to be a writer? All circumstance seemed to be at his elbow to prompt him.

> Mirrors will drink your image with intensity
> and bleed your spirit of its density,
> for they are thirsty for the inner man
> and pasture on his substance when they can.
> The double image upside-down
> They drink their fill – you never drown.
> They echo fate which is not kind
> O sweet blood-poisoning of the mind!

It was not too bad a description of the acute narcissism necessary to become a poet. He was anxious to be away south but the Probate people kept him an extra week. It was a strange new sensation to have money in the bank, to be able to write out quite decent-sized cheques. His allowance had been a very modest one, and he had tailored his needs to meet it. Now he bought some clothes which he much needed. But the result of all this was a bad attack of panic-meanness, and for a few days he lunched in a pub on short commons, almost choking himself with Scotch eggs and other such heavy fare. Back in London things were rather different. There was some sense of urgency. He met fellow under-graduates already in uniform and talking of foreign postings. Air raid sirens were in full rehearsal. The newspapers were full of hypothetical battle fronts bristling with arrows. A national daily asked "Where are the War poets?", and the Ministry of Propaganda set about creating some, though this was difficult, as to be really efficacious they would first have to die, and at the moment there was so little chance. Or so it seemed.

But Austria! The bombs, the parades, the curfews self-imposed from panic, the bands of uniformed thugs roaming the streets all night, surely all this was moving in the right direction? In London the left-wing poets announced that Plato was a Fascist and his mature thought was exemplified by Hitler. It was Syracuse all over again. Blanford had no literary contacts, only a few donnish ones. He aspired mildly to be a historian and apart from a few sporadic attacks of verse had little interest in the world of so called literary values. The scene was not wildly exciting. It was still fashionable to fustigate Lawrence, while at home the "serious critic" devoted energy to wondering if Walpole had genius. But Austria was another matter!

All this was preoccupying Sutcliffe no end, for he was stuck in Vienna, waiting for the treatment of Pia to yield some "concrete results" – what a cliché! He was waiting for her to "come to herself" – what a cliché. And this new science was a sort of hedgehog of cross-reference in which one could only have an approximate faith. He spent most of his time in a pastry-shop round the corner, on the square by the Somethingstrasse, 'twixt the so-called Rathouse and the office for the registration of foreign labour. His German did not exist, so he lived in a sort of fearful fog. He waited for his darling, engulfing the while, at breakneck speed, those ponderous sweetmeats, puffs and flans for which the capital was famous, and feeling himself covered with spots at each new intake of sugar. They lived in a small hotel-room where they returned each night in trembling silence to eat a sandwich while he brewed a coffee in the lavatory. Then slept. She turned her back to the horrible folksy wallpaper and sighed and trembled and talked in her sleep all night. There was no more communication between them; there was nothing they could say to one another that would not wound, would not spoil the chances of this fragile "treatment". It was a real war situation, and moreover it was a costly one. Blanford was touched by his plight and sent him quite a large cheque which was no sooner cashed than swallowed up by the treatment. But Rob had discovered that all the barbers in the capital were females – there were no male figaros. In black dresses with white frilled collars and cuffs they attended to the male scalp at all hours of the day and night. It was his only solace, to be soothed by the fingers of one of these amiable maidens and have his scalp tingled by some alcoholic concoction which made him feel as if he had gathered a halo.

In that small world of neurological patients and terrified Jewish intellectuals who could see the world coming to an end, they made a number of good friends, but the best among them was a dramatic and beautiful Slav whose extravagant and fleshy *ampleur* was somehow wonderfully sexy and composed. She was a writer and a new disciple of Freud, and she spoke of poets then unknown like Rilke and even of Nietzsche whom she claimed to have known – which made them laugh in secret. But they liked her, and she developed a deep fondness for poor Pia.

He stood in the late spring wind – cutting despite the time of the year – and watched his newly acquired motor-car hoisted up into the air at Dover and then plonked down with a shudder on the deck of the ship in which he proposed to travel. He was fearful lest the bump damage its interior – which he visualised vaguely as something very fragile: an engine made of china and supported by hairpins. But it worked well enough when it was discharged again and he set off in a gathering twilight for Paris, driving with immense devoutness on the wrong side of the road. He had been assured that he would soon get used to it and indeed by the time he reached the capital he felt quite at home in the new vehicle. He had avoided thinking too explicitly of Livia partly because he was still in a state of concern and distress about the news Constance had brought, and feared to force a breach between them by demanding an explanation: and partly because with one side of his mind he was troubled by the vague intimation of a side to her life which might in the long run prove fatal to this painful attachment to her.

To his surprise, he was reassured to find the flat empty – or apparently empty, for after a long moment of questing about for evidence of her possible presence in the form of cigarette-butts or journals, he became aware that there was indeed someone in the bathroom at the end of the corridor. He heard the flush clank, and then the sound of running water in the basin. There was light also shining through the fanlight over the door. In this new mood of hovering irritation mixed with sadness, he tapped lightly with his finger and turned the handle, to find that the door was unlocked. As he did so the girl standing naked in front of the long mirror turned also and confronted him with a bold and impervious stare. No, both adjectives were quite incorrect – it was simply the calm animal quality which made him qualify her gaze thus. It was as if he had interrupted some self-assured pussy-cat at her ablutions. In fact she had just finished shaving under the arms with a small safety razor which he recognised as his own. She had swabbed the pits with a sponge and patted them with a rolled towel. Now she was simply there, and her great bronze face with its marvellous Easter Island eyebrows gazed equably at him full of a keen friendship. A vivacious light shone in those sumptuous eyeballs, the light of tropical islands, where all thinking is muffled by sunlight. "She went this morning," said the Martiniquaise hoarsely, setting her fine head back to clear her helmet of dark hair off her shoulders. "But only a moment ago."

This was the girl whose French was so "killing"; and in her satiny nakedness she was of great beauty but also of great strength. The figure was athletic – that of a discus thrower or an Amazon of the javelin. But she was friendly, and had no thought but to please.

It was indeed her professional cue to be so and an endearing paganism shone warmly out of her eyes and mind. Those little tip-tilted breasts she leaned towards him now in a soft gesture of shy friendship. "Take me," they said, "I am all antelope. I am all musk-melon. I am spice-islander." He raised his hand perhaps to slap her but she did not flinch, she almost appeared to welcome the blow – perhaps as a sort of expiation; his hand fell to his side again. He stood there quite still and listened to the ticking of his own mind – no, it was his wrist-watch. The woman said, "All finish with her – *fini. Elle a dit à moi*!" She tapped herself on the breast-bone, stretching her long throat-line the while, with the dignified mien of some Polynesian queen. Yes, it was finished. He suddenly realised that, and, wondering at the irrationality of the human mind, he asked himself which of two reasons was the stronger. Was it because of the sexual betrayal as much as because he had discovered her opening his letters? Curiously enough the second reason seemed every bit as wounding as the first. He had old-fashioned notions about marriage and privacy, the fruit of his English education. "You say nothing?" said the woman, and he agreed, shaking his head and staring steadily at her until he felt the small prickle of incipient tears starting up. He felt ashamed of them.

She moved towards him in sympathy and then his hand, groping for a handkerchief, encountered the black rubber dildo which was still attached to her pubis, buckled on to her body by a section of dark webbing with a fastening at the back, over her rump. He took it awkwardly in his hand. There were little metal buckles round the crown of the penis, presumably to add pleasure. But what an extravagant invention, and how coarse compared to the tender and sensitive organ for which it was so pathetic a substitute. She poked it against him and laughed. Then with hands behind her back she undid it, with the gesture of one who unbuckles a sword, and let it flop to the floor where it lay, a grotesque trophy of their coupling minds. He turned on his heel and went back into the small salon, where a tremendous confusion reigned. In his haste he had overlooked this tangle of lipstick-marked towels and torn paper wrappings – marks of a hasty packing-up and departure. Through the open door he could see the unmade bed, with the pile of old newspapers lying beside it. Standing there, breathing softly and con-sidering, he felt the weight of his grief mixed with both anger and relief. But where was the letter of farewell which she must undoubtedly have written and left somewhere? The dark girl must have scented his confusion and divined the reasons; she went to the cupboard and opened the door. It was there with a few of his clean shirts. It was terse and to the point. She was going into Germany and not coming back if she could help it. They must divorce.

About the sense of failure there was no doubt, but it was perplexingly supplemented by a feeling of freshness – the fresh wind of freedom which quickened all the staleness of the last few weeks, all the doubts which he now realised that he had been stifling. It was with a pang of remorse for this feeling that he watched the dark girl change into a clean frock and express herself as ready to accompany him towards the inevitable consolation of a drink which would topple sadness and free him once more to see the world for what it was ... an absurd way of putting it. The new world that was beginning to emerge from the slime of history – would it be so very different from the old?

> Boys and girls come out to play,
> Children of the *godmichet*
> Now let each seraphic mouse
> Between the thighs keep open house
> Let their uncanny kisses rain
> Upon the upturned face of pain
> In grief at having lived in vain.

In the Sphinx all was light and the pleasant frenzy of welcome by all the acquaintances he had made when he was last there. The Martiniquaise disappeared about her tasks of pure ablution round earth's shores – his Keats was rusting visibly – and left him to the silence and introspection of his notebooks which even by then had started to gather their aphoristic fungus, their snatches of verse and prose. He plunged his hearing into the swathes of coarse talk and laughter, his sense of smell with delection into the smoke of cigars and Celtique cigarettes. Friends came up to salute him, students from the Midi with warm accents so different from the curt Parisian parrot-accent. *Didonk mon gar comment sava* – his ears transliterated sound and conveyed it to his limping understanding. No, his French was not bad, just rather slow. It would have been appropriate to reply: *Cava très mâle* – with the circumflex. But really he was too despondent about his circumstances to appreciate his own feeble witticism. He set himself to drink ardently in the traditional manner of the jilted Anglo-Saxon. Later he would break up the bar, get himself knocked out and put in custody for the night. This would obviate sleeplessness and idle thoughts about suicide which would be simply anachronistic – since the whole of Europe was bent upon that course. It would be pretentious, an individual act of the kind. Even if the hemlock, love's castration-mixture, worked. Who did he think he was, Socrates? Passing to and fro, leading her clients up the stairs or dismissing them at the foot, the dark girl took the time to stroke his shoulder or hair. Was she trying to fire him? He bent more closely to his book.

The fatal absinthe did not so much fire the blood as alter the heartbeat, anaesthetise one; one became steadily gloomier and more wretched until, just before the cataleptic trance of oblivion, one was seized with a positive epilepsy of joy, a frenzied ecstasy in the mode of St. Vitus. One pulled beards, danced with chairs, imitated famous ventriloquists. The police came. He had never as yet gone beyond a second glass of the mysterious and milky liquid. Yet already the first stage – that of an unsteady torpor – had seized him. His desires had become unwieldy, infused by a sort of sulky passion. He gazed around at the long bar with its patient and attentive clients sipping their drinks and allowing themselves to be fondled into heat by the all-but-naked girls. Trade was brisk. In the outer café beyond the bead curtain a harsh music burned like straw – *la vie* forever *en rose*. The next time she passed and placed her hand on his head he was sufficiently emboldened by hemlock to run his fingers up into her fork and touch the moist fountain of youth under her sarong. "*Viens, chéri*," she breathed, and buttoning up his *serviette* to secure his precious notebooks he lurched to his feet and obeyed. Quick as a swallow now she ducked back to where the Madam of the house sat, enthroned in wigged splendour like a very very old ice cream of a deposed empress, watching keenly over the form of her female stable. The girl took a *jeton* and was given a fresh towel which she draped over her arm like a waiter. They then mounted the stairs, negotiating them very successfully, and at last entered the little cubicle which was white and clinical and decorated only by a hideous eiderdown on the bed and a crucifix over the bidet.

The divine spasm assuaged nothing, nor did it modify the hunger it was intended to cure. He saw it now – with a phantom of disgust – as an act of barren retaliation. But skin was as glossy as ivy, breath as sweet as newly minted cocoons, so who was he to challenge fate, especially after his second hemlock? It was later that he discovered that she had managed stealthily to empty his wallet; happily his rentier's low cunning had foreseen something of the kind and he had placed two-thirds of his *fric* in the hind pocket of his trousers which he kept firmly in view at the end of the bed. It remained only to catch a homely clap now and he would be all artist. The serpent lay beside him breathing softly, waiting for him to recover his strength, fondling him the while to see if there wasn't another kick in the old *manivelle*. As a sort of testimonial to his masculinity she sowed a few love bites, little *suçons*, upon his throat and shoulders. Heigho! So this was the creative life as lived in this seamy capital? He had begun to feel somewhat of an initiate by now, though his mind still flirted with anger and sadness.

But here was a new problem – his walk had gained a strange swaying amplitude which was unwonted; coming down the stairs he had sudden flashes of vision which made him feel that he was falling backwards into a prism of yellow light. Dismayed, and a trifle alarmed – he was perfectly sober, only his legs flirted with gravitational fields beyond his knowledge – he hung himself on the bar again, in order to gain time. Though he asked for nothing he found another bloody hemlock standing before him and in his shy confusion drank it. Faces were pivoting in the mirrors, other girls seemed eager to share their favours with him. He clutched the wad of notes at his bum and allowed an attack of meanness to overwhelm him. By breathing deeply and evenly he steadied the optic nerves and then steered his way majestically into the night, tenderly unhooking the ivy-soft arms and fingers which sought to stay him, and keeping tight hold of his diary-notebooks.

At the Dôme there was a crowd gathered in the inner dining-room around a radio from which poured stream upon stream of terrifying rhetoric in a voice which by now the whole world had come to know only too well. The barmaid – a rather handsome little second-hand widow in a good state of repair – had provided this curiosity for them, though she knew that almost none of her customers understood German. It was simply the spectacle that riveted them, the phenomenon of that grating snarling voice; the sense they might well guess. And then the roaring applause. He thought of Livia. But what was he doing here? What had prompted him to enter another bar? The answer was a thirst, a raging thirst. He realised the folly of drinking so much Pernod, and called now for a pint of champagne. It hardly mended the situation, except that the coolness was invigorating. But now he was really drunk and his subsequent wanderings gathered impreciseness as time wore on. He lost his briefcase and his umbrella. Thank goodness he had had the sense to leave his passport back in the flat with other and more valuable papers. . . . He nearly fell over the Pont Neuf, enjoyed the conversation and esteem of several hairy clochards, and was finally knocked down by a taxi in the Place Vendôme, whose driver, appalled by what he had done, had the humanity and despatch of his profession, and loading him into the back raced hotfoot to the American Hospital in Neuilly where his confusions were worse confounded by drugs intended to secure him some sleep while they investigated his bones.

He informed the doctor seriously: "The whole of humanity seems simultaneously present in every breath I draw. The weight of my responsibility is crushing. A merciful ignorance defends me from becoming too despondent." He was told to shut up and sleep, and was reassured that while no bones were broken he had been much "concussed", which accounted for some of the bells ringing in his head.

Deus absconditus, the shaggy God of all drunkards' slumbers, now invaded him, and in his mind's mind he found himself wandering the ever green lanes of a southern landscape, hand in hand with the sort of Livia he had dared to imagine – one he was never to see in reality; or else seated at the stained old table in the garden covering page after page of his notebooks in a hand which he vaguely recognised as that of Sutcliffe. Time stretched away on either side of the point-event of each drawn breath, back into the subfusc suburban past, forwards into a veiled future, but somehow as yet void of significance. The writer, *l'homme en marge*, writing the Memoirs of a Marginal Man. On the title-page he had written, in this large flamboyant and rather hysterical hand: "All serial reality is by this writing called into question." The radio went on and on in his head, roaring and foaming. An ape fingering a safety catch – Europe was holding its breath. He bent his aching head lower and wrote on, "I have no biography; a true artist, I go through life like a character in one of my own books." To this S added, "My first experience of an audience was when, as a fattish youth, I played Adipose Rex in the school play. Since then I have often dreamed of living in a deserted school (life?) full of empty rooms, open doors and clean blackboards; yes, life waiting for the scholars of breathing. Comrade, continue that poem in invisible ink, ask yourself why the Dalai Lama has no Oedipus Complex." "Silly, because he has no parents. . . ."

The sirens wailed once or twice briefly like supercats *en chasse*. These were practice calls only but they wrung the heart. Marriage to her would be like drinking wine from a paper cup. What he had really needed was the smell of warm sirloin, smell of cooking in fair hair which had bent over the stove, the scent of celery in the armpits. Already he seemed to have lived a dozen lifetimes with her, all in the same cottage. For years afterwards they would remain, the claw-marks on the door where every night the dog scratched to be let in, the scratches she had made with her key around the lock. Suddenly the voice of Sutcliffe admonished him: "Aubrey, you have a mind like a fatty chop. Be silent or be completely fascinating. Never bore." The poor fellow could not have felt in any better humour than his bondsman yet he persisted in being flippant – though at times his voice was quite squeaky from fatigue. He quoted:

> Our old telluric artichoke,
> We sucked her leaves but nothing woke;
> The cactus of the primal scene
> Had mogrified her sweet demean.

Blanford, always slow to retort yet determined to get some of his own back, sat up and said: "Rob, you haven't the talent to rub a bit of polish off the primal apple; you are simply an old football full of pus."

Somewhere in the course of his military training at Oxford he had come across the expression "omega grey", and had been told that it was the scientific designation of the deepest grey before complete blackness; now as his troubled sleep swirled about him, changing form and colour and resonance, it seemed to him that the whole of the outer world beyond the window of the white ward was painted in this colour – the almost black of death. Omega grey – the phrase echoed on in his mind, though whether he was asleep or awake he could not guess. This drug-bemused reality was filtered through a mesh of discrete sensations, containing fragments of the recent past juxtaposed or telescoped upon fearful contexts. He saw the body of his mother transformed by a neo-Cubist painter into a series of porpoise-faced nudes. Her teeth were all but opaque, her gums fashioned in gelatine.

Swollen to enormous size she floated over the Thames to defend it against enemy aircraft; moreover she was all grey, camouflage grey, *omega* grey, the last colour before the dark night of the soul settled over them like a new ice age. There would hardly be time enough to achieve that state of beatitude and equilibrium which for him was already associated (wrongly) with the creative act. What was he doing here in this molten bed, fuddling while Rome burned? He should have been telling his beads and praying aloud.

He pressed his palms on his eyelids and sent showers of sparks flying across his eyeballs. Yes, it was there, the state he vaguely hankered to achieve! It already lay somewhere inside him in a completely unrealised form – or rather he knew it was there without being able to locate it. It was like hunting through the house for one's spectacles when they were on the top of one's head, perched on one's crown. A vomit of words, linked by pure association, floated below his visions like the subtitles to an incomprehensible film written by a lunatic. (The drunkard's word list is sometimes the sage's also.) A vision of Livia with her finger to her lips.

> The weather is breaking up, my puss,
> The cards are down in autumn stars

In his dream he told her: "The maddening thing is that what is to find cannot be looked for. You are trying desperately to acquire what you already possess but do not recognise. Meditation brings on a state of perilous heed – it is not mere daydreaming. All this would be risible if it were not so serious a matter." To which she replied sweetly, shaking that fine cervine head: "At any moment tell yourself that things are much better than they have any right to be." What sophistry! In the streets he saw the faces passing, omega-grey glances upon pavements of omega grey. Yes, there was nothing that did not lead somewhere – yet everything also had a built-in trap that at any moment could become an obstacle.

Suddenly the scene changed to a basement in Vienna – he knew it to be Vienna without knowing how he could know; for he had never been there.

A swarm of violins started up somewhere and through half-closed eyes he saw the fiddlers performing their hieratic arabesque – girls combing out their long hair. Bearded candles in the darkness gave them not rose or carmine, but the uniform pork tint of omega grey. A slowly folding line of music from some fugue wrapped them all in a melancholy tenebrousness. There were a dozen or so people there, but he only recognised the faces of Sutcliffe and Pia. There was something startling about their attention and he suddenly realised that they were listening, not to the music which welled from the radio, but to the distant crepitations of musketry and machine-gun fire, punctuated from time to time in the furthest corner of space by the soft thud of a mortar. There was trouble almost every night, they told him, and they were forced to live by a self-imposed curfew, more or less. It had, however, not been going on long, but the persecution of the Jews was beginning.

Then, abruptly, as if the scene had been "cut" like a film sequence, they found themselves walking timorously among deserted squares and startled public statuary, with a light spring snowfall blurring everything and obliterating skylines. They were heading for a quarter of the town which was predominantly inhabited by the intellectual élite of medicine and the arts. Here were the practice rooms where right round the clock one heard pianos playing scales and snatches of classical music, heard sopranos giving tongue, heard the gruff commentary of tubas practising. The nationalists had been busy wrecking this quarter during the earlier part of the evening and had been driven off by police, or else had had their attention diverted by other prey in other quarters where the inhabitants were easier to bait or intimidate. They had, however, left a legacy in the form of two large bonfires burning away – mounds of medical books doused with petrol. All the windows were open and the flats from which these articles had been seized and hurled into the street appeared now to be empty. All the lights burned on, furiously on, as if outraged, but there was no human form to be seen. Then Pia saw the old-fashioned sofa half in and half out of the window on the third floor, and she gave a wild sad cry. These were the old consulting-rooms which the penurious medical crew could hire specially cheaply, for they were subsidised by the university. The sofa! She had recognised one of the old consulting-rooms which an impecunious Freud had shared with Bleuler when they were making their first halting steps towards a theory of the unconscious. It was the same old leather-covered monster of a committee-room sofa upon which the master had (it seemed a century ago now) invited her to recline. On it, writhing to and fro like someone in a high fever, she had embarked on that strange adventure which as yet seemed to be never ending; one promise succeeded another, one remission followed another relapse. Now this fond critical instrument of torture hung there like a maimed crocodile.

In the wild cry of recognition with which Pia greeted this spectacle was mixed all the anguish and reverence she felt for this shabby symbol posed so outrageously upon the window-sill – like a woman too fat to get out or in now, irretrievably stuck, waiting for the fire brigade to rescue her. As a matter of fact they could be heard approaching some streets away, though their customary moaning signals were mixed with the sinister mesh-like sound of caterpillar-tracks upon concrete. A light tank prowled across their line of vision a couple of street corners away. They had been joined by a small group of medical students who were in a high pitch of excitement – they all looked as if they had been drinking.

Now a man had appeared at the window from which the sofa protruded – a sort of janitor it would seem, from his green apron. He had been going round turning off lights and closing open doors. He paused irresolutely for a moment before the sofa, obviously wondering what to do about it. It protruded so far that it was impractical to drag it back, though he seemed at first tempted to try. It was hanging by its back legs above the burning street. The students began to gesticulate and shout in a desultory fashion, though without any clear idea of what might be done to ameliorate the present situation, the smashed lamp standards, the burning books. Suddenly the concierge at the window came to a decision. With a heave he disengaged the back legs of the ugly old crocodile and catapulted the whole thing into the street, where it fell upon one of the burning piles of books. The sirens had come much closer. "Quick!" cried Pia, quite beside herself with anxiety, for the sofa had begun to smoulder at the edges. "Quick!" People gazed at each other wondering what she could mean, but she herself had darted forward and caught the old crock by the shoulders, pulling it with a frantic, almost superhuman force, until it was clear of the flames. "We must save it," she said. "Rob, for Christ's sake . . ." Bemused and puzzled as he was he broke into a clumsy run and, without for an instant understanding what their objective might be, helped her tug it clear. Other students now, equally in the dark, came to their aid, and acting like lunatics they picked it up and set off at a trot for the nearest shelter. The whole performance was totally spontaneous and unplanned. It had been sparked by the intensity of her cry and the concentrated passion of her actions – she looked like someone in a trance. Obviously this tattered object was of the utmost value and importance to her. Obligingly the crowd helped her save it and drag it to the relative safety of an air-shelter with a wall where they placed it under a tree. They were all panting and yet somehow exultant. From the other end of the square now burst the police and the fire-engines, dramatic and noise-bearing as a whole opera. It was time to shrink back into the shadows and disappear. They left the old sofa sitting there in the light snowfall.

Events had moved so fast and so dramatically that they themselves were quite out of breath with astonishment at what they had done. "What will you do with it?" cried Sutcliffe now, aware that they could hardly house it in their little hotel, and she thought fiercely for a moment, her pale face bowed. They were already walking fast, almost running, towards their hotel, trying to select untroubled streets where they would not meet patrols. Friends were waiting for them at the hotel – among them the Slav girl – and they ordered coffee in the tiny shabby lounge where they would, as was customary, hear an account of the day's happenings both in the capital and in the world – the outer world which loomed over their daily minds like a storm cloud. "Whatever happens we must keep it," said Pia decisively, in the middle of a conversation about something else; and he knew she meant this stupid old sofa for which he himself felt nothing. Had she gone mad? He asked her, but she was already explaining what they had done to her friend whose face lit up with a triumphant and generous approval. The two women, he thought, were as superstitious as savages. What would they plan next?

The outcome was even more unexpected than he had any reason to suppose. Medical students, friends of the Slav, now arrived upon the scene, and they warmly approved of this absolutely medieval gesture. (They would be selling indulgences next!) They were young and impetuous and determined to rescue the totem. The only problem was to decide what should be done with it. There were several lines of thought. One wished to give it houseroom in his flat, another thought it should be carted to the Faculty and placed in the hall – but of course the medical authorities, who had hardly heard of Freud, would have had a fit at the very suggestion. Suddenly Pia pronounced upon the matter with so much vehemence that everyone knew that she would not be gainsaid. "It is mine," she said, "and I intend to keep it. I shall send it to my brother in Avignon. I have quite decided." There was no more to say; all that was left was to decide upon the details of transport – how the devil could one send a sofa? Obviously by rail. Yes, but what about transport to the station? Here one of the students, who worked part-time with an undertaker, suggested that he borrow the hearse to transport the holy relic. "Yes! Yes!" she cried and clapped her hands exultantly. "That is what we must do. I shall telephone to him tonight."

So it was that, at five in the morning, Mr. Sutcliffe found himself seated with an air of ludicrous amazement in a large black hearse, in front of what to the average passer-by must have seemed something like a very large corpse wrapped up in a brown-paper parcel. They had indeed enveloped the charred old article in several layers of brown paper, the better to label it, and to their surprise there seemed to be no problem about sending it. It would await arrival in Avignon.

Blanford had followed all this hazily, through the heavy meshes of his dream, and he conveyed his approval of the whole initiative through the usual channels – the pulse-beat of the blood. But he had decided that Constance must have the relic, not Pia; and as he carried more weight in everything to do with real reality, he knew that he could override the present decision, and persuade a carter to take charge of the sofa and ferry it up, not to Verfeuille but to Tu Duc. He said as much and to his surprise Sutcliffe did not demur – it was a measure of his indifference to the relic. He had come to hate the whole science of psychowhatsit, which promised the moon and came unstuck at every corner.

"Very well, *maître*," he said ironically, "if you say so. How is Paris treating you?"

"A pleasing priapism rules the waves," said his incoherent and maundering *alter ego* or *summum bonum*. "The croissants are brown as mahogany. I saw her at dusk, reading in a public garden, and I longed to approach her and ask where she had been. She had disappeared for nearly a week. But I dared not. I sat on an adjacent bench and told myself that it was not her, it was just someone who resembled her. She was reading one of my unwritten novels – with pious intensity. Beside her lay a bag with a half-eaten croissant in it. She was sunk in profound thought, I could see that, and would certainly be sulky if approached. I closed my eyes and waited. When at last she got up to go I saw that indeed it was not her but someone who resembled her. The discarded paper bag lay where she had abandoned it. I scattered the croissant for the birds and went home by the lake in order not to give her the illusion of spying on her. But of course when I got back there was, as usual, nobody at the flat."

> Little grains of splendour,
> Little knobs of lust,
> Make a writer tremble,
> Loving is a must
> Nor can he dissemble
> When his heart is bust.
Let all young women bring me their emulsion,
Gods are born thus with every fond convulsion!
THUS SPOKE ZARATHUSTRA!

He went on foundering more and more deeply in these patches of dream-nightmares which stretched away on all sides of him to the horizon, feeling his mind being feverishly ransacked by the combined fevers of medicine and alcohol. The dark streets of Vienna had been replaced by Paris. Night-watchmen everywhere, a tribe of scowling lurkers, loveless as poets whose minds had become viscous with fatigue, waiting for dawn. Broken glasses, club feet, *arthritis deformans*, huge clubbed thumbs. He kept waving his arms and protesting, trying to obliterate these images of menace, but they persisted, they gained on him.

His eventual release from hospital, albeit rather reluctant, was something that he simply had to accept – it would have been malingering to stay comfortably between the sheets with nothing worse than post-alcoholic depression and a touch of shock. The kindly taximan who had knocked him down came to see him and offered him a free ride back into his *quartier*. The young doctor, who was called Bruce, saw no objection. The hospital cashed his cheque without a tremor, leaving him enough change to resume civilian life once more, so to speak. Back then to the empty flat, deposited at the Dôme by his kindly overturner. But once home he became suddenly aware of his weakness, and sat down on the unmade bed with a thump; his desolation continued to manufacture discordant images of loss, but they were more inconsequential now and less forceful. Where could he find some rest – the loneliness in this little box-like flat was intolerable. If he went back to the Coupole or the Sphinx he would be undone. He hid therefore in a local cinema, feeling the fleas jumping about his thighs while he watched the amours of that most congenial of all funny men, W. C. Fields. "Dharling banana, where's your sense of humour? Fragrant yam, you are my dish." Wondering vaguely – the subtitles were hairy with age – how all this would translate. Provide your own version. *"Clafoutis imberbe! Potiron du jour!"*

When at last he struggled to his feet and sought the exit, night had already fallen, the mauve-magenta night which was part street-lamp and part aerial radiation of white light against the blue-black sky of cheap fur. He was hungry; he scuttled to the Dôme and ate bacon and eggs with energy, gazing round with distaste at all the other representatives of the arts and crafts who surrounded him. Pride of lions, skirl of loafers, extravagance of poets. No, he would go far away, he would eat liquid mud on toast in far-away Turkish khans. Far far from the dungy altars of the Nonconformist mind. He would order a clyster for all parish Prousts of the Charing Cross Road. He would . . . On the cusp of a mere nod the waiter replenished his glass. He realised that he was still calamitously drunk in a reactivated sort of way. His blood coursed. He was surrounded by Africans with beautiful fuzzy heads and booming tones. They had all come to Paris to gather culture. Here they were, screaming for worm-powders. What was to be done? Great sweet turbines of black flesh innocently cutting slices of Keats or Rimbaud for their evening meal. A wholesome cannibalism when you thought of it. *O Grand Sphincterie des Romains*! O spice routes of the poetic mind which lead to the infernal regions below the subliminal threshold. Metaphors too big for their boots, literature of the S-bend. Wind in an old chimney – fatherly flatus? He should be more modern, go into business.

> To shit, to codify a business lunch
> A pint of lager and a brunch.

He had ordered various things for which the tally of saucers did not work, so the waiter had issued him with little price slips. It was on one of these that he jotted down a few figures, trying during a coherent patch in his thoughts to mobilise his reason and estimate what his expenses might be when he left Paris on the morrow, as he now intended to do. When it came to pay the waiter tore up these slips as he cleared the table. Then he noticed that they were scribbled over and he turned pale. "*O Monsieur!*" he exclaimed, beside himself with vexation, "*j'ai déchiré vos brouillons!*" He was under the impression that he had inadvertently destroyed the rough notes of some foreign poet of genius. His confusion was touching, his relief when he was reassured on the point, hardly less genuine. Blanford realised that he was madly in love with Paris. He had much to learn from these extraordinary people, for whom the word artist meant so much.

He felt steadier now in wind and limb, and visited the garage where he had left his car, to reassure himself about the servicing, and as to whether he might find it available for him at six in the morning, for he planned to make an early start and perhaps lie for the night at Lyon. All was in order, happily.

He went for one last drink to the Sphinx with the intention of bidding the Martiniquaise goodbye – with the present ambiguous and ill-regulated state of affairs he felt that he should really tell her of his movements, in case Livia reappeared and wished to know where he might be found. But the girl was not there that evening, she had gone to the cinema, though nobody knew which. He wrote her a message and left it with the presiding Mama who regally accepted to see it delivered. Then he drank his drink and departed, making his way back to the sad little flat, so empty now of resonance and tone – as if even its memories of the events which had taken place within its walls had gone dead and stale.

Nor could he sleep – images floated him beyond reach of it. He was hunting down the great rat of the emotions with a heavy stick in a dark house, creeping from staircase to staircase, pausing to listen from time to time. The night was full of the noise of cats feasting on garbage and each other – stale cats, the fitting symbol for temple women, all faceless claws and minds and civet. He threw up the window and stuck his face against the sky – the whole of space, sick as an actress, living in a state of permanent and thoughtless manifestation. He would be glad to get away from the Sphinx where trusting little Benzedrine Papadopoulos opened her twiggy legs to show a black bushy slit with a red silk lining. Farewell to Livia and the dry copyists' succinct word for craving – four letters beginning with L. Avignon radiated the memory of peace and contentment, and tomorrow he would be on the road once more.

In contrast to the affairs of the world, his own were more or less in order; the little flat would revert to its owner automatically for the rent had not been paid. He had wound up all household bills, debts to the newsagent, and the like. He was vacating Paris – it was a hollow enough feeling. He passed by the Dôme and scanned the letter board which contained as always a wealth of messages which waited patiently to be reclaimed. There was nothing from her, and he was a fool to have expected anything. On an impulse he copied out a poem from his notebook and placed it in an envelope with her name on it. It was valedictory enough to suit the occasion; he felt inexpressibly sad about the whole business, about the whole failure to connect, to unite. He was also alarmed for her safety – for he was, unaccountably, still deeply attached to her.

BURIED ALIVE

for Livia

A poem filling with water,
A woman swimming across it
Believing it a lake,
The words avail so little,

207

The water has carried them away
Frail as a drypoint the one kiss,
Renovation of a swimmer's loving.

Attach a penny calendar to the moon
And cycle down the highways of the need,
The doll will have nothing under her dress;
With an indolence close to godhead
You remain watching, he remains watching.

When she smiles the wrinkles round her eyes
Are fitting, the royal marks of the tiger,
The royal lines of noble conduct.

Virtuous and cryptic lady, whom
The sorrows of time forever revisit,
Year after year in the same icy nook
With candles brooding or asphodels erect,
Stay close to us within your mind.
These winter loves will not deceive,
Unplanned by seasons or by kin
They feast the eye beneath the skin.

SEVEN

Prince Hassad Returns

NOR WAS HE THE ONLY ONE RETURNING TO AVIGNON, he discovered, for he later found it bruited that Lord Galen and the Prince had already come rumbling and roaring and careening out of Germany together in a high state of emotional and intellectual disarray. It had not taken long for the gimlet eye of the Prince to pierce to the heart of Galen's romantic folly; he could hardly credit what it revealed of the whole catastrophic investment. Among so many miscalculations of the same order, this one stood out as a monument of the purest insanity – and so fearfully expensive to boot. Never in Galen's long career as a "gentleman-adventurer" (he was fond of the phrase) had he committed such a fearful "bloomer" (another he favoured). Indeed the blow appeared to have all but demolished him – at all events temporarily. His sang-froid had turned its back on him. He walked with a stoop, giving the impression that the disaster had actually aged him. You felt he was worn out with the long and humiliating journey back to sweet reason. At all events they drew up at Les Balances in Geneva for an orgy of accounting and numerous vital meetings with paler and paler executives. To tell the truth Prince Hassad was less bruised, less cast down, for he had invested nothing in the scheme. In fact he hovered on the edge of smiles, although his cumbersome coach caused endless annoyance in the parking spaces of the city and his staff much excitement. It was Galen who bore the brunt of it all; try as he might there was no disguising his asininity.

The Prince had, heaven knows, been the soul of tact, but from time to time a mortal chuckle escaped him. He struck his knee and wrinkled into lizard-like smiles of a private nature; but Galen could quite well guess why. Though the little man in his royal green-striped flower-pot actually *said* nothing his chuckles lodged like barbs in the tender cuckold flesh of his associate's consciousness. Things had gone so far that they had actually been threatened with arrest unless they decamped – and this by the Nazis! Galen rather wished now they had been arrested – his sadness would have been sublimated by an expiation of sorts. "Well," said the Prince, "it is no use just going on brooding. We have made a ghastly incoherence. You must save what you can." He was kind enough to pretend that he had shared the misfortune. "Look on the brighter side," he said, turning Stoic. "In two or three months we shall all be dead – you have read about the nerve gas in the *Tribune?*" Galen obediently thought about his approaching death and felt quite cheerful of a sudden. Yes, there was no use brooding. The Prince picked his teeth and reflected; he had spent all day at the Egyptian Embassy, telephoning and sending telegrams in cipher. "My dear friend," he said, "you will go on to Provence and arrange your affairs. I have things I must attend to. I will follow in ten days' time and we can decide everything else."

"You aren't leaving me?" said Galen, pulling his underlip and pouting. "Only for a while," said Prince Hassad, "and I think the best thing for you, my friend, is to wind up things here and then go back south. I will send off the coach ahead. In ten days we meet again and then there will be big decisions to make. I fear I must leave all my new friends in Avignon and return to Egypt for a while, until we see what form this war takes. There is a big Italian Army on the frontiers of Egypt, for example, and we don't know . . . well, *anything* as yet.* As for you, it is impossible to disguise your

* See Appendix.

incoherences." (His perfect English had nevertheless small and unexpected flaws of usage.) "So why not make the best of them and just be frank. Eh?"

Lord Galen considered being frank, with his head on one side, like a fox-terrier. "Just admit I've been a fool?"

"Exactly."

"I never thought of that," said Galen and looked suddenly relieved. Nevertheless his sorrow and humiliation were not unduly lightened by this decision of the Prince to desert him in Geneva for a few days and take the express for London and just when he needed company and sympathy too! But Hassad insisted that he had a number of things to attend to before returning home, and that these must be despatched before, in the popular phrase of the hour, "the balloon went up". The image of a bright Montgolfière – Europe itself no less – floating up and out into the unknown empyrean of the future was suitably frivolous.

After the comparative calm of Geneva, the cud-chewing capital *par excellence*, it was strange to sit in a first-class carriage of the Golden Arrow as it drew away from frenetic and gossipy Paris where one could secure a laugh at cocktail parties by giving the Nazi salute. (The Prince was terrified when he thought of it.) He sat bolt upright in his corner seat mechanically doing the *Times* crossword puzzle and waiting for the lunch gong to summon him swaying down the corridor towards a hearty but insipid meal.

Yet the quicksand of an international lethargy was still the factor which so mysteriously dominated everything. Time, from being a solution, had become a jelly. On the outer fringe of things everything seemed in a state of violent agitation. There were trumpet-calls, denunciations, sabre-rattlings, government pronouncements . . . but the whole in a sort of void. People scurried about like rats, hoarding food or making testamentary dispositions or booking tickets for

America. But these gestures were somehow shapeless and without pith because, in fact, nobody could believe that human beings in this present stage of civilisation could conceive of a war – after the lessons of 1914. The little man said to himself: "It is because it is quite unthinkable that it must happen. People want death really, life poses too many problems." Things proceeded, he had observed, by cruel paradox. He sighed heavily, for not the least of his concerns was with the vulnerable and defenceless England towards which his train was racing, shrieking aloud in tunnels, and leaving behind it a thick black plume of smuts which always managed to settle themselves on his grey spats and on the astrakhan collar of his finely cut overcoat. Everything would have to be cleaned the instant he got back to: London! The word made his heart race, for surely there would be a letter from his little Princess in the diplomatic bag? It was cruel to have left her for so long alone in the dusty old palace on the Nile with nothing much to do save to paint and read and dream about his return. "My partridge!" – the endearment escaped him involuntarily as he thought of her.

The ceremony of the passport control, followed by the abrupt change in the scale of things – the new toy landscape after Dover – set his thoughts wandering in the direction of his youth as a young secretary of Embassy in an England which he had loved and hated with all the emotional polarity of his race. How would she withstand this cataclysm? Would she just founder? He trembled for her – she seemed so exhausted and done for, with her governments of little yellowing men, faded to the sepia of socialism, the beige of bureaucracy. And Egypt, so corrupt, so vulnerable, was at their mercy, in their hands. . . . Long ago he had made a painstaking analysis of the national character in order to help in the education of his Ambassador, dear old Abdel Sami Pasha. But it had been altogether too literary, and indeed altogether too wise. He had distinguished three strains in the English character which came, he was sure, from Saxons, Jutes or Normans – each Englishman had a predominance of one or other strain in his make-up. That is why one had to be so careful in one's dealings with them. The Saxon strain made them bullies and pirates, the Jutish toadies and sanctimonious hypocrites, while the Norman strain bred a welcome quixotry which was capable of rising like a north wind and predominating over the other two. Poor Sami had read the whole memorandum with attention, but without understanding a word. Then he said, "But you have not said that they are rich. Without that . . ."

The long struggle against his English infatuation had coloured his whole life; it had even imperilled his precious national sentiment. How would they ever drive them out of Egypt, how would they ever become free? But then, would it make sense to replace them with Germans or Italians? His glance softened as he saw the diminutive dolls' houses flashing by outside the window, saw the dove-grey land unrolling its peaceful surges of arable and crop, like the swaying of an autumn sea. Yes, this country had marked him, and his little Princess used often to tease him by saying that he even dreamed in English. Damn them, the English! He compressed his lips and wagged his head reproachfully. He lit a slender gold-tipped cigarette and blew a puny cloud of smoke high into the air, as if it would dispel these womanish failings of sentiment! Womanish! The very word reminded him that the whole of his love-life and his miraculously happy marriage had been tinged by London. He hoped that Selim had not forgotten to book the suite at Brown's Hotel – the Princess loved Brown's and always sent the porter a Christmas card from Cairo.

But then Egypt was one thing and the Court quite another; their education had modified fanaticism and turned them willy-nilly into cosmopolitans who could *almost* laugh at themselves. It came from languages, from foreign nannies and those long winterings at Siltz or Baden-Baden or Pau. It had etiolated their sense of race, their nationalism. The French distinguish between knowing a language and possessing it; but they had gone even further, they had become possessed by English. The other chief European tongues they knew accurately of course, but for purely social purposes. There was none of the salt in them that he found in English. . . . Nor was everyone at the Court like him, for some were more charmed by French, some surrendered to Italian. But it was his first firm link with Fawzia, the passion for England. Even when he was at Oxford, and writing anti-British articles in *Doustour* under his own signature! And paradoxically enough she loved him for it, she was proud of his intellectual stance.

The thought made him stamp his spatted foot on the floor of the compartment, stamp with delight like a little Arab horse. He had first met her at the Tate; poor darling, she was piously copying a Cézanne, pausing for long drowsy moments to dream — so she afterwards averred — of a Prince who would suddenly appear from nowhere and ask for her hand in marriage. This made her copying somewhat haphazard. She was chaperoned by the widow of a Bey whose son had been at Oxford with him, and this gave him the excuse to exchange a few words with her, and then to be presented to the Princess. She curtseyed in an old-fashioned manner, and he bent over those slender fingers, feeling quite breathless. Indeed they both paled at the encounter. "It was a moment of silk," in the Arabic phrase. Her dark eyes were full of ardour, idealism and intelligence. He put on his gold-rimmed spectacles in a vain attempt to seem older than he was. The three human beings — everything had become dream-like and insubstantial — took a slow turn up and down the gallery, emitting noises about the paintings displayed. He could feel the words coming out of his mouth but they were like "damp straw". Inside him a voice was saying, over and over again, "Fawzia, I adore you!" He was terrified lest his thoughts be overheard, but she preserved her demure disposition, though her heartbeat had reached suffocation point. The kind duenna absented herself for a moment and they talked on. He was electrified. *She appreciated Turner!* "We must place him beside Rembrandt," she said firmly, indeed a little school-marmishly. But how right she was! He felt he would start vapouring with devotion if this went on, so he abruptly took his leave with a cold expression on his face which dismayed her for she thought that it was due to disdain for her artistic opinions. She stammered upon the word "Goodbye" in a way that made his heart exult, though he continued to look grim as he stalked out of the gallery. Outside he smacked the back of his hand with his grey gloves, then smelt it to see if any trace of her perfume remained before continuing this reproachful simulacrum of self-punishment. Towards the next religious festival he permitted himself to send her a large and handsome folio of colour reproductions from Turner, expressing the hope that she did not own it already. She did, but she pretended the contrary, and expressed a rapture not the less sincere for being feigned. They met briefly at a number of functions and exchanged quaint fictions of conversation in public, almost suffocating with desire as they spoke. He did not quite know how to advance from this point. He was now a graduate, yes, and though heir to a large fortune in cotton and land, had no precise job. Moreover, their attachment having been launched upon such a high romantic keynote, could not be allowed to sink down the scale and revert to the humdrum. I suppose it was very Shakespearean, but they both believed – privately, secretly, separately, passionately – that nobody had ever loved with such intensity. He was anxious to keep their love free from every taint of Parisian frivolity for he considered French notions about love to be so much straw, vanity and *trompe-l'oeil*. In this period of indecision they made several important discoveries. She found, for example, that his eyes turned violet-green under the stress of aesthetic emotion, as when he spoke of the Turners in the Tate. On his side, he became more and more enraptured by her small vivid hands, so swift in action, and yet folding into her lap like rock-doves. His doctor told him that he was suffering from heightened arterial tension, and gave him a sleeping draught, but he preferred to lie awake and think about her.

Then the way opened before them. His father, after a second heart attack, wrote and told him that he must really consider getting a job and also open negotiations for a wife. He proposed to use (he said) some *piston* in the first instance, (he preferred French culture to English and thought his son's passion unhealthy and indeed unpatriotic): the second contingency he left open, being a wise man. So it was that the Prince found himself a young diplomat *en poste* in his favourite capital; and the young lady received a formal letter which had first been submitted to her aged mother, asking whether he might declare his intentions towards Fawzia. The Arabic he chose was pure though somewhat florid. Afterwards he found that she had been much amused at being referred to as "the person in question" and for a while she signed her love letters with this sweet superscription. Yes, permission was given for them to meet, to speak. The die, as they say in bad novels, was cast.

His good genius, too, must have overheard his prayers, for his choice of a meeting place for the critical encounters with his beloved could not have been more happily chosen. He would call for her, he said, towards the late afternoon and take her for a short drive along the river. She must bring a shawl as the evenings were sometimes chilly and he proposed

to show her a sunset before delivering her safely back to her
mother's house in Kensington. Call he did, but in one of those
smart horse-carriages, with a cockaded and billycocked
driver in the Victorian style. There was a whole rank of these
smart vehicles, drawn by beautifully groomed horses, which
occupied a station near Buckingham Palace – a perfect draw
for the sentimental tourists who loved to be photographed in
them when visiting London. He was not too formally dressed
– just enough for a London sunset. She had put on some finery
and had obediently borrowed a shawl from her mother –
shawls were old-fashioned articles of a past decade, so this
was rather distasteful to her, but it was too early to be
disobedient.

She was charmed by his originality and rendered slightly
tremulous by his presence. She had practised accepting his
offer of marriage in a variety of voices but could not quite
decide which to choose. She was going to leave it to fate to
decide. For his part he was equally mixed-up but deep down
he felt that, in some obscure way, the issue would be decided
not by him, but paradoxically enough, by the painter Turner.
He began to talk diffusively, discursively, about him, his
secret life, the magnitude and simplicity of his vision which
ran counter to that of his whole epoch. He quoted, with
flashing indignation, the judgement of Constable. ("Paintings
only fit to be spit upon.") And she trembled with sympathetic
pain and sadness. What pitiable blindness! But his eyes had
turned colour again and she felt the deep stirring of her
emotions, so deep in fact that she squeezed her thighs hard
together in order to allay them. They jaunted out of the Park
and took the river at Battersea Bridge from which they could
already see the preliminary conflagration of a late spring
sunset with all its sultry brutal saffron and carmine. "We
shall be just in time," he said. "Do you always do this?" she
asked and he nodded with fervour. "Ever since my first

Turner," he said, "years ago now. It is different in each season." He took her hand and pressed it. "It is so very personal," he went on, "and nobody seems to know it. It is his store cupboard, so to speak." Then he broke off to inveigh against the Tate for keeping the vast quantity of the artist's paintings in a cellar and refusing to expose them. And then against Ruskin for exercising censorship. "Shame!" she cried.

How broad it was, and how placidly it flowed, the Thames, under the massive and thickset old bridge. There was little traffic on it at this hour so that they were able to hear the rustle of river traffic, distant hootings, even voices. Spars moved upon the evening sky. All London lay around them in the expiring light. The note of the horse's hooves deepened as they reached land once more, and quite shortly the driver turned sharply to the right, to follow the long sad walls of a factory upon whose river frontage they would later notice the florid legend Silver Belle Flour. On weekdays one could peer through the gates and see flour-whitened figures like snowmen going about their tasks with the air of participating in some medieval rite. But on Sunday all was quiet. Only the children of the poor played their eternal cricket and football upon grass trodden bald by their boots. It was a depressing corner, slummy and down at heel, and she wondered idly where they were going. But it was not far, their destination, for the little church of St. Mary the Virgin still flourished like Martha's Vineyard in the midst of these gaunt deformities of factory and tenement. When they drew to a halt at the slender iron gates which opened upon a green lawn, she saw that there was a great sweep of skyline open to the west with no cumbersome buildings to break it down and arrest the mind. She looked keenly about her with her bird-like grace. "You will see with His eyes!" he cried suddenly, exultantly – and indeed on an almost theological note, so that she wondered for a moment whether there was not to be a touch of religious fanaticism underneath this exuberance. "Whose?" she asked, turning quite white, her pulse a-flutter. "His!" he said sternly and would vouchsafe no more.

So the year 1777 came to meet them across the river water in the form of St. Mary the Virgin, with its four eloquent pillars holding up, caryatid-like, the deep-roofed porch. The spire, the clock, the green belfry – so spare yet so vivacious in execution – set off the whole with unemphatic charm. The whole thing seemed to them a paradisiacal model of what village church architecture should be, should stand for. The growling circumambient toils of London around them faded before the calm of these innocent precincts. The grass was crisp and bright before the church, and was studded with a few tall trees. But it was small in extent and ended in the stout sea-wall against which lay a couple of ships, marooned by the tide and lying on their sides with their spars almost in the garden. She did not dare to exclaim, "How beautiful!" for that might have seemed banal. Instead she murmured the Arabic word "Madness!"

The angle of inclination to the place, too, was inspired and set it at a slight cant towards the curving western corners of the further river, where the dense forest lands gave it a shapely horizon full of screens through which the late sun filtered. The view, so light and airy, could have hardly been any different when the church was first opened to the parish of Battersea five years before Blake elected to marry his Kate there.

Mr. Craggs, the verger, was waiting for them faithfully with the keys, as he always did, for the Prince took the precaution of phoning ahead when the weather promised a fine sunset. Despite the rules, Mr. Craggs had been suborned by the munificence of the Prince's tip. "Never less than an 'ole suffering," he informed the awestruck clients of The Raven, or those equally awestruck in The Jug and Bottle or

The Old Swan, which practically abutted upon the little
church. The Prince had once read in a novel by Thackeray
that a sovereign was an "adequate recompense" for a special
service rendered, and though the coin was no longer in
ordinary use he had his bank send him a dozen every month.
It worked wonders, he found. But apart from this he and
Craggs had become fast friends, and now the verger was enslaved by the Princess; he helped her down ardently if somewhat creakily, for he was a martyr to lumbago. "Well I never,
Master Ahmed," he said, "what a nice young lass." The
Prince blushed proudly. But today Craggs happily could not
stay, for he had a meeting of the Legion – or so he said. "I
shall 'ave to 'op it I'm afraid." But he had placed the old oak
chair at the strategic place. "I know I can trust you to replace
it, sir, and put the key in the 'ole in the wall." It was ancient
ritual all this, and the Prince nodded. "Have a nice sunset,
then," said Craggs agreeably, winding his woollen scarf
round his neck and placing a battered bowler hat on his head.
The operation gave him a moment of polite and very tactful
hesitation – time to enable the Prince to extract a whole
suffering from his waistcoat and press it upon his friend?
Craggs gave a false start of surprise as he always did, and then
promised to drink Egypt's health and the lady's, before
stumping off into the evening. It was so calm. They were
alone. The cab withdrew to the pub to wait.

"How kind he is," she said. She had already climbed the
two stairs to the deep balcony of the church front. "He has
even put a chair out for you. I understand everything now.
What a view!" She sat down in the clumsy oaken chair and
gazed past the balconies of The Swan to where, on a level
horizon and fretted by forest, an unframed Turner sunset
burned itself slowly, ruinously away into a fuliginous dusk,
touched here and there with life as if from a breath passing
over a bed of embers.

"No!" he said, with the same extreme bliss written on his face. "As yet you do not understand. Fawzia, you are sitting in His chair, in Turner's *own* chair which he bequeathed to the church! He sat just here to study the light effects, just where you are sitting, for God knows how many years. . . ." He all but choked with his ardour. To see her there, seated in the Master's own chair – the cockpit, the vantage-point from which he had embarked upon the great intellectual adventure of becoming himself! His fingers touched the expensive engagement-ring in his pocket – he had had it specially made for her in Nubia. He placed it on her finger now and she submitted with bowed head, only giving a small sniff, perhaps a suppressed sob. And suddenly he felt triumphant. "Of course you will, won't you?" he said, sure of his response; and like a rock-dove she replied, "Of course I will. Of course I will."

He sat himself down on the steps at her side, and thus they waited for darkness to fall, hand touching hand, speechless with joy. Even when it came time to replace the holy chair by the pulpit in the dark church and replace the keys in the 'ole, they did not utter a sound for fear of shattering the gorgeous complicity of the moment. She felt as if the ring weighed a ton.

So they clip-clopped home in lazy and loitering fashion, and she was glad of the shawl as they drew near Kensington and her mother. The entire contents of the casket labelled Human Happiness appeared to have been emptied upon their heads from a spring sky. He saw her to her house porch without a word and then, dismissing the cab, set out to walk across London to regain his flat. He felt like a comet, trailing the fire of the painter's inspiration which chance had bestowed on them.

From thenceforward, he reflected now, as the train ground its way towards the capital, everything had borne fruit, and their marriage had become the envy of less lucky friends. She had asked the young Farouk to give her away – her father was dead, she had no male relations, and she had the right to do so, for soon the stripling would be King. This the young man did with grace and style, surprising everyone by his gazelle-like adolescent beauty and his courtier's address. How he had changed now, thought Prince Hassad, stubbing out his cigarette. The caterpillar-like sloth, the sudden rages and fits of weeping . . . What a fate! Yet when he began his reign it was like the début of a Nero, an auspicious entry upon the world of power, full of authority and idealism. He sighed as the new image replaced the old in his memory.

Then followed the good years in London as a young attaché. The wind had set fair for them, London liked them. Their children were beautiful and clever, without problems.

The magnetism held, and here his little wife showed brilliant insight for she adopted more than one role with him. When she was pregnant with their second child they ran away to France and played at being artists in a secluded *mas* near Avignon – two months of bliss. She let herself go, was dishevelled and out of breath as she bent over the cooking pots, while he reverently prepared her vegetables. Her breasts were full of milk from which he drew frequent swigs. They were both of them none too clean, too, like joyous peasants. Her hair smelt divinely of cooking, her body of spices and sweat. He adored her *boeuf en daube;* she admired his wood-cutting and fire-lighting, as well as his fashion of polishing glasses. He snuffled into her wild eatable housewife's hair like a truffle hound on the scent. All this was very good for the gestation of their little son. In the years to come his love-making would profit from all their happy abandonment, their sensuality. "From your way of making love," he said, "one can see that he will print up quite beautifully as a man, little Fouad." They avoided all that was fashionable but they did visit Saint Tropez, a tiny hamlet of scarce a dozen cottages, where already the famous and inebriated Quin-Quin had opened her shop and offered to sell Fawzia a scent which was really vulgar, something from the bazaar. A scent which threw open its arms to you and said "*Me-voici!*" But the Prince was doubtful about its propriety if she wore it in London. "You would excite the whole Embassy unbearably," he said.

Of course there were mishaps as well and shoals to face, as in every marriage, but nothing can withstand devotion. During her third confinement he contracted a vexatious though slight venereal infection from a young lady-in-waiting fresh from Cairo and was very much cast down by the misadventure. But Fawzia took the whole thing in her stride and nursed him with a passionate devotion. She was glad to have an excuse to show the depth of her attachment to him; she almost thanked him for giving her the chance to show how irreplaceable she really was and how magnanimous. He was overwhelmed with wonder and joy. He suddenly realised what a real woman is capable of facing. It was a little frightening. He swallowed his humiliation and submitted to her tender care like a child, glorying in the feeling of security and forgiveness. (The lady-in-waiting was banished back to Cairo, however, in very short order.)

Far from separating them, this little contretemps brought them closer together. He could afford to be weak with her for she scorned to take advantage of his weakness. "Goodness!" he said. "You are extraordinary!" He meant it.

She smiled grimly, almost scientifically.

"I love you," she explained in her somewhat inconsequential fashion, "not because you are my husband but because you are such a man!" He echoed the word feebly though he did not contradict her. Long may she cherish the

illusion, he told himself. She kissed his brow and he fell
asleep filled with the density of this loving memory. The other
children were told he had gout.

So life led them on in tranquil fashion until it became
obvious that he would soon, by pure gravitation, rise to a
rank which entailed responsibility as well as hard work –
neither was really to his taste. And in the more recent years
they had both rediscovered Egypt and found that Cairo had
begun to occupy a much larger place in their thoughts than
hitherto. It was not to the detriment of London, far from it,
it was simply that they both felt the need of a change of
scene. They wintered as often as possible in Upper Egypt,
and always left it with a pang. Perhaps a new posting? He
tried to lobby himself something in Alexandria, but failed.
There remained a distasteful choice between the Embassy
in Moscow or the one in Pekin – neither tempted him. Then
the brilliant notion dawned – why not become a private man
again and really take in hand his large property holdings,
together with the three or four old palaces which his father
had left him, for the most part tumbledown edifices in
handsome gardens lying along the Nile? The single one they
had done up for themselves largely satisfied their ambitions
and their needs. With the others, she had started to play –
for her architecture was a game, an eternal improvisation, and
he loved to see her haphazard fairy-tale palaces being realised
on a more modest scale in mud brick and cement. Business,
too, diverted him in such a slippery capital as Cairo. He had
a marked aptitude, he discovered, for bluffing and performing
confidence-tricks – all business in the Middle East is a variety
of poker. It was a relief, too, to finish with protocol and
precedence, the ramifications of which he had found so silly.
For example, the courtesy rule which forced one to keep a
person of superior rank always on one's right, even walking
down a street, even in a taxi. One had always to be scuttling

round people or cabs to see that this silly custom was observed – or else your visitor treated you with marked coldness, or went downright into a diplomat's huff. Phew! All that was over. He could play cards all night, even cheat if he wanted. One of his first civil acts was to win a large sum (by cheating) off Lord Galen who fancied himself as a brilliant courtier and card-player but who was as innocent of guile as a newly born child.

The last kilometre or so before they entered Victoria was taken at a walking pace – why, nobody could tell him, but it was so. This enabled Selim to walk along the platform beside his carriage, however, and make agreeable miming faces. The Embassy had sent a car for old time's sake, and Selim who was acting as chargé came with it to bring him his correspondence. He held up three magenta envelopes which contained letters from the Princess and smiled broadly. Selim of the quiet studious foxy expression was a Copt and had all the reserve and resilience of that enigmatic race or sect. He smiled rarely, and always grimly, for preference at the discomfiture or defeat of others less wily than he. But he was an admirable diplomat. They chatted like old friends in the car on the way to Brown's, and the Prince delivered his news which Selim was burning to hear. "As I told you in my telegram from Geneva – not the one *en clair* – Lord Galen committed an incoherence in Germany, but it was useful to me. I have it from the highest authority that they will not move for a while yet. These peace parleys and last-minute attempts to find a solution will be allowed to fizzle away for a while. Then . . ." He cut the air with his palm. "As for the Italians they have orders to do nothing for fear of upsetting Arab opinion. The build-up is purely a defensive act; even the British are not unduly alarmed. They know the Italian capacity for making mud-pies." So the talk went on, and the gloating Selim was delighted by Hassad's lucidity and the compactness of his mind. There were at least two long telegrams in the matter.

Meanwhile Abdel Sami Pasha, now long retired, had asked him to lunch at his club, and all that remained was to ask for official permission to send a private telegram *en clair* to his wife. There was nothing to fear about this either, in spite of the dramatic overloading of the wires due to the war situation. "The only thing," said Selim, "is, I did not ring the verger of St. Mary's – it looks like rain today." The Prince said that he would do that himself after lunch with Sami; Selim bowed his head, and after consulting a pocket memorandum said that that was all the business he had for the Prince. "How long will you stay?" he asked. "Just a couple of sunsets! After that I must get back to Provence and get the P. and O. to cart all my affairs back to Egypt. It's all arranged. And Farouk is sending the royal yacht to Marseille. No problems at all, as you see, my dear Selim."

They embraced warmly, with genuine warmth, for had they not been brothers in arms "in the Diplomatic"?

It did not take Hassad long to arrange his possessions in the Hotel and then to take a taxi to the gloomy old reception rooms of Sami's club in Burlington Street. They had not met for quite a time and the older man had become very white and frail. The Prince greeted him tenderly and said: "Excellence, you have venerable-ised and so have I." It was the polite way of dealing with the matter in Arabic. They talked shop for a while and his European news was duly delivered and debated. For his part the old man announced that the British would buy the whole cotton crop for that year – one problem less. "But," he went on sadly, "poor Egypt, so divided! Everyone is on a different side. Everyone hates the English, yes, but who loves the Germans except Maher? Farouk favours the Italians, but only because they are weaker even than us. . . . What a business!" They ate their slow lunch to the tune of a good wine. "As for you, young man," said the old diplomat, "I do not wish to reproach you, but from what I hear your life has become very . . . very *vivid*!" The word was exquisitely apt. Sami prided himself upon the fine apposite Arabic of his despatches. "Vivid is the word," the Prince admitted, and hung his head. "What does Fawzia think?" said Sami – he loved them both like his own children. The Prince said: "She gave me a terrible shock and that started everything off." He sighed heavily. Sami said: "Was she untrue to you?" The Prince reflected deeply and laid down his knife and fork before he answered. Then in a low choked voice he said: "She became a journalist."

Sami was silent – a silence of sympathy and commiseration. "Goodness!" he said at last. "Under her own *name*?" But here the Prince shook his head; at least it had been under a pseudonym. But the basic fact was there. "We drifted apart after that, I don't know why. In Geneva they tell me it is the menopause, that it will last three years, and then go away."

"That is quite different," said Sami with relief. "If it is an illness. Now my prostate . . ."

The conversation prolonged itself over coffee and cigars until it came time to say goodbye which they did with a tender sadness – who knew when they might see each other again in this uncertain world? Rain had begun to fall, a light spring rain, and the whole prospect became blurred like a window-pane. The porter's taxi drew up and the Prince got into it ordering the cabby to drive to Battersea. It was a very unpromising weather for tea-time and he hesitated a moment, wondering if he should not rather go to Simpson's for a crumpet and an Indian Tea. But he wanted to read his beloved's letters at St. Mary's, so that he could tell her so in the long cable Selim would send to her tonight. The place would most likely be locked, but if by luck the key was in the 'ole . . . It was! The creaky lock turned and admitted him to the empty church which smelt of varnish and industrial floor-polish. He tip-toed in, why he did not rightly know; perhaps so that he should not disturb old ghosts? The rain rustled on the roofs and on the water of the river. A wind shook the foliage of the trees. There was only just enough light to see. He sat in the Master's chair to read his precious correspondence which was full, not only of the unwavering affection of this model wife, but also with the delicious small-talk of family life – essential information about children's teeth and examinations and local scandals. The Nile had behaved very capriciously and had risen by fifteen feet in a night, washing away the little turret and hexagonal tower which she had been building for him – somewhere where he could "get away from everything and just sit and think". "Drat!" said the Prince. It was an old-fashioned expression he had picked up from his nanny. "Drat!"

Ruefully he thought of the period when he himself had been just as zealously faithful to her, just as single-minded. For years. Then suddenly in middle life shadows had fallen upon him; irrational fears of impotence, of glandular disorders, had been among them – and others less tangible. But he felt that he could not discuss such matters with anyone in any detail – unless it be a psychoanalyst of equal social rank to himself. And where to find such a person? It was a real dilemma! He had even consulted witches: to no purpose. Ordinary doctors gave him ordinary advice, prescribed tonics with unnerving names. But he hoped that they at least would be proved right, and that this period of delightful frenzy would come to an end and leave him in peace once more.

He read on slowly, voluptuously, and as he did so the evening outside suddenly lightened with some rays of un-expected sunlight. Tucking the letters back in their envelopes, which smelt of frangipani, he crossed the church with his light step and threw open the door. The whole sky was a sheet of flame! It was as if Turner himself had come back to welcome him, to give him a last sunset before the end. It might be years yet before he saw another. He did not take the heavy chair but sat upon the steps to inhale the dying light of the sun as it bobbed down to the rim of the horizon. It was like watching a stained-glass window being slowly shattered. And it was for him he felt – for them both. He took the letters out and kissed them for the sake of old memories. A line came into his head, "An Empire upon which the sun never sets." It was setting now over England! And by the same token, towards the north a balloon was going up – lurching heavily, greasily, awkwardly, up above the river. But what nonsense! The real Empire was in the primacy of the human imagination and that must always outlast the other kinds, or so he had believed. The sun was setting, the balloon was going up. He must return to his hotel and make his plans for the end of the week. He replaced the key reverently in the 'ole and walked back to the bridge.

At the hotel he found that Sami had sent his manservant with a bottle of medicine for him – for his "condition", so the visiting card said. It had a terrifying Arabic label and was clearly full of sherbet, the standard Cairo cure for impotence. It was called SFOUM, and that was roughly the noise it made when water was poured on it. One dose was enough. The rest he emptied down the sink. That night he walked a while in the park and then took a cab for half an hour to see the sights, Piccadilly, Oxford Street, the Palace. Who knew how long before he might see them again? But his long cable to his wife went off punctually, as Selim had promised.

EIGHT

Lord Galen's Farewell

DIRECTLY UPON HIS ARRIVAL IN PROVENCE LORD Galen, with a characteristic gesture, invited everyone to dinner – as one might call a committee-meeting to announce a bankruptcy. It was rather fine of him; one saw his essential kindness and innocence. He did not wish to disguise his shame; he stood in front of his own fireplace, empty in the summer save for a basket of blue sea-lavender which gathered dust but withered not, and he allowed a tear to course down his tired cheek as they came into the room, Felix, Constance, Blanford, and Sam resplendent in his "heroics", as he called his service-dress. The old man held out his two hands, asking only that they should be pressed in sympathy after his tragic blunder. Blanford found it moving so to demand the silent commiseration of friendship from them, and his heart went out to Galen. Max blew his violet nose in noisy sympathy and prepared them drinks – whisky mostly, from the ancient cut-glass decanter which had been the gift of a business friend with good taste. The Prince had not yet arrived. Galen hoped he wouldn't suddenly give his eldritch chuckle during dinner.

"I do not need to tell you about my mistake," he said meekly, without theatre, "for you know already! The Prince and I escaped just in time. I have lost a fortune and betrayed my own folk. Nobody will ever speak to me again in Manchester." He hung his head.

He had actually prepared them for this dénouement in the document he had sent Constance by way of a dinner invitation. There was nothing to say; he was most lovable at that moment.

He turned, sighing, to place his glass upon the mantel-shelf; the remains of his old cat Wombat gave a low gasp. It reminded him for a moment of the Prince's chuckle, and he frowned upon the memory. "It has been a calamity," he admitted, "and the whole thing my fault. Crest-fallen is the word. Yes, I am quite crest-fallen!" He bowed his head briefly and in some mysterious way managed to give the impression of an old rooster with bowed crest.

Shyly, from the depths of their youth, they raised their friendly glasses to toast him and to register their concern and affection; and at that moment there came the characteristic rumble of the Prince's coach as it drew up before the house, all its damascened paintwork glittering with high polish, and even its horses burnished and cockaded in the best pantomime tradition. Blanford had last seen this sort of thing at the Old Vic, when Cinderella was carted off to the ball in her transmogrified pumpkin. Quatrefages rode with the little man. He had become very friendly with the Prince, who for his part treated him with affectionate familiarity, often throwing an arm round his shoulder as he talked. ("*Il est redoutable, le Prince,*" explained the lean youth to Blanford during the evening; "*il connaît tous les bordels de la région.*") It was not surprising, for the Prince like a good Egyptian had taken the precaution of calling on the Chief of Police during his first week in the city, and of inviting him for a ride in his coach. His knowledge now (compared to the limited knowledge of Quatrefages) was all but encyclopaedic. Lord Galen, however, while full of respect for the blue blood of the Prince, steadfastly refused to share the pursuits of the royal amorist. "He must have his little spree," he might say, cocking his head roguishly, "but I need my eight hours!" Nor did the Prince insist, for he had all the tact of a gentleman of the old school. He went about on his lawful occasions, secure in the knowledge that apart from the factor of diplomatic privilege accorded him, he also enjoyed the esteem and respect of the Chief of the Police des Moeurs, who was not above giving him a ring at the hotel to pass the time of day. But he had, in a relatively brief delay, accumulated a lot of new acquaintances whose appearance was not somehow altogether reassuring to Lord Galen. There is an indefinable something which makes a gentleman who belongs to the *milieu*. It exudes from his person – some of the heavy slothful quality that emanates from the person of a great banker, or a promoter of national schemes which collapse in dust, or of an international criminal, a diplomat, a Pope. The Prince's hotel was now full of sinister silent oracular personages, who spent hours locked up with him, discussing business or (who knows?) pleasures as yet to be experienced. There was a heavy air of mystery which hung about the velvet-lined double suite of the Prince. The telephone was always going. They smiled, these dark hirsute people, but the smile was not full of loving kindness; the smile was like the crêpe on a coffin.

"I wonder who all these new people *are*," said old Galen in perplexity. "I ask him but he just says they are associates." He was a little bit put out by the Prince's discretion, and also a tiny bit anxious lest promising business mergers might be taking place just behind his back. At any event it was past worrying about, as he had decided that, in the light of the general war situation, his best move was to return home and brave the critics. After all, not everyone might be abreast of his activities; and this fearful mistake might as yet be hushed up. But he was very sad, he lay awake at nights and brooded; and in the deepening twilight of peace, dissolving now all round them, he felt the renewed ache of his missing daughter. So far all his expensive researches had yielded nothing concrete, though at times Quatrefages hinted that fruitful discoveries were just around the corner, not only on this topic but on the more challenging one of the

Templar treasure – that mouth-watering project which, though he could not foresee it now, was to cause him the unwelcome attentions of the Nazis who were to prove hardly less romantic in their intellectual investments than Lord Galen himself.

But all this lay in the fastnesses of the futurity; tonight was a quiet and sedate affair, imbued with a valedictory atmosphere. He bade them welcome to one of the finest dinners one could command in the region and the amateur gourmets of Tu Duc did ample justice to it. But they were sorry when the old man said: "I have just decided to return to London the day after tomorrow. Things are slowly going from bad to worse and I feel that I must be at my post in the old country if the die is cast and England finds herself at war." It was true, he was moved by a patriotic impulse, but it was mixed with the feeling that it would be more prudent to be nearer his investments. (As a matter of fact, as the Prince explained to Quatrefages, he was not going to London at all, but to Geneva.) He was just naturally secretive, he did not want gossip. And yet, with half his mind, he felt the welling up of warm sentiments for the Old Country. Tonight he talked in a warmly human way of what might be expected to happen after the hypothetical war – for even now the whole thing seemed such madness that one half expected a last-minute compromise or perhaps an assassination to change the trend of things. "We must move steadily towards greater justice and great equality of opportunity," said the old man, appearing to be unaware that such sentiments had been expressed before. He filled them with his own pure and innocent conviction. At such times he would actually inflate his breast, almost levitate, with idealism and emotion. He wished the whole world to have a second helping. Usually this was after dinner over a *fine à l'eau* and with his Juliet drawing smooth as silk.

The Prince also seemed a little sad and withdrawn into himself; he did not like partings and there were partings in the air now – just when he had stumbled upon several very promising lines of activity with his new associates. When Galen first probed him he did not reply directly in order not to shock the old man unduly. It was also a bit from a desire to keep his new friends as far as possible to himself. He had been carefully and conscientiously studying their portraits in the police files which had been placed at his disposal by the head of the Gendarmerie, who had himself been offered a marvellous job in Cairo at an excellent salary, in order to train the Egyptian police. The whole situation was full of promise – only this wretched war threatened to compromise his initiative; if only one could be sure that France would remain free. . . . He thought of the great gallery of photographs of his new friends: Pontia, Merlib, Zogheb, Akkad. . . . Such prognathous jaws, such cuttlefish regards, such jutting forelocks, such rhinoceroid probosces! It was wonderful! Yet they all looked just like great religious figures, like Popes in mufti. He stroked their images mentally like so many imaginary cats. Perhaps he should tease Galen? He gave his dry little clicky chuckle, and saw his host stiffen with pain. "You ask about my new associates?" he said. "I wonder if you would be surprised if I told you they were all bishops and abbots and chaplains and parish priests – all *religious* men?" Galen looked really startled and the Prince released another dry click of a chuckle, though this time he softly struck his knee and followed it up with a laugh, a small laugh, aimed at the ceiling. He looked like a chicken drinking. Quatrefages, who was in the secret, gave a hardly less wounding guffaw. But Galen could now see that his leg was being pulled. "Indeed so?" he said, slightly huffed, slightly pipped.

"My dear," said the Prince, "I was choking. You must allow me my little choke from time to time. *They are all great criminals.*"

"*Criminals?*" echoed Galen with a swishing indrawn breath. "You are associating with criminals?"

"Alas," said the Prince, "I wish it *were* so, for they would be so useful. But the situation does not permit me to risk any Egyptian money on their schemes. This wretched war . . ." It was as if every thought ended in the same *cul de sac*, the brick wall of the war situation. The Prince now explained that in France, when the great criminals became too hot to hold, they were submitted to a sort of exile in one of three great provincial towns, Toulouse, Nîmes, Avignon. They were forbidden to return to Paris. But in these towns they could reside at liberty and cool their ideas. How lucky, he added, that Avignon turned out to be one of these towns. It had provided him with a host of new contacts of the right sort, and had things been different he would by now have initiated several new schemes on behalf of the Egyptian companies he represented. Galen listened with popping eye.

Delighted by his theatrical effect the Prince permitted himself to embroider a little in his almost lapidary English. "Though they are all well bred," he continued surprisingly, "yet there may be one or two who would think nothing of sentencing a rival to *death!*" He paused for a moment and then continued, "They simply have them clubbed insensible and then thrust through the medieval *oubliettes* into the Rhône!" He talked as if the river were choked with corpses. "Goodness me!" said Lord Galen, startled by his obvious relish. "What an idea!" It gave a whole new dimension to business methods.

A few more such sallies followed, but to tell the truth Blanford felt that the evening had begun to lag on in a rather spiritless fashion, as if its back had been broken by the approaching war and the impending separations. Outside the moon was high, and the vines seemed very still, with no breath of wind to stir their loaded fronds. Quatrefages

became very thoughtful and sad when Galen told him that he must, in the coming week, close his office and transfer it back to London. "So soon?" he said and Galen nodded decisively. "I know it's hard," he said, "but something tells me it is time to move."

It was, and for once his intuition was correct. But how ironic it seemed that the weather was maturing towards a record harvest – never had the prognostications for the wine been so full of tremulous optimism! "I could, of course, stay until after the *vendanges*, if I wished," said the Prince. "*Après tout* Egypt is to be neutral so I could do as I please. Nevertheless I fear I must go too. The yacht can't wait for ever." He was thinking lustfully of all the up and coming young wines which were raising their proud crests upon the gentle slopes and terraces around them: and not less of all those shaggy old champions once again distilling and renewing their golden weight among the hundreds of square kilometres of vine stretching away on both sides of the swift green Rhône. The very thought made him thirsty. He suddenly became as merry as a cricket. "Must you really go home?" he asked again, and again Galen said he must. "Well, so be it," said the Prince, raising his paws to heaven; and he closed the subject with an invocation to Allah, the Decider of all things.

"But I must not overlook anything," said Lord Galen extracting from his breast pocket a tiny scarlet memorandum book which contained all his engagements written down in a minute spider-scrawl. "I must not forget to go down and play with Imhof once before I leave. It's over two months since I went, and he must get awfully lonely down there in Montfavet surrounded by lunatics and alienists. He loves a game of trains!" Trains – it was the magical draw of the model railway which the authorities had permitted Imhof to construct in the hither end of the asylum garden! Blanford had been invited once to accompany Lord Galen to see his

unfortunate ex-associate in his confinement. "Because," he said, "you have a very soothing presence I find. You say little but when you talk it is with a public school accent. Imhof will like that."

It was somehow typical of the essential inconsequentiality of Galen's nature that these arresting things should be said, one after another, as if they were all of the same order of thought; for him, Blanford reflected, nothing was really unusual – it all flowed together with a phenomenological impartiality which carried the colour and tone to Galen's innocent mind. "It must be dreadful," the old man continued while they were bustling down the green lanes leading to Montfavet, nestling in its bowers of roses, "to be condemned to excrete always through a slit in the stomach wall directly into a rubber envelope. Yet he doesn't seem to mind, he is positively *cheery*. He has had a very bad time has Imhof." He went on to describe the slow downfall of his partner's reason in equally colourful terms – terms which startled Blanford out of his ordinary equability and made him glance suspiciously at Galen, wondering if perhaps all this rigmarole did not stem from some secret sense of humour. But no, he was quite serious. It was no leg-pull. He described the first symptom which betokened the overthrow of Imhof's reason. "He went into shops and asked the price of things. Then he would just give a high cracked laugh and leave. It startled people."

Imhof, it turned out, was a massively built, red-headed man who looked like a market-gardener or a station-master with his crumpled black suit and heavy cheap watch-chain. He was rather unshaven as well and smelt strongly of shag. But he gave no sign whatsoever of recognising Lord Galen, and stared at him uncomprehendingly. His model railway was, however, rather an ambitious affair, with several large stations and plenty of engines and rolling stock. But it was

obviously too big for one man to enjoy and he grunted with
pleasure when Lord Galen started to behave masterfully with
switches and points, and make coal and passenger trains
perform their various functions. They did not speak but exchanged little grunts of pleasure now as they played like a
couple of absorbed children, a perfectly mated couple. They
got down on their knees and directed expresses to race in
various directions. No words were needed, the railway was
in the hands of two experts. Blanford felt deserted. He sat for
a while on a bench, and then went for a little walk among the
magnificent rose gardens from which the establishment took
its name. It was from one of these corners, hedged in by
vivid flowers, that he saw emerge a tall frail girl with long and
shapely hands. She came towards him, slowly drawing a
shawl about her narrow shoulders. Her dark wavy hair
framed a face which was beautiful but too thin; her shoes had
very high heels. She advanced slowly with a smile and said:
"So you are back? O! how was India? I am dying to ask. How
calm was India? Nowadays at night I seem to hear Piers
walking about in the other room, but he is never there when
I run to see. Did you meet him in India? Does the smell of
the magnolia still remember me supremely?" Blanford did
not know how to react. Though obviously an inmate, her
speech was superficially so coherent and her pale beauty so
striking.

They stared at each other for a moment in silence while
he hunted for a word or a phrase which might suit so strange
an occasion. She smiled at him with a tender familiarity and
reached out her hand to place it on his elbow, saying: "Of
course you did. It is obviously there you met him." Blanford
nodded, it seemed to be the right thing to do. They took a
few steps and on the other side of the flower-bed he saw an
open French window giving on to a room furnished with a
certain old-fashioned luxuriousness. There was a tapestry on

the wall, and a concert-grand in the corner. Scissors and a bowl of flowers on the terrace explained what she had been doing when the sound of his step on the gravel had disturbed her. "I knew it all the time," she said again, "I knew you would come from him, from Piers." At that moment a flight of birds passed close overhead, and at the whirr of their wings a panic fear seized her. Her face clouded, her eyes became wide and glittered with apprehension. "It is only the birds," he said, hoping to soothe her, but she gazed at him wildly and repeated hoarsely, "*Only* the birds? What are you saying?" Huddling the shawl round her thin shoulders she hurried away towards the terrace and the open window. He stood quite still until he heard the latch click home. Then he made his way thoughtfully to where the two grunting men moved about on the ground like apes, releasing their marvellous models with a high skill and a perfect enjoyment.

It was a full couple of hours before Galen came to himself; it was as if he at last awoke from a deep trance of perfect, transcendent happiness, and sighing, took his leave of Imhof who gazed unfeelingly at him, watched him move away, and then bent down resolutely once more to his trains. Nothing was said about the public school accent. There had been little chance to use it, so mute had been the harmony of the two train-lovers, so deep their concentration. As they drove away Galen said, sighing with repleteness, "Poor old Imhof. I so often think of him. He made just one big miscalculation and pouf! it played on his reason. A fearful bloomer! Shall I tell you? It was during a water shortage in England, a scandal. All the newspapers went on about it, and the Government asked people to save water as much as possible. Then the press said that the Englishman's bath was the reason and gave statistics about the millions of tons of water we waste. It was here that Imhof got the idea of buying all those bidets – hundreds of thousands of them. He said that if England could be got to accept the bidet we could all make do with one bath a week. The saving in water would be immense. I forget the details but he spent millions on advertising his idea, and at the same time, not to be caught short, in buying up all the bidets he could find. A massive investment all lined up in warehouses on the coast waiting to invade across the channel." He gave a sad chuckle. "They are still there. He seemed not to realise that one of the hardest things to do is to get a national habit modified. Bidets!"

Remembering this occasion, Blanford reflected compassionately upon Imhof and his bidets while the old man thoughtfully circumcised a cigar and struck a match to light it. He leaned back now in his chair and smiled round at them; he had expiated his guilt by his sincerity and now felt calmly himself again, though of course still saddened by the whole affair. Constance and Sam said little, and it was assumed that they were preoccupied with each other and deaf to the appeals of mere sociability. But she was filled also with a weight of apathy and weariness which astonished even herself. They were like people living upon the slopes of a volcano, Vesuvius or Etna, resigned to the knowledge that one day, nobody knew when, the whole of the world they knew would be blown apart by forces beyond their imagining. And yet they continued to respect social forms like automata, like the Romans of the silver age, when the Goths were already gnawing at the walls of the civilised world. As if he had intuited this feeling of remorseful apathy in her, Lord Galen patted her hand and sighed deeply. "If this goes on," he said, and everyone knew what he meant by that, "why, money will become quite worthless." He looked round the table. "And it's a great pity. It has given us so much pleasure. Indeed there is something very inspiring about money." The word was strangely chosen, but one could feel what he meant. Money, thought poor Felix, working his toes in his dinner shoes. He had contracted a hammer-toe from his solitary walking about the town. Money – if only he could get his hands on some. Blanford himself had a twinge of panic. "I suppose all investments will collapse?" he said with some alarm. The Prince nodded. "It depends," he said, "some will. But if you have armament shares. . . ." Lord Galen now called to Max to wind up the old horn gramophone and set off the traditional *Merry Widow* waltz which closed all his dinner parties. They took themselves to the quiet terrace where they were supplied with drinks hard and soft and tobacco for Sam's pipe. It was curious that no mention had been made of Livia, and Blanford wondered suddenly if they knew anything about her – was it perhaps a tactful silence? But then on the other hand nobody had mentioned Hilary either. The moon shone upon their glasses. There was no wind, but away over the hills there came a tremor of summer lightning like a distant bombardment going on, which must herald one of the thunderstorms which traditionally ushered in the harvest and the autumn. The Prince asked Blanford whether he would not like to visit Egypt. "I would be happy to engage you as a personal private secretary if that were the case. You would live in the Palace and meet the best people, the *top-notch*. It is a very picturesque land."

The proposal was startling and novel and tickled the youth's fancy. He asked for time to consider. As yet his own personal affairs were not sufficiently in order, or so he felt, to embark on what promised to be so exciting and enriching a career as that of social secretary to a prince.

Now, turning aside, the Prince addressed himself to Felix Chatto. They took a turn up and down the balcony and on the lawn, linked arm in arm. Felix was very flattered to be treated with the deference due to a senior diplomat, as if he was in possession of state secrets of the highest importance. The Prince gave a résumé of the political and military state of things and asked him to comment upon it with a becoming modesty and a keen attention. Rising to the occasion Felix did his best to present the balanced analysis so dear to the hearts of diplomats and leader writers. As usual it all depended on If, When and But. The Prince thanked him warmly. "In a few days," he said, "I am going to have a little *spree*. After Lord Galen goes. Do not be offended if I do not send you an invitation, my dear. It will be rather an advanced sort of spree and you have a professional reputation to look after in this beautiful but somewhat sinister little town. But don't take offence. You will understand everything when you talk to your friend Quatrefages." But Felix needed no briefing, he could imagine very well what the little spree would entail. "I must pay back some social debts to my new friends," explained the little man, and the young consul saw in his mind's eye all those faces like crocodiles and ant-eaters and baboons, all dressed in dark suits with improbable ties and fingers with black hair sprouting through their rings. "I shall quite understand," he said seriously, "and I take it as a compliment, sir, that you should bother to explain to me." The Prince squeezed his arm and gave a ghost chuckle.

They broke up relatively early that evening, pervaded by a sense of weariness and loss. Perhaps because he felt that this was probably the last occasion they would meet round his table, old Lord Galen tried to infuse the occasion with a touch of valedictory ceremony. He called for a toast to the Prince and to Egypt which was willingly drunk, and which, by its unexpectedness, pleased the Prince very much indeed. He for his part replied by calling for a toast to His Majesty the King of England. He sprang up as he uttered the words with alacrity and a genuine enthusiasm. He had been received at Court with great kindness, which had seemed to him quite natural and unaffected. Besides, one of the younger members of the Royal Household had elected herself his mentor and

Muse. What he admired so much, he told Chatto, was that in England you could do almost anything without getting into the newspapers. You felt so safe, while in Egypt those dreadful socialist and communist papers were always on the lookout for scandal. "They don't like the upper class to have a little spree. Why are Marxists such spoilsports? I have never been able to understand it, especially when you think of the morals of Engels."

The car came, with a tearful Max at the wheel, and they all said goodbye to the Prince with a genuine pang. When would they all meet again? Nobody could tell, nobody could say.

The inhabitants of Tu Duc took their leave with Max in the old rumble-dusty vehicle of Lord Galen; Quatrefages and Felix, since they were going into the town like the Prince, were offered the trip in his coach. The journey passed in friendly silence; the Prince spent most of it exploring the cavities between his teeth with a silver toothpick of great elegance. He said no more about his spree until the changing tone of the horses' hooves upon the cobbled avenues of the town told them that they were almost home. "The little spree I spoke of," he told Quatrefages, "will be at the end of the week, perhaps when Lord Galen has left the country." Quatrefages asked if he could be of service in the matter and received the reply that everything was going to be arranged at an official level. "It is much safer that way. But I hope you will honour us with your presence. I think the occasion will be a memorable one – in all this fearful war-indecision which prevents us all from thinking or planning. They ring me up all the time from Abdin Palace with rumours and scares, telling me I must return. The palace yacht is already at Marseille waiting with steam up. But I think all this is quite premature."

The others elected to be dropped at Tubain, and to walk

the rest of the way in the deep moonlit dust, under the long avenues of planes and limes. And in silence for a change. Not necessarily the silence of despondency, but a silence which held the whole world of futurity in solution, as it were; the silence in which one waits for an orchestra to strike out its opening statement. Constance linked her little finger to theirs and walked with her face turned upward towards the moon. On the way, flickering among the trees like a firefly, came a bicycle-lamp which fluttered towards them and stopped. It was the son of the post-master of Tubain who had been up to the house to deliver a late telegram, and found nobody in. It was for Sam and they all knew what must be in it. It was only the date of his recall which was in question. He tipped the boy and said goodnight to him before opening the slip of blue paper. Blanford struck a match which gave a yellow hovering splash of light sufficient for him to read the contents. He gave a sigh. "I leave on Sunday," he said, in a tone of elation; it was understandable. It was far better to know for certain – at least one could prepare for the event. Yes, they all felt better armed against the future this way. They would have a few more days together before the parting. Constance was going back to Geneva for her work – she would quit Sam in Paris. Blanford would stay on for a while with his little car (which was at present in a garage, being repaired and serviced), and wait upon events. Never had he felt more useless, more undecided about his direction. The Egyptian project was most tempting; but would a war not qualify it? He presumed he would be called up, and as he could not conscientiously object, he would soon find himself in uniform like Sam.

They crossed the garden in single file, under the cork-oaks with their snowy crests, and turned the creaking key in the tall front door. The familiar smell of the house greeted them in darkness; it smelt of long forgotten meals, of herbs and of garden flowers, it smelt of cobwebs and expired fume of candles. All at once it seemed a pity to go to bed without a nightcap. In the kitchen they lit a paraffin lamp and by its mild unhovering yellow light sat down around the scrubbed and sanded table to brew tea and to play a hand of gin rummy. Blanford opted for a glass of red wine instead, however, despite the lateness of the hour and his general abstemiousness. It was late when they at last bade one another goodnight, and even now with such a fine moonlight outside it seemed a shame to go to bed; so he walked down to the water and took a silent, icy swim, letting the rushing wings of the water pass over him like rain. Closing his eyes he seemed to see in memory all the black magnetism of the dark light which shone out of the earth, whether among these trees and vines or out of the bald stone garrigues and pebbled hills with their crumbling shale valleys. Among these rambling dormitories of shards Van Gogh had hunted the demon of his black noonday sun – and found it in madness. Only when one was here did one realise how truthful to the place was his account of it. He was beginning to realise the difference between the two arts, painting and writing.

Painting persuades by thrilling the mind and the optic nerve simultaneously, whereas words connote, mean something however approximate and are influenced by their associative value. The spell they cast intends to master things – it lacks innocence. They are the instruments of Merlin or Faust. Painting is devoid of this kind of treachery – it is an innocent celebration of things, only seeking to inspirit and not coerce. Pleased with these somewhat rambling evaluations he scampered back to the house and to bed, shivery with cold all of a sudden, so that he was forced to climb between the sheets with his socks on. He would have liked to read for a moment or two, so delicious was the moonlit air outside, but sleep at last insisted. He sank to the pillow as if beheaded.

Down below, in the sleeping town, the pro-consul

paced out his long penitential walk from bastion to dark bastion; the moonlight only emphasised the shadows, creating great caves of pure darkness out of which he dreamed that some brilliant gipsy might emerge and pounce on him; but more likely it would be a footpad. His fingers tightened upon the little scout penknife he carried on his person, not so much for security as for tedious pro-consular uses, such as cutting up string to make parcels. The prospect of the war filled him, strangely enough, with elation which was somewhat shame-making. Naturally he would never have confessed to such a thing publicly, for he wished nobody harm and was person-ally too much of a coward to hanker for firearms – he was in fact rather gun-shy. But the reality of war if it came. . . .

If he had been guilty of imitating the rather pretentious formulations of Blanford he might have told himself that the reality of war (death) if it came would render back once more all the precious precariousness of life which had become stale with too much safe living. It was not a question of swimmers into cleanness leaping à la Brooke, but simply a breath of fresh air in a twice-breathed suffocating age. If it came he would join up at once. He would welcome all the restrictions which went with the uniform. He would glory in the savage discipline, for too much freedom gives you vertigo – you are looking out into nothingness all of a sudden. Nothing-ness – your own portrait! Much later he would realise that this feeling was echoed by the whole of the Nazi Youth!

Apart from that, he had started a course of physical culture with some vague notion of fitting himself for the fray. He read a cheap pamphlet on yoga and realised that he was walking in the wrong way, his breathing rhythms were at odds with his steps. This made him walk in a self-conscious, rather stilted fashion as he remembered the instructions of his pamphlet. "Ordinary people breathe eighteen times a minute but in the best yoga practice you can get down to less than ten and that will do. But three a minute is really good!" Three a minute? He found himself counting the paving stones and holding in his breath, only to express it in a swish when the strain became too much. Surely this was not right.

But at dawn even he found relief in his weariness, hurrying home along the empty streets now drained even of the moonlight. Time was still there, a slowly discharging wound which the daylight would stanch. But first a little rest. He too climbed into bed and slept, but not before passing in review the sleep of the others which he could picture so clearly. Blanford all tousled, with his head under the pillow, Sam snoring, Constance invisible. Somewhere quite nearby the Prince lay, with a small piece of muslin over his face to defend him against moths – he dwelt in mortal terror of being eaten up by a moth, like an old tapestry. He had wrapped his one false tooth in silver paper, to avoid swallowing it in his sleep. It lay beside him with his beautiful ivory-covered Holy Book. Up there in Balmoral Max snoozed in a sort of cupboard which smelt of dead mice. The poor little secretary preferred a hammock in the garden. Lord Galen lay in his great bed all serene. He wore a night-shirt with frilled white cuffs which he got from Mannering's. It had his monogram on the breast. He slept with his mouth open and from time to time squirmed out a great snore which might be phonetically transcribed as "Gronk-phew"; Felix remembered the Prince saying, "He is such a good man that he is prone to be *spoofed*." And now war was coming.

> Once it was Bread and Circuses,
> Now it is all Dread and Carcases.

Where had he read that?

Yes, Blanford slept, but in his excitement he woke early while the others were still asleep, and tiptoed to the kitchen to make himself coffee. This he took back to bed where, lying luxuriously half asleep, he sent his roving mind as Felix had done, to visit his friends in their several sleeps and to try, by projection, to realise them more fully. Did he know what they felt or was he simply privileged to imagine – the writer's illness? He hardly knew. Yet it was so clear to him that the girl who slept in the afterglow of Sam's embraces was already ahead of them all in a certain domain whose real existence they hardly as yet realised. As for Sam, still drunk on the huge honeycomb of these first kisses, there seemed little beyond death and separation to consider, to evaluate. He had suddenly started to realise that he was now dying, quite softly dying. Mind you it would take time, but it was quite irrevocable. Most people hid their faces and refused to look this moment of realisation in the eyes. He slept on triumphantly in a cone of silence. The realisation itself was a victory, and it had nothing to do with the war. It would have come anyway, simply because of the contact with Constance, she had grown him up, though he would have been hard put to it to describe just how and why.

Even the notion of death offered a sort of hidden glee, it had been mastered! This whole absurd and mysterious business had been sparked off by a simple conversation in which the girl had said, "It will seem to you quite mad but from early on in my adolescence I seemed to have set myself a sort of task. I was trying to want only what happened, and to part with things without regret. It made me sort of on equal terms with death – I realised that it did not exist. I felt I had begun to participate in the inevitable. I knew then what bliss was. I started to live in a marvellous parenthesis. I also knew that it wasn't right to know so much so young. . . ." The effect of these words on Sam was indescribable. He was struck dumb. It was as if he understood exactly what she meant, but that the words had by-passed his reason. Later, much later, she would be able to add to this in a letter to Blanford by saying: "An overwhelming thirst for goodness is a dangerous thing and should be discouraged. I hunted not an ethos but the curve of a perfect licence charged with truth – however disconcerting pure truth might be! I was an alchemist without knowing it. Idiot!"

There they were, sleeping all, quite unaware that their dreams were models and outlets for their future acts. He had fallen asleep again, Blanford, and this time it took Sam an effort to wake him. "No time to lose," said Sam, "these last few days are precious. To horse!"

In some old book of aphorisms he had been surprised by the observation: "A superlative death costs nothing. The lesser ones are the more expensive." Was it Montaigne? He could not remember.

The Spree

THE PRINCE'S LITTLE SPREE PROMISED TO BE OF SUCH
royal magnitude that the excited Quatrefages, when he
got wind of the details from the inhabitants of their
brothel – their common brothel, so to speak – at once borrowed
a bicycle and scorched (the metaphor is an exact one, for it
was at noon) out to Tu Duc with news of it. It must somehow
be seen, he said, despite protocol considerations; even if
only from afar. He himself was, of course, actually invited,
but out of considerations of delicacy the Prince had decided
to omit their names from his list of matchless crooks –
perhaps just as well. But . . . he had rented the whole Pont
du Gard, and with it the whole of the ancient Auberge des
Aubergines which abutted thereon. He was already busy
transforming the place to suit his notions of how a spree
should work.

The Auberge was a strange, rambling old place,
admirably suited to this kind of initiative, with its collection
of Swiss chalets hugging the cliffs of the Gardon, buried in
plane-shade, leaning practically over the green water. Though
it was not a residential hotel it had a series of large inter-
connecting upper rooms which in summer managed to
accommodate tourist groups or clubs devoted to archaeology
or Roman history who selected the monument as a point of
rendezvous, and sometimes camped out in the neighbouring
green glades along the river. The cuisine was what had
made it famous, and this was, of course, an important part
of the spree. But it was not all, for the Prince, who was a
man of the world, knew his France well. He knew that in
this spirited Republic any citizen may call upon the *préfet* of

any region to floodlight a notable monument at a purely nominal cost, simply to grace his dinner. When he himself had been young and madly in love with his Princess Fawzia he had offered her dinner here, served on the bridge itself by his liveried waiters; just the two of them, quite alone. He always remembered this early part of his married life with emotion. And now the great golden span of the Roman aqueduct was going to hover above their revels, its honey-gold arches fading into the velvet sky of Provence. His heart leaped in his breast when he thought of it. He became absolutely concave with joy. No detail must be left to chance.

Quatrefages had participated in some of the discussions as a friend and helper, and was able to attest to the Prince's thoroughness. He retailed these scenes with amusing irony, even imitating the Prince's accent to perfection. When he had asked, *"Et le gibier?"* the Prince had given him a reply straight from the heart of Cairo: *"Ne t'en fais pas, Bouboule,"* which came from some old musical comedy which time had encrusted in the Cairo soul. His henchmen were already out on their errands. Even the *gibier*, the game, was coming to the party from several different corners of the land, mostly Marseille and Toulouse. The Prince had announced that he liked the girls to be *plantureuses, bien en chair*, which explained the huge collection of cartoons after Rubens which finally arrived at the Pont du Gard. Whenever had one seen so fine a collection of sleepy sugar-dolls in all their finery, and their war-paint, a-jingle with doubtful jewelry and glinting with *toc* – the very perfection of the Arabian imagination? It was clear that the old Prince had been stirred by inherited memories of the Khedival entertainments of Cairo a century ago.

Quatrefages was so engrossed in his exposition that he did not hear the sound of the approaching car in which Felix sat bolt upright in a straw hat looking like a rabbit, and tremulous with indecision. He was still not fully confident of this steel animal. Now everything had to be repeated for his benefit, and he listened with a slight pang of envy, simply because it sounded such a picturesque notion to give a party there, in the heart of the country. Preparations were already advanced; period furniture from all over Avignon, rented at ruinous prices, was being bundled into lorries and trundled out to the Auberge. In actual fact, they would only be about a hundred strong. "But the fifty girls are all *en or massif*," said Quatrefages, involuntarily licking his lips. "Marseille has outdone itself to provide sumptuous dollies."

"But where do we come in?" said Constance, who was also beginning to feel that they ran the risk of missing a treat, purely by being regarded as too virtuous to participate in it. "Indeed?" said Blanford. Quatrefages chuckled and said, "The roads after eight o'clock will be closed to motor-traffic by the gendarmerie at the request of His Highness. Obviously you won't be able to get in. But I have an idea. You can watch it all from the top of the Pont du Gard – the ballroom windows open on that side and you can see in. I know because once when I was spying on a girl who I thought was doing me down I came there and sat on the top with glasses. She was dining with a man I suspected. I saw them both quite clearly. If you take those little opera glasses you have, you will also see everything from the top."

"Yes, but to get to the top . . . ?"

He gave an impatient shrug of the head and took out a fountain pen. On the local newspaper he swiftly outlined a sketch map of the country immediately surrounding the aqueduct – a drawing which stirred their memories at once for they had walked here. "Do I need to go on?" he asked. "Here is the sunken road near Vers. You climb that slope following the broken arches and the masonry. Then suddenly you turn a corner and . . ."

Yes, you walked out into the sky, and the great crown of the aqueduct with its deep water trench lay beneath you. You walked out, in fact, upon the top of it as if upon a bridge.

"I see," said Blanford thoughtfully. "Yes, it would be possible."

"Of course it would be possible," said the impatient clerk, irritated by these slow English lucubrations, this slow chewing of the cud. "You would have a ringside seat."

"When is it to be?"

"Tomorrow. You will *never* regret it!" His solemnity was amusing.

He went on with his exposé of the details and they could see that indeed this was to be no mean entertainment, but one worthy of such a splendid setting and . . . so, well, gallant a company. Yes, they really must go! If nothing else it would take their minds off the perpetual nibbling of thoughts and doubts about the war and about the impending separations. How well such an event would have rounded off a normal summer holiday, how well it would have suited the time too, situated on the cusp of the harvest, with the closing festivals of wine and bullfighting to look forward to! Never mind. Go they must.

So they set off from the house after dinner the next day, by a low and rather famished moon – late in her exaltation and fast in her setting; a deep autumnal haze lay over the land which hereabouts looked so Tuscan in its rounded forms and paint-brush cypresses, its hamlets and villages all to human scale, its rivers small but sturdy and full of trout. Soon the greenery would give place to the more dusty uplands of the garrigue, all stone and shale, and for much of the time regions both parched and waterless. They followed the instruction of Quatrefages carefully so as to avoid the traffic restrictions of the gendarmerie. When they reached Remoulins, for example, they did not cross the bridge – they

saw lights and gendarmes on the further side. They turned
right, as if for Uzès, and rolled along deserted roads which
fringed the river bank, swerving from side to side to follow
broad sweeps of the Gardon. The Pont du Gard was already
lit up for the feast, its great bronze form lying in the sky like
a stranded whale. Underneath it, on a flat mossy glade among
the rocks, the Prince had caused a brilliant marquee to be
run up, where he sat on one of his pantomime chairs to
receive his guests. They were disgorged by their cars among
the groves of willow and walked the thrilling fifty yards or so
freckled by the light of reflectors, advancing dramatically
towards the theatrical hovering aqueduct above.

The Auberge was warmly lighted also, and the whole
upper storey had been converted into a sort of harem, with
its walls covered with priceless rugs on hire or loan, and
cupboards and coffee-tables and filigreed mirrors fitting
enough for the Grand Seraglio itself. All the antiquaries of
Avignon had contributed their mite to this impressive display.
Pinned to a curtain was a beautifully lettered panel which
read LADY BOUDOIR POUDRERIE WATER CLOSET. It was
comprehensive, it left nothing to chance. On the morrow
Quatrefages was to steal it and give it to Blanford who
attached it to the outdoor earth closet at Tu Duc, being
always glad to point out the felicity of the Cairo French, for
"poudrerie" means not "powder-room" so much as "powder-
magazine". The great open hearth of the Auberge was ablaze
with dry vine-tendrils, crackling and snapping away like the
horns of enormous snails. Somewhere in the inner heart of
the establishment an orchestra was tuning up softly, suggesting the presence of a dance floor or a ballroom. Everything
was in hand.

In order not to over-complicate matters they had
elected to travel in one car, despite the crush; this had the
further advantage that Felix was able to loan the consular

car to his invited friend for the trip. Quatrefages in *tenue de ville* looked splendid, though somewhat nervous. He had actually seen a few of the arrivals from Marseille who were to be accommodated on the morrow at a hotel. He was enthusiastic. "They all look as if their periods were overdue – it gives women a wonderful neurotic magnetism. I saw at least two superb dollies like great caterpillars, covered in pollen." Felix was a bit shocked by the relish of his friend. Quatrefages had drunk a whisky or two with the Prince's major-domo and was in a fine state of exaltation. "Remember the message of the caryatids?" he asked, shaking his finger at the abashed consul into whose car he had now inserted himself. "A girl should always try to look ever so slightly pregnant." It was an old chestnut, invented in the past by Blanford and which had tickled him enough to stay in his memory. "Whatever happens, dear Felix," he said, "don't miss it."

So here they were bowling through the sweet glades of cherries and mulberries; from time to time the brilliant aqueduct emerged upon the blackness to their left, and was then swallowed up by the greenery. They could hear the river grinding its teeth down below to their right. Then came the left turning which normally would carry them right up on to the bridge itself, and here stood a policeman with a pious air and a white barrier which he had placed across the road. But they now pretended they were heading for Uzès and passed him by with a wave, to curl down the long avenue of cool planes until the sunken road by Vers came up and here they drove most carefully on an appalling surface until they came to an olive grove which crowned the slopes. Here it was not possible to continue by car and they started to walk on the shaly slopes among the snatching bristles of holm-oak and thorn. It was harder to navigate in the darkness than by daylight.

The hill was a wilderness of dividing paths and fire breaks; but ahead of them was the furry white light of the reflectors and they navigated upon that until, with the sudden surprise of actors who walk unwittingly out upon a lighted stage, they reached the culvert which marked the first arch. And here began the circumspect descent upon the crown of the aqueduct with its metre-deep gulley – the channel through which the spring water of Vers was conveyed to Nîmes in Roman times. Here they could perch like birds in a high tree and rest their elbows on the side of the trench, to gaze down upon the princely revels below. The idea of the opera glasses was also a brainwave. They had originally been bought for the performances of the Opéra de Marseille, but lately had been much out of use, lying about the house. Now they trained them like sharpshooters upon the Auberge below, and found that, as Quatrefages had said, they had an excellent view of half the great dining-room, one side of which opened into a sort of sun verandah.

The proceedings had already begun with a certain regal formality; the male guests, who were all unaccompanied, had been received in the pavilion and had been offered an aperitif of the Prince's devising – possibly laced with cantharides? Quatrefages indeed wondered about the matter as he gulped down his portion of the fiery colourless brew. The company looked even stranger at night than by daylight. They were all dressed in dark suits which were uncomfortably warm for the time of the year, and they gave the impression of being weighed down by their cravats and heavy rings, and greased hair. At this stage there was no sign of the women. But at last, when the assembly was complete, the Prince beckoned to his guests to follow him, and led them, as if they had been a cricket team, through the glades towards the Auberge, which had stayed all this time in almost complete darkness – just a candle-glimmer here or there which betokened movement. The Prince held in his hand his little gilt fly-swash with its length of white mare's tail hanging from it. It was rather like a conductor's baton. With it he tapped on the closed doors of the Auberge and they sprang open at his behest. At the same moment the whole dining-room was flooded with light and the advancing cohort of guests gave a collective gasp of pleasure. To the right of each male guest there was to be a *naked lady of pleasure*! Those already in place clapped and shouted and vociferated in ladylike fashion as the dark-suited men advanced with a thirsty air, each to find his place card with his name upon it.

No phantasy had been spared, it was clear. Constance chuckled almost continuously at the scene as her glasses picked up now one corner and now another of the ballroom. The men, as befitted their superior sex, sat on chairs with high gilded backs, like thrones; the girls upon velvet piano-stools. The Prince dominated the table as a good host should. Behind his chair stood the three dignitaries of high office clad in the most wonderful service robes of scarlet and gold, with green facings. One was the official food-taster, who would not be pressed into service tonight; the other two, one on each side of his chair, were bearing on their right wrist a tall hooded falcon. The Prince's rank entitled him to this dignity, just as a Scottish aristocrat is entitled to his bagpiper. The dinner began with a swirl of conversation and popping and waiting . . . a little sticky as yet, despite the fiery aperitif.

The men looked like shy honey-bears at Sunday school. "But not for long, I don't suppose," said Constance, who had voiced this thought to the others. The scene was full of variety and charm. In the bloom of the candles the women looked as sumptuous and grandiose as the requirements had stipulated. "*J'aime les grands balcons arrondis*," the Prince had said, perhaps with his guests in mind. And here were the great rounded balconies in all their splendour, covered in fresh violets and jewels and scented in a thousand extravagant ways. The merriment was slow to emerge but it was just as well, for this sort of dinner-party, in which so large a part of the thrill is the marvellous food, should begin on a note of attentive reverence. This fête was no exception. They were, after all, Frenchmen, which meant that they had an innate culture of the table, and also of the human heart and person. Even the most curmudgeonly and bearish of the guests was a born appreciator of *la bonne chère* and turned his eyes to heaven from time to time with ecstasy; some kissed away bunched fingers in the direction of the *cuisine* and the cook. With the tucking of napkins into collars a new ease asserted itself and the conversation flowed in harmony with the excellent wine. Quatrefages, who was not particularly attracted to balconies, found himself with a big shy round dolly with a vulgar laugh, but with all the right instincts for she pressed his knee throbbingly and gave him infinite seafruit to sup. Slightly fuddled as he was, he nevertheless realised that he had never in his experience eaten food so exquisite, yet so simple. The shade of Brillat-Savarin must have turned mumbling in his grave to bless the table of the Prince. So exceptional was it, that he thought for a moment of saving the menu to bestow on Constance, and then he realised that it was useless – it would be like confiding the programme-notes of some superlative performance to a friend. What could they imagine from such a bare recital of the elements of this divine repast?* Where the devil had the old boy found the champagne? Lost in wonder and ecstasy, he allowed himself to be tweaked and tickled and fed like a Strasbourg goose. The watchers on the top of the aqueduct were vastly amused by his beguiling air of helpless content.

It was long, the banquet, but so full of fascinating detail that they were completely absorbed in the watching; towards

* Nevertheless see Appendix.

the end some scattered little sorties took place, to enable couples to dance a stately measure or two on the dark balconies outside. These took place with a slightly absurd formalism, which suggested that the dancers were none too sure of their feet. The orchestra remained invisible, but waltz and tango and "slows" figured on a repertoire which was calculated not to prove too tiring for people after such a mammoth dinner. But to the regret of the watchers the lights progressively became more and more discreet – one last cavernous flare as from the mouth of hell took place with the *crêpes flambées*, that was all, which conferred on each hairy face the kind of dark light which Rembrandt has marked as his own. It was a tremendous success, the snapping of paper favours and even – a stroke of genius – the wearing of paper hats which pushed the scene from the plain picturesque to the absolutely side-splitting. Elderly rats in strange paper hats, waving their cigars at the universe! What a marvellous touch of lunacy was conferred by this simple touch. And the dancing became a trifle more treacly – the ladies swathing themselves more amply, more amorously about their partners, or spreading their arms wide like galleons in full sail – or combine harvesters, to select a metaphor by Felix who found it more appropriate to the approaching *vendanges*.

So things went on in a slightly more sentimental key – even the Prince trod a bird-like measure, but his affections seemed to vary a good deal; several large unplucked-looking girls were competing for his attentions. All that money! All that food! "He has found another lovely word," said Felix. "He says 'spiffing' when he means 'top- hole'."

Their spirits began to droop a little – perhaps because of the notion that the visible part of the revels was finished. Constance thought lovingly of the Thermos of hot wine and the sandwiches which awaited them in the car. Then suddenly the universe was blown out and the whole darkness of the sky came down on them as forcibly, as palpably almost, as a lid. They could not even see each other and the distance between them and the revels seemed suddenly to have lengthened, so that they felt miles high in the sky, seated as if in an aeroplane. Caution also was indicated, for a frolic up here in the darkness could cost a life or a limb. They waited to let their eyes accustom themselves to the dark, but before this happened another kind of light assailed them.

From below there was a succession of bangs and strings of coloured snakes hissed up into the air around them, only to spit out their hot coloured stars and plumes and subside groundward again. They scored their beautiful trails on that dark lambent sky, and their stuttering, pattering trajectory carried them right over the bridge on which they lay. It was relatively short as firework displays go, but the colours and forms were choice, while down below, at water level, fizzed some grand yellow Catherine wheels, and a set piece which looked somewhat like a *santon* of Provence eating olives at the pace of St. Vitus. From afar off they heard the distant clapping and cheering, and now, since the new darkness seemed to be permanent, they crawled back along the stone tunnel and up onto the hill. It was a bit of a scramble, but once on the other side they made better time with the aid of a torch. It had been worth it!

A dense dew had been falling, ripe with the premonitions of the harvest; it dripped from the quiet olive under which they had parked the car. How welcome the wine was. Yet a heavy mist hemmed in the further visibility. As they drank their drink there appeared a sort of secondary cloud, moving up the hill towards them, and they recognised the character-istic clatter of hooves and tonking of bells which betokened a shepherd, who came across to get a light for his cigarette, and was glad of a sip of wine. He spoke in a sing-song southern French. As he puffed and warmed his palms with the cup, his dogs crouched beside him attentively, and the frieze of sheep strung out on the hill behind. Their hooves bruised the sage and set up a dense perfume in the windless orchard. The old man said: "The War has begun," but his tone was one of such incomprehension and unconcern that they could hardly take it seriously. How did he know? He had heard it at the Mairie at midnight. But in a land so poorly equipped with wirelesses rumour makes do for fact to a great extent – and this particular rumour had been often encountered already. And yet ... It was disturbing. They said goodbye to him, shaking his rough hand, and piled back into their car which took some moments to start.

The heavy ground mist cleared after they had negotiated Remoulins and were safely launched upon the road to Avignon; for about ten minutes there was some disposition to doze, but as they fronted the last hillside before the famous bridge, they all came full awake again and began to debate whether to go home, or whether to go into the town in search of coffee and croissants and some truthful account of what was happening in the outer world. "It's too late to go to bed, and too early to get up," said Blanford, "and Felix is the only one who feels normal at this hour." As a matter of fact Felix was elated – almost the whole night had passed in delightful fashion for once, and here he was, happy and wide awake – only a little disquieted by the peasant's remark about the war having begun.

To town then, but Avignon itself was as dead as a door-nail – even the bakers had not started to warm their ovens, while no cafés were open, not even at the Gare. They tried a last chance and crossed Les Balances on foot, skirting its sordid and gipsy-ridden tenements, worthy more of Cairo than of a European city. They dumped the car at the Papal square. But here too, alas, the little Bar de la Navigation was shut fast. They began to feel dispirited.

But in one of the side-streets near the ancient tanneries with their foul network of canals, they heard the throbbing and pulsing note of a powerful engine or turbine. It sounded like the engine of a ship. "It's an old friend," explained Felix, "come and have a look at it! It follows me in my wandering at night, in the first week of the month every six months it 'does' this quartier during the hours of darkness. Then it moves on round the clock." It looked to them like a variety of fire-engine, and it bore the arms of the town painted in gold on its muddy flanks. "What is it?" asked Constance and Felix replied with a knowledgeable air, "It's the *pompe à merde*. You see, there has never been any main drainage, here all the houses have pits, dry pits for their only sanitation. Well, these are sucked out during the night by this old mastodon of a thing. They are all proud of it. They call it 'Marius'."

Mastodon was the word, though it had a long rubber proboscis like that of an elephant which had entered a front door and descended into the cellar where the privies were. The sucking and slobbering were fearful to hear, and the shuddering and drubbing of the pumps fearful to behold – it was like a clumsy animal, sweating and straining at its task, Blanford thought. "It is sucking out the intellectual excrement of the twentieth century in a town which was once Rome. The dry pit of the human imagination perpetually filling up again with the detritus of half-digested hopes and fears, of desires and resolutions." It was a bad sign he thought, frowning, to see metaphors everywhere; though he was not the only one. Constance said softly, "An anal-oral machine most appropriate to our time. Like the Freudian nursery rhyme."

But here afflicted by a sudden modesty she decided not to repeat it aloud; she would whisper it to herself instead.

When the bowel was loaded
The birds began to sing;
Wasn't that a dainty dish
To set before the King?

There was a light in a nearby bistro where the driver of
"Marius" was already ordering his coffee and a small marc
to drive off the excrementitious odours with which he was
forced to live. Well, it was a profession, just like any
other. . . . The others joined him at the *zinc* but Blanford
stayed behind, fascinated by the old machine sucking and
slobbering its way through the centuries. On one side, the
old wrinkled dawn was coming up in coral and nacre, and
down here at the same time the stench of excrement was
spreading over the whole quartier. Soon it would be time to
wind up the rubber hose and drive "Marius" away to its
stable, for this kind of sump-cleansing was only done during
the night – for the sake of decency, he supposed.

But now he was really tired. A quotation came into his
mind. *Inter faesces et urinam nascimur*. Yes, it was appropriate
enough. It had been, after all, Augustine's "City of God",
transplanted once upon a time to this green and innocent
country.

Appendix

* page 18
Full text of the 12 *Commandments*

1. *Faut pomper la momie allégoriquement.*
2. *Faut situer le cataplasme de l'art chauve.*
3. *Faut analyser le carburant dans les baisers blondes.*
4. *Faut faire faire, faute de mieux et au fur et à mesure faire forger.*
5. *Faut oindre le gorgonzola du Grand Maître.*
6. *Faut respecter le poireau avec son regard déficitaire.*
7. *Faut scander les débiles sentimentales avec leurs décalcomanies.*
8. *Faut sauter le Pont Neuf pour serrer la main d'une asperge qu'on trouve belle.*
9. *Faut caresser inéluctablement la Grande Aubergine de notre jour.*
10. *Faut pondre des lettres gardées en instance, tombées en rebut, Poste Restante, l'Amour O crème renversée.*
11. *Faut dévisager la réalité à force de supposer.*
12. *Faut cracher les tièdes et décendre les incohérents.*

* page 210
Readers who remark a slight divergence between so-called "real" history and the order of events adopted in this novel will, it is hoped, accord the author a novelist's indulgence.

* page 258
MENU POUR LE BANQUET DE PRINCE HASSAD AU
PONT DU GARD

Consommé glacé à la tortue
Gratin de crevettes roses en bouquet fait
Darne de saumon sauce Léda
Cailles aux pêches du Pont Romain
Médaillons de veau Sarah Bernhardt
Gigot d'agneau Grand Pétrarque
Aubergines en bohémienne
Champignons truffés Sautebrau
Salade Olympio
Plateau de fromages des douze Césars
Fruits rafraîchis des premières cueilles
Crêpes flambées à la façon de Madame Viala du Pont Romain
de Sommières
Café et Marc du Grand Daudet

❖

Blanc Aligoté 1927
Rosé de Pierre-feu
Morgon 1937
Champagne Mouton Rothschild
Quinze liqueurs

❖